CAPTURED BY THE ORC KING

THE PERISHED WOODS

TRACY LAUREN

❀ Created with Vellum

PROLOGUE

Petra Gunnora, The Witch-Queen of Envercress, the
Eternal Princess...

*I*t began a long time ago, right in this very castle. A magical place, in the eyes of a young village girl. It was like something pulled straight from a fairytale—with rolling, green lawns and majestic spires. Manicured perfection was to be found everywhere one looked, coexisting with a vast history, an ancientness delightfully paired with the type of modern beauty that only great wealth can buy. How easy it was, to imagine that a place so wonderful could hold more than just the ordinary.

The Castle at Envercress.

There was a King who lived here. A widower with two children—a boy and a girl. He was a kind man, a doting father, simple in his ways, with a good heart. He found deep joy in his kingdom, but alas, he was lonely *and* he was a romantic.

It would have been easy for this King to wed another royal. Smart even. There are people who arrange that sort of thing with the other kingdoms and if he had let them, how different

1

our paths would have been. But *this* King wanted love. The real kind—love at first sight if possible, because that's the kind of man he was: filled with good-natured hope and overflowing optimism.

And when you are that sort of man, you tend to find what it is you're looking for. His heart's desire came in the form of a peasant seamstress, living down in the village. My mother. Beautiful and compassionate, possessing great strength of character, loved by all who knew her. She was a widow herself, and looking back, just as lonely and romantic as the King.

I wasn't there when they met, but I've imagined it so many times I think I can see it just as it was.

The royal carriage coming up the road, my mother out on the path, arms laden with parcels, pausing to cast her gaze back at the sound of approaching horses, a look of awe crossing her face as she took in the beauty of them. Seeing her from the window, the King would have ordered the carriage to stop.

I remember she was in her lavender dress that day...such a good seamstress, one of the best in the village. My mother always turned out so nicely in her dresses. With long, chestnut hair worn down—it must have been glistening in the sunshine. But I imagine it was her pale blue eyes that captivated—morning-sky eyes, I always thought. Any man would have stopped for her. Even a King.

He bounded down from the carriage, hurrying to lessen my mother's load and they laughed together as he stumbled.

"I'd watch where I'm going but I find it difficult to take my eyes off of you."

"You flatter me, Your Highness."

"I speak only the truth." And his voice was always so rich with sincerity. "Please, you must allow me to offer you a ride home."

"I couldn't possibly." My mother blushed.

"But I insist."

"Then I must insist on offering you a cup of tea."

"I would be inclined to accept that offer."

Just like that, *the King himself came to our humble cottage!* It seemed as if the entire village was standing outside our gate, watching with interest. That part I remember: walking home from my lessons and seeing the crowd. There was a nervous feeling in the pit of my stomach. I hadn't seen so many people gathered together since they came to tell us about my father... about the accident. But this was different. I could see as much. The faces weren't so solemn. No, people were *smiling*, they were chittering with excitement.

I paused where I stood, across the road, watching them all. Little did I know that inside, my mother was serving tea to the King. She told me later that they spoke of the Queen—who had passed some years before during a miscarriage. And of my father, who was a mason. He suffered a fall during one of his building projects. His skull was crushed and he never came home.

The King and my mother, they both knew loss. I imagine there's a kinship in that.

The conversation shifted to work when the King noticed my mother's dresses lying about—her sewing projects, her mannequins. She confessed that she was a dressmaker and he asked her to come the very next day to the castle to start on a gown for Princess Meredith.

That's when I ventured inside.

"This must be little Petra!" he exclaimed happily, and he was genuinely pleased to meet me. I imagine he thought it was perfect that this woman, who he was so smitten with, had a child near in age to his own. In fact, I was the same age as that baby would have been—the one his wife had lost. Yes, the King thought it was fate. Even on that first day, he envisioned us as a family just coming into fruition. "Bring Petra tomorrow," he offered, beaming a smile at my mother. "Meredith would love a friend to play with."

The next day a carriage came for us.

"Mama! Mama! It's here!" I called—thrilled as any child would be.

When I close my eyes I can still hear her laughter, like gentle bells, as she admired my wide-eyed awe. The day got better from there. At the castle, the King had a doll waiting for me. The most beautiful doll I'd ever seen. I have her still, tucked in a case of things I'd hate to forget. He must have ordered it right after leaving our cottage. For it was a custom sort of thing, with its hair and eyes *just* like mine.

He was thoughtful. As a matter of fact, it's what he was best at—making people feel loved. I think often that he would have had a good life as a farmer or a country pastor...a longer life. I muse over it, all these years later, mentally dressing him up as a commoner. Even in ragged clothes I think he'd have stood tall, with that absurdly happy smile on his face. He didn't know negativity, deceit, anger. The one tragedy he'd experienced in life was the loss of his first wife and the baby, yet he was able to remain impossibly hopeful. Never could he have fathomed the idea of someone plotting to overthrow him. In his mind, all people were wholly good, kind, generous, always trying their very best.

I still remember that shocked look on his face, the complete lack of comprehension, the disappointment. As if disappointment alone was enough to make one's enemies repent. That is just who he was, charitable with all souls.

The people of this land still remember him as a good man. He led with his heart and believed fully, deeply, that heart was enough. It is a sweet notion, wonderfully sweet. Close to a hundred years later, I look back and smile—wishing it could be so. But if heart were all it took, life would indeed be a fairy tale.

For some of us, however, it is a curse, a burden to bear. The

King couldn't grasp that weight of the world is heavy. He certainly wasn't prepared to carry it, nor was he capable. Not like I am.

Running my fingertips across cool stone, I think back on the moment it started. For me, it wasn't that day in the cottage. It was some weeks later, just after the wedding. There was a big party and a feast, but the King brought us—his family—to a private parlor. He didn't care much for all the pomp and circumstance. All he really wanted was to be a husband and a father. He wanted to solidify our family. So, he put a ring on my mother's finger and for me...he had a special gift.

A fire was blazing in the lavish hearth. Meredith and Prince Belric sat close by, always carrying an air of regality. My mother and the King knelt before me: excited, happily gazing into my eyes. I remember how pleased my mother looked, how content. It was as if a light was emanating from deep inside her, from her heart. She *glowed* with joy.

I was nervous with all these eyes on me. I wanted to fit in. I wanted to make everyone else happy. That's what I was comfortable with. But they all looked at me, trying very hard to make *me* happy, to make *me* feel included. I shifted on my feet as the moment came. The King held out a beautifully carved box in his hands.

"Petra," he said, eyes twinkling. "You are a daughter to me, *family*. I love you so much little one, just as much as my own flesh and blood."

I looked at my toes, blushing, feeling shy and out of place.

"That's why I'm giving you this."

He held that box out, urging me to pull back the ribbon—pink, satiny, beautiful in and of itself, a treasure for a peasant child. It slipped to the floor and the King pulled back the lid. Inside sat a necklace, lying on a velveteen pillow. It was...*extravagant*. Gold filigree, adorned with glittering gems—all of which complemented a curiously unique stone that hung as the centerpiece.

"It's been in the royal family for hundreds of years." The King spoke, not knowing what he was starting, what terrible cascade of events was to come: His death, the fall of his family, the overthrowing of his kingdom. Not by his enemies, I couldn't allow that, but by me: the twelve-year-old daughter of a seamstress. A peasant girl. More than that, I was a serious and observant child, willing to do what was necessary in a monstrous world.

"It's beautiful, isn't it?"

"You could have made her something *new*, Daddy," Meredith had said, coming to look over his shoulder with a grimace. Meredith. She was a *real* princess. Hair golden and styled fashionably. Her dresses were impossibly fanciful, like something imagined out of a dream. She wore shoes with heels and walked daintily in them without wobbling ankles. I was in constant awe around Meredith, for she embodied perfection in all ways. Even her voice was royal.

"Something prettier," she pouted. "With diamonds. Not an old rock." She wasn't being mean. She was trying to be generous in her own way. She thought I should have something new and stylish, like the things she wore. But the King was searching for something beyond a pretty trinket. He wanted to give me a gift to symbolize my inclusion in his family. A ring for my mother and an heirloom for me. But that stone, *my stone*, it was so much more than an heirloom and the poor, sweet, simple King had no idea.

"Nonsense, love. Petra can have a hundred diamond necklaces if she likes, but this is special. This means"—he pulled the necklace from the box and unclasped it for me—"we are family."

And it *felt* special. The stone wasn't some perfectly cut gem, there were cuts and polishes, but in some places it was raw and natural. Reds and violets...I couldn't name all the colors I saw swirling in it. It was intense and awe inspiring. I could tell it was old and not just from the King's words. I could *sense* it. I could *feel* an ancientness about it. More than anything else, I knew this necklace was for me.

"I got it from the family vault," he said, fixing it around my neck. I felt the change right away, though I didn't understand it. A connection to a greater knowledge, a life-force, an entity...

My stepsister frowned, chastisement in her tone. "There are so many *nice* things in the vault, Daddy."

The King gave an exasperated smile. "And if I were choosing something for you, Meredith, I would have chosen differently. But to me, this said *Petra*."

He wasn't wrong.

"Do you like it, sweetheart?" he asked.

"Yes," I replied, mesmerized—confused by the magic I sensed. My stepsister may not have found the stone visually appealing, but I was enthralled by it. The style was so...*commanding*. Not intended for youth, but for someone with great power, with intense strength. And I loved it, for it was *mine*. It spoke to me. It was a necklace meant for my very soul, I thought.

A twelve-year-old girl on the outside, but inside, I was different from other children. So solemn, so serious. Always analyzing. Clever. Too clever, they said—for a girl, for a child. The villagers didn't like it, but I sensed that the stone liked me just as I was.

I had opinions on things, big things, that other children never seemed to consider. As much as I loved my stepfather, as excited as I was for this new family...I knew the King wasn't fit to rule. It felt dangerous to have a man like him, so soft and weak, responsible for the well-being of so many. He would have made a wonderful farmer, with a big family and fat, contented animals. But he had no business being King...and the stone agreed.

7

TRACY LAUREN

It was after his fall that things began to happen so quickly. I had nothing to do with that, by the way. But the stone had warned me. I didn't believe the visions at first, then I saw them coming true and I knew I must act.

What a frightening time...those first horrible portents the stone granted as a trust was built between us. I saw the future ahead was dark, not just for my family but for the entire Kingdom. It *warned* me. Someone had to take charge. Someone had to do what was necessary to lead Envercress into a brighter future—no matter how terrible the deeds.

Still, I wavered.

The crown went first to Prince Belric. He was a spoiled child, selfish, a glutton at heart. The future with him leading us was the darkest. The things I saw...I had to *protect* everyone from it. So, into the pond he went. My first spell. The stone told me how it was to be done and I wept afterwards. I didn't want to cast him into that place; I *had* to. He was still so young and he had been a good brother to me. But I *knew* what he would have turned into and I couldn't let it come to pass.

Then, Meredith was crowned. I thought that would be the end of it, that the stone would go silent. We could put the ugly past behind us and focus on the future. But that wasn't the case. Poor Meredith. Her assets were in her beauty, not in her ability to lead. The stone showed me that. War would come with Meredith on the throne. The other Kingdoms wouldn't respect her. They would come and they would take from her. They would *ruin* her and this land. So, the stone told me to put her in the pond with Belric, but I said no. Belric might harm her, out of spite, out of his hatred for me. I told the stone: I didn't want any harm to come to Meredith.

So, it showed me another way.

It wasn't the stone's fault. I was a child. I didn't explain myself clearly. But I learned from Meredith, from all the things that went wrong.

At that point the people were suspicious. Two peasants move into the castle and the royal family is so quick to fall? They looked at my mother, of course, but she was looking at me.

She could sense the change. She couldn't have guessed what it was. Who would have? But my mother was no fool. Maybe she saw me whispering to the stone, sneaking about the castle, dark circles under my eyes from sleepless nights. I was less like a child than ever. Worry, constant worry, plagued me. I felt no guilt, no remorse. My deeds, though gruesome, were a dire necessity. Panic was my primary state as I tried in secret to get the Kingdom back on the right path.

I paid little attention to her. There were far more important things going on than her pain—things that I was responsible for taking care of. No one else had these visions, the stone trusted only me. But she was heartbroken, a phantom of that glowing version of herself, newly wed to a King. Now two times a widow, she didn't have eyes for the big picture. All she saw was what she lost. All she had was suspicion for who might have taken it.

True love. Fairytale lives. A happily ever after... If only I could have allowed them to have it.

Even now, it makes me sad, for I did love them. All of them. Gladly, I would have given each their own fairytale. But my power wasn't what it is now. I was young and I was scrambling, desperate to save my Kingdom from all the horrid possibilities the stone showed on the horizon. What were a few lives when balanced against that? What did my own happiness matter? A big choice for someone so young, but the stone knew me well. It knew I would make the right choice and sacrifice my family to save the Kingdom.

The King wouldn't have made the same decision. None of them would have. I was the only one. That's why I couldn't tell. I couldn't even tell my mother. But, as I've said, she sensed it and so she went to the garden.

"What is there to fix today?" I ask. More than eighty years have passed since then. Perhaps it's been closer to a hundred? Still, I am thinking—always thinking—of my Kingdom.

Out on the terrace, the warm sun is on my face and a gentle breeze makes the whole world seem to sway. In the village, life goes on. The people are happy. They're safe and prosperous. They fall in love and build families, all thanks to the sacrifices I made so long ago. Thanks to the sacrifices I continue to make. I live only for them. My work is for them and I have my stone to help guide me.

Each day, from beginning to end, the stone and I gaze bravely into the future. We assess all paths and together we decide the fate of our world.

I, Petra Gunnora, was the last in the family to be crowned Queen of Envercress. It hasn't been the fairytale life I thought was awaiting me when the King first proposed to my mother, but that's alright. I don't mind bearing the weight of the world. I've come to think of it as a job made just for me. There is no one else in all the land who could do what I've done—I know, for I've checked. I smile over that, proud of myself, proud of my strength. I am nothing if I am not the woman who gave up all she loved to protect her Kingdom.

All along the terrace, the curtains dance lazily. It's quiet here, save for the softness of the breeze. Not a soul to be heard. Somewhere there are servants, of course. Throughout the castle —cleaning, working, always keeping out of sight.

They stay away from me as a general rule, unless necessary. It's been that way for years, though I don't know why. I take such care to appear sweet and meek, like the girl I was when I came here from the village. And yet they never seem comfortable. So, I offer pay too good to refuse and that keeps my castle staffed. The silence doesn't bother me, for I'm not so alone as they think.

I peer across the land through a spy glass. My blessed companion hangs round my neck, always showing me the way. When it grows silent, I coax it. I test different paths, different ideas. I offer options until it glows bright and talks to me the way it used to. It's been quiet lately. Thoughtful. Particularly when I look south, toward Pontheugh.

"Talk to me," I whisper. We are like old friends. I run my fingers tenderly across the surface, knowing every facet of it. Of course I do. How many years have I gazed into its center—searching for answers, for the right path to take?

I gaze into it now and see that castle in the distance, far better than I could see it through the magnifier. It's not my Envercress, but a castle beyond a great lake. Pontheugh. I frown, feeling nothing but disinterest and disgust. Silence has lasted between our Kingdoms for a decade at least and I'd be glad to allow that silence to continue. It is their King who disgusts me. He is a fool, a directionless fool with no love for his land, nor his people. I wouldn't concern myself with him, if it weren't for the stone's urging.

My concern is for *my* land. *My* people. "I don't want to care about anyone else. I've got Envercress."

The stone disagrees. It thinks there is something I should know.

"Some threat to my kingdom?" I wonder. Maybe that is why it shows me this castle again and again, day after day.

"I'll protect Envercress, you know I will. But must I extend the same care to Pontheugh?" The thought sours my stomach and my mood. I long only for my own land. I want to pour myself *only* into my own land. The stone knows this and still, it shows me Pontheugh.

"What would you have me do? What would please you?"

The stone shows me the castle. Slowly moving inside, I see the throne and I grimace.

"I have a throne to sit upon *here*. I cannot abandon it." Nerves take hold, making me sweat and I rush around my terrace with the spyglass so that I might look at what I love, ensure my land is still there and my people are still safe.

"Does Pontheugh threaten this?" I demand, and the stone shows me the castle again—insistent.

Yes. It is telling me, *yes*.

I sigh, hanging my head, trying to talk myself into drawing up more strength. I've done this all before. It's been years since I've had to take control in a violent and forceful way, but I am capable. The stone knows I am. The stone knows the lengths I will go to. I *will* protect my people at all costs.

Click, click, click. Footsteps approach, steady across stone. I hardly allow them to enter my consciousness, for my mind is otherwise occupied.

"Your Highness—" A lady's maid curtseys and I turn to face her, adopting the persona of a sweet, young monarch. She does not venture to make eye contact. "I have your tea."

I take her in, noticing that she's older. Grey hair and an overall formidable appearance. Sturdiness—that's what stands out. She's got broad shoulders and a hard jaw. I smile at her, finding it all so very interesting. They used to send young women to serve me—to tend to my dresses, to my rooms, to my hair. Now they send women like this—cold and hard, women without superstition, women who aren't so easily frightened.

But what in the world is there to be frightened of? The whole of my appearance has been crafted to elicit only a sense of peace in my people. To be sure, I cast my eyes to the mirror behind her. Certainly, I've taken great care. Reflected back is a youthful and pale face—admittedly somber, but I've got doe eyes, soft curls, and a modest dress. There is nothing here that one might accuse of being dangerous or frightening. In their eyes, I am hardly more than a girl.

"Hello," I say softly.

She keeps her expression flat and I keep my smile meek.

"What's your name?"

"Agatha, Your Highness." She doesn't whisper. She speaks in a firm, confident voice. But she won't look at me.

"Have you had your afternoon tea, Agatha?"

She pauses for a scarce second, perhaps unsure how to respond. "Yes, Your Highness."

"Oh. Well, one can never have *too* much tea. Join me for a cup, here on the terrace. We can look at the garden together."

"No thank you, Your Highness." She curtseys again and takes a step back, but I stop her.

"I take great pride in my garden Agatha. Objectively, it is beautiful."

"Of course, your majesty."

"And yet you won't join me?"

"There is work to be done, Highness, and a woman of my station shouldn't be wasting the time of someone like you."

"I wouldn't think of it as a waste—"

"I mustn't."

"Tell me, Agatha," I press, taking a step to follow her. "What are your thoughts on Pontheugh?"

"Your Highness?"

"The Kingdom of Pontheugh? Are you familiar with it?"

"Aye. I am. My oldest son farms land belonging to Pontheugh. On the outskirts, still near enough to visit."

"Is he happy there?"

She nods in a curt sort of way.

I inch closer. "Do you love him?"

Agatha's already hard jaw tightens. "You will have to excuse me, Your Highness."

"I've plenty of tea for the both of us—"

"Thank you for the offer." She curtseys in a rushed and fluid motion and before I can say another word she backs from the room and the clicking of her shoes is notably at a faster tempo than when she approached. I stare after the formidable Agatha. Formidable enough to deny a Queen.

Strange...when I look like this. One would think...*I thought*...that they would love me. Decades of prosperity, no war, plentiful farming, our villages have flourished...you would think they would love me. It isn't as if anyone is around who remembers what happened. Sure there are stories, but it's all been so long.

Perhaps it's this ageless face frightens them or the disappearance of village girls that makes them wonder. But what can I do? The stone calls for certain things. It *needs* to be nourished just like any living creature does. I can't help that. Sacrifices will always have to be made and I'm the only one willing to do the hard deeds.

It's for the people, and I would do anything for my people.

I bring up a smile. "Let them think what they wish." I'm happy to sacrifice. Generation after generation, I'll be here, loving them, watching over them. They are like my children and I would never allow anyone to hurt my children. My smile falls away and I cross the terrace. The sun is beaming down, all across sweet Envercress. My one and only love. I *live* for this land.

But in the distance, across an expanse of countryside and farms, there lies another kingdom. *Pontheugh*. I haven't loved Pontheugh. I haven't *wanted* to love Pontheugh.

"It's hard enough," I mutter, my fingers coming back to the stone. I touch it with affection, with adoration. My only partner for all these years. How could I turn my back on the stone? I shake my head. Never.

"What is it you want me to do?" I offer. "Must I take Pontheugh? Another child to care for?"

The thought is overwhelming...a struggle to comprehend.
"But she's so far. Surely we can find a compromise. A path that might allow me to remain here, in Envercress?" Envercress is my love. My darling. I can't go far, not unless absolutely necessary. To leave here would make me angry. "I can't leave my Kingdom unattended...*vulnerable*," I plead as I peer into the stone, into the veins of light that seem to course like blood through my charmed necklace.

What a pitying description. *Charmed.* It's more than a charm. It's *so much more.* I couldn't make anything like this. No matter what power I've attained over the years, I could *never* charm an object in such a way. My necklace is *imbued* with power, great and ancient power. It is a force. A lifeforce perhaps. Something far beyond my understanding. There are no writings that speak of it, no ancient tomes that lend a hint. Oh, and I have searched. Far and wide I have searched, but it remains a mystery. A terrifying and awe-inspiring mystery. One that I am grateful for. A curse around the neck of most, but for me...it has been a gift. Despite everything, this necklace has been a gift.

I stroke the smooth bits, giving it love. It doesn't speak to me in the traditional sense. I hear no words or whispers. But it conveys everything of importance. It always has, since the very beginning. Since I was a child. It has told me all I must know; all I must do. The stone has trusted me.

"Please, a compromise?"

The vision within the stone changes, shifting like the wind, like clouds in a storm. I see fighting. I see *war* and I gasp, horrified. But I'm relieved to see it isn't my land. It isn't my precious Envercress or my darling people. Gazing more deeply, I see it isn't people at all. What I see are...*beasts.*

"Orcs?"

I hurriedly point my spyglass toward a dark band of green in the distance. A woodland that borders Pontheugh, not Envercress. I have little concern for it. Little concern for anything besides my Kingdom—Envercress is my obsession. For the first time in a long while, I place my attention on that cursed forest. *The Perished Woods*, they call it. A land of monsters and fiends.

"Orcs?" I say again, searching my mind. They come from the mountain. I know that. And I can see it even from this distance, standing taller than the trees. Black and ugly. I care nothing for it.

"What would I do with orcs?"

I clasp the stone and look to it for guidance. What I see...*makes me laugh.* "An orc sitting on the throne at Pontheugh! This is a joke. Surely, you've suddenly developed a sense of humor?"

But the vision becomes more clear, more vibrant and real. It is indeed an orc sitting on the throne and around his neck is a medallion—with the emblem of Envercress on it.

I laugh again, this time without humor. "Is this *my* orc? Does he rule in my stead?"

The view shifts, showing me war, fighting, brutality—it is the path to Pontheugh. Cruel as it is, I don't care, as long as there is no threat to Envercress.

More deeply now, I consider the prospect. "I suppose it would be good to claim Pontheugh. I admit, I have worried about that King on more than one occasion. If his land were mine, I would never have to think about our shared border again. From here to the sea would belong to Envercress."

It is a possibility...

"Where is he now, this orc?" The stone offers a window and I see him through a haze, deeply absorbed in battle. I study the background, the surroundings. "It's Black Mountain, isn't it?" Might as well be pulling him from the depths of Hell.

"The magic it will take to call him from there..." But the stone already knows.

"Orcs...they are beasts. They are vicious monsters. They rape and kill indiscriminately. To work with an orc, would that

CAPTURED BY THE ORC KING

not be dangerous? Would that not be welcoming a threat to my own land?" I huff and frown, feeling trepidation. Surely, there must be a better way forward. It would be nice to have Pontheugh, but I've always worked alone.

"No. There has to be something else. Show me another option."

The vision comes quickly, too quickly for my liking. War on my border. Pontheugh's banners flying over *my* land. Their disgusting King...coming for *me*. My throat tightens and I watch my people's crops wither. I can hear them, in their homes, wailing as they starve and I am powerless to help. Outside the castle, my own garden turns black. My statues, so many of them precious to me, are shattered beyond repair.

"Well, we can't have that."

Already my feet are taking me back inside, to a vanity, to a drawer, to a familiar little bauble...a medallion. It is *the* medallion from the vision, the one the orc was wearing. I pull it free and turn the metal disk over in my hand, only to toss it back roughly.

"An Orc..." I say again, this time to myself. "What do *I* want with an orc?"

The vision burns brighter—in my mind this time. I can see him on the throne...scarred and grey... The stone is persistent. It's been a long time since it has *pushed* me so hard. Not since the beginning. This must be important.

"Fine!" I cry out, my eyes drawn to the medallion. "If he's a beast, that means he can be trained." I retrieve the metal disk, already planning my course. "A curse, to control him?"

The stone doesn't argue. *Good.*

"But there are a thousand orcs slithering around in the belly of that mountain. What am I to do? Go down there and get him myself?"

The stone shows me a door, a passage from there to here, but the stone is impassive. It points the way without emotion. It cares nothing for what lengths I must to go to in order to conjure that door. I huff and cross my arms over my chest. "If this is the only way, then I will do as you ask."

In the facets, I see blood. I see war waged by an orc army. I see the castle at Pontheugh falling. The King and his daughter brought to me—their blood so precious, so crucial for my spells. There is much death. But it is not the death of my people and that is all I care about.

"And what will I do with an army of orcs once the war is fought?"

The stone shows me more blood, more death. "They are a tool? Nothing more? Use them and then eradicate them?" That doesn't sound so bad.

The image in the stone becomes clear: Envercress, the land I love. The sun shines upon it and I can see years into the future, years of peace and prosperity. It soothes me.

"And I'll get to stay here? In my castle? In my beloved Envercress?"

There's a soft glow from the stone, bringing me a deeper sense of peace.

"What about the King? His heir?"

It is confirmed. More death, more blood, and my stone... bathing in it. The glow shines brighter than I've ever known it to shine and my eyes widen.

"Oh, I see."

This is about so much more. I must maintain the stone's power to care for my Kingdom and in that, I will bring an end to all future threats against my land, my people, and our prosperity. Not so bad a deal when put in perspective.

"Pontheugh..." I frown over them, my heart softening just a bit. "No one loves them as I love Envercress." That's a sad thought and I begin to toy with the medallion, whose future is already planned, already envisioned in the stone's center. I move to one of the archways to gaze out at the horizon—toward

Pontheugh. I have so much love to give. It's selfish really, to harbor only this one love, this one child. With all the resources available to me, I could love and protect everything from here to the sea.

"Is the Orc King *really* necessary?"

The stone obliges me with another vision, ever so convincing. It shows me scenes of a war raging across farmland, of orcs wiping away all the would-be soldiers in between. These are the soldiers who might fight me, who might contend my leadership if I sought to lay claim to their Kingdom. I try to imagine a future without the orc and the stone grows grey, faded, unclear.

With an irritated huff, I instead picture the beast where the stone seems to want him. In that vision, the sun shines and the land is prosperous. It extends far beyond the current boundary of Envercress. A surge of love fills my chest. Love for Pontheugh *after* its purge.

"It needs a purge, doesn't it?" Wipe away the ugliness. Cleanse the land. The puppet orc can remain on the throne, a placeholder, a husk. But when I get rid of the orc army, the people will love me. They will enter an age of prosperity like the one Envercress has felt. They will know that it was I who saved them and *I* will know that I saved them from their wretched King—self-centered, greedy sloth that he his. He doesn't love them. Not the way I love my people. I could...I could love *all* the people. The stone warms, it brightens, and I chuckle to myself.

"Yes, my love is without limit."

It's decided. It has been from the start, hasn't it? For I am bound to my stone. Never would I ignore its call.

"And all I must do is make a door for this orc to walk through? Give him a charmed medallion that will whisper my wishes and control him completely? You're sure? It is an *orc* that you want?"

The answer is an affirmative. The future I am shown isn't as defined as I long for it to be, but it is clearer than it's been. This is the path the stone desires and once I have the blood of the King and Princess, all will become vibrant—perhaps more vibrant than ever.

I think something must be happening in Pontheugh, a turning of tides. A change in fates—a change so intense that the stone believes it will eventually threaten Envercress.

"You know I'll do anything it takes," I tell it. "I've no intention to give up now."

Closing my eyes, I try to follow the course of the future laid out by the stone, but there are blank spaces, clouded areas, faces I cannot see. Red. Anger. Heat. Change. The winds of change, beating through the air and the shadow of a monster flying overhead. I see death and I sense the King and his Princess. I feel no love for them, only the desire to get them out of my way. The stone wants their blood? I will feed it their blood. I long for the future to be more precise and there is only one way for that to occur: I must begin.

Here and now, I step onto the path. Pulling back a tapestry, a door is exposed, leading to my hidden magics room. It swings open for me. Perhaps there was a time when the servants knew of this door, but decades have passed since and women like Agatha never linger and snoop in the rooms of a witch, whether they believe in them or not.

I descend a stone staircase, feeling the chill of the room. Down, down, down I go. A different sort of mood overtakes me. My appearance is unchanged, but I am no longer the doe-eyed girl, the embodiment of the face I show the world. It is the power in me, the strength, the fortitude to do all that is necessary that shows itself now.

If only I could make another stone like mine, I think to myself, chuckling. But that would only help if I could find a person to *truly* care as I do. There was a time in which I tried, a time where the weight of this thing frightened me so much that

I longed to be free of it. Only, there wasn't anyone to take my place.

The truth of that is evident even now. No one can lead Pontheugh the way that I can, even from afar. My task isn't to find another Petra or to convince the orc to value what I do. My task, *my spell*, is to make him feel *my* drive—connect him to me, like an extension of myself. And that's simple. A charm can do that. A curse can do that. It can make a link to the orc, make him feel this intrepid force, I can make him care so much that it's all he can think of, all he hears, all he sees and anything that might stand in his way will be maddening. He will be powerless to refuse the call.

Yes. Even a lowly orc can serve obediently, given the right curse. I consider the path ahead, happily planning. I will remain here in Envercress with my precious stone, in the Kingdom that I adore. With this spell, the orc will want what I want. He will be as consumed as I am while I remain free to stay here. Right here. Forever. Yes, I smile, fondly caressing the stone. This will work wonderfully.

"You are very clever, you know that? I'm sorry it took me so long to see it your way. I need convincing at times," I whisper apologetically. The stone warms, forgiving me.

"You always send me in the right direction. I know there is work ahead, hard work. But after it's done I will never have to worry about Pontheugh again, or think of their filthy King. With the right charm, I won't even have to think of the orc." This spell I'm to craft, it will be so potent that the beast will act as my puppet, moving only as I command him to.

Joy fills the space beneath the stone—my heart. Yes, I can put in a little work to conquer a kingdom. It's been a while, but I've done it before, when the stakes have been much higher.

"Better to take care of these problems now before they get out of hand," I say, conversationally as I start the fire. But I'm thinking ahead, giddy at the prospect that I won't ever have to leave my home. Two viscous liquids are the base of my potion, I mix them together. From the corner, I hear a gentle moan, but my mind is elsewhere.

And what all will this journey bring? Nourishment for the stone and another 100 years of peace and prosperity. This time, for two kingdoms.

I toss the medallion into the cauldron and smoke fills the room. And there it is: I am well on the path to claiming Pontheugh.

CHAPTER 1

Thorn
A long time ago...

D eep in the heart of the Perished Woods stands Black Mountain. I am told you can see its terrible peak from as far away as man's land. Beyond that, not much is known. There are whispers about it, of course, but no bold talk. *Think of that*—even in a cursed forest, ruled by chaos and beasts, Black Mountain breeds fear.

I heard once that it is a gate to Hell. Maybe it is. One thing I know for certain is that Black Mountain is the birthplace of my people—the orcs. But I am not of this mountain. I am half-blood. Born of a witch and an orc, raised in the cursed forest with my brother...*Ash*. We went our separate ways.

He always was so content, while I felt some crucial piece of me was missing—calling from a faraway place. Thus began my journey.

* * *

I RAM my body into the nearest grey-skinned beast, toppling him. He falls into the mud and muck; my sword drives through his heart and his mouth twists in a pained scream that bleeds into the din of battle. Orcs push up from the pit. An endless stream. An army being born. I wield my blade, fighting to get past them. Seems like I've been fighting for years—forcing my way against this current. It's maddening.

How long have I been here?

Red heat from the earth rises all around us—stifling steam. It's difficult to breathe. Sweat blends with blood. The stench is appalling—the offensiveness of it never seeming to fade.

Sometimes I recognize faces in the battle. A friend perhaps? A kindred spirit? Or just other orcs fighting the current? We are neither allies nor enemies. We simply fight the same fight, unwilling to relinquish the meaning this place holds, which is unique to each of us.

To me, the depths of Black Mountain is the only place I might find the answers I've been searching for. If I can cross this river of warriors, if I can work my way into the pit—get to the source—perhaps then I will understand my purpose. I can get to the root of who I am and what I am meant for. *Where this ache in my chest comes from and how I might fill it...*

A blade swipes across my bicep, inciting a subtle sting amid mass numbness. I track the fighter and gut him, tossing the corpse aside. There are so many corpses. I climb over them. Hands grab at me, trying to hold me back. I'm so close. It's nothing but a sea of grey bodies being pushed up from this gash of Hell.

The air is thin. Too many mouths fighting to breathe. A hand grips my ankle. I sever it and press on. I am always pressing on. Scrambling over the bodies, making my way to the center, fighting for a way back down into Hell.

The Devil will answer to me.

Miles and miles into the earth. Months upon months of struggling to survive. So close now. Closer than I've ever been.

I'm forced to abandon my blade as I squeeze past writhing bodies. There is no more air. Orc blood courses through my veins. The beating of my heart pounds in my ears. War drums. I clench my teeth and cry out in primitive and guttural strength. My vision fails me. And then...I'm falling down into Hell.

At first, it's like leaping off a cliff. Wind rushes past. I spin and so does my stomach. Then, very suddenly, it is more like magic. The fall becomes slower and slower. I see nothing but black...save for two small flames flickering in the distance.

My lungs gulp crisp air. I close my eyes and savor the cool feeling against my face. Then, my feet touch ground. I look down.

Dust. Soft and fine. Before me is an ornate door—gold leaves scrolling across onyx. It's cradled by torches.

Looking around, all is dark. Or more accurately, I'm surrounded by the absence of everything. A void. An abyss. The only dust is that which the light of the torches reaches. Beyond that: nothingness.

My gaze comes to the door. Flames whip. There is no call to hesitate, for I am steadfast in my conviction: I came for answers. Striding forward, my hand meets door. I push it open. Bright and blinding light floods my vision. I shield my eyes and step forward onto stone.

I can't see a thing...

"Welcome."

The voice is soft and feminine. I'm still blinking against the sun, trying to focus on the form before me. A woman. No, a girl. My eyes adjust and I see that she's neither.

"I've been waiting for you." Hair long and in waves, a delicate crown set atop her head. Unimposing, she watches me from behind doe-like eyes and a somber brow. If she were what she appears, she'd be trembling before a beast like me. And yet, she doesn't seem afraid in the least. Makes me wonder...

"What is this place?"

"You are in my home."

I curl my lip in challenge. "Lies."

But the girl gives a gentle smile and holds her hands out, palms up. "This is the Castle at Envercress. I am Petra Gunnora, Queen of this land."

"Never heard of it and I've never heard of you, *Princess*." I sneer. She wears the mask of youth.

"Queen," Petra corrects. Her tone is ice and my muscles start to twitch.

What the fuck is this place? I stride across the room. Stone floor, stone walls. Not coarse rock, but *cut* stone—carefully placed. Open windows arch behind the supposed Queen (I know what she really is). Outside there is blue sky and we seem to be overlooking a vast garden.

"You are in the Land of Man. Or, *woman*—as the case may be."

"I am in the belly of Black Mountain."

"Not anymore you aren't."

I point toward the door I just walked through. "Black Mountain is on the other side. That means all of this is nothing more than a witch's parlor trick. *It's fake.*"

An amused smile forms on youthful lips and I cut my gaze back to the door. Onyx with gold leaves. I was delivered to it after finally breaking through the pit. Now it's gone. There's a wall there instead, with a framed painting showing a King with two children to his right, his Queen beside him, and a third child clinging to her skirt—separated from the others. Though Petra Gunnora appears slightly older now, I recognize the solemn, nut-brown eyes.

"What is this?" I demand.

"I tell you, Thorn. You are in my home. I brought you here."

I growl. "I've no wish to be in *Envercress*. I came to see the Devil."

"Well, I'm afraid I'm the only one here. And anyway, what would you want with the Devil?"

I scour the room. It's sparsely decorated, but what is present is quite fine—finer than anything I've ever seen. From the furniture, to the curtains, and rugs. I've never been in a castle, but I do imagine this is what a castle would look like. "How? How could I get from *The Pit* in Black Mountain to *this* place? And tell me, witch, how is it you know my name?"

"I've been waiting for you."

"Me?"

"Well, an orc anyway." She raises a brow. "And I suppose you count."

I bare my teeth, detesting the insult set upon me. "The orc blood coursing through my veins is all I recognize."

Her eyes take me in, head to toe. There is only assessment in them, calculating assessment. Petra crosses the room, giving me a better view of the costume she wears.

Her dress is subtle, exquisite, but subtle. Mauve with a rich forest green bodice and accents at the wrists and hem. The skirt doesn't puff out in the way one might expect from a princess and her crown is nothing more than a whisper. She wears no other adornments, with the exception of a heavy ruby stone hanging from a chain around her neck. It strikes me as out of place considering she's worked so hard to present herself as this humble and unimposing girl.

Standing there, looking about eighteen years old, I realize she's allowing me to form an opinion—to make an assessment of my own. "It's a good disguise," I say finally.

"Disguise?" Petra questions the assertion, but I can see the curve to her lips.

"What are you really?"

She laughs, taking measured steps toward a credenza where

she retrieves a towel and holds it out for me to take—another calculated move on her part. Imagine, a Queen serving a half-blood forest dweller like me. "You're getting blood and sweat everywhere."

I look down and see that she's right. It looks as if I just crawled from the belly of Hell and I think perhaps I did. Taking the towel, I wipe blood from my face, chest, and arms. Very little of it is my own and I watch this supposed Queen without trust while I wait for her to speak, to tell me how and why I am here. Unless I have finally gone mad, she truly did pull me from Black Mountain.

"Why don't we take a walk in my garden?"

"Now?"

She nods.

"Wouldn't a Queen need guards to escort her?" I cast my eyes to the halls on either end of the room, but no one seems to be here to protect her. In most cases that would make me feel opportunistic, being one-on-one with a foe. But in this moment, it only instills the prickling understanding that this one has power.

"I'm not worried about it, Thorn. Come, let me show you my garden. It is famed for its beauty."

"I'm not one for gardens."

"I think you'll enjoy mine and anyway, you said you have questions. Maybe I can help answer them?"

"I wanted to ask the Devil."

She inclines her head. "Alas, I assure you, the Devil isn't here."

"I don't quite trust that, but you can show me this garden if you must."

Petra leads the way and my eyes scrutinize everything, gathering information. *Know your opponent.* I've fought rough beasts, but the battle this one is starting here…it isn't obtuse, like the swinging of an axe. There is an intricacy at play and I welcome the test to my ability to strategize. I can rise to any challenge. As a matter of fact, I crave a new one.

Petra's castle is large and airy. Sunlight seems to pour in from all directions and I can smell the flowers blooming outside. It is such a stark contrast from the hellish place I came from that I touch everything in reach, proving to myself that it is no hallucination. All evidence suggests I really am in this place called Envercress. This witch *pulled* me from Black Mountain. Her power must be great.

"If I attacked you now—"

"Oh, I hope you don't." Petra chuckles, her body inclining as if to show me she is indeed a young and blushing Queen. It is a role she plays well, but a role nonetheless.

"What would happen if I did?"

The smile remains on her lips and her eyes meet mine. "I'd have to stop you."

I hum in acknowledgement and, other than our footsteps, all else is silent. Eerily so. I get the impression that servants are around somewhere, but none make an appearance. Of course, that might be because I'm here. Orcs, even half-bloods, were exiled from man's land hundreds of years ago. I don't imagine a Queen would want anyone to see her walking with a monster like me.

And yet, side by side, we make our way down a spiraling staircase. It opens right out onto a too perfect, lush, green lawn. I am forced to pause. Indeed, this is quite the opposite of Black Mountain. This is unlike anything I've ever seen before.

"Beautiful? Isn't it?" Petra gazes out at her gardens with pride—rolling green hills, perfectly cropped bushes, fans of flowers, and pristine, stone paths.

I frown at it all in dismay. "Strange is more like it."

"*Strange?*" Her expression tells me she approves of my forwardness. "No one has ever referred to it as strange. Envercress is famous for its gardens."

"I imagine no has told you how strange it is, because you frighten people. So does this place."

My words earn a frown, the first true display of emotion I've seen from the witch. And that's what she is. Maybe she is the Queen of Envercress too, but more than anything else, more than being an 18-year-old girl, Petra is a witch.

"Are you telling me you're scared, Thorn?" Her eyes scan me in that assessing way and I shake my head.

"Not scared. *Aware.*"

I cast my attention across this overly manicured land. You don't see such order in the Perished Woods—everything is wild in that place. But the unnaturalness isn't the only thing that strikes me about Petra's garden. It's all the faces and the bodies. A sea of statues striking odd poses—poses that look more like people frozen in a state of horror than art. Petra pushes on, her pace slow, and I watch the statues—who seem to watch us right back.

"Why don't we start with those questions?" she suggests.

I clasp my hands behind my back and draw in breath. "Alright. How about this: Do you know what I went through to get to Black Mountain? Or how long I had to fight to get into The Pit?"

Her lips quirk. "Do *you*?"

My nostrils flare in anger. "You said I could ask questions. Is that not true?"

"You have the answers to these ones. Why not ask me something you don't know? Like why I brought you here."

I clench my jaw and stare at the white-marble statue of a man with his arms outstretched before him, the muscles in his hands flex as he reaches. It's as if he was stopped just before strangling a foe. I stare at it for a long time before I turn to Petra. "Who would make a statue of such a thing?"

She frowns. "Yet another question you already know the answer to. Thorn, you disappoint me."

"*You* made this."

"I made all of these." The admission is flat and my lips remain sealed. The Queen's patience thins. "What stops you from asking what you set out to know? Is it this *costume*? Did you expect a demon in red? Or is it my womanhood that offends you, half-blood?"

Anger rises in me. "Maybe I did expect a little more pageantry."

The queen scoffs. "Is transporting you all this way not enough? Gods, Thorn, you are difficult to please."

I let out a growl of warning. Another time, I'd thrill at this game—this challenge. But I was on a pilgrimage. My journey had *meaning* and this child-like witch plucked me from my path. "I was expecting to face off with the Devil himself."

"Don't you sound self-important?" Petra strides away and I follow her, wanting to dump my anger on the girl, but I'm drawn by curiosity as well. She might not be the Devil, but she has power—and lots of it.

Water babbles. There's a large fountain, embellished and feminine beyond anything else I've seen thus far. If there is one thing about Petra Gunnora that is obvious, it is her minimalistic style. She is not ostentatious in the least, though judging by her castle and the wealth it must take to maintain, she has the means to be as ostentatious as she pleases. So, where did this extravagant fountain come from?

"Not exactly your style, is it?" I see her eyes cut to the center, to the flourishes of water spraying around a focal point of flowers and fairies. There's a pedestal there and on it sits a woman's crown...dripping with diamonds. *Definitely not Petra's style.*

"This isn't for me."

"For the girl who wore that crown then?"

Petra cocks her head, setting her jaw and steeling herself against my needling. I search for more clues in the garden—

from the face of each desperate statue to a massive, white cage with nothing but an empty swing inside. The breeze gives a nudge and its chains whine in protest. A game of chess sits at a garden table, half played. I make for it, but Petra stops me—her tone firm.

"Don't touch that."

And I don't, but my eyes narrow. "We're dancing here."

"And I happen to find it exceedingly dull," she barks back.

I'm forced to laugh at the flash of her true-self. I like these bits of reality more than the show she seems so accustomed to. "Gods forbid I bore a Queen."

I consider her. This isn't the way I imagined things, but I find myself in a position to get the closure I set out for so long ago. All those questions that drove me, that set me on my path, far from the life I knew and the only family I had. It all felt so maddeningly important. Only, as I stand here, pondering the questions again for the first time in a long while...they fall away. The words I'd practiced, the fire behind them...they don't matter in the same way they once did.

"I..." I'm forced to laugh, deep and true. "I was an angry thing in my youth."

"What a revelation," the Queen says drily.

"Indeed, it is." Apparently, in all the fighting, I learned something about myself.

I rub my chin, contemplative. Ash was leaving, spending more time out on the trails and I was resentful of the fact that he didn't think like me. *He* wasn't as angry or as burdened as I felt. So, I left him. I told myself I'd go to the Devil and find out why I was made. Why he keeps making orcs only to relegate us to the cursed forest—with no true place in this world, conquered by man.

I wanted to know my purpose, to find out where my mother had gone, and why my father didn't care to return. I wanted to know why I felt so painfully alone all the time. But more than anything, I wanted to run away from Ash. Not because he was different from me, but because I was so frightened of being abandoned.

He was my little brother, but I had raised him. He gave my life meaning. Every day I got up—hunted, traded, foraged—all for him. Without my brother, I might have killed myself. I had been so utterly alone until he came along and suddenly he was all grown up and that void in my heart returned. It terrified me. So I ran to Black Mountain. I built it up in my mind.

I turned my anger on something safe—*myself*. I looked in the mirror and saw an abomination, a visage that prevented me from being anything more than a forest-dweller. A *cursed* forest dweller at that—and what good is there in a cursed forest? Wasn't I meant for something more, something great? Wasn't I *deserving* of a place in this world? I thought so. I could feel it in the very blood coursing through my veins. *I* was meant for something bigger. It was out there and it was calling to me. Even now, I can feel it. I told myself it was my blood—my orc blood calling. I rub at my chest, at the place right over my heart and the emptiness...

"More's the pity," I say. "I find I've no questions to ask. Only a statement to make."

"Consider me your captive audience."

Somehow I feel I am the captive here, but I speak my revelation just the same. "I was meant for something more. That's what I would have told the Devil."

A smile, wide and true, spreads across the Queens lips. She clasps her hands before her chest, and for a bare moment, she *is* the young girl she pretends to be. A ghost of something long since passed. "Well, I'm glad you're here, because I think so too."

Petra touches my arm, leading me. I furrow my brow at the momentary connection, being far more used to fear—even beasts recoil when they see my monstrous face. But not Petra.

"This is where I come to think," she tells me.

We stand on a small bridge arching over a pond. It is as clean and white as all her other garden ornamentation. Staring into the water, she toys with the gem at her neck.

"Do I detect nervousness?"

The Queen gives a soft smile. "Mmm. I confess, I do find myself nervous at the moment."

"You show no signs of fear, yet you are in the company of a monster."

"I am not scared of you, Thorn."

"No, you aren't. Which makes me wonder, what in the world might make you nervous?"

The side of her lips curl into a half-smile. "Honesty."

I raise a brow.

"I'm considering sharing quite a bit of the truth with you, Thorn. More truth than I'm used to sharing."

"Why would you do that? You don't know me."

"No. But I need you."

I'm unconvinced. "Why?"

Her fingers toy with that stone. "With this, I can see the future. Or possible paths anyway…and do you know what I saw? An orc."

"There are many orcs. Thousands in the belly of Black Mountain alone."

"How many of them did you kill?"

I shrug. "Plenty."

"So you're a warrior."

"Princess, I'm one of the best."

Her expression is flat and I laugh aloud, happy to have needled her.

"I don't think you like being called Princess."

"You know what I am, I see no need for pretense in this arrangement."

"Prefer I call you Witch then?"

CAPTURED BY THE ORC KING

Single-minded, she ignores my taunting. "I need someone I have faith in."

My eyes widen skeptically. "You have faith in me?"

"I have faith in my stone. And anyway, I can see *you* just as well as you can see me, Thorn. If not better. I know exactly what trials you faced in Black Mountain. And...I know what sent you there."

My chest tightens and I think of Ash.

"You were determined to find your purpose. You *knew* you were meant for great things. Don't you see? Your path led you here! *You* are the orc I need."

I relax, letting the memory of Ash fall away. I've the stark impression that I wouldn't want him here, around this woman. "What exactly do you need me for?"

I follow her gaze into the water finally. Brightly colored fish swim lazily beneath the surface. Our reflections stare back. And beside us stands the reflection of another. A young man, loathing in his eyes as he glares at Petra. I snap my attention to the place he should be on the bridge, but no one is there. The reflection lives in water alone. The Queen watches him without malice...perhaps only with a bit of regret.

"Many years ago I came to this castle as stepdaughter to the King."

"How many years?"

She shakes her head. "It doesn't matter."

"Then it shouldn't matter if you tell me—you said you wanted to be honest, did you not?"

Her voice is low. "Eighty. Maybe closer to ninety now."

"That's a long time to be a Princess."

"I am a Queen, Thorn. I didn't want to be. I *never* wanted this burden, but at a point it became clear that I was the only one fit to keep this land safe. Maybe my people do fear me, maybe they think I'm strange, but *I keep them safe.*"

"And where do I come in?"

"There is a threat on the horizon and I'm not one to sit on my hands."

I stare at the angry reflection once more. Looks as if he's screaming in rage, but no sound comes from the water.

"The King in Pontheugh is mad. More than that, he's absolute trash, running his kingdom into the ground. His people suffer and the suffering will only worsen the longer he's in power."

"Not your kingdom. Who cares if they have shit for a King?"

"Let me explain. I consider myself more of a shepherd than a witch."

I throw my head back and laugh.

"That wasn't meant to be a joke."

"What you're saying is that you're *controlling*."

"If someone else is fit to be in control, send them my way. I'll happily relinquish the burden."

"I'll wear your crown if you hate it so much."

Petra raises a brow. "That's what I was hoping you'd say."

Sobering quickly, I tell her, "I don't believe I follow you."

"If I continue to ignore Pontheugh there will be a war. The King will send his army. He will wound my land and my people. I can't allow that."

"How do you know?"

"I can *see* it."

"What are you going to do about it?"

"I'm going to send my own army first. I refuse to allow blood to be shed in Envercress."

"But you don't mind spilling it in Pontheugh?"

"There are only so many options available to me, Thorn, and I am forced to choose the one least damaging."

"You didn't like the way things were run around here, so you took over. Now you don't like the way they do things in Pontheugh, so you're taking that kingdom as well."

Petra shakes her head. "No. You're going to take it for me."

"Me?"

"Yes, you. I can't be in two places at once. I need someone I can trust to wear the crown there, to commit to doing things according to my...*methods.*"

"How do you know you can trust me with such a task?"

"I've seen it."

"You've seen *me* ruling over Pontheugh?"

"It is one possible outcome."

"I thought you claimed to see the future?"

"I said I can see *possible* futures. And right now the one in Pontheugh is...too murky for my liking. I want to send you there. I want to claim the most favorable path now, before it's too late."

"Why should I help?"

"You want purpose and I seek to give it to you. You'll have an army of orcs, and once you take the castle, capture the King and his daughter for me, you'll have a crown and a kingdom to rule over. Orcs will be freed from the Perished Woods and you will have a place above all others. You will be King. Isn't that what you wanted?"

"Well, not exactly, but it doesn't sound bad."

"Then align yourself with me. Ride on Pontheugh, stir terror along the way, and when you get to the gates..." She looks down at the stone but seems disappointed. "When you get to the gates it will all become clearer. I will be able to guide you to victory."

I turn my back on the pond and stare up at the castle. It's magnificent really, like nothing I've ever seen. And this Witch-Queen, this Eternal Princess, is telling me I will have one of my very own.

"Seems mad."

"What does?"

"That you have more faith in a monster than you have for the man in power."

"Appearances are such a small thing, Thorn. It's what's on

the inside that counts. Look at me. I wear this mask for the benefit of others, to give them peace. Don't fool yourself into thinking you're different."

"I wear no masks. I'm as real as they come and I don't think this face gives anyone peace." I jab my thumb at the scars across my cheekbone.

Petra levels me with her gaze. "You wear a different type of mask, but a mask nonetheless. The exterior is harsh, but inside, you're—"

"Are you trying to say I'm weak?"

Petra purses her lips and shakes her head. "I think you're strong, I think you love fiercely, and I think there are few people in this world as principled as you. That's why you made it here and that's why I've given you more honesty in the last hour than I've given anyone in the last 90 years."

There is passion in her words and it speaks to me.

Looking back over the course of my life and at the times I felt the greatest sense of belonging. It wasn't when I was fighting in the belly of Black Mountain—though I was quite good at that. I felt most at home in myself when caring for Ash. He's grown now, gone. But maybe I can reclaim that feeling, that sense of leadership. There's an entire kingdom out there, waiting for *a shepherd*.

I turn to Petra. "I will give you the victory you desire, Princess, if your promise is indeed to make me King."

"As I said, I have a certain method. As long as you can place your trust in that method, we have an alliance."

I reach for the Queen's hand and she takes mine, but doesn't let go.

"There's one more thing."

"What's that?"

From her pocket she produces a gold medallion. Like a large coin, hanging from a heavy chain. "You must promise to wear this—*always*."

I narrow my eyes at the thing. "Always?"

"It is a link between us."

"Magic, no doubt?"

"Of course it is magic. It will help me communicate with you, and you with me. *This* will keep you safe. It will make you stronger."

"I'm strong enough."

"A war is coming; you can never be too strong or too safe."

"It's really not my style—"

"There is no deal without the medallion." Her expression is so ridged and serious; it seems uncanny on the face of such a youthful girl.

I click my tongue at the shinning piece of metal. "Then I suppose I have a new piece of jewelry." Petra watches, leaning forward with anticipation as I slip the chain around my neck. The second it hits my chest…I stagger under the weight of it.

A cloud blows in, making the air seem heavy and the sky dark. My muscles twitch with need. Pontheugh is so far away, but it's calling me.

"Thorn?"

I scan the horizon for it.

"Thorn? Look at me. Can you hear me?"

The clouds are churning and I find it impossible to keep my eyelids open.

CHAPTER 2

Alba

Presently...

There's laughter spilling out onto the dusty main road of Aberdeen. From inside the tavern I hear a stool scrape across wood floors. It's followed by a loud thud and more of that raucous laughter. My stomach is in knots. I stand there, wincing, trying to gather enough courage to breach the walls of this awful place.

The door swings open before I do, and out of the alehouse tumbles a ruddy-cheeked Jacob Tilbury, with a chicken tucked under one heavy arm and a woman under the other. The woman is the blonde-haired and buxom Jacquette. It's hard not to know everyone in a small village like this—and while I don't *know* Jacquette personally, I certainly know *of* her.

She's a *woman of the night*...though it's only midafternoon. Already, she seems to be in her element, hair mussed and the lacings of her bodice only half-tied. Jacquette offers a passing glance and Jacob doesn't seem to notice me at all.

They leave the tavern door ajar as they go: an invitation. I take a deep breath and straighten my spine, before I march my way inside.

Immediately, I'm hit with stale and muggy air. It absolutely reeks in here. I'm forced to wrinkle my nose at the onslaught of body odor and spilt beer. It's dark too—with very little light permeating grease-clouded windows. All the patrons seem to be crowded at the bar, around a brunette who has the men's attention—at least, those men who can still keep their heads up. Lavinia is the woman and I know her only by her affiliation with Jacquette. She spots me right away.

An amused twinkle in her eye, she calls out, "Be gone with you, nag! No wives allowed!"

The men cast glazed eyes in my direction and throw their heads back, laughing when they see me looking every inch the nagging wife I'm about to prove myself to be. I clench my jaw, utterly mortified, hating even the idea of having to be around people like this. But I came to retrieve my husband.

"I'm here for Luther," I call back, though my voice doesn't sound nearly as powerful as Lavinia's. It's more like a question, as if I am only here to ask if he might eventually decide to return home.

She smirks and nods her head toward a booth along the far wall. "He's indisposed." And indeed, there is my husband, passed out on a bench. Luther's mouth gapes, spittle wetting a chin that hasn't been clean shaven in days. His hair is disheveled and his shirt unbuttoned. He looks like...an embarrassment.

I start toward him, but Lavinia speaks once more. "I wouldn't if I were you, honey. He's apt to be in a mood." Her words stop me in my tracks, making me second-guess myself. I've still got bruises from the last time Luther was in a mood.

But this isn't right. He shouldn't be here, wasting the day, spending all our coin on...on this *ugliness*. We barely have enough to feed ourselves. I don't even want to think about how much he must have spent to get into this shameful state.

Oh Luther! We haven't been married a year yet and already I'm miserable. I never imagined life like this. Marriage was supposed to be a fairytale—especially with this man. I had admired him for so long. Oh, and Luther was *so* handsome; he could have had anyone. But he chose me and I thought that meant something. I thought he loved me. Only, Luther doesn't seem to love anything besides himself and this awful place.

I square my shoulders, determined. This is *not* the life I'm going to have. Voices hush as I march toward my unconscious husband. I'm too ashamed to send angry glares at the others. I just want to get Luther and get us out of here. Close enough to hear his snoring, I hesitate, unsure of what to do next.

I clear my throat. *"Luther?"*

Still sounds like a question. I try again. "Luther." Sounds a little firmer now, but he doesn't budge.

Finally, I lean over him and give my husband a gentle shake. My own body is cold, yet I'm sweating. *Nerves.* Luther's eyes flutter. He's beginning to come to. I force a serene and loving smile to my face as his eyes focus on me. "Luther, darling. It's time to come home now." I'm careful to say the words oh-so gently. Truth be told, I'm terrified of setting him off.

His brows furrow and he lifts his head just a little to confirm where he is. "What are you doing here?" he asks, sounding disoriented…and annoyed.

I avoid the question. "Come on. Let's go." I reach out, trying to help him, but he shoves my hand away and sits up on his own. I straighten. Behind me, I can hear the others snickering; I can feel their eyes on my back—gleefully watching this pathetic display unfold.

Luther can barely open his eyes. Squinting, he scrubs a dirty hand down his face. "What the fuck are you doing here, Alba?"

I'm still trying to stand tall, but it feels like a lie. Awkwardly, I shift on my feet, questioning myself. Maybe I shouldn't have come here. But what am I supposed to do? *Truly, what am I supposed to do about all this?*

Unable to cobble together any words or reasoning, I try—cautiously—to reach for my husband again. I only want to help him home. He's drunk—eyes bloodshot, swaying as he sits. He *belongs* at home, sobering up.

But he slaps me away again, harder this time. His hand connects with my chest. There's a hollow thunk, knocking the wind out of me. I'm thrown back onto my ass. For a slim moment there is silence, and then an eruption of laughter from the bar. Luther laughs too and I scramble to my feet—eyes stinging.

Lavinia, humor in her tone, shouts, "This is why I say no wives allowed!"

I make for the door.

"And don't come back!" someone seconds.

Their laughter follows me, nipping at my heels in my humiliating escape. Only, I bump into Jacquette as she's coming in.

"*Watch it, you twit!*" Her face is twisted in a hateful scowl and she shoves me too. Everyone laughs harder.

"What's her problem?" I hear Jacquette question as the door slams shut. I'm out on the dirt road again, hot tears streaming down my cheeks. I point myself in the direction of my father's shop.

* * *

THE DOOR IS OPEN, flies buzzing in and out. His cleaver comes down on the counter as I slide to a halt inside the threshold.

He looks up. Seeing that I'm not a customer, the warmth in his expression vanishes. "What's wrong with you?" he grumbles.

"It's Luther. He's drunk again, down at that tavern." I wipe the tears from my cheeks. "I went to get him—"

My father's face screws up in surprise. *"You did what?"*

"I went to get him. To bring him home."

"What'd ya do that for?"

"He's drunk!"

"The man likes a little ale. What's the big deal?"

"We've got no coin—"

"So *that's* why you're here." He points his cleaver at me. "I ain't giving you any handout—"

"That's *not* why I'm here. I came for a little help, some guidance! Luther is at that tavern, drinking himself half to death with what little coin we have. How are we supposed to *eat* if he spends everything on ale?"

My father shakes his head, focusing on the work of dismembering a pig. He's the village butcher—has been my whole life. And the smell in here is worse than the tavern, but it's a smell I'm used to. Dried blood and dead flesh. Even the upstairs smells of it. I was raised above this shop. Just me and Dad. No mother to speak of. For a while there was my grandmother, but she passed when I was still very young.

"Just like a woman." He spits. "You expect everything of the man and aren't willing to do a thing yourself."

"What am I to do? Tell me and I'll do it."

"How about you take in a little sewing work? Or some wash?"

"I don't have the coin to buy needles or thread and we barely have enough soap to do our own wash!"

"Excuses. That's all I hear from you."

"That's no excuse. It's reality." I hold out my dress to show him un-darned holes along the seams.

"Then garden, why don't you?"

I grit my teeth. "I try. It isn't enough."

"Sounds like *you're* not enough. That's why you can't keep your husband at home."

My throat tightens. Secretly, I fear he's right. Maybe I'm a terrible wife and that's why Luther doesn't love me and why he escapes to the tavern every chance he gets.

"You know he hits me."

My father sets his cleaver on the counter with a loud clank. When I raise my eyes to look at him his face is stern—angry. "Get out of here."

"*What?*"

"You heard me. I said get out."

"But I..."

"You're just like your mother. *Entitled.* You think this world owes you something. For what? Because you have a pussy?"

My cheeks heat and I have the urge to run again.

"Be a better wife. How about that? Don't come around here trying to make your husband look bad, trying to make everyone pity you—"

"That's not what I'm trying to do at all! I just...I need help! This isn't what I thought marriage would be!"

"Get your head out of the clouds and grow up, why don't you? You've a duty to that man and you're lucky to have him. If it weren't for what happened to Adelaide, Luther would have *never* chosen you. Think about that next time you want to complain that your husband isn't good enough."

I feel punched in the chest again. "I don't know why I thought you'd understand."

Now my father's face screws up into something truly angry and he strides round the counter with such aggression that I fear he might hit me too. I skitter back. "Don't you embarrass me or Luther like this again. You stay out of that tavern; you hear? Get your ass home and start worrying about what *you* need to be doing."

I stare at my father towering over me—the bulging vein that runs between his eyes and over his bald head, he's wearing the same blood-soaked smock he's worn since I was a girl, and the same hateful grimace. I'm his daughter, his only child, but we were never close, were we? I've no memory of him putting me up on those tall shoulders. There were never any stories before bed or laughter around the table during a meal. Why did I come here thinking he might help? Probably because I have nowhere else to go.

I square my shoulders but look at the ground. "I apologize."

"*I apologize*," he mocks, relaxing his body and making his way back to the pig, swatting at flies along the way. "Little fucking brat. Just like her mother." He isn't talking to me anymore, but under his breath and to himself. I tell him goodbye, but he makes no indication I was heard.

Calmer now, though nothing solved, I leave my father's shop and start down the road toward home, keeping my eyes down the entire time.

What am I to do? All I ever wanted was to be a wife—Luther's wife, to be exact. But this is *not* how I imagined our life together.

Luther set his sights on me after Adelaide was no longer an option. They seemed like an obvious match. Two beautiful people. But Adelaide went mad with grief after the sudden death of her parents and she never quite recovered, not in the way the village wanted her to anyway. *Contrary* is what folks called her...among many other, much nastier things.

In any case it was my lucky day. With Adelaide unavailable, I was the next best thing. The runner-up. Luther aimed his beautiful blue eyes at me and I thought it meant something. I thought we were going to live happily ever after.

But as soon as the ring slipped round my finger, he became a different man. Or maybe he finally showed his true face. Luther is a beast. A monster. And I'm at wits' end. My husband is drinking us out of house and home, he spends all his time in the company of drunkards and whores, and when he does bother to show his face...it's worse than him being gone.

"What can I do?" I mutter. I've been grasping at straws, trying to please him—to clean just right or cook his favorite meals. I walk on eggshells whenever he's around, terrified of setting him off. Today I thought, maybe I need to put my foot down? Maybe that would get through to Luther. But it didn't. It was just another humiliating ordeal.

I'm consumed by my thoughts and I don't notice another traveler on the road until a loud gasp draws me from my rumination.

"*Alba!*"

I startle, looking up to see Margery Carter on the path before me. My mother-in-law. She's got a basket on her arm with a kerchief tucked around its contents. Perched atop her head is a very out-of-fashion floral bonnet. The high-necked dress she's wearing is so confining around her thick neck, I imagine she must feel half-strangled.

"What in the name of the Gods are you doing out here?"

I feel strangled as well, but I manage to find my words. "I suppose you've heard about what happened at the tavern?" My cheeks heat and I wonder if the whole village knows of my pathetic attempt to bring my louse of a husband back home.

"Look at your face!" She's horrified—her mouth open and curved impossibly downward. Worried eyes scan our surroundings, making sure there are no witnesses. She rips the shawl from her shoulders and begins to drape it over me—as if to hide me from view.

"Margery—" I'm both startled and confused.

"*What is wrong with you?*" she hisses, still pinching the shawl around my head and shoulders.

I stare at her, dumbfounded and she reaches out, pressing

her thumb to a yellowing bruise on my cheek bone. It hurts and I suck in a breath while trying to tear from her hold.

"Do you *want* people to see you like this?"

I'd rather not be bruised in the face at all, but I bite my tongue.

"You *terrible, terrible* girl. You'll be the embarrassment of my family. I warned Luther about you."

"You warned him about me?"

She squeezes her lips together as if something sour is setting on her tongue. "No mother. Of course you don't know how to act."

"How do you propose I act when my husband drinks away the sunlight day after day? Or when he sets his fists on me after having one—*or ten*—too many?"

She turns her face away, the truth being a vulgar thing. "Oh! My Luther! My baby!" She wails. "How did he ever end up with such an awful wife?" Margery pulls a second kerchief from her waistband and holds it to her lips. "Go home, girl. Don't come out with your face looking like that again."

"Who will do the shopping? Am I allowed to fetch water from the well? Or are you worried I might bring shame on the family from my own garden?"

Margery raises a brow and drops the lament from her tone. "That garden brings us all shame."

I'm in a stupor—I feel as if I'm going mad. Luther's actions are so vile, yet I'm the only one who has a problem with them. As a matter of fact, everyone seems to view *me* as the problem.

"Your son is a drunk and a lowlife."

Margery wails loud enough to block out my words. Trembling with rage, I shout louder.

"HE'S IN THE TAVERN NOW WITH DRUNKS AND WHORES!"

"No, no he isn't! You're a liar!"

"HE HITS ME, MARGERY. YOUR PRECIOUS SON BEATS HIS WIFE!"

"You deserve it, you disgusting thing. How dare you try to bring my family low! Go home this instant. I can't stand looking at your awful face." And she won't look at me. I might as well be a pile of cow shit steaming in the center of the road.

I shake myself, ready to leave the interaction behind, but before I can take two steps toward home Margery calls out. "Launder that shawl before you return it."

With wide-eyes, I realize her stupid shawl is still draped around me. I tear it off and scream—a deep, belly scream. No words. Just hot rage. Surely my face turns beet red, but I don't care. I scream in Margery's direction and throw her shawl into the dirt. "Wash it yourself!"

And I don't stand there a second longer, an audience to her feigned distress.

"I'm going home!"

A short while later I'm turning down the path to the one-room cottage I share with Luther. My eyes stinging with angry tears, but there's no one out here to see me, so I let them flow without shame.

Am I going mad? I feel like it. I'm certainly acting like it. Going to the tavern today, that was out of character for me. Screaming like a banshee in Margery's face was new as well. But I'm miserable and I've tried everything I can think of to get Luther to change. What a hopeless endeavor…trying to change a person.

My shoulders slump and my feet drag, but the world around me cares nothing for my misery. The sun shines, birds sing, and flowers seem to be blooming everywhere but in my own garden. I stop to stare at my home with a furrowed brow. It's uninviting, cramped and dusty, with no one to talk to. Memories of Luther's ugliness have been punched into the walls—

quite literally. Every moment inside that place leaves me haunted by my past and wary of my future.

I don't want to go in.

So I stand outside, options exhausted. I know I have to prepare dinner and I've chores to do that won't get done by any other hands. Even with no drive to speak of, I'll do it all. I'll do it so Luther doesn't have another reason to hit me—though I've given him plenty today.

A lump forms in my throat and I rub at it as tears slip down my cheeks. *What can I do?* I beg the Gods to send an answer.

As always, they are silent—with the exception of a branch snapping nearby.

I startle, spinning to see where the sound originated. But there's nothing there. Fields of green wheat grass wave gently. The nearest neighbor is a mile up the road. Clenching my jaw, a child-like fear coils in the pit of my stomach, and I turn toward the tree line.

It isn't just any tree line. It's the gateway to the cursed forest, pressed right up against the border of Aberdeen. Though I'm scared, I force myself to search the shadowy woodland with my gaze. Mist hangs thick beyond the blackened trunks. Every muscle in my body tightens the longer I stare. If there is something out there, I need to know. It isn't as if there is a man here to protect me.

The longer I stare, the more certain I become...I'm not alone. I see nothing unusual, of course. It's just a feeling mounting in my core. I'm being watched.

I open my mouth to speak, but the words get stuck. Clearing my throat, I try again. *"Hello? Is someone there?"* I call.

We've all heard the stories, of monsters and beasts that reside in that unhallowed land. I don't know that I believe in them, but I do believe in evil. Luther could be out there, trying to frighten me—a punishment for this afternoon. But I don't know that he's brave or fool enough to step beyond that boundary.

I remember once, when I was a child, there was a little boy who did. A flash of a memory deepens my terror—a swollen and purple hand hanging from beneath a death shroud. No priest would bury him.

Another snap of a branch and it's too much for me. I make a mad sprint for my dark and unwelcoming cottage.

CHAPTER 3

Thorn

So many villages to burn on my way to the castle...it's tedious. It's muck I must wade through before I arrive at the place I truly wish to be. The urge to force my way is incessant. I desire nothing other than to ride on the kingdom that is meant to be mine and claim the throne that awaits.

But that is not the way her majesty wants it.

Instead I'm forced to plod along the boundary of the Perished Woods, committed to her method. *Petra.* She makes my muscles twitch. It's as if there is something foul about her, just on the edge of my perception, always slipping away before I can grasp it.

The all too familiar scent of moist soil and rotting leaves distracts me, filling my nostrils. I breathe it in. I breathe in deep —doing what I can to calm the thunder clouds within—to be present in this moment. Conquering will come. Until then, scouting helps.

Learning the enemy focuses my attention. Not that humans have proven to be much in terms of opposition. The villagers have shown themselves to be insufferably weak and there are few warriors among their clans and settlements. Reconnaissance is, at the very least, a challenge to my mind if not my sword.

I spend my time out here, treading the outskirts of this place that was once my home, inching closer to man's land. The trials of Black Mountain are of the past and here I have some semblance of quiet, forcing me to face a stark and painful truth: *I am lonely.* I miss Black Mountain if only for the fight. I had brothers there, in a way, didn't I? Hard to remember now. What I really miss is the intimate companionship that Ash and I shared. And while I march with an army numbering in the thousands, it simply isn't the same. I feel so far away. Surrounded by orcs, I'm as alone as ever. Alone as I was on the day I turned my back on Ash. And I ask myself, should a King have to burden such an emotion? Doesn't seem right.

Leaves crunch beneath my feet, thoughts swim. Voices contend in my mind—calling me to the stone spires far in the distance. A maddening hum follows me everywhere. In camp, it ratchets—always drumming, drumming, drumming. All the time. Then there are the witches. They followed us from the woods. Masked in beauty, they dance and they fuck, but I can hear the dark magic buzzing around them, like flies to a corpse.

I've come to crave these moments away, where I can focus on a task, where I can chase some echo of my *own* voice. I catch whispers of it—of concern and regret. I remember how much I miss my brother and the fool notions that led me away to begin with.

Perhaps, once I take the castle, he will hear of me and venture out of the Perished Woods. Ash will come and we will be family again.

That's what I think about that anyway, when my mind is calm. I think of Ash.

Moving among the shadows and through the mist, there is a

whole world beyond the veil of the cursed forest. Man's land. I can see it, bright and hot. *Too* bright. *Too* hot. It doesn't appeal to me. I'm drawn to the moist soil of the forest, the dank scent of nature in decay. The medallion around my neck hums angrily and an incongruent voice whispers in my mind, telling me I'm wrong, that the castle is out there in all that bright heat and I *want* that castle.

What I want is that awful voice out of my head. I crave silence and the throne is where I will find it. But there are still so many villages between me and my destination, villages the Eternal Princess wants to see engulfed in flames. Burn them, strike fear into the hearts of the leaders of Pontheugh, she says. These country hamlets pose no oppositional threat. But they can be *used,* she tells me, to show our power and mercilessness. They can be *used* to influence their King. It is through fear that Petra will get into his mind...

My own temples throb as I push myself to maintain concentration.

Another nameless and dusty village. Insects hum from the fields. Still on the outskirts, I've passed a few quiet and lonely houses, but haven't seen a soul. Not even a single dog to bark warning of my presence. This tiny village is nothing more than fodder. Particularly sad fodder at that. The homes will go up in a flash and I probably won't even be able to pillage anything of value for my tent.

It's with that morose thought in mind that I pause. The crunch of dirt beneath shoes meets my ears and I spot a woman coming up the road. With narrow eyes I assess her. She's young. Her hair blonde, like honey. She's the first person I've seen in hours and though her presence is of little value to the task at hand, the afternoon is late and I am bored. So, I lean against a tree to watch...vaguely curious.

Focusing, my mind seems to clear ever so slightly and I try to imagine what this young woman's story is. There's a heat about her, anger and tension held in the shoulders, in her stride. But with every step, the woman weakens. She bows a little more inward. An invisible weight bears down. *I wonder what her name is.* She turns up a path, coming closer, and I cast my eyes to her destination.

A woeful little cottage, in my opinion. And I grew up in a dilapidated witch's shack in a cursed forest, so that's saying something about this girl's place, now isn't it?

Even on a bright day like this, there's a shadow hanging over her home. I try to discern if it's a trick of my unruly mind. But no…the cottage is grim and foreboding. When I look back at the honey-haired woman, I see that she has stopped too, to stare at the house.

Dread? Hopelessness? I try to read her. One thing is certain, she's weeping. And tomorrow will be more weeping for her. Weeping and then death. A swift one if she's lucky.

It strikes me as a bit sad, that her last day of life is spent like this…so forlorn.

Hmm. I think to myself. Maybe I can influence her in some way? I search my surroundings. Tree trunks, mushrooms, grey-green leaves, a few dry and brittle sticks. This will do. I bend over and take one of those sticks in hand, toying with it as I watch her. She's just standing there on the path. Frozen.

With a smile curling my lips, I break the stick in two and thrill when I see her startle. Doesn't take long before her eyes dart in my direction. She doesn't see me of course, but she stares long and hard, her back straight as an arrow. It tickles me. There's something naively brave about it.

"*Hello?*" she calls. "Is anyone there?"

I bite my bottom lip, wanting so very badly to return her call. Wouldn't that be amusing? I can't imagine she expects an answer, but if she got one…I'd love to see the look on her face.

It is quite a pretty face. Inhaling deeply, I catch her scent on the air. It's soft, like roses. My smile fades and suddenly I feel cold despite the heat of the day. I don't know why, but I find it distressing that this woman is going to die tomorrow.

Strange. I've never felt that before.

I break the stick a second time and discard the pieces, watching her sprint—with impressive speed—toward her grim, little cottage.

"There. Not sad anymore. Just scared." Perhaps fear will serve her better than pain.

I don't know why, but I watch that cottage just a bit longer, half-hoping to see a pretty face in one of the windows.

CHAPTER 4

Alba

*H*eart racing, I bring the latch down and wait with my back pressed against the door. My breath is ragged and I clutch at my chest, eyes squeezed shut. Moments pass, painfully slow. I'm sure someone or something is coming. My ears quest for any sound that might confirm my suspicion, but there's nothing.

Still, I scan the room, combing for signs someone was here. Everything appears as I left it. YET I remain unconvinced and scramble to the nearest window, careful to stay out of sight.

That feeling, out on the path. I *knew* something was there, watching, toying with me. But now that I'm surrounded by the safety of these four walls, I begin to talk myself out of it. Hurriedly, I check all the windows only to find nothing beyond a familiar and lonesome landscape on the other side.

There is nothing out there.

I lean against the wall, hand on my forehead, laughter bubbling up. "Probably a damned squirrel. And here I am sweating." I laugh a bit longer and it makes me feel light—it makes me feel like *myself* again. I'm not the nagging and worried wife, wondering how we'll make ends meet, or if I can get through a day without being hit, screamed at, or made to feel a fool.

Dropping my head back, I stare at the ceiling, revelation washing over me. This is about Luther, isn't it? These past months of marriage have me wound so tight I'm likely to snap. *Oh*, but I *did* snap today! And at Margery, no less. The memory has me buckling over, laughing again. I can picture her face. Cheeks puffing in and out, sputtering as I bellowed. I'll pay for it later, but for now it's hilarious. So hilarious that laugh until I'm crying again.

I press my palms to my cheeks, feeling wet tears. This has to end. Truly, how much can a woman take?

Time ticks on. The room grows darker with each passing minute. There's no telling when Luther will be home again. But he will be angry. The only thing I can do now is have the house clean, dinner ready, and anticipate all the things that are apt to set him off. It's going to be a rough night.

With a deep breath I push myself up, feeling like I'm wading through molasses, but I can't let that stop me.

* * *

THE SUN IS long since gone by the time I finish chores and dinner. I bank the fire, keeping the coals alive and Luther's stew in a pot hanging over them. It will be warm and ready when he does stumble in—hopefully too drunk to remember the scene I made this afternoon.

I check the windows one last time, staring long and hard into the night. It feels as if something *could* be out there. But the only thing I have to fear is Luther. I climb the loft ladder up to our bed. It's as cold as it always. Unwelcoming, even to the weariest soul.

The problem isn't the sagging mattress, but rather, my

racing thoughts. Sleep has been elusive; my mind simply won't settle itself. Still I lie down, going through the motions, allowing a restless slumber to harness me, if only for a short time. Maybe it's minutes. Could be hours.

My eyes shoot open in the dark and my ears prickle. It's childish, but my first thoughts are of monsters spilling from the cursed forest. My bones rattle and muscles clench. Then, I hear cursing and the telltale shuffle of a drunk's boots on dry earth.

Luther's home. My heart seizes—*and I forgot the latch.*

Scrambling from my bed, I can tell he's already at the door— fumbling with it.

Shit, shit, shit.

Down the ladder, across the room, I pull up the latch—the door bursts open, slamming into me as it does. I stifle any cry of pain, I'm in too deep as it is. Even a whimper is apt to set him off.

"Locking me out?" He's slurring, his eyes bloodshot and barely open.

"No, I'd heard a noise and—"

"Fucking bitch. You locked that damn door to piss me off, didn't you?" He's in my face already, voice raised. I can feel the hot stink of his breath on my skin. My jaw tightens and I struggle to maintain eye contact.

"No! There was a noise earlier. I was scared and I forgot to unlatch it. I'm sorry. It was my mistake."

"Damn right it was your mistake. You trying to fucking blame me? Locking me out of my own house. YOU can't lock me out of my house."

"No, of course not. I'd never try to do that."

He pulls his arm back. I've time to flinch before his palm connects with my cheek. The hit is hard enough to make my ears ring—an all too familiar sensation. Instinctively, I draw my arm and shoulder up, readying to block the next hit.

"DON'T FUCKING BACK-TALK ME. This is *my* house.

Think you're so big because you came down to the tavern today? Thought you were going to make a scene?"

He pushes past, roughly knocking me with his arm. I breathe in through my nose and bite my tongue, still angry and embarrassed about it all.

Luther draws short before the table and throws his arms into the air, expectant. My eyes are wide, heart racing. He wants me to read his mind, *but I can't.* I try to anticipate his needs, to know ahead of time what is going to upset him—but no matter how hard I try, I will never be able to read his mind. Still, I stumble forward, wanting to comply—wanting to do anything to keep from being hit. Because I know it can get a lot worse. Hell, I was lucky to get an open hand. More often it's his knuckles.

"Where the fuck is my dinner, Alba?"

"Oh!" I jump into action. Pulling down his bowl, the cutting board, a bread knife, and the loaf I'd bought fresh...but now it's stale, nearly a day old.

"*Oh? Oh?* Are you fucking stupid? I've been out all day. What the fuck do you expect? Of course I'm hungry!"

"Of course you're hungry," I echo, wincing at the bread and how dry it's become. I'll cut from the middle, put some butter on it, lay it on thick. He's hungry, drunk. He probably won't notice. But I've got that choking feeling, like icy hands creeping up my neck. *He's going to notice. He's looking for reasons to be angry. I'm fooling myself if I think this night is going to end with anything less than a black eye and a split lip. The bread could do it for me. The bread could set him off.*

My hands are shaking. I hear Luther grab a bottle from a small stand by the door. My throat tightens even more. I've been watering that old bottle down—and it isn't even because I'm afraid of Luther when he's drunk. The problem is, we don't have money to buy more wine. But I can't tell him that, can I?

It's just another thing he'll blame on me, another thing to take out on me.

He pulls out his chair, dropping into it with an ugly grunt. I wipe bread crumbs from the board, trying to conceal any signs of dryness. Then, I head to the pot over the hearth. The stew is warm inside, even though the coals are nearly dead. I give it a stir and ladle it into my husband's bowl. When I serve it, it's carefully and from across the table so Luther can't reach for me.

My eyes dart to the bottle. He's got no cup. I watch as he drinks straight from it—sloppily. A red stain dribbles down his chin. He doesn't bother wiping himself clean. Luther glares at the meal, while I wring my hands.

He's searching. Searching for something wrong. Something to be angry with. And I'm searching my mind, wondering if I *did* make a mistake. Too much salt? Is the meat dry? Chewy? I can hardly breathe, worrying about it.

Eventually, he leans forward and tucks in. My shoulders relax. Maybe he's drunk enough to pass out after this. A fool's wish. I think the truth is Luther is waiting for the right moment to explode. It's a sick game he's drawn me into. I made my move and now it's Luther's turn to take his.

I knew the odds were against me. It was a gamble going down to the tavern. I just thought that maybe it would show him how serious I am—how wounded I've been over our romance, if you can call it that. If nothing else, I hoped he might be concerned with his reputation. But I was wrong, wasn't I?

"What the fuck are you doing?"

I startle, dropping my hands to my sides. "Nothing."

"You just going to stand over me and stare?"

"What do you want me to do?"

"Act like a normal fucking person, will you?"

My mouth works and I look around the room for a place to take up less space, to become invisible, to fit in, *but I don't fit in here.* I don't fit in this house, this village, and certainly not this marriage. I snap. "NONE OF THIS IS NORMAL!" I scream.

I don't know where to go or what to do, because there is no place that won't offend Luther. There is no magic seat in this house to make me invisible. And Gods how I've tried to be invisible. Every move and every inaction is grist for his mill of hatred. I'm on eggshells. I can't win.

Luther sits back in his seat, a cruel smile on his lips. He knows he's won. I've raised my voice. He's free now, to do whatever he wants—to punish me anyway he sees fit.

"None of this is normal?" His voice is low, measured. He's like a cat toying with his prey. He wants me to play the game, to cower in the same way I've done just about every other night since our wedding. But today is different. *I'm* different.

"No! None of this is normal! You think it's normal to spend every day at that tavern, drinking yourself into this disgusting state? To be newlywed and not want to touch your wife with affection? We should *love* each other, Luther! I thought we were going to *love* each other!"

His head bobs in amusement. "You thought this was about love?"

"You...you asked for my hand in marriage..." I'm already stuttering, losing the conviction to my tone. "A man does that when he cares for a woman—"

Luther interrupts. "I married you because you had the best dowry—and don't get on your high horse about it. Just because it was the best doesn't mean it was much—but eventually your father will die and I'll inherit his business, his house, his land... That's why I picked you. That's the *only* reason I picked you. You stupid, wilting flower."

His words hit hard as fists. I squeeze my eyes shut and drop my head, so saddened by this news. So stupidly saddened. Luther never loved me. Without moving, I ask, "Did you ever *like* me? Did you think that maybe we were at least a good match? Even if there wasn't love between us?"

He slaps his hands together, the clap so loud I almost think I've been struck again. It resonates off the empty walls of our cottage. Luther throws his head back, laughing as if I made the most outlandish joke.

"*A good match?*" he asks finally, wiping a tear of mirth from the edge of his eye. "You're no match for me, Alba. Look at you." He makes a sweeping gesture with his hand. The look on his face...I can read it well, because I suppose I feel the same thing for him at this point. Disgust. "Who would want you?"

"I'm not homely. I clean, I cook for you—" I can hear my voice cracking. It's embarrassing really. I don't know why I take this man's words to heart. Maybe...maybe it's because I have no one to tell me he's wrong. Maybe it's because he sounds so much like my father always did and these are the same words I've been hearing my whole life. Perhaps I fear they are true. "I try to be a good wife."

"Your tits are too small. Your voice, your fucking voice, it's *grating*. You can't fuck to save your life. Your pussy is as dry as this fucking bread." He knocks the plate with the back of his hand, sending it and bread crumbs flying. "And worse of all, you're no fucking fun." Luther scoffs, shaking his head at me. "Yeah. You make a *great* wife."

I search for some kind of retort, but talking like this—so boldly—isn't familiar to me. "I'm a better wife than...than... those *whores* at the tavern would make!"

Now Luther's really laughing.

My hands find my hips and I try to stand a little taller, a little braver, and be a little more confident in my words.

"Gods, if they came with a dowry I'd have had either one of them over you. Least they get my dick wet when I stick it in them."

My stomach turns. Luther must see the shock on my face,

the silent question written there. I don't dare speak it aloud or even acknowledge it fully. To do so would be too painful, especially with Luther watching.

His eyes widen in delight. "Oh! Oh, you thought I only fuck *you?*" The notion pleases him above all else. "Tell me, Alba, you think there's something sacred about that dry cunt of yours? You got something special between your legs I don't know about?"

I think I might be sick and so I turn away, needing to create some distance, feeling the urge to run, but not having anywhere to go.

Luther pushes out of his seat, with nothing short of menace. The chair falls back, banging loudly on the ground. I cast my eyes to him, but it's so hard to look at that man's face. I see the cruel smile and how gleeful this all makes him. Luther is only happy when he's hurting me and he just struck emotional gold. His hand catches my arm and I try to wrench away, but his grip is strong.

"*STOP!*" I scream. I hate him so badly. I want to scream it in his face just as I screamed at Margery. Unfortunately, it wouldn't have the same effect. While my mother-in-law prefers to pretend this family has no problems, Luther thrives on them.

Soon he has me by both wrists and I'm struggling, trying to avoid his eyes—fearing the evil I might see there.

"I don't want this anymore!" I sob the words.

"What don't you want?" he coos, pressing his face uncomfortably close.

"I don't want to be here! I don't want to be your wife! I don't want to waste another moment living with you!" It's honest… too honest, but I can't fight the stream of words needing to escape me. I'm at the very end of my rope. Spending my days like this, it's torture. I feel as if I'm going mad. I can't take it anymore. I can't.

"You'll live on the streets?" Luther questions, a teasing hint to his words.

"I don't care if I have to live in the cursed wood, as long as I don't have to endure one more second of this HELL."

He chuckles. I'm sobbing, hardly standing on my own accord. It's his grip on my wrists that keeps me on my feet. "You'll end up like Jacquette or Lavinia. Is that what you want? To be a dirty whore, begging for coin?"

"Stop it!" I'm choking on my tears. I wish he would shut up. I wish he would shut his fucking mouth and never open it again.

One of his rough hands snags my jaw, forcing me to face him. "You'd die without me. You know that, right?"

I wrench my body, trying to break free. It only makes Luther grip tighter. He wraps his arms around my torso in a suffocating bear hug. I can't stand it. I feel as if I could faint. I can't draw in a breath of air. I don't like being held down like this, but even more so—I can't stand my husband touching me.

"You love me."

The words make me freeze—my eyes shoot open and finally, I look at him. His once beautiful blue eyes are bloodshot, his breath reeks, his face is unshaven, and his hair is dark with oil. I'm horrified at the accusation.

His smile widens showing wine-stained teeth and he smashes his face against mine in something hardly resembling a kiss. I scream against his mouth, finally managing to scramble free from my husband's hold.

I wipe at my lips, revolted, and put the table between us—feeling more like the mouse to this cat than ever.

"Don't touch me."

"I thought you wanted me to touch you," he teases. "Isn't that what you said? A husband should want to touch his wife."

"Not like this." My heart is pounding so hard I can feel it in my throat. He paces side to side and I skitter in time with him, trying to remain as far away as possible.

"I know what your problem is."

I'm afraid to respond. Luther has a crazed look about him. I was expecting a beating tonight, but there's something escalating here. We are in uncharted territory and my fear is greater than ever.

"You need to be put in your place."

I don't dare respond to that.

"A wife belongs at home."

"I won't go to the tavern again," I promise. And I'm not just saying that to pacify Luther's rage. I don't ever want to go back to that wretched place.

"A wife should do as she's told."

I purse my lips.

"She should cook for her husband—"

"Your dinner is always ready for you—"

"Clean."

The cottage is spotless, save for the mud Luther dragged in.

"She should please him. That's a wife's job."

I'm trembling now, like a leaf. If I could make it to the door I'd run right out into the night and never return.

"But you're more like a dog, aren't you? Following me to town, whimpering like a *bitch*. Maybe I should keep you out in the yard? Make you sleep there." He pauses, waiting for me to protest. And when I don't, he presses: *"Do you think anyone would say a damn thing if I did?"*

I shake my head.

"No. Because this town fucking hates you. Even your father, Alba. He was glad to be rid of you. He *paid* me to take you off his hands."

The words hurt, making me feel like a fool. Like garbage…

"Maybe I should gag you? Shut that mouth so you stop complaining."

My feet feel like lead, but the tension in the air is mounting, leading to something terrible. Luther makes his move—grabbing the table. It drags across the floor, sounding like the roll of thunder. I think I scream. Maybe I even try to escape, but I don't make it far. His hands dig into my arms.

The motions we play out are dizzying. The perpetual fight has become a dance between the two of us, but the music we step to has grown discordant and intense. I twist against him and he forces me into place. Pain stabs my body as I'm thrown into furniture. His fists strike my cheek, but I'm able to catch my fall along the table. I cling to it, desperately sucking in air.

When I'm able to gain some sense of what's happening...I realize Luther is tugging my skirts up around my waist.

My brows shoot up in horror. *"What are you doing?"* The words are screamed, frantic and angry. "Stop that!" I roll against the table but am unable to stand upright. He's got me pinned.

"You want me to touch you."

"NO! Get your hands off me! Luther, stop this! Stop this now! *Stop!*"

I think I might be sick. His hands are under my skirt. I hear fabric tearing. I scream so hard it feels as if my throat is tearing open. And then...I kick him. It's nothing intentional—just my limbs flailing wildly. But I think I hit him in the knee, in just the right place. My husband buckles.

There is this slim moment of give. I slip from between him and the table. Luther's eyes snap to me. The "fun" is gone from them—that teasing twinkle he gets when he's exhilarated by causing pain. Now, all I see is red-hot anger. It's primitive. Like a predator setting sights on his next meal. And maybe my next move is just as primitive—for I grab the knife I'd been using to carve my husband's bread.

Luther sees what I've done and lets out an enraged roar before lunging. It feels as if the whole house crashes down on me. It's an instant, nothing more, all happening within the blink of an eye. His weight is atop me and I can't breathe again. I think perhaps I might die.

His hands grab. I clench my eyes shut and fight back as hard as I can, but it's alien to me. I feel woefully inept—scratching, clawing, beating fists against his chest.

By some miracle, I manage to scramble out from beneath Luther. I've no sense of direction, because if I did I would make my way to the door and bolt—never to return. But instead I find myself scurrying toward the hearth on hands and knees. Red embers feel warm against my face.

A hand grabs at my ankle and I scream, but slip away. Luther doesn't drag me back.

I turn, expecting another attack, and am surprised to see Luther still lying on the ground. He's face down, propped on his elbows, back hunched over. I think perhaps the alcohol has finally gotten the best of him. Is he...*passing out?*

No.

Luther groans and rolls onto his back. That's when I see it— the knife sticking straight out of his chest. Blood is steadily soaking his shirt. His lips are wet and red. My own eyes wild, I look down at myself and see crimson covering the front of me. It's on my hands...it's everywhere.

Luther turns and the words he speaks come out soggy. "You fucking bitch." My husband's typically ruddy face is rapidly growing pale. "I'm going to kill you. I'm going to *fucking* kill you."

He's looking right into my eyes as he says it and there's an honesty there—something I'd be fool not to trust. Luther rolls to his side, pushing himself up. *He's coming for me.*

And I...I don't know what I do. I'm not thinking. It's just fear. Animalistic fear. I grab the only thing within reach—the pot over the stove. Heavy, cast iron, still hot. My skin sizzles, but before Luther can make it to his feet, I bring that pot down onto the back of his head. Sounds like the tolling of a bell.

He's on the ground again and he rolls onto his back, face up, eyes on the ceiling, mouth open. He doesn't move, but I feel like he's going to grab me, wrap strong hands around my ankles and drag me down. I fear he's going to kill me. So…I bring the pot down on his face…again…and again…and again.

I do it until my arms are weak, until I can't manage to lift the pot one more time. It slips from my hold and rolls beneath the table. I fall back onto my ass. The cottage is silent. Save for my shaking, of course. Save for my breath. Save for the aching sobs that come after I finally realize what I've done.

Luther is dead. I've killed my husband.

CHAPTER 5

Alba

*W*hen rational thought returns to my mind, the first thing I think of is Margery. I imagine a knock at the door. My mother-in-law showing up unannounced, coming to tell Luther how I treated her on the road. I can *see* the fake tears glistening in her eyes as she dabs at them with one of her many handkerchiefs, and the smug grin she would wear, knowing I'll be beat for my transgression.

But I won't be beat. Not this time. Not by Luther anyway. Because my cruel scoundrel of a husband is dead. So if Margery comes, it won't be to stir a beating for me. It will be to discover her son's corpse rotting on our cottage floor.

The scene plays out in my mind, her jaw dropping—real emotion crossing those pinched features of hers. She'd scream. She'd scream so loud someone would hear. Never mind that no one ever hears me when *I* scream—no neighbor comes to my aid when Luther has had one too many and lays into me. But in this instance, Margery would be heard and the whole town would come.

I push to my feet, scrambling back until I'm up against the wall. In horror, I stare down at the mess I've made. *Luther* is a mess. Unrecognizable. I'll hang. Or worse. They'll drag me into the street and stone me. I can already feel it. Like fists tearing into me, breaking bones. My vision tunnels and I realize I've got my own hands wrapped around my throat, squeezing. I'm hyperventilating. A cold sweat is soaking my dress. I start for the door, needing air...but I trip over my own undergarments and remember that Luther was going to rape me.

Bile rises up in my throat and I dive for the door. The weight of my body pushes it open and I collapse on the ground, emptying the contents of my stomach onto the dirt. Seems like an eternity of retching. When I'm done I look up to see the sky beginning to tint grey. Morning is coming...and I've a body to hide.

I salvage an overturned wheelbarrow and shovel from behind the house and formulate a plan to take the corpse to a small, vacant plot on the other side of the village.

That plot was gifted to Luther and me on our wedding day. In my mind it represented a future fertile with possibilities. But Luther only saw coin. He sold it quick, one night at the tavern— for a pitifully low price.

He was drunk and thinking only of his next bottle. Later he rationalized it as stupid to have land so far from home, that we would do better investing in our own garden. But he *never* invested in our garden. The damned wheelbarrow isn't even ours. It was something Luther borrowed and never saw fit to return—sitting untouched for months in the spot he had sworn to plant squash.

Now it's his death carriage. With much strain and effort, I load him in and unceremoniously balance the shovel on top. He can't stay on this land, haunting me and our cottage. And anyway, wouldn't Margery notice a Luther-sized patch of freshly overturned soil in the garden?

But out in the field, if I bury my husband deep enough, he might go undiscovered. Luther sold that plot to Jerald Godfrey, another drunk, and it's sat baking in the sun ever since.

My blistered hands grip the coarse handles of the barrow and the toes of my worn shoes sink into morning-moist earth. I duck my head and press on—I press on as I've done for months on end and perhaps my whole life.

I never wanted our marriage to end like this. I never wanted it to be so ugly. But I'll be damned before I hang for this man.

Heart racing, terrified of being discovered, I realize I feel no remorse. Luther was a monster. He derived pleasure from torturing me and he got what was coming to him. If it wasn't my hands that killed him, it would have been the drink, or the hands of an angry neighbor. Luther was no stranger to a drunken brawl.

The early morning is silent. I hear only my struggles and the gentle swaying of wheat grass. The air is crisp and a chill feels like a blessing against my sweat-soaked dress. Ahead I see the barren plot—a godsend as the blisters on my hands tear open. My back aches and my hair clings to my neck and forehead. I all but toss Luther to the dirt as I use what feels like the last of my strength to come to a halt.

But it can't be the last of my strength. I've got a grave to dig and it's got to be deep. So deep that no farmer will ever find bones when tilling this soil. I draw in air and sweep my hair back as best I can. Then, I take the old shovel in my hands and drive it into the earth. Feels like digging through solid stone. "I'm strong," I tell myself, spearing the ground. A little bit at a time, the grave carves itself out.

Hours pass. I sway under the sun's heat and drop the shovel. My hands...I don't know how I'll explain my hands. Red and bleeding. Filthy too. I tell myself the dirt will wash away. They sting something fierce, but I'm nearly done. I use those raw hands to climb up out of the waist-deep hole and I look at Luther for the first time in hours.

While I don't regret what I did, I feel as if I'm in mourning. Not for this bastard, but for the life I thought I was going to have. Maybe it's exhaustion, but the tears flow again—hot and heavy. Luther is in a heap, bloodied face in the dirt, and an arm bent behind his back. "All you had to do was be a good man," I mutter.

Squeezing my eyes closed, youthful wishes invade my thoughts. Simple things really. A husband to hold me at night, who would laugh with me, tickle me until I squealed, and gaze upon me with...with love in his eyes. *Is* that too much to ask? I can picture this image of a man, sneaking up as I work on our dinner, just to goose me. I'd curse him with a wide smile on my face. If I woke with a nightmare, he'd sleepily run his hand down my arm until all fear subsided. And me? I would be devoted to him, with all of my being. Love would be enough for me. It would be more than enough.

With resolve, I grab Luther by the arm and drag him to his final resting place. It's more than he deserves. I could have tossed his corpse into the Perished Woods and been done with it. No one would have found him there. This is a favor. One last favor honoring my duty as a wife. He gets a decent grave.

It's a strange feeling to grab hold so boldly of a man I had grown to fear. The very sound of his footsteps used to make me tense. But now I drag him across the dirt and his body makes a sound I don't think I'll ever forget as it lands in the bottom of the grave.

My toes edge closer and I look down at him. He isn't handsome anymore. He looks like a monster. His face finally congruent with his soul. Slowly, I breathe in and gather my thoughts. I'll tell everyone we fought and he left me, he left town to be rid of me for good. That's not so far-fetched. In his drunken state he would often speak of leaving this village.

Margery might be suspicious, but she won't have evidence to prove otherwise. Hell, she might even take my word for it and blame me for driving her son away. Let her. Yes. As long as I can clean up the cottage, everything is going to be okay.

I'm about to reach for the shovel when the sound of footsteps on dry ground startles me. I duck low, searching for the origin, and my eyes find Adelaide, of all people, coming up the road.

Fearful of being discovered, I do the only thing I can—I drop down into the grave with Luther. It makes me cringe. There's something terrifying about it. It almost feels as if he's going to wake and grab for me. The hair on the back of my neck stands on end and I watch Adelaide.

She looks upset, I think, as she wades into a field across the dusty main road. We're at the end of town, a secluded place. Her side of the road butts up against the cursed wood. Seems dangerous to me, in more ways than one, to be alone and so close to that awful forest. There are monsters of course, but perhaps even more dangerous is the threat of someone like Margery seeing her and crying out *witch*.

With a furrowed brow I watch. Slowly, fear subsides and I feel oddly kindred with the red-haired beauty. Luther claimed the whole village hated me. I think the same can easily be said of Adelaide. Poor thing. Lost both her parents when their carriage overturned. She was never the same after that and no man would have her as a wife.

She pulls a branch from a tree, heavily laden with berries, and settles into the shade. I watch her and think to myself. Perhaps after this I'll...I'll go knock on her door. I think Adelaide and I might find friendship in one another.

The fantasy doesn't have time to unfold before a scream tears through the day. My heart drops and my blood runs cold. It's Margery. It has to be. She's found the blood. She knows Luther is dead.

It's a senseless rationale, of course. The cottage is so very far away. Still, to my mind there could be no other answer. Until I see smoke rising into the air. I look across the field and find Adelaide, her gaze fixed back on the village. There's terror written on her face and she grips the tree like a life boat in the midst of a stormy sea.

In the distance, chaos erupts. The screams are bone-chilling. I haven't got a view from my vantage point. Desperate, I lock my eyes onto Adelaide. Her back heaves, deep breaths drawing in and out. And then, so very suddenly, she bolts—making her way right for the cursed woods! I suck in a breath, my hands slapping over my mouth, lest I be discovered and I watch that girl disappear into the mist.

My mind is aghast, disbelieving. I can't fathom what would make anyone run into that horrible, horrible place. Not until I see three dark figures pursuing her. Dropped down onto all fours, they run with inhuman speed. Monsters. *Orcs.*

Our village is under attack by orcs.

I tumble back into the cool soil, tripping over Luther. Falling right atop him. Wide-eyed, my face is inches from his and it dawns on me—we might be sharing this grave.

CHAPTER 6

Thorn

Smoke clouds the once blue sky, but it does nothing to impede the heat—the oppressive heat of man's land. Sweat wets my brow. It mixes with droplets of blood sprayed across my chest. It slips in ribbons down my arms as I wipe the blade of my sword clean once again.

The screaming has subsided. Replaced with the sound of fire, cracking flames and buckling support beams. It fills my ears. I can feel the heat on my face as I stride through it all. The carnage.

All around me my orc army pillages and I curl my lip at them —the undiscerning scavengers that they are. There is nothing of value here. Still, they break out windows and knock down the last standing doors. They'll be lucky to roll a few barrels of ale from the remains of this village's dismal little tavern. Trash is what they'll reap. I'm ready to move on.

Arran, my general, frees me from my thoughts. "Orders, your Highness?"

I blink at him. Remembering something faraway. Did I see

him before all this? Back in Black Mountain perhaps? A head taller than me and as wide as an ox. Arron doesn't bother with adornments; he dons only a pair of boots and a worn, leather waist cloth. The simplest of blades are sheathed on his back— axes. A pair. They aren't sleek nor were they made by master craftsmen. They are ugly and heavy like the orc who brandishes them. But they kill with precision just the same.

I think I can remember Arron from Black Mountain, but those memories are like whispers in my mind, contending with the beckoning call of the castle. I narrow my eyes, trying to discern more. I know he is more principled than the others. But I don't know what drives him, or if he can be trusted.

"Thorn?" he asks in a familiar sort of way.

"I'm ready to ride on."

"I'll tell the soldiers—"

I hold up my hand. "Let them pillage. I'm riding ahead."

"With an accompaniment?"

"Alone," I insist, with a curt cut of my hand. Orc company makes my skin twitch. Of them all, Arron is the only one I can stand, but I can't keep my mind clear enough to want to ride even with him.

Funny, I seem to remember feeling so lonely. But this army is akin to crumbs. They do nothing to satiate my hunger for companionship and I'd choose silence over riding with beasts even on the most desolate road. Anyway, in silence I can hear my thoughts and I chase those moments of clarity with desperation.

"Shall I order one last sweep of the village?"

I cast my eyes over black smoke and skeletal remains of homes and businesses. What would it matter if any of these people escaped? Could one country farmer truly thwart Petra's great plans? Seems dubious to me, dubious at best. Still...there is Petra to think of. The Eternal Princess and her unrelenting grip on control.

I shrug my shoulder. "You make the call. Have you seen my horse?"

Arron points up the road and I spot the black stallion. He's found the edge of a field and is nosing at the grass. I start toward him, knowing Arron will indeed sweep the village—because he is smart and rightfully fearful of the power Petra has at her disposal. But those thoughts quickly escape me. With every step, I get farther from the remnants of chaos and closer to the castle. Closer to sanity and peace...

My steed is chomping on wheat grass when I make my way to his side. I hum a greeting and run a hand along his inky, black coat. I'm just about to mount when a curious scent catches my attention. I grow still, hand on the horse's reins.

What *is* that smell?

It's like a faint memory mingling with death. I can't place it. I can't find the sweetness for all the rot. Curious, I search the fields stretching away from the Perished Woods. The grass sways in the wind, but I can't hear it. I see it move, but to my ears there is only silence. The scent pervades all else.

Drawn by it, I leave my horse to his meal and start blindly across the farmland. It appears to be a whole lot of nothing. But it isn't nothing, is it? I smell death out here. Death and something hiding just beneath it.

Brows drawn. I don't know what I'm looking for. The wind shifts and I'm further from my goal. Then it shifts again and I think I'm right on top of it.

Blood.

My pace quickens and then I see. A rough hole dug in an unplowed plot of land. A grave. The scent of death is strong here. Too decayed to be a result of my raid on this village. I close my eyes and breathe in that putrid odor. What is hiding amongst it? Something fresh that doesn't belong...roses perhaps?

Carefully, I approach this half-finished hole in the ground and find myself quite shocked when I view the contents.

Sure enough there is a dead body inside—twisted, bloodied, an absolute mess. And curled next to it, fast asleep, is the young woman I watched just yesterday; alive and well, if not exhausted. I chuff, smiling to myself and surveying the surroundings. A wheelbarrow. A rusted shovel. Nothing else.

The girl, she's wearing the same tattered frock I last saw her in. Only now it's filthy, covered in dirt and blood. Even with her hair hanging down I can see bruises on her face and I inch closer to get a better look at the man. The scent of liquor is easily detected, stale and foul. His hair is greasy and what's left of his face is unkempt, as are his clothes. I can still draw up the picture of her, staring at the cottage, loathing the idea of stepping inside. Doesn't take great cunning to figure out what's happened here.

I squat beside the grave, smiling and impressed. Seems fear did indeed serve her. The man must outweigh the girl by a hundred pounds at least, but she didn't let that stop her. *She is strong.* And brave to lie beside a mess like that.

My heart softens and I gaze at the golden locks that have swept over tired eyes. The storm in my mind falls silent and I imagine what life has held for this young woman in the hours since I first spied her. Fear, desperation, a fight for her life. All alone, she had to dig this hole. It's no small task. I can see why she's fallen into such a deep sleep. She's spent.

Frowning, I turn back to consider the village. That dismal cottage is likely gone and I doubt she'll find anything of worth in any of these burned-out houses. She's got nothing beyond the filthy clothes on her back and I don't even see a waterskin lying about.

She was in a rush, of course. I toe dry earth and cast my eyes up to the sun beating down from overhead. She probably didn't expect to be out here so long. But there was the raid and she needed to hide. Lucky. A grave really is the perfect place. But it is hot and she's been out here for a while I guess.

It would be a waste if she died now, wouldn't it? After she's already fought so hard to survive. The decision is a simple one. Quietly, having no desire to wake her, I tug my own waterskin and coin purse free from my belt and set them on the ground. She's more than earned it. Perhaps these small things can serve her on the next part of her journey. I can linger no more. I've work to do.

It's only when I turn my back, heading for my horse, that the storm returns to my mind. Screaming my name, like a terrible siren. The castle is impatient. It waits for me.

Mounting my steed, I gaze in the direction of that brave, blonde villager, hiding in a grave she dug herself. As long as she waits out my army, she won't die today. I feel good about that. I don't know that Petra would. But what harm can one woman do? It isn't as if this lone survivor can somehow foil the Eternal Princess's plan to claim the kingdom of Pontheugh. I pardoned one, single, precious life. I think I'm allowed a good deed among the mass of death and destruction I've left in my wake.

Ashes swirl in the air around me. With a deep breath smelling of smoke, death, and the faint hint of roses, I close my mind to that morbidly resilient girl with honey-hued locks. I'm exhausted too. Heavy-lidded, I shut my eyes and succumb to the burning call of the castle. With a rough spur to my horse, I take off down the road, one village closer to claiming my throne.

CHAPTER 7

Alba

I wake feeling dizzy and baked by the sun. Though shade has enveloped me, my tongue is plastered to the roof of my mouth and my lips feel ready to crack. I blink—dazed, eyes adjusting. The shape of a face takes form only inches from mine. I keep thinking it will morph into something familiar—My husband's rough jaw, oiled hair falling down over his tan forehead, bloodshot eyes...

Instead, I see Luther as he is now. Utterly destroyed. He's horror and gore and the memory of last night comes rushing back like an icy wave. Our terrible fight, the threat of rape, Luther's vow to kill me, all the cruel things confessed! By the Gods! I've been living in Hell, married to the devil himself.

I'm still not sorry, but seeing what I've done makes me sick. My stomach turns and I push up, hissing. My hands! They're blistered, crusted with puss and dirt. They *sting* worse than anything and my lips do indeed split open. I'm sunburnt and thirsty; my head throbs. The scent of smoke hits my nose and my eyes shoot wide. *The attack! Orcs!*

My heart begins to race and my vision tunnels. I don't know how long I've been here or if the attack is still underway, but I do know I need to escape.

My ears prickle. Desperately, I listen for screams—for anything that might clue me in on what's happening, but there's nothing. Only silence. Looking into the bit of sky I can see, there's smoke, but it's the light kind. Like a fire on its way out. I turn to Luther, as if he might provide some insight. His hideous face does nothing but stare, likely sending wishes of harm from his place in Hell. Looks like I've got to figure this out on my own.

Pressing myself to the wall of the grave, very slowly and very quietly, I rise. I see the fields of tall grass, but I can't see much beyond them. Gazing across to where Adelaide once stood, my heart aches when I remember how she thrust herself into the cursed wood. Suicide. A frightful thing to witness. If those orcs didn't get her, surely something else did.

I watch and listen for a long while, but hear and see nothing. It's time to move on. Without grace, I claw my way out of the grave and remain low to the ground. I've a sinking feeling in my gut, as if Luther might grab my ankle and draw me back in. But he doesn't. Luther doesn't move a muscle.

With sadness I take one last look at him, trying to decide if I should cover this hole before I leave. Only, it doesn't seem so imperative anymore. If someone does find him I can always blame his death on the orcs.

I'm about to leave my husband, once and for all, when I notice some items lying on the ground. The breath is stolen from my lungs. Sitting just beside the mouth of the grave is a waterskin and pouch.

I snap my attention all around, searching for eyes that might be watching. For someone *was* watching. They saw my wretched hiding place and my crime, yet they left these precious things behind. Who could have done such a thing? Curious, I inspect the pouch—black leather, soft and velvety, a fine pattern stitched into it. I've never seen anything like it. Inside I can sense the unmistakable weight and shape of coins. I loosen the drawstring and take a peek, only to draw it tight again.

My face grows hot and I clutch that little pouch close to my chest, fearfully casting my eyes about. Still, I am alone. Hastily, I tuck the coin purse into my bodice and greedily tear into the water, gulping it down. It hits my empty stomach and feels impossibly heavy. Nausea is instantaneous. Only a little bit at a time, I tell myself.

Allowing a deep breath to fill my lungs, I get to my feet. For the first time in hours, I have a view of Aberdeen and it's staggering.

Smoke billows into the sky, making twilight all the hazier. My village, the only village I have ever known, is nothing but a blackened skeleton. I see not a single rooftop still intact. No villagers roam the street, there are no farmers in the fields beyond. All is silent.

I stumble forward, feeling only half alive. Led by an inexorable pull, I no longer fear Luther being found or my crime being discovered. Let someone see the blood stains down the front of my dress and my suspiciously wounded hands. The only thing I desire is to find another living soul.

Tripping through the field, nearly at a run, I get closer and closer, until finally, I break out onto the main road. It's heavily trodden. No longer packed earth. Instead, it has been turned to mud and it wets the hem of my dress, causing a fresh, red stain to appear.

"Gods..."

I hurry onward, my eyes racking the hollows of every building. A beam weakens and falls within a nearby structure, crashing into the ash. Smoke rolls and curls around it. I nearly jump out of my skin. And that's when I see it...the first corpse.

My mouth opens and I realize I'm about to call out, to ask if they're alright. I press my fingers to my lips, horrified. The body is unrecognizable. Man? Woman? I don't know. It's curled in on itself, nothing more than charcoal in the shape of a person.

My pace quickens, my eyes search more hastily. I spy something in the mud. Just a dirty little bit of something. But I squint at it, drawn to it, perhaps recognizing it on some unconscious level. A bit of fabric?

Oh. It's a lady's handkerchief.

My spine straightens, a lump forms in my throat, and hot tears fill my eyes. I blink them away. Slowly, I look around only to find two bodies on the side of the road, not far from one another. A pair of elderly women. Margery and Celia— Adelaide's aunt. Friends. Objectively awful women, and yet still not deserving a fate like this. A sob rocks me and my knees go weak. That's when I think of my father.

My legs break into a full sprint, carrying me to his shop. I know. I already know. I can see it in the ruins, I can hear it in the silence. The shop won't be there. Neither will my dad. That man who raised me, demeanor always cold and mean. His unhappiness evident. Still, he was the only father I knew and despite myself, I loved him.

I skid to a halt, not hardly recognizing my childhood home or the small shop I was raised above. It appears as if a cleaver sheared the top right off the building. The front window is broken out. Most of the meat display is gone. What's left smells of rot, flies cling to it.

The doorframe is still there, however, and my feet shakily carry me toward it.

"Father?" I call, eyeing the road. It's my first utterance in hours and the word comes out a croak.

Broken glass crunches beneath my shoes. Night and the darkness that comes with it is creeping in, but I can still detect a splatter of blood across the wall. My eyes follow it downward and I catch sight of my father's legs. He wore the biggest boots in town—that's what the cobbler always said—and I stare at the bottoms of those boots. He was a big man in so many ways. Imposing. When I was a child I used to pretend he was a giant holding me captive. Neither then nor now could I imagine anything cutting him down.

The scent of the shop overwhelms me. I don't know if it's rotting meat or my father's corpse. The thought is simply too much. I stumble out onto the road and heave up the water I drank.

Painful thoughts assault my mind. *Everyone I know is dead. The entire village has been razed.* I stare at my feet—at my shoes caked in mud and the crimson hem of my dress. The beat of my heart can be felt in my temples, pounding. It will be dark soon and…I can't stay here.

I look down the road toward my cottage knowing it's no longer there. There's nothing in that direction. Miles and miles before the next village, land governed by another kingdom. But the other way…there's Birchloch and Willowbend, then, the castle at Pontheugh.

In all my life, I've never stepped foot outside of Aberdeen. Never had the freedom to make a decision on my own. I scrub a rough hand across my forehead, feeling grimy but resolved as I remember last night's urge to run into the darkness alone, to keep on running, never to return to this place.

I suppose this is my chance.

CHAPTER 8

Thorn

"I don't want to go out there," I growl in irritation.

"And I didn't ask," is Petra's response from the other side of the mirror. Framed in gold, this is one treasure that didn't come from the pillaging of burning villages. It came from the Eternal Princess herself. Cursed, as is everything she touches.

I turn my back on her, temples throbbing. "You don't understand. The *noise—*"

"I said, *I didn't ask*. It isn't a request, Thorn. It's a command. Do you understand?"

I claw at my hair, pacing lush rugs stacked haphazardly atop one another. All of them, stolen from homes that no longer stand. There's chaos outside. It's like I'm back in the belly of Black Mountain. Only the noise, *the constant noise*, it isn't just surrounding me. It is *in* my head, directing every thought. A cacophony of discordance and thoughts that feel as if they are not my own. All of it, driving me mad. The closer I get to the castle, the further sanity slips from my grasp. And yet, the castle seems to be the only answer.

"You need to show strength."

"*I am strong.*" My words are insistent. "Why must I prove this? Haven't you seen my strength?"

"This army of yours requires a constant display. Really, Thorn, I shouldn't have to explain such a simple concept." Petra clicks her tongue as she wears an expression of distaste. "Those creatures need to see you in command."

The condescending tone agitates and I bare my teeth at the witch-queen. It only makes her gaze turn icy.

"You will go out there, you will wear your crown, and you will sit on the dais. Feast, if you like. Celebrate your victories, fuck some of those slave-girls you like to keep. It's all a show, Thorn. Might as well have fun with it."

Fun? I'm apt to go mad and Petra speaks of fun. "I will ride ahead. I can start on the next village—"

"Listen to me: they *need* to see your power or they will turn on you. We are talking about orcs, for goodness' sake! If they don't see you, they will forget you. If you don't maintain the presence of a King, they will fail to recall you are one."

"We are not as simple as you think, *Princess.*"

"If you were smart you would do as I command."

My skin twitches, I feel as if I am losing this battle. Petra's voice nags and the chain round my neck seems to grow heavier with each passing second. My voice is shaky. "I'll ride ahead and bring back heads to put on pikes. There's a show of power for you."

"That's war and they can *all* wage war. What makes *you* their King?"

"I can fight better than any of them."

"And they'll make you prove it if you aren't careful."

I glare at Petra, stalking to the mirror and gripping the

frame in my hands. "Then I will prove it. I survived Black Mountain. I can take this entire camp—"

"But you won't. You will go out there, as I am commanding you to, and you will lead your people."

"My people?" I huff. They make me sick, adding to the turmoil of my thoughts, constantly reminding me how alone I am. "I can take the castle without them."

"You will do as I say."

"Why? You see something playing out in that little charm of yours?"

Petra rolls her eyes, uninterested in the jab against her power source. "What I see isn't your concern, but what I advise must be obeyed. It is in your best interest after all."

I bite back a growl, wanting to take her neck in my hands and squeeze. But it is only a reflection I see. Petra is miles away. "Since when does a King obey any command above his own?"

"Don't make me laugh, Thorn. The only reason you are a King is because I have declared it so."

I shake my head. "I heard the call. Long before you set your sights on Pontheugh, *I* heard the call to greatness."

The Eternal Princess dons a placating smile.

"I hear it still."

"You heard nothing. You were scared and running. I found you and I gave you the gift of direction."

My jaw tightens. She might be right. I can't remember all the details, not with all this damned noise. There was Black Mountain, I was battle weary, and then suddenly there was Petra. But how did she pull me in? I can't fathom, because I loathe her now. I loathe the suffocating hold she has on me.

"We've already agreed, Thorn. When I tell you to do something, you will do it and you will do it *my* way."

Frustrated by ephemeral thoughts and memories I don't trust; I squeeze the mirror until I hear the frame crack. "I don't need a crown to tell me who I am and I certainly don't need you to either."

"You're confused. Go, be with your people. It will set you right again." Petra, in her taciturn, stone hideaway in the castle at Envercress, backs away from the mirror. The image fades, but her eyes burn into me—leaving a searing heat. She might wear the mask of youth, but this isn't a child's game she's playing at. The woman is as serious as death.

Though I wish to speak, I bite my tongue as she vanishes, because I am King and I will not be reduced to begging for permission to hide from the strained madness of camp. *Kings do not beg.* A cloud fills the mirror and it isn't until a rush of wind cuts through my tent that it clears and finally, I see only my own reflection once more. A scarred face with tired eyes. They seem hollow, even to me. I'm missing something.

I place a hand over my heart, but there is a barrier there, warm metal in the form of a medallion. It hums, urging me. It won't go silent until I do as Petra wishes and I wonder how long I can fight the itching insistence...

I am not free to contemplate for long, for the flap to my tent flies open. My gaze snaps to it and my hand shoots to the hilt of my sword. But it is only Arron standing there, steely-eyed. "Your Highness. I beg your pardon for the interruption, but we've retrieved something of yours from the wood."

"Something of mine?"

He grunts and steps aside. My confusion deepens when a woman, bound at the wrists, is ushered in by two guards. Not one of the witch-dancers or the slaves. This woman isn't of our camp. She's fair-haired, her dress is fine, and she wears fear in her eyes. It calls forth a memory, seemingly from long ago. A village girl, asleep in a grave, nestled bravely beside an ugly corpse...but this isn't that girl. The hair might be similar, but it isn't her. The scent is all wrong. I don't know who this is. She's a stranger to me. But the way her eyes widen reveal...*she knows exactly who I am.* It is recognition beyond my reputation as the Orc King. How does she know me?

"You say this woman belongs to me?" I ask Arran.

"Your soldiers found her in the wood trying to escape."

"Hmm. I wonder what do they do to women when they try to escape our camp?"

Arron stands a little taller, but does not answer outright. "I noticed she has your scent on her, so I had them bring her back."

"Didn't touch her?"

"No, sir. I wouldn't allow them touch something of yours."

"Good, good..." I murmur.

I rise and approach her, feeling a stirring in my chest —*excitement.* Something important is happening here. My instinct tells me so. But what? Who is this mystery woman who seems to know me so much better than I know her?

"Thorn?" She gasps my name.

I cock my head and take in her scent, paying close attention. Recognition is instant, it hits me like a physical blow. I stumble back and everything else washes away. I'm dizzy with joy. I *know* that smell. I know that smell! And I know exactly how this woman knows me!

My heart rages with elation like I have never known. Could it be? Could it truly be? I cast eyes to the mirror. Did Petra know this was coming? Or were her visions clouded again?

It doesn't matter—I don't want to think of her now. This woman, she is mine. All mine. My secret, my joy. Petra need not know. Yes, it will be my secret. My heart and mind reach a stalemate in their battle. There is a delicate balance between the two that vaguely resembles calm. Finally, everything is going to be alright. I'm not alone anymore. Thank the Gods, I'm not alone! I'll have the strength I need to take the castle for Petra, to bring her the King and his heir. Companions—they will make me feel sane. I will be myself once more.

CAPTURED BY THE ORC KING

"Arran! I have questions!" I bellow, my thoughts race as I assess our captive. "You know who I am?"

The girl nods, her eyes drinking me in with severity, while I'm practically shaking with excitement. I can smell it so potently. It's as if she's bathed in the odor. I throw my head back, laughing. Arron thinks the guards retrieved something of mine. They thought she was mine *because she smells like me!* Who else, in all this mad world, could smell like me?

Careful to conceal my thrill, I crouch, inching closer, conscientious of the woman's fear. I want answers. I want *all* of the answers.

"Seems as though Petra will indeed have her way," I tell Arran. "There *will* be a feast tonight and I think the guest of honor isn't long behind this one here."

"I'll inform the cooks."

Waving Arron away, eager to focus on the woman, I inch closer to her still. "Tell me," I ask, voice strained, painstakingly working to balance my mind. *"What does my brother say of me?"*

91

CHAPTER 9

Honora

Orcs beat their drums and witches dance under a starless sky—their feet bare in the mud, long hair whipping to the rhythm of war music. I sit on the outskirts, legs crossed beneath me, observing the scene. So many orcs, spilt out of the Perished Woods by that Eternal Princess of Enver-cress. What a lovely mess she has made in the land of man. I admire her. The supreme power that woman has...the wealth. I want those things. I want them badly and I always have. Ever since I was a girl I've known I was destined for more. When my mother was burned at the stake, when the priest took me in to save my soul, when I snuck night after night back into the Perished Woods, I knew what I was destined for. Greatness, of course. The type of greatness magic can bring.

"There you are, love," Marie says breathlessly, dropping down onto the bench by my side. "You're missing the fun."

"It's early still," I murmur, not shifting my gaze from the slow assembly of the army in the heart of camp. Flickering torches cast their light on milky-eyed orcs. Soulless, vicious warriors. They hulk, waiting for permission to partake of the food and women. But *why* do they wait?

Marie twists herself to pull a discarded half-mug of ale from the table behind us. She drinks it down in one long, inelegant gulp. I bite back a cringe but say nothing. It serves me better to feign an alliance with the other women, so I do.

"What do you think all this is about?" I ask.

"All what?" Her attention is on the slave girls carrying out platters loaded with meats and roasted vegetables, dripping with gravy, and hot, fresh loaves of breads. The spoils of war—stolen from sad, dried-up little villages that the orc army graciously burned to the ground. The memory of my own sad, dried-up little village floats to the surface of my mind. Malice washes over me and I hope it's been burned too...with all the people in it.

"The *party*, Marie. What else would I be referring to?"

She shrugs, pinching a cluster of grapes off one of the heavily laden platters. With a simple, happy expression she sets to popping them into her mouth. "It's just a party. There are loads of parties. It's what I love about this campaign. Who knew war could be such fun?"

I shake my head. For all that Marie loves divination and her cards, she truly lacks the foreknowledge and intuition necessary to ever be any good at it. I think she must be quite stupid. "Don't you ever use your head, Marie?"

"I use it to suck dick," she guffaws, then puts on a confused expression. "Wait, no. I don't use my head...I *give* head." She slowly pieces her joke together.

"Very good, but I'm asking if you think for yourself."

She gives a nonchalant laugh. "I do indeed. I happen to think this party has gotten off to a lovely start. I think the food is divine *and* I think I might let some of these delicious brutes fuck me stupid before the night is over. How is that for thinking?"

I don't think dick will make her any stupider than she is

already, but I don't say that. Instead, I grab her by the chin, squeezing slightly harder than necessary. I point Marie's oblivious eyes toward the dais.

The throne sits atop that raised platform. Usually it is dark, with Thorn spurning the party, allowing his followers to have all the fun. But not tonight. Tonight it is surrounded by torches, flames bright and flickering. Slave girls ready fine golden pitchers and goblets for use. Garlands of rosemary and sage are hung in anticipation. Obviously, the Orc King will be joining us tonight. And why? Did we obliterate some pivotal outpost belonging to Pontheugh? No. All our conquests of late have been simple villages with simple people. No castle guards, no weaponry, no anything of note. Just sleepy farmers with plump wives and plump pigs and stores of food that this army will burn through in a day.

"What is so special about tonight that his Highness will be gracing us with an appearance?"

"Maybe he's bored?" Marie offers, not truly caring. I cross my arms over my chest, annoyed at how lacking she is. "People get twitchy sometimes, they need a good party to let off the steam."

I roll my eyes. My tone is laced with sarcasm. "Truly, you think that's all this is? His highness just wants to unwind?"

She shrugs again. "Why not?"

"I don't know how you forecast anything with those cards of yours. You've no vision of any kind."

Marie laughs, her light mood undeterred. "And you have a single-track mind. There is a party, love. Good food, flowing drink, cock for days! Why don't you relax? If his Highness can unwind, so can the great Honora." She says my name like a title. I should like a title. I should like this whole camp to bow to me, Thorn included. And I mean to make it so.

"Don't worry about me. I'll have my fun."

"Good," Marie says happily, producing another mug of ale

from the table behind us and shoving it into my hands. "Let the fun commence!" I set it aside as her attention is drawn to an orc with a freshly opened bottle of wine. "Fancy sharing that?" she coos, lighting to her feet and sliding a hand suggestively up his muscled arm.

The orc leans into her, heavy jaw jutting out. His free hand wraps round her waist in that dominating way orcs have. "And what do you plan on sharing in return, witch?"

"Something just as wet, I can assure you." They're laughing as I leave them, hands shamelessly moving across the planes of one another's bodies. I don't begrudge Marie for it. She isn't wrong. The parties are quite fun. The food is lavish in all the ways I like and while orcs can be such ugly things, there isn't a better fuck in all the land. They're absolutely spectacular beasts when it comes to sex. Not an ounce of restraint. And those cocks! Twice as big as any man's. Long, thick, adorned with piercings that tease in all the right places. I sigh at the thought. I do love a good party. When I am Queen there will be a party every night.

But I am not Queen yet. I won't feel secure until I am wed to that half-mad orc we call King. And for some reason I feel even less secure tonight. My intuition is tingling, telling me that something is about to happen and soon. It's in the air. I can feel it. *But what?*

I fall back into the shadows to watch the scene without disruption and soon see the King's general, Arran, lumbering from our master's tent. A command is whispered amongst the soldiers and I watch them disperse, slowly creating a perimeter around the party—the dais at its center.

I narrow my eyes at the scene.

Thorn has yet to show his face. Curiosity burns. Arron is probably the cleverest of them all, but he isn't worth the effort of talking to. A girl could get more from a stone than that silent, overgrown beast. It's a shame he's such a stoic one. Arron is actually good-looking for an orc. Big and scarred, but too smart for my taste—too smart for my purpose.

My eyes fall instead upon a wiry orc who all but vanishes among the other soldiers—easily camouflaged by his unremarkableness. I move from the shadows, following him with interest. His hand is on the hilt of his sword and his gaze remains not on the dancers, but on the darkness beyond the reach of the fires.

He's looking for something. Waiting. It's time to work my magic. Not spells. In this case feminine cunning will serve me. I might even have a bit of that fun Marie was talking about.

Pushing my hair off my shoulders, I let it flow down my back, providing an unobstructed view of my most ample assets. My gossamer dress is as dark as the night, as are the strands of beads hanging between my breasts. I like the way they conform to the curves of my body, accentuating what men are always hungry for.

Men. Simple creatures. I've found no difference among orc, human, or troll. An ample pair of tits can manipulate the entire lot.

Casually, I move nearer and begin a seductive dance while studying the subject of my attention. This orc isn't particularly familiar to me, but who's to say we haven't fucked before? There are so very many orcs in camp and it is hard to keep track. But I guarantee, if he's had my pussy before, he'll want more of it. And if he hasn't, he'll be desperate for his first taste.

The orc-soldier's ghost-like eyes search the darkness, but I'll have his attention soon enough.

Rhythmically, I roll my head from side to side—exposing the slender, cream-white column of my neck. This orc will want to take a bite, I suspect. Imitating a desperate need to be touched, my fingertips trail from rounded hips, up, up, up, until I am caressing my bountiful breasts. I play with the weight of them, moving my fingers to gently tug at my nipples. I close my eyes and dip my head back...mock-ecstasy. When I open them again

—the orc is staring. Of course he is. I gift the fool with a smile. An authentic one at that. For I am so very good at this.

Taking on a light and playful air, I dance close enough to feel his already erect penis jutting against my hip.

"May I dance for you?" I ask coquettishly, chin dipped, eyelashes all but fluttering.

I see his throat bob as he swallows. "I'm working," he grunts, his eyes dart about. This orc isn't fooling anyone. Already he's lost sight of his task. He's looking for Arron now, making sure he won't get in trouble if he fucks around a bit.

"Working?" I gasp. "But it's a party!"

My fingers find his chest. He might be lean, but he's solid. Hard muscles ripple beneath his skin. I drop my gaze to see his long, hard cock throbbing for me and I make a show of widening my eyes, as if I've never seen a cock so grand.

"I think you'd prefer to enjoy the party," I purr.

A growling comes from deep in his throat and he snaps at me with fangs that could tear skin. "I've orders..."

"And what if I were to order you to play with my pussy?"

He groans again and looks down at the curls on my mound, teasingly on display through the sheer material of my skirt. What a simple creature, so easily molded to fit my needs. I've just got to get him talking before he starts fucking.

"What orders could be more important than that?"

"Orders from the King," he says, puffing out his chest.

I make my mouth into an O. "My, you must be important."

He gives a curt nod and looks around again, making certain that no one of true importance is watching. A rushed and clumsy hand works past the slit in my skirt and starts a sloppy fingering of my pussy.

An exaggerated gasp escapes me. "I wouldn't want you to get in trouble." Furtively, I wrap my hand around his cock. It's quite long. I think it will feel good spearing into me. "I can help. I can be a second set of eyes."

I like the way he's working me and I lean my body against his, breathlessly whispering my next words into the crook of his neck.

"What did the King order you to watch for?"

"Who said I was watching for anything?"

"A woman has a way of knowing," I say impishly as my other hand skates to his balls. There are piercings there—as the orcs like to have. I slip my finger through one of the rings and tug. His face contorts and seed starts a slow trickle from his tip. I wet his dick with it.

"A guest is coming...supposed to be here soon..." He grunts the words through thickly fanged teeth and a frown forms on my face.

"A guest?" How unusual. We don't get guests at camp. We get new slaves at times, but nothing more than that. "Someone important, is it? That wretched Princess perhaps?"

"No...not the creature from Envercress."

"Then who?"

"Don't know. Something to do with the woman they found in the woods."

I know nothing of any woman found in the woods and I'm beginning to grow quite annoyed with my mark. *Details.* Men never tell a story with any Gods damned details.

"The King has her in his tent now."

My mouth forms a thin line. "He has this mystery woman in his tent? But who is she?"

"Dunno. Just a woman. Human. Made him real excited though. Been running around ever since. That's why he's done it up big, this party." His hands forget their task of trying to pleasure me, and wrap around mine. He works his dick into them, harder and faster—trying to cum. But I want to know more.

"Was she pretty?"

The orc huffs, hot air coming out his nose. Stupid question

from his perspective. These beasts would fuck anything, what's pretty got to do with it? It's Thorn who has the discerning eye.

"Tell me about the guest."

"What for?" His chin comes down and a frown appears on cruel lips.

"Because it excites me." I play with the cum beading on the tip of his cock, sliding the pad of my thumb over his sensitive tip. "All this secretive planning. I bet it's not a welcomed guest. If I had to bet, I would say there is going to be blood shed tonight."

The orc growls, his clawed hands grabbing the globes of my ass. Roughly, he draws me against him. His hard cock jams against my front and my breath hitches. What fun it would be if he held me down and jammed that dick into one of my holes. "You're wrong there, witch."

"Wrong?"

His hands grow impatient, but it doesn't matter, I think we are reaching the extent of his knowledge on the matter. Roughly squeezing my breast, he sneers, long tongue sliding out of his mouth to lap at my neck.

"We aren't allowed to kill him. Supposed to just let him in, pretend we don't see him coming."

Curious. Very curious *and* out of character for our King.

"Then what?" I press.

I feel a third hand join the party. Another orc—stout and wide-shouldered, with a bald head, and a fat belly—reaches between us to pluck at my nipples. He twists them, teases them. I send him a sultry smile, a silent plea to keep going.

"Then nothing. A party. A feast." He thrusts his cock forward. "Some *fucking*. The King is playing a little game. We can play too."

"Mmm, a game..." I murmur suggestively. But it seems my informant is done playing. His hands move to my shoulders and he sends me to my knees. The stout orc ebbs closer, pulling out his cock and offering it up. I take it in hand. Not as long as my wiry friend here, but twice as thick. I gaze up at him from under my lashes, letting him know I approve. I start a vigorous stroke whilst opening my mouth wide for my talkative friend. He's given me plenty to consider—as well as some good fun to start the night.

The taste of salty manhood—of sweat and cum—it floods my tastebuds and I float between sensation and curiosity.

Thorn has a woman in his tent, does he? Doesn't matter to me in the slightest. Let him fuck another woman. What do I care? It will be me he ends up with.

Fingers bury into my hair, pulling my face closer. That long cock delves deep down my throat. I can feel the body before me tensing. I think this one likes what I can do with my mouth. I think Thorn does too. Doesn't matter if he does have a new pussy to play with. It's always me he comes back to. I'm familiar to him. Even when he can't remember one moment to the next, when he can't think straight, when that cursed medallion is humming so loud that even I can hear it—even *then* it's me he likes best. Out of all the girls in camp, he fucks me the most and if this new thing thinks otherwise, I'll just have to let her know.

I'm confident and it brings a smile to my lips as the orc rips his cock free, ropes of saliva still connecting my lips to throbbing manliness. In an instant, the stealthy beast has flipped me ass up. He rams his cock into my dripping pussy and drives all the way to the back wall. I open my mouth to cry out, but a fresh, thick, cock is being pressed against my lips. Who am I to deny it?

New women in camp are always a burden to be dealt with. But she isn't the person these guards are looking out for. Who in the world could be coming here tonight? Who could warrant such a reaction from the reclusive Thorn?

I simply can't imagine anyone our King would go these lengths for. He loathes parties and crowds—anything noisy

CAPTURED BY THE ORC KING

really. Hells, I can't even imagine him *remembering* anyone long enough to go to all this trouble for them.

It must be someone important. After I'm good and fucked I'll have to keep my eyes peeled for our guest of honor. I can't have anyone disturbing the equilibrium I've created. On the other hand...I might be able to profit off a change in the status quo. Thorn has been slipping lately, deeper into that cursed abyss. A change might be exactly what I'm looking for. Yes. If I play my cards right, this might be my chance to finally ensnare the Orc King.

CHAPTER 10

Honora

"*B*ack to work," the wiry one grunts, shaking off his dick. I press a kiss to his shoulder and allow my fingers to trail across the other's arm in farewell. A firm hand slaps my ass as I go and I toss them both a grateful smile. But the moment I turn away it is back to work indeed. My brow furrows and my eyes move to Thorn's tent.

My curiosity is thoroughly piqued. I don't like my position at present. Not having a hand in this matter—being so completely uninformed. If only I could make my way over... eavesdrop a bit. I glance around the celebration. Everything seems to be amping up—energy coils. I think something might happen soon. The guards can sense it as well.

"Why've you got such an ugly look on your face?"

I press my lips together. Marie. My damned shadow. "I'm thinking is all, what's your excuse?"

She bumps my hip with hers and drags me to a nearby table for us to lean upon. Somehow she manages to produce two goblets of wine. If she's got any magical prowess, it is in her uncanny ability to make alcohol appear—apparently from thin air.

"How are you enjoying the party, my love? I don't like to see you sulking about with a frown on your face. You should be smiling, dancing, *fucking*." She draws the word out, laughing, and the wide grin she wears is of true satisfaction. I think she adores life here, among the camp—the excitement of it all. I like it well enough. For now. But I'm after more. I want what lies at the end of this road. With this army and the power of the Queen of Envercress—Thorn will soon sit on the throne at Pontheugh. And Gods damn it all, I want to be the witch sitting next to him.

"I've already done many of those things this evening," I tell her drily, only half-minding the conversation as I focus on the guards and where they place their attention. I'm searching for a sign from one of them that this mystery guest has indeed arrived.

"Oooh, do tell."

"Hmm? Oh. Nothing to tell. Just a little fun to serve my needs."

Marie pouts, her shoulders slumping just a bit. "Oh Honora. You can make just about anything sound dull."

I stop searching the party and cast my eyes to her, conceding. "I had two wonderfully proportioned dicks and I came atop each of them. Is that better?"

Marie holds up two fingers as if to say, just a bit. But she's got a sly grin on her lips and I soften, if only for the sake of maintaining an alliance. "There's my girl." She clinks her goblet against mine and I give in to sipping at the crimson drink.

"What are you so serious about?"

"Same thing as always. My plot to capture our King."

"Ah, Queen Honora. Tell me, will you relax once you're ruling over the lot of us?"

"Yes. I shall be very relaxed once I'm bathed in jewels and

finery. I'll even toss you a few hand-me-down dresses here and there, so don't mock me now, Marie."

"I wouldn't think of it, your Highness."

"What's your scheme to win him over tonight?"

Frustrated, I puff my cheeks out and frown. "Well, thus far I'm not dealing with so much of a scheme as I am a mystery. There is a surprise guest who will be arriving shortly."

"*A guest?*" Marie grasps the uniqueness of the situation. "For the King?"

"Yes. Has something to do with a woman that was found in the woods today. Have you heard anything about it?"

"Of course not. You know I'd tell you straight away."

I hum in acknowledgement, my tone flat, and I nod toward the positioned guards. "They wait for him, this mystery man."

"Oh my. Would you look at that. How do you know all this?"

"The simplest magic: tits and ass."

Marie laughs. "Oh, these fool creatures. It's hardly fair. Like puppets for pussy."

"I wish Thorn were so easy to control," I mutter angrily, harboring a grudge against that witch who rules Envercress. If only I had power like hers. Well, I wouldn't need Thorn if I did. I should like to have that much power one day. Having a crown on one's head and a throne under one's ass would make it all the easier. Anyway, she's the only person to wield any power over our King. If only I knew how to control it... I chew at the side of my nail, thinking.

"A woman in the woods and a man coming after her..." Marie recounts, deep in thought. I don't think she'll make anything of it, but it doesn't hurt to let her try.

"That's the gist."

"Have you seen the woman?"

I shake my head, aware of the scowl on my face. I don't like the idea of Thorn being alone with her—whoever she is.

"Nothing to be jealous of, I'm sure."

"I'm not the jealous type," I spit.

Marie snorts and sips at her wine, loudly saying nothing.

"I'm not jealous. Not in the traditional sense anyway."

"No, I suppose you aren't. It isn't as if you're in love with him."

I scoff at the notion. "There's only one thing I covet."

Marie stops short of another sip of wine. Her eyes go wide. I follow her gaze to see movement at our King's tent! We hurriedly discard our goblets, rushing to get a clear view. *"What's this?"*

Thorn appears, clad in a long, hooded cloak. With great ceremony that is not typical of him, he and a procession of guards make their way to the dais. The orcs howl at the sight of their King. The witches dance with passion and force, slaves pour from the cook tent, bringing a fresh wave of elaborate dishes. And the intensity of the drums, they make my entire body vibrate.

"Put your game face on," Marie whispers, elbowing me in the ribs. I run my fingers through my hair and push out my breasts, hoping to catch Thorn's eye. But he's got that fool hood down so low. I watch as he takes his seat—*I should be up there, beside him.* Then, I see the girl. I practically growl at the sight of her.

"Pathetic thing," I hiss, but Marie isn't listening. She's already distracted, her hips swaying to beat of the drums. Tight, vibrant, red curls bounce as she moves and she doesn't bother looking at the sniveling damsel Thorn has parading on his dais.

That girl. She's ghost white in the face, horrified by the scene playing out around her. Monsters. I imagine that's what she thinks when she looks at us. Like all those other sniveling little things I grew up with after the priests burned my mother. My lip curls in disgust.

Her locks are fair and her features are boring and innocent. She wears a frock that is dirty, but I can tell, even from this distance, it is made of fine material and craftsmanship. She's a city girl, I'd bet my life on it. Sheltered and protected from the wild. Probably has got shit for brains. But she's the kind of thing men covet. A virgin, no doubt. Every orc in this camp would love to ruin a soft little wretch like that.

Hand on my hip, I roll my eyes in the most unforgiving manner, forgetting all about the man the guards are waiting for. My focus is on the whimpering blonde. I hate her. I just hate her and mentally, I tear her to shreds.

The orcs are barking and riotous until someone on the dais cries out: "The King's woman isn't dressed appropriately for a party!"

My eyes widen and white-hot rage fills my chest. *The King's woman!* Is that right?

Marie claps her hands, laughing, cheering. I cut my eyes to her with malice but the words sink in. *Oh.* The modest dress isn't to our King's liking. A slow smile sneaks across my face. I guess there's only one thing to do about that. The blonde gets it too and she's shaking her head in horror.

Thorn means to make a show of shy, meek, little virgin! He's going to strip her down in front everyone. *How thrilling!*

Taking my cue. I saunter up to the dais, grinning and triumphant. How could I have ever thought Thorn was interested in this pathetic creature? I nearly laugh aloud. Joy blossoms in my breast where rage simmered only moments ago.

This girl's a party favor—nothing more.

The orcs guarding the dais smirk approvingly, allowing me to pass. I attempt to catch Thorn's eye, but that fucking cloak is in the way. Anyway, I'm on the dais, just as I should be and I make a sultry show of slipping my dress off one shoulder at a time and shimmying out of it. I stand nude before the party —*proud* of my body. Unlike the trembling wretch clinging to the neckline of her stupid, filthy dress.

Thorn himself takes my cast-off and holds it out to the girl. She tries to skitter back, but she's stopped by the guards. They

grip her shoulders and force her forward—her heels ineffectu-
ally scraping across the dais. I'm grinning from ear to ear, absolutely giddy. I really can see why the orcs would want to ruin
this girl. I want to ruin her too. As a matter of fact, I think our
King is being a little too easy. If he let me take the lead, I might
use a blade, cut her a little. Really put some fear into those
pretty blue eyes.

"Take her clothes," the King commands the guards.

The exhilaration builds in me like an orgasm. I'm trembling,
on the precipice of complete delight, ready to tumble into
ecstasy at the sight of this woman's ruin—but the feeling is
sapped from existence when a blade slams into the skull of one
of the orcs holding her.

Thorn shoves me aside—not out of the way of harm mind
you, but out of *his* way. As if I were nothing more than an
obstruction to his line of sight. The slight goes unnoticed by
everyone but me. A thousand sets of eyes snap to the origin of
the blade.

The crowd parts and a twin cloaked figure stands among
them. The most shocking sight: a mirror image of our King. My
mouth falls open. The quiet is so stark you could hear a pin
drop. It's laughter that breaks the silence. A deep barking laugh
that I have never heard before. *Thorn's laugh.* Stunned, I watch
the scene play out. Our King pulls back his hood, revealing
himself.

"The guest of honor has arrived!" he bellows. "Let the celebration begin!"

Barks, roars, howls. Thorn dismounts the dais, striding—
even his step is unfamiliar, looking more alive than I've ever
seen—he opens his arms to this stranger.

"Come, sit with me, *brother.*"

This isn't a mirror of my King; he is his flesh and blood.
Family. That is problematic to say the least.

I slip away, disappearing into the crowd. I need to think

about what this means for my plan. Thorn is half-mad, easy to fool, to manipulate. But with a brother here…it might potentially make the process more complex. Obviously, he came for one reason and one reason alone. Scraps. He wants to sit at the table. He wants to be royalty and to wield the power that comes with it. He won't want to share.

Marie is quick to find me. "What do you make of it?" she whispers conspiratorially.

"I don't know," I glare back at the interlopers—the brother and the girl. "But I don't like it. Not one bit."

"Nor do I." Marie shakes her head. "They give me a bad feeling, those two. Harbingers, I should think."

Harbingers or not, let Marie try to divine something in her cards about it. All I know is that they stand between me and my prize.

CHAPTER 11

Thorn

The fog bleeds chaos in my mind. I wanted to tease my brother, to stir him. I suppose that's because I'm still angry from all those years ago. What I really wanted was for him to come crawling back. To beg forgiveness. I wanted Ash to tell me how sorry he was that I left, to tell me how badly he needed me. I wanted life to have stopped in my absence.

But that's not the way it happened.

I could see his feelings in his eyes—fear, anger. He looked at me as if I were a stranger and it only made me grow more upset. It made me want to turn that stirring into a rough shake. *Love me!* He's the one who drove me away in the first place. If it weren't for Ash always looking outward... *We had each other back then.* If he'd have stayed, I'd have stayed too. Then I wouldn't be in this mess. I could think straight. I would have my own mind.

I breathe, telling myself it doesn't matter anymore. He's here and hasn't got a say now that I'm King. Nor does this woman of his. My eyes shut and the storm abates ever so slightly—enough to be assured that everything is going to be okay. My family is with me. I can let the past go. What matters is that Ash is here now.

Honora throws long, raven locks over her shoulder, tsking as she riffles through a battered trunk. My mother had one like it, filled it with vile and dangerous things.

I can remember when Ash was a child and I was his only caretaker. Mother, father, brother—all in one. I warned him to stay away from that loathsome old box, fearful that he might get into something that could hurt him. He was the only thing I loved and I wanted so badly to protect him. But I never needed to worry about Ash, not when it came to magic. He hated magic. He blamed it for the way Mother was—her obsession. No. Magic was never the problem with my brother. The problem was wandering and I worried, even then, that my brother would one day leave me.

"I can't say I'm impressed."

I hum—acknowledging that the witch spoke, but uninterested in her opinions.

Gracefully and barefooted she glides around her shabby tent, lighting candles as goes. "He should have bowed to you. Instead, he comes here, to *your* camp, to a party you threw just for him, and he throws a knife."

Is that the way it happened? It's a struggle to piece together the night. My temples pound in protest when I try to think of anything besides my objective. Petra's objective.

The castle, Thorn, the castle. It's like the beating of war drums, only it never ends.

"Ash was always good with his blades," I say dumbly, losing myself to memory. I can't see the witch for all the memories floating to the forefront of my mind. My brother—young, happy, smiling. My only companion in a cursed forest. I chase those memories; I try to grasp hold of them as my temples beat, beat, beat.

"But poor with his manners."

A small laugh escapes me. "I don't think I know anyone good with manners."

I picture my brother's youthful face, eyes twinkling as he practiced his accuracy. I can *hear* the sound of metal delving into the hard trunk of an oak and I squeeze my hand, staring at the bloody wound there.

"Things got out of hand tonight."

"How many of your soldiers did he kill?"

I shrug, still staring at my bloody palm. Ash's blade pierced straight through. I remember now, it was meant for my heart. And for what? *That woman of his.* She must be important. There must be something to her that I'm not seeing.

"I don't care that he is your brother," Honora tells me, dropping her wares onto the table. Wrapped herbs, vials, a bit of gauze, an unlit candle. "He stepped out of line. If I were you, I'd have slit the girl's throat."

I blink, finally seeing the woman before me. "You think I should have killed the girl?"

"Your brother needs to know how he's expected to behave around here. *Show him you are the Orc King.*"

I feel nothing in Honora's presence. No connection, no sense of confidence, no interest. Dealing with her...it leaves me painfully aware of the hollow sensation I carry in my chest. "A King doesn't need to *show* anyone anything. He simply is."

Honora stills, realizing her misstep. Her eyes meet mine and she contorts her lips into a false smile. *Masks. These people only show me masks.* "Of course, your majesty. I spoke out of line." She says the words with sugary sweetness. "I hope you will forgive my familiarity; our time together has made me feel..." Her hands take my wounded one. She is gentle in her touch. It is a gentleness as fake as the smile she wears. "...a certain *closeness.*"

Disinterested, I watch the hole in my hand as Honora administers potions. This witch is cut from the same tired, old cloth as my mother—hungry for power and willing to do anything to get it. All her falseness repels me.

"What will you do with her, my Lord?" Her tone is too tight to be sincere; it frays at the edges.

"Who?"

"*The girl.*" Tighter still.

Oh yes. The girl. My brother's woman. He loves her, doesn't he? It wasn't me that he came here to find. It was her. Ellyn. Ellyn was the one who drew concern. That's important. There's something important there. I can't quite make sense of it, but I know enough to know it is important. "I'll keep her, of course."

"Another slave? A dancer for your soldiers?"

I shake my head. "My brother is fond of her. Very much so. I suppose that means I'll make her my Queen."

Those cold and pacifying hands go rigid and a brittle laugh slips from pretty lips. "*Your Queen!* Isn't that sudden?"

"I trust my brother's judgment."

"The same brother who tried to kill you?"

"I've only got the one," I say with reverence.

She presses her lips together and tears at a bundle of herbs, rubbing them roughly into my wound. "Well, far be it from me to challenge a King who has made up his mind."

Pulling from her grip, I light the candle for myself, finishing the healing charm. When I rise, Honora dons the mask of a wounded lover. Perhaps it is this mental turmoil of mine that helps me see emotion so clearly. Half the time, I can't make sense of the things people say, but I can see their energy and desires.

"I didn't mean to upset you." She pouts.

"Witch, you haven't the power to upset me."

Taking on a seductive pose, she tosses that long black hair once more, accentuating full and rounded breasts, barely hidden beneath a sheer gown. "Stay longer, lover, talk to me. Speak of your plans."

"There is no secret plan. My brother is home." It is no longer a matter of convincing him to stay—to stop his incessant wandering. I will simply command him. "This is where he belongs, with me."

A slow smile crosses the witch's face. "Simple as that, is it?"

"Of course it is. His throne will sit beside mine in the castle at Pontheugh. His woman will have every desire met and then some. There will be riches and power beyond imagination. Who could refuse that? An offer to reign over a kingdom?"

"Not I," she murmurs, her eyes cunning.

"As I've said, I've got something he's fond. My brother will come around to my way of thinking. So will the girl." Why wouldn't they? The offer is a great one for both sides. I can provide everything they've ever wanted and in exchange I get companionship.

The three of us will be a family. All I must do is claim the throne and bring an end to this madness. Then it will be done. Finished. I can rest. As soon as I take the castle...

Even within the confines of Honora's tent, I can't help but turn toward Pontheugh, to search for what is mine through thick canvas walls.

"Well, I hope you're right. There is only so much I can do with potions and if the blade were to hit home..."

I grunt, not bothering to let her words sink in. I'm finished here. I want to be out of this tent, in the open air—to alleviate the terrible pounding at my temples. If only I could lay eyes on the castle, if I could find it on the horizon it would ease me.

With a wave of my arm, I stride out. There's a scurrying behind me.

"Do us all a favor and stay clear of your brother's blades," Honora says, hurrying after me—like a dog at my heels. My brother's blades. The simple words bring a flood of memories.

I draw to a halt under the pale moon. Past blends with the present—the sound of a knife cutting through air, my brother's youthful grin. Or was he frowning, angry and older? Clad in red and black? I can see the two versions in my mind's eye. We aren't in the Perished Woods anymore. We are in my camp and Ash...Ash was angry. *With me.*

I can't quite remember what I did to upset him. The realization frightens me. My hand aches, but when I look down...the wound is gone. I question whether it was ever there at all.

The more I try to focus on what happened here tonight, the more thunder it creates in my mind. My thoughts turn to echoes. Intangible...always leading me back to the castle. All I can think of is that damned castle. Thunder rolls and I search the sky—but it is cloudless.

"Thorn?"

I'm tethered by Honora's call—forced to wonder how long have I been standing here, searching the sky for a storm that exists only in my mind. The witch scrutinizes me in that wolfish way of hers. Always searching for the chance to take a bite out of me. I've no use for her. I am being pulled in another direction.

"Your medallion..." she squeaks unnaturally, pretending to be concerned. Only, it is curiosity that I recognize in her gaze. *Interest.*

Chuffing air through my nostrils, I shake away my disorientation. Or I try to at least. But it snakes around me—worming through my brain. *Keep hold of what matters,* I tell myself. Ash has come home to me. I can win him over. I can have a partner in him—a companion. I won't be alone any longer. I...I can set things right. But the more I grasp at that goal, the more I try to orient myself towards it, the sicker I feel. *I'm getting worse.*

Honora's fingers grip my wrist and I wretch away. When I focus on her, her narrowed gaze is fixed on the weight around my neck. The medallion. That's what's choking me, isn't it?

In a hushed tone and with greedy eyes, she speaks. "It's practically glowing. Thorn...the power coming off of that thing..."

"DON'T TOUCH IT!" I've lost my calm, my inner strength, that piece of me I cultivated during my years of isolation. That piece that held fast in the belly of Black Mountain. That piece that makes me King...more than any crown ever could. Suddenly, I feel more orc than man. Or maybe even more beast than that.

I'm a wild animal, chained. I'm a horse, bit in mouth. My rider driving straight for the edge of a cliff. Instinct tells me to turn back, but I move as though I am a puppet.

Honora's eyes are wide. Her mouth agape. *She wants my medallion.* The thought is like searing heat. I cut my hand through the air and finally, she draws up short. This time, when I stalk away, the raven-haired dancer knows better than to follow.

Alone at last, I claw at my temples. I can have it all, I insist: a family *and* the throne. Whispers seemingly coming from within my own mind say otherwise. I try my best to hold them at bay. Despite the chill of the night, sweat cascades down my body in rivers. Emotion wars with drive and I wince, trying to find myself, trying to keep it together. Yet, I think I must be falling apart.

CHAPTER 12

Honora

$\mathcal{J}$ press my lips into a firm line and watch Thorn go, half-staggering. I've never seen him this bad before. As we've neared the castle, sure—he's gotten worse. But I believe his brother turning up has complicated matters.

Standing out in the cold won't solve anything. It must be near dawn now. I turn back to the tent I share with the other women. Now that our King has gone, they slip from the shadows and descend like flies into our living space. I cringe, trying to shut out their insipid chatter. But it is no use. Lydia whistles at me, pulling pins from her hair, tossing them frivolously onto the vanity. I notice she's wearing some of my beads and I stare at them pointedly.

"That was one hell of a show." Her long, horse-like face, cracked with powder, is alight with excitement. The fool.

I'm silent, moving to my own dressing table to wipe the rouge from my lips. Marie is the only one with any semblance of intelligence and she's gone straight for the cards, spreading them out across her blanket. She studies each with a frown.

"*Well?*" Esme demands, sliding up behind me to squeeze my shoulders. She's a mouse of a thing: small, with a little tapered nose, and ugly ears she hides beneath a mass of frizz. I extract myself from her grip.

"Well what?" My expression is blank.

"Are you going to tell us anything?"

Rolling a shoulder I open a trunk, pulling out bed clothes. "What is there to tell? We all saw what we saw."

"And his Highness spoke no more of it while he was in your care?" Their eyes are unbelieving, but they don't know Thorn like I do. They don't know how aloof he can be. To them, this has been one long party. An adventure out of the Perished Woods. To me, it is everything. It is my future—the one I deserve.

Nicolene drops onto her bed, propping her head up with the palm of her hand. She is more beautiful than the others, though her eyes are a little too closely set for my taste and she watches me with an amused smile. Clicking her tongue, she instructs the others: "Hush. Honora will speak when she has space to."

"And what shall I speak of?" I challenge, sending her my own smile, though amusement is not what I feel.

"The wheels in your mind are turning, my dear. It is plain to see."

"Perhaps they are, but it's nothing to do with the King's brother."

"It truly is his brother then?" Esme thrills. "I tell you; I sort of like the look of him better. Handsome, don't you think?"

I give a slight curtsey. "It is Thorn who has my heart."

They throw their heads back and cackle. Even Marie lifts her chin to smirk at my words. And I laugh too, callously. "I'll need to work on that." I slip into a night dress and fix a dressing gown around myself, my hands sliding over the smooth silk. I'll have a hundred of them when I'm Queen, in every color imaginable. "But, yes. That was his brother," I admit, speaking only for the sake that conversation sometimes stirs my own imagination. Once in a great while I can even glean a little insight from the others. Rare as it is, for these are very stupid women.

"And that bleating little sheep he brought with him?" Lydia asks.

"Wretched, isn't she?" I hold my tongue on the bit about Thorn wanting to make her his Queen. Rash words of a man half-mad. He might just as easily forget all about her. Then again, he might not. "The woman is of no consequence," I insist to the others. "Just a toy to tease the brother with."

"You know, I missed the first of it. His arrival," Esme says.

"Threw a knife from the crowd!" Marie fills in the drama the rest of us had the pleasure of witnessing.

"I thought there was going to be a blood bath right in the middle of camp," Nicolene says in a placid sort of way.

"I simply can't believe Thorn didn't kill him—or at the very least the girl."

"My thoughts exactly," I mutter.

"Kill the girl, teach the insolent brother a lesson. It's simple."

I hold my hands up. "I agree. It is the only sensible course of action. Of course, our King is not a sensible creature." Not with that medallion round his neck. I throw myself onto my own bed, my thoughts working.

"Did he fuck you?"

"What's that?" I stall.

"Did the two of you fuck tonight? When you tended to his hand?" Lydia presses the question.

"Of course we did," I lie.

"Lucky girl. I've only had the pleasure of his company once, but I won't soon forget it."

"Honora has always been his majesty's favorite," Nicolene says in a knowing way. In a way that tells me she can see through my lie. How she can see anything with those close-set eyes, I'll never know. Anyway, it doesn't matter if we fucked or not, because I *am* his favorite. He frequents me over all the others. I've got the best tits. The most beautiful hair. I fancy I'm the most beautiful altogether. As I should be, Gods know how much magic I've put into appearances...

Nicolene addresses Marie. "What do the cards have to say?"

Marie shakes her head. "Nine of swords...mental anguish, The Emperor—I can guess who that is...and The Moon—deception, confusion, strife," she sighs unhappily. "Then there's The Tower, followed by Judgment, then Death. What is there here but a warning? Danger is coming, ladies, and this is where it begins."

The others grow still, their eyes are fixed on Marie and the light-hearted atmosphere is sucked from the room. She's got a reputation for being good at her cards. But I am quite good at what I do as well. I twist the meanings in my mind so they work for me. "You make it sound so ominous!" I laugh. "The Tower can represent *any* unexpected change."

"I've got to acknowledge the context of the surrounding cards, love. This isn't a happy story they tell."

I push myself up and saunter over to Marie's bed, allowing my dressing gown to catch the air, fluttering around me as I move. I can imagine one far more regal draped around my shoulders. "I see a distressed King longing for reprieve."

"The tower is danger, I assure you."

"I look at it and I see change." I drop my nail down on Judgment. "A decision to be made. Followed by—"

"*Death.*"

"A new beginning. What is the death of one thing but the birth of another?" My smile is triumphant, my chin lifted. "Call me an optimist, dear, but I think this reading was meant for my ears tonight. I do believe it is a call for me to step up my game."

"Do you now?" Nicolene sings from across the tent. She thinks she's so clever, but she's got no ambition. Not one ounce of it. And how clever can you be if you've no aspirations in life?

"Indeed, I do. We near the castle. Our King's task is nearly complete. While I have thoroughly enjoyed our time together in this tent," a bald-faced lie, "I think it is high time I became a more constant companion to our Lord and Master, Thorn."

Esme glows at the idea. "Honora, I think it could be! I really do! You could be Queen! Imagine that. A humble witch from the Perished Woods, ruling over man's land!"

"Who said I was humble?" We all laugh over the notion, all of us except Marie. She runs her fingers over the cards, contemplative. I have no time for negativity. Thorn loses more of himself each day; the arrival of his brother and this woman are no help in that matter. Given his current state, Thorn is apt to make a rash decision. He might even marry that wretched little thing from the city. That is, if no one takes the initiative to stop him. The time has come. I've got to claim Thorn now. As soon as possible, I need to become his wife.

"What about this woman in his tent?"

"What did I say? A toy to tease the brother. Thorn has no interest in her otherwise." I say it with harsh confidence. "But it is a good thing the brother is here."

"Why is that?" Lydia asks, leaning forward with interest.

"Why, of course we will want family at the wedding!"

Nicolene snorts. "*The wedding.* Indeed."

"Yes, indeed. My wedding to the King. Careful the way you talk to me or you won't be invited."

"Of course I will." She waves away the suggestion. "We all know what orcs expect from a party. There are a lot of cocks and not nearly enough pussy in this camp." She slaps between her legs. "I'm absolutely raw! What we should do is put the brother's girl to work."

"It will be my first royal decree, I assure you."

"That's all fine, Honora. I think you are the perfect match for Thorn, but the cards—" Marie protests.

"The cards are nothing more than an urging for me to tighten the noose."

"And how do you propose to do that?"

"Womanly wiles."

Nicolene has that slightly amused, needling look about her. "They haven't worked yet."

Well, Thorn has never been so lost in his madness before, is what I'm thinking. But I keep that to myself. Mentally, our King is at his weakest. I saw it tonight, didn't I? With my own eyes. I saw the power of the medallion taking over. I know for certain, *that* thing has been controlling him. I'll let it too. With his mind consumed, a few whispered words and a warm, wet pussy can steer even the most powerful King. This is my chance.

"It's a matter of suggestion and convenience at this point. A simple thing, really." For a simple and fragile mind. I open a drawer at my vanity and retrieve my favorite perfume. "I'll make him think of me when I'm not there...desire me in an insatiable kind of way. And when he comes looking, there I will be. Always at his beck and call. The woman he can trust—"

Nicolene snorts, laying her head on her pillow and closing her eyes.

"Well, maybe 'trust' is too strong a word," I say reflectively. "But I'll be there and I've *been* here since the beginning. In that sense, I am loyal."

"Loyal to your ambition."

"Loyal all the same. Loyal...and determined." I hold the little bottle of perfume between my fingers, plotting the beginnings of a plan...and a spell to go with it.

CHAPTER 13

Thorn

The days bleed together, muddying themselves in my mind. Everything feels so damn pressing, but I'm lost in a directionless fog, never seeming to make any headway.

"I worry we are losing focus," Arron says. He is keeping stride with me and my harried pace. I cut my eyes to him, angered.

"Have there not been enough deaths? Have you run out of villages to burn?"

His jaw juts out, he's stewing in his own tempered anger. I can feel how coiled he is. And me? I feel frustrated.

"Spit it out already. I haven't the patience for games."

Arron halts, his tone gruff and urgent. "I am not one to play games, sir. Nor do I take pleasure in questioning your motives..."

"And yet?" I practically snarl at him in accusation.

With a great huff, Arron casts his eyes about and steps closer, keeping his head bowed and his eyes on the ground. "I am *concerned*, Thorn. You have not been yourself."

"Then tell me, Arran, who am I?" I growl the words; my mind is being drawn and quartered and now I must deal with this? What is this but an annoyance? I've no desire to answer to anyone, to explain myself to anyone!

"This situation with your brother, sir..."

"What about it?" I start back on my path, but realize I don't know where I was headed. The air is thick and hot. I'm sweating. It drips from my brow, slipping into my eyes, burning them.

"Ever since he came here you have been a ghost."

I laugh. "*A ghost?* Please, Arran, I'm not dead yet."

"Not yet? Do you plan to die soon then?"

The question sobers me. For I don't know the answer. I scan the landscape for help. Grey. Everything is grey in this godforsaken camp.

Arran's urgent whisper brings me back, feeling like trumpets in my ears. "*This isn't you.*"

I can't quite remember who I am. There's so much noise. Incessant noise. Voices commanding me this way and that...

"He's poisoning your mind."

"Who is?"

"This brother of yours. This *obsession.*"

"My brother loathes magic. He would never poison me—"

"I didn't mean it like that."

I wipe sweat from my brow, feeling as if there is some place I am meant to be.

"The Eternal Princess is growing impatient. Angry even—"

That catches my attention. My eyes widen and I feel...afraid. "You've spoken to her?"

Arron shakes his head and I wonder suddenly if I can trust him. I stumble back; worry flashes in his eyes. I can hardly recall the past days. Only flashes of Ellyn's fear, beacons of my brother's outrage. Over and over again, they renounce me, lie to me, betray me. I press my palms into my temples.

"Let me help you, before anyone else notices..."

I pull back fast, my attention focused hard on Arran. "What would you do?"

"Figure out this problem, of what your brother is doing to you."

"My brother isn't doing anything to me!"

"Then how do you explain this…this…*confusion?*"

I squeeze my eyes shut. "It's simple. I'm being pulled in too many directions. My thoughts, Arran, you don't understand. When I try to focus on something other than…" I can hardly say it. *The castle.* It makes my stomach roll. I want to break out into a run. If only I could head right for it and leave the rest of this behind.

But I don't want to leave it all behind. The camp, sure. My army? I don't care. But not Ash. Not my brother. Not even Ellyn. There's something about her. He thinks there is anyway and I want to see her through Ash's eyes. I wish I could. I don't understand what it is they have, but damn it all to Hell—*that* is what I really want. Not a damned castle. I want people. I want people who are *mine.*

"We've known each other a long time…" Arron says. My eyes snap open. I look at him. I'd forgotten he was here.

My brows draw down in confusion. A long time? Have we? I don't speak the words though, in fear of being found out. I don't want him to know how lost I am. Truly, this madness is consuming. If only, if only, if only…I've got to find a way out of this fog.

"I'll take them away from here."

"*Who?*" I startle.

"Ash and the girl."

I hold my finger out in accusation. "Don't you dare. Don't you for one second dare to take them from me. They're mine. Do you hear that? I need them."

"*Why?*"

He doesn't understand. He isn't a half-blood like me, like

Ash. Arron is all beast, relishing only in the fight. If this were his own brother throwing a wrench in the plans of the Eternal Princess, Arron would kill without a second thought. But Ash is my blood. My family. I need him. These monsters will never be able to understand. "I'll take care of it."

"When?" The patience leaves him.

"In *my* time! Since when does a King need to follow the timeline of another?"

"When he is acting as the sword of the most powerful witch in all the land." His words are spoken low, filled with apprehension... Arron casts his eyes about the tents and mud surrounding us. He's fearful of being overheard. Does Petra have spies then? I scan too, suddenly quite suspicious. "I don't trust her, Thorn."

Petra, a monster in the mask of a young woman. Her fair skin, those feminine gowns, the soft curls to her hair. It's the eyes that cannot fool. The eyes that are ancient and cold, they cut through man and beast like knives.

The medallion weighs heavily and the hair on my neck prickles. I can feel her watching. Whispers invade my thoughts, urging me toward the castle. Like needles, whispers like needles, stinging...

"If they were gone you could focus on the castle."

I dig my fingers into my hair, pulling it at the roots, trying to relieve some of the tension. The castle, the castle, the castle... He's one of them, isn't he? One of Petra's spies.

"At least let me have one of the witches make a potion, to alleviate the stress."

I scoff. "You think I should place my trust in them? You think those *hags* from the wood could compete with the witch at Envercress?"

His wide jaw tightens and he looks up to the clouded sky, searching for an answer. "I don't know."

"I do. I won't have any potions from them, Arran."

"Then what will you do? It can't go on like this. The Eternal Princess will come and if she does…"

"It won't go on another night." I square my shoulders and search for an elusive sliver of myself among the madness. "I'll end this. Right now."

"How?"

I grasp for ideas, but there is only one. "My brother's woman. Ellyn."

"What about her?"

"She'll have the answer."

"What answer?"

"I don't know, Arran! Some kind of womanly answer! She's enthralled my brother, turned him against me! If I can get through to her, she will fix this. SHE is the answer." My stomach sours. Even in my madness, I know it wasn't Ellyn who turned Ash against me. I did that, many years ago.

"Well, she's in your tent readying herself for you. A meal has been prepared."

"Good." I nod, pulling my hair back, trying to return to some state of decorum.

"Do you need me there?"

"I can do this."

I see the doubt written on my general's face and somewhere, deep in my mind, I know it is an unfamiliar look. Does he speak the truth, have we known each other long? Had faith in one another? Been friends even? I simply can't recall. Who is Arron and can I trust him?

"Tonight," I repeat. "This ends tonight." I say the words with such surety, even I believe them. Anyway, I'm desperate to. Desperate to end this new depth of insanity. I think I'll die if I don't. Truly, it's killing me.

CHAPTER 14

Thorn

Ellyn is uneasy when I come to her. Always uneasy. I try so many things and always, she fears me.

"Sit," she urges. "Please."

Her voice is stressed. Her features tight—so strained is she in my presence. That's not the way it's supposed to be. I can feel the emotion coming off of her in waves and it sickens me. It isn't joy, it isn't ease, or companionship. It's fear in all its ugly forms and it makes me hate myself.

Still, she has asked me to sit. I am finally making headway. And despite her lack of trust in me, I feel as if it is only she and my brother who I can open myself to. "This hasn't been easy, you know?" It's a confession. "All I wish is to be a family. To *understand* this thing you and my brother share. I want it so damned bad—"

You desire nothing but the castle... a voice contends. Not Ellyn. I push it away and endeavor to focus on what matters.

Clearing my throat, I watch her reaction. "I'm lonely here,

Ellyn. I can't imagine that's been a secret to you. For years, I've hoped Ash would find me. Only, now that he has…"

"It isn't going the way you thought, is it?" She's frank. I like that about Ellyn. Business-like and proper. Completely unlike any woman I've met before. I feel as if I should desire her in a deeper way. But I don't and it only makes me more confused.

I look down at the food spread across the table, but I feel nothing. Not even hunger. Eventually, my hand settles on a bottle of wine. Uncorking it, I top two glasses. "I always knew he'd need convincing. I suppose I'd hoped the years would have done it for me." I go on. "And maybe they would have, if *you* hadn't beaten me to him. The thing I'm coming to realize is that he can't see past you, Ellyn. It is as if you have enthralled him."

She swallows uneasily. I watch her throat bob as she does. Why must she always be on her guard? If only Ellyn would relax. She says nothing. She *adds* nothing to the conversation. Damn it all, it makes me prickle. Finally, I am forced to spur her.

"Has he done the same for you?"

But I know the answer, don't I? Of course I do. Yes! Ash has her heart. She loves him. And how can it be? A woman. A human woman. Not a witch, but a good, honest woman—has fallen in love with a beast.

All my life I have been taught of the discrimination, *the hatred*, humans feel for us. It's why we were banished. Exiled to a dangerous land. And yet, this thing between Ellyn and Ash…it seems so balanced. Not a one-sided affair. She is as committed to my brother as he is to her. If only I could understand the how and the why of it, then I could figure out how to align myself with them, to *feel* what they feel.

Ellyn searches my face, almost in a pleading way, as if she *wants* to understand me. I want it too! "I care for Ash," she tells me with precision. "More than anyone I've ever cared for in my life. He has my heart."

"I know he has your heart. But how? Have you no regard for what he is? Don't you see? He's an orc, a monster from the cursed wood."

She presses her lips together and tilts her head in consideration. "His appearance was different to me at first, I can't deny that, and I was taught to believe many falsehoods about the people of the Perished Woods. But Ash, he's...How can I say this? How can I make you understand? I've gotten to know him and *who* he is matters more than anything else."

Who he is. I know who he is.

"And *I'm his brother.*"

I growl the statement angrily and set my wine glass down with an abrupt clatter. Rising from my place at the table, I stride to Ellyn. She's up too and she retreats until she can go no further. If orc blood doesn't matter to her, then shouldn't I be just as worthy of affection?

Close to her now, so close I can breathe her in, I whisper. "Could you care for me the way you care for him?" Her eyes go wide with discomfort over the question, but I press. "Could you devote yourself so blindly?"

"I don't know what you're asking."

My head pounds in irritation and I raise my voice. "*Could you love me the way you love him?*"

She sputters but says nothing.

I'm not getting through to her. All she has to do is say yes. All she has to do is treat me with love, with affection, with devotion. If only she would love me, Ash would see and Ash would love me too. Somehow, I've got to get her to agree.

I search my mind for a solution. Fuck me, I search for a *compromise*—that's how bad it's gotten. The great Orc King is willing to compromise. "What if I said you could leave here?" I ask in a rush, grasping onto an idea. "That I'd take you far away to someplace safe and you'd never have to look back?"

"You'd let us go? Just like that?"

I laugh without humor. "No. I could let you go. But Ash—he stays." With Ellyn gone he might forget. I'd be his only companion. Eventually, he would have to be my brother again. He'd let down his guard if he didn't have Ellyn to protect. We could talk and laugh again, like we used to.

Her eyes grow discerning and she narrows them at me. "You're willing to make a deal?"

A deal. I consider it. Have I stooped so low? Do Kings make deals? Do Kings beg as I have? I stare down at my hands, feeling too far away for them to be mine. It is as if I have lost control and I don't know where I left it. "I've been known to make deals."

"Let him go and I'll stay instead." The suggestion startles me and she hurries to explain. "I'm...I'm not promising to love you, but I can be devoted."

My lip curls and I shout. "*I want you to be devoted to ME. Not him!*" Sacrificing herself. How fucking heroic. What is this offer but an allegiance to my brother, undying allegiance even in his absence. That isn't what I want. It would never satisfy the craving in my heart.

Hurriedly and with worry in her eyes, she slips around me, trying to put space between us. I stalk after my prey.

"I don't know how to do that!" She's nearly screaming the words in frustration. But what is her frustration compared to my own?

"Love, devotion, loyalty. Is that really so much to ask?" I continue my advance, but Ellyn is backed against a dresser. She presses her hands against my chest, keeping me at bay.

The touch calls my attention. I drop my eyes to the medallion as her fingers graze it, ever so slightly.

This is the thing. This terrible thing. It weighs on me. I can feel it pulling even now. All this business with Ash and Ellyn, it is like swimming against a rushing current. The more I try to swim toward them, the louder the water rages in my ears. I know what the medallion wants. It wants me to leave this tent, to continue my journey to the castle, to claim it in the name of Petra Gunnora, to capture the King and his daughter, to give them over to my master... The castle, the castle, the castle. An image of it flashes in my mind.

"We should discuss this over dinner." Ellyn's voice sounds far away, but it brings me back. I nearly stumble and her words settle in. A command. I huff. She's issued a command.

"You and my brother are the only ones who don't treat me like a King. What you fail to realize is that I needn't *discuss* anything with you. I can simply take what I want—I can even take you."

"That isn't how love works," Ellyn tells me, her eyes pleading. I don't like to see her like this—cowering and small. I want her to look at me the way she looks at Ash. I want someone to look at me and see *the man,* not the monster. I turn my head away, ashamed of the thought. I am not a man. I am a bastard, one foot in each world.

"Fine, let's eat," I grumble, giving in, turning toward the table with the stupid, grand feast set upon it. It's a meal to be shared, but it grows cold while we argue.

"Wait!" Ellyn all but screams, quite nearly startling me. The woman's pale hands clutch at me and I grimace at this sudden and intense contact. I should feel something when she grabs hold of me, shouldn't I? A thrill maybe. Desire? *Anything?* Instead, I want to peel her away.

"What is it?"

"Before we eat...I just want to know...uh..." She searches for words as she wrings her hands. "If that deal sounded at all possible to you? Would you let Ash go in exchange for me?"

Sizing her up, I'm utterly perplexed. It's like being back in Black Mountain, fighting that long battle to reach the core. Only, here I fight hard and make no progress. I don't think I've ever felt so helpless in my life...so confused. If only I had an ally.

"I want to know what Ash sees in you. I want to *feel* what he does."

"Well, what about that girl you were with the other night?"

I don't remember.

"The one with the long, dark hair?"

I snarl in disgust. Honora, the deceitful witch. "I deserve more than that, don't I? I'm a *King*, Ellyn, and you'd have me keep a whore as my Queen?"

Her face pinches in perplexity. "What do you even mean, *Queen*? You keep saying that, but I don't—"

I could scream, but I tighten my jaw and force my tone. "How many times must I explain? I want you to be mine in all ways. I want your loyalty, now and forever, as undying as your love. You could be my wife. That is what I mean when I offer you the title of Queen. It should be simple!"

"But...But...*Why?*" She seems distracted. "You don't know me, Thorn. If not the...*whore*, as you call her, then why not find someone you actually care for?"

I hang my head. Gods, the energy this takes. "My brother knows you. There's something about you in particular that he likes very much. And despite everything, I trust him. I don't have time to search for a more suitable partner, nor would I know where to look. Besides, if we keep you, it solves more problems than one."

"How's that?" She glances behind me. I start to turn to the table, but she grips me tighter.

"We could share you, Ash and me. That way we both get what we want."

Ellyn doesn't like the suggestion. As a matter of fact, she seems almost threatened by it and I notice her hand slip conspicuously to her coat pocket. I'm forced to bite back a smirk. She's hiding something in there. Doesn't matter. I'll let her. What have I to fear from a soft, little woman from the city? My guess is that she's got hold of a weapon, perhaps a knife from the dinner table. I could take it easily, of course. So, if it makes her happy, I'll allow her to have it. As long as she plays nice.

"*Share me?* That's, uh...that's certainly a unique idea."

"I can be practical at times."

"Yes, well..."

Fatigued, I cast my eyes back to the table. "You're hungry, Ellyn. Let's eat."

I pull out a seat, bidding her closer with a warm smile—a conscious effort to put her at ease. But it is a chore, isn't it? My brow sweats and my temples beat a steady rhythm. I teeter as I stand there, holding the chair out. Still, Ellyn looks nervous.

Tentatively and with eyes darting all about, she comes to the table. How nervous she's grown, I notice, leaving her at one end of the table to take my seat on the other side.

Then, we proceed to stare at one another. Silence stretches on uncomfortably. I don't think this is how it is supposed to be. If it were her and Ash, the atmosphere wouldn't be so painfully solemn. Eventually, I pick up my glass of wine, sipping from it in a melancholy way as Ellyn takes to poking at her food.

I study her for a while. "He'd never leave without you. You know that, right?" This deal of hers. It's flawed to the core.

"Yes, I suppose I do. Ash isn't like that. He would never leave anyone behind."

I snort in amusement. Or the lack thereof. "No, your darling Ash would never leave anyone behind. Except for me, of course. Except for his own flesh and blood."

She stares at her plate, her fork clicking against it ever so quietly. "If you truly love him as you claim to, you could just let us both go."

Everything in me coils. It's as if all my words are said in vain. No one hears me. My restraint falters and I slam my cup down on the table, causing wine to slosh over the sides. Ellyn jolts in surprise. "I don't have to let *anything* go. I don't ever have to do that again. I'm a fucking King, Ellyn. A fucking *King.*"

She starts to nodding, eager to make my anger dissipate. But she's got no true concern for me or the things I want. She just wants to placate me. "You spared my friend the other day. A guard from Pontheugh that your army captured. I begged you and you released him," she hurries to say. I hardly remember it. "I want you to know I'm grateful for that."

"Show me your gratitude then!" I bellow.

"I'm sorry?"

"Come and show your King how grateful you are for his mercy."

Ellyn grows pale and she makes no move other than a quick shake to her head. I lean back in my chair and laugh. This woman, she *pales* at the suggestion of touching me. Of *loving* me. My blood heats, turning into unconcealable rage.

"I'm an orc, Ellyn. A *monster.* My brother tries to deny that piece of himself, he ignores it. But I'm not him, don't ever mistake me for—"

Suddenly, a wave of warmth washes over me. It's peaceful really. Almost like being drunk. My anger softens, the noise dims—inside my head, that is. And I'm able to lean more gently into this craving for companionship and affection. The medallion still feels hot against my skin, but it is as if I have taken a step outside myself and I am only vaguely aware of the pain.

I turn my full focus on Ellyn. She's a lovely woman, the most beautiful in my camp. But what do I feel when I look at her? Sadly, nothing. What does my brother see? What angle did he look from to see it? I'm willing to bend. For this, I am willing to bend. "If I taste you, Ellyn, do you think then I would be enthralled? Would you have me in your grasp, just as you have him?"

Taking the offer as a threat, she pushes back from her seat at the table. I can't find it in me to be upset. No. I'm suddenly quite tired. Unnaturally tired. My head tips as she rises and I notice her hand once again, snaking to that coat pocket.

"What's that you have there? You keep touching your pocket, Ellyn. It's quite telling, you know." A dark idea suddenly crosses my mind. But no. That would be absurd. Still…I lift my glass, swirling it in my hand, examining the contents before bringing it close to inhale its scent.

I close my eyes and a memory floats to mind. Something from my past. From long ago. I'm taken back to the Perished Woods, to the valley I grew up in, where stood my mother's shack. Inside was that wretched trunk of hers. Suddenly, my eyes open wide. I know this scent. *It's poison.*

Ellyn. She's killed me. The realization is like ice water to my veins.

With a swipe of my arm, the table and all its lavishly prepared contents go flying. I wanted it nice for Ellyn. I spared nothing. I tried, I tried so hard to reason with her, to impress her. I tried to show all I could offer.

She stifles a scream, fingers clasped over her mouth. I rise, but my head is spinning, causing me to stagger. I clutch at my head. "I can't believe I didn't see it—I don't know *how* I didn't see it." I close the distance between us in two short strides.

"What you're talking about?" She has the nerve to feign surprise.

With rough, angry hands, I pull her close and glare into her eyes with accusation. "You're a *witch*," I growl.

"A what?" Ellyn draws back, showing nothing but more confusion. It's a well performed ruse. A needless one. Her job is done. I know that scent. I remember my mother brewing the very same death-draft.

"Show it to me," I demand, reaching for her pocket, but before my fingers can wrap around the vial surely concealed there, something strikes me hard from behind. Glass shatters and I fall to the ground.

Were it not for this wretched poison, were it not for this roaring chaos raging once again in my ears, such a blow would never have dropped me. Warmth cascades down my face. I'm incensed and I bound to my feet—only to lay eyes upon my own flesh and blood. My brother. His hand is in this. In my death.

They wear masks of horror as they gaze upon me, but they do not know true horror as of yet. Blood, hot and red blood, spills from the wound on my head, wetting my lips as I snarl my betrayers. "All your high and mighty talk of magic and look at you—you're *fucking* a witch. And now, she's killed me!"

Ash, in his loathing of me, produces a vial from his pocket and throws it venomously at my feet. The contents are black and they rattle when they hit the ground. Time stalls and I stare at it—so familiar. Memories threaten to overwhelm me. Childhood, the fear my mother could instill, hiding, shielding my precious brother from her evil, from her cruelty. He despised that wretched woman and yet it was her spell he used to kill me.

It wasn't Ellyn. I want it to be Ellyn, but it wasn't. It was Ash.

A guttural growl rips from deep inside my soul and I dive for my brother. In the blink of an eye we're both on the ground, rolling over pieces of broken glass. I'm wounded. It isn't the gash in my head, nor the madness, nor the poison. It is the dark abyss my brother has cast me into. He has abandoned me once and for all. I mutter words of hate, of loss, and despair—and Ash, Ash tries to strangle me. The next horror is my own, as my hand finds a shard of glass and I drive it into the only family I have ever known. The only person I can say with absolute certainty, who I love.

Time stops. The fight pauses. Ash looks down at his side. His eyes meet mine. How, he seems to be asking. How did it come to this? But all he had to do was surrender. If only he would have surrendered his will.

I strike my brother across the face and he tumbles onto his back. "Try to strangle me?" I grit out. My own fingers dig into his neck and I squeeze. His hands are feeble against my own. I've rage on my side. My brother. I can feel him kicking, but he can't gain purchase. Does he truly think he can best me in a fight? "I am a King," I mutter.

Then, the game changes impossibly fast. There's a sensation across my throat that doesn't quite make sense. Hot, red, blood sprays across my brother's face. The shock of it makes me draw in air—only I can't. It's as if I am suddenly drowning. I suck in breath, but it is wet.

Ash kicks free and scrambles for his woman. Her hands have blood on them. *My* blood. I reach for my throat and can feel it gaping. "Tried to take me down to the bone," I say, but it is sputtering to their ears.

It is hopeless trying to stop the rush of the blood. My life spills from me, scorching and wet. Ash and Ellyn watch. Their cruel mouths hang open, but they say nothing. They inch away, abandoning me even in death. What merciless hate, I marvel.

I force words from my broken throat. "We could have...been a family. A brother...a sister..." I made promise after promise. Concession after concession, and still, they refused to yield! I can't wrap my mind around it, my blood boils at the thought—and I've so little space left for thought.

I blink once, twice. It's a tremendous task. Crimson heat spills down my front and I fall to my knees, vision tunneling. I can't form more words, but inside there is a storm raging. Thunder rolls—endless noise.

Ellyn buries her face against Ash, taking solace in him and he in her. He cradles his woman. Something about all of it shreds my very essence. I'm torn in different directions. My mind goes one way and my heart another. Even now, in my death throes, the drive for the castle bears down on me. But the core of my being is screaming for something else—for something more than stone.

Knees no longer able to support me, I fall the rest of the way to the ground. Numbed by the poison, I watch my brother's feet as he and Ellyn make a harried escape from my tent. There are no goodbyes. No apologies. Not a word. If I could call after them I would, but every time I try, blood fills my mouth. This is not the way Kings are meant to die.

Wave after wave of emotion rocks me. I'm a slave to it, I realize, and that doesn't sit right. How can I be King and slave at the same time? It's impossible. I am one or the other. Never both. But I was meant to be King, was I not? Didn't I hear the call long before the Eternal Princess plucked me from Black Mountain? I close my eyes and will the wheels of fortune to give me another chance. I command it—*I am meant for more in this life.*

My medallion seems to hum in agreement, growing hotter and heavier by the second. It burns, searing through the numbness. If I could move, I'd wrench it from my body. Thunder rolls again. I can feel an electric tension building in the room. My hair stands on end. There's a crackling, like ice readying to break. Then—the lightning finally strikes.

It's a curious thing, for lightning to strike in one's tent. I would very much like to see what exactly is happening, but my muscles refuse to respond and the only thing within my line of sight is a blood-soaked carpet. The edge of my vision turns black. How quickly I fade. My breath is shallow. I think this is the end. But someone else is in my tent now, grumbling and cursing. I already know who, for I've only one ally in this world.

A satin slipper toes me in annoyance. A woman's voice curses again, taking in the severity of my wounds. Then, Petra bellows.

"ARRAN!" There's an urgency in her that doesn't quite match the mild-mannered persona she tries so hard to exemplify. It's so entirely out of character that I'd laugh if I could, but instead, I pass out.

CHAPTER 15

Thorn

Flashes of a castle I've never seen burn into my mind. Stone spires overlay dark clouds. All the windows are empty. There are no sentinels along battlements, no archers at the arrow slits. Not a soul to be seen. It holds no appeal and I turn away. Only, it doesn't hurt anymore. In the darkness, I place a hand over my heart and look inward, demanding answers.

"With no desire for the castle, what's left?"

Loneliness.

I'm startled by a response. I spin, searching all around me, but I am surrounded by a pitch black darker than night. I see nothing. "Is that what I'm to be left with?" I call. "After everything?"

Silence.

"After years of wandering, searching for answers, for my place in the world. After war and bloodshed—you propose to leave me with nothing?"

You'll have exactly what you started with.

My anger rises. "To Hell with you!" I challenge this new voice. It isn't the call of the medallion. Nor is it Petra and her suffocating drive. It's something else. Something familiar and yet, at the same time, not. "I was born to be King. Everything I've done has led to the castle at Pontheugh. This was meant to be mine. I was called here! I followed the call, didn't I? All of my days, I followed the call."

Have you?

"I followed it," I insist. "It took me all the way to Black Mountain, to Envercress, and now here. To *my* castle."

Sweat forms on my brow as silence drags on. I still feel the presence of another here in the dark with me. I feel knowing eyes looking, seeing me as...as only *I* can.

There's no use in lying to one's self. Is that what I'm doing here?

I allow the question to permeate my mind. What if I no longer want the castle and this path I've been on is leading me somewhere else, somewhere unforeseen? I've been blind. All this time, I've been lost.

It incenses me.

You've followed anger, groveled at insecurity, traversed rivers of blood—and for what? For all your efforts, you are no closer to having what you desire. You call yourself King, but what are you the King of?

I clench my jaw and try to turn away, but it is impossible to turn away from oneself. Deep am I in the grip of emotion. "My brother left me," I say finally. An admission. A shameful one. For a second time, I was unable to keep the person I love most in this world.

What were you searching for in him?

I nearly laugh. "That should be obvious."

It isn't.

Blowing out a beath of air, I hold up my palms. "Family, connection, an equal..."

Loneliness...

"I admit that I am alone. But solitude does not rule me. Not even emotion can rule a King."

You say again and again: you're King.

"As I was called to be."

The silence that ensues says more than any words could.

I bare my teeth, gnashing them in anger. Words get stuck in my throat. The pain is searing. Blood fills my mouth—warm, tasting of iron. I try to spit, but more blood comes up. So much blood, I could drown in it.

"*Thorn.* THORN!"

I try to ignore the urging.

"Thorn, look at me!" Hands grip my shoulders, shaking me with violence. "So help me—"

The dream fades. The sense of a presence I had only a moment ago is suddenly gone. I'm alone once more. Alone except for...

My eyes slowly blink open. Petra stands over me with blood on her hands and all over her fine dress. There are circles under her sharp eyes and her hair, usually so perfectly fashioned, is touseled. Her pupils...dark, angry pinpoints are focused on me.

Raising my head is a struggle. But I push myself, driven by confusion and my desperate need to gain clues as to what is going on. Candles cover every surface in my tent and a perfumed smoke hangs in the air. My body feels weak and my head aches. Despite all that, there is a clarity to my thoughts that I haven't felt in a long while.

Petra collapses into a nearby chair, looking drained. "Oh, thank the Gods," she gushes, having no patience to her tone.

"Wasn't the Gods that saved him," Arron mutters. I sense more than see him lift something unwieldy and carry it from my tent. I wonder again about the blood all over Petra and who it might have belonged to. But I say nothing, absorbed in

TRACY LAUREN

exploring this sudden stillness in my mind. The peace of it...it's
startling. I push to my feet and the world around me spins.

"What are you doing?" Petra complains, meeting me, urging
me back to the bed.

"I'm no invalid, woman. Leave me be!" The words...the
sound of them...I clutch my neck. The wound there is still
tender and my voice sounds monstrous—like rocks tumbling
down a mountain. Confusion grips me.

Ah yes, I remember now. Sweet Ellyn slit my throat just
before she and my brother abandoned me. A strange heat stings
my eyes and I squeeze them shut.

"I need a drink," I grit, roughly grabbing a nearby decanter
from one of the many chests in my tent. My hands shake, so I
don't bother with a glass. I throw my head back—a dizzying
motion—and make an attempt to swallow. The rum burns like
acid and I cough and sputter.

"You idiot. Get back in bed."

"Never took you for such a forward thing," I tease grimly.

Petra huffs. "Don't flatter yourself. I put a lot of work into
saving your life and I expect you to show gratitude."

I turn away from her, not feeling any.

"The bed, Thorn. Now."

I cut my gaze to her, rage simmering, just about to boil over.
"I am not your slave."

Her eyes narrow and her jaw grows tight. "We have an
accord."

"I agreed to be your partner."

"You agreed to doing things *my way*."

I shove the decanter back onto the table with a rough clank.
One of the other bottles falls, breaks, and the sharp scent of
liquor fills my nostrils. I shove all the rest of the bottles to the
floor with it. Petra crosses her arms over her chest.

"Are you quite done?"

My answer is no, but I say nothing.

"You've allowed yourself to be distracted and I've had enough of it. I don't know what it is that has your attention, but I can guess. I can smell her cheap perfume in here, this tent reeks of it. I'm telling you right now Thorn, do whatever you need to do to get your head together or I will take more drastic measures."

"You won't find anything here to distract me." And that's the damn truth of it. Ash is gone and Ellyn with him. I'll never see them again. I grip a heavy dresser with my hands until I hear the wood creaking beneath my grip.

"We've a job to do," she presses with that impatient air. All she cares about it herself, about controlling this whole damned world and everything in it.

"You mean I've a job to do, don't you? I'm the one doing all the work, all the killing, all the leading—"

"*Leading?* HA!" she exclaims. "You don't know what it means to lead, you haven't a clue at that particular burden—"

I round on her, cutting my arm to the tent flap and the army outside. "You think I don't lead them?"

She straightens. "You do as I say, per our agreement."

I stalk a little closer, feeling weakness in my limbs. "I don't remember agreeing to anything other than claiming the castle—"

"*In my name.*"

"And what if I claim it in my name?" I shout the words, impertinent and angry. A change comes over her Highness and all the air is sucked from the room. Electric tension mounts. I can feel it tingling across my skin. Then, I'm choking. My sore throat begins to close. A fresh surge of blood rushing into my mouth and Petra stands before me, her eyes no longer pinpoints but daggers. Her face completely blank.

Quietly, she begins. "I've worked hard for this, Thorn. I won't let you take it from me. Not a whim and not because you're melancholy. Do you know why?"

I clutch at my throat, but there is nothing there binding me. Still, I cannot breathe.

"Because you haven't the power to take anything from my grasp."

The candles in the room dim. Some sputter out. I think I might be like one of those delicate flames, I might simply go out.

"I'm the only one. The only one worthy. The only one *willing* to sacrifice, to do what it takes. I wish it weren't the case, but wishes change nothing."

Whatever mystical hold Petra had over me is released. The room brightens, the static feel subsides, and I fall to my knees, dragging much needed air into my lungs.

Petra pads over, only her slippers and the hem of her dress revealing themselves to my vision. "Whatever it is you're clinging to, whatever wish or hope, I implore you: bury it. Bury it deep and focus on doing what you're told."

My teeth clench and my very soul recoils at the suggestion. When I turn my eyes up to her, Petra's got the medallion in her hands. I shake my head at it.

"You will put it on." It's a command. But I am no dog, I am no slave, I am the King of Orcs.

Only, my limbs are impossibly heavy, I can't move. I'm glued to the carpets as the witch lowers the chain around my neck. Even before she lets go, I can feel the destructive weight of it. This is my madness. It is how she's controlled me and kept me outside myself. If it weren't for this curse, everything with Ash and Ellyn might have gone another way. They might be here, with me, right now.

She releases it. Sensations of heat and ice burrow into my mind. And that noise, that ceaseless noise—the sound of a storm, rolling thunder, and rushing winds. Relief lies in one direction and one direction alone: the castle at Pontheugh.

"There we are," Petra says, her tone satisfied. She cocks her head to the side, inspecting me. "That's better, isn't it?"

I make no effort to answer, my mind is reeling.

"This excursion cost me greatly, Thorn." She tsks. "The magic that was wasted...I hate to think of it." She leans in, aiming for clarity perhaps, but instilling icy fear. "If you allow it to happen again, there will be grave consequences. Do you understand?"

Petra—her hand reaches out, as if she might touch my shoulder...and offer comfort...but her fingers simply hang in the air between us.

"I am a compassionate Queen. I hope you can appreciate this second chance I've given you. There won't be another."

And with that, the most powerful witch in all the land rises and makes her way to a framed dressing mirror—tall and thin. There's that sound again, that I heard while I was dying. The sound of ice stiffening, bending, cracking under pressure. The mirror moves like water, and Petra steps through it like a doorway. Thunder snaps and then she is gone.

I take a deep breath, allowing my muscles to relax. When I push myself up, I check that mirror, just to be sure, knocking it with my knuckle. Only glass. Then, I am prompt to break it, along with every other mirror in my tent. I don't stop there. All of my pillaged goods, my hoard, my treasures from villages burned —they are all victim to my wrath. I destroy everything in my tent with a violent rage and, in my madness, I find that little vial that Ash brought. Small, innocuous, but filled with bones, darkness, and death's accoutrements. Bending to pick it up, I allow myself a moment's rest, to tumble onto my ass and look more closely.

The drive for the castle is already in my mind, steadily mounting. But the wounds—the heart wounds I have—are great. I lost him. Again. The thought is troubling, to be caught in a cycle and unable to change its outcome. Not only with this cursed medallion, but with my brother as well. I am trapped. A prisoner. A dog. Not a King at all.

My fingers release the vial and move slowly to the medallion. Hot. Pulsing, like the beat of a heart. It's poisoning me and I know, with absolute certainty, I need to get it off. Now.

CHAPTER 16

Alba

"It's going to be a week at the least, but I'd guess you're really looking at two."

"You must be joking!"

Gerald. The churlish man won't look me in the eyes. He rubs at his scruffy chin and absently scans the sickly crowd of refugees packed into the Copper Coin. It's dark in here. The light dimmed so people can rest. There's not much else to do. Food is scarce with the orc army just across the great lake. You can hear the coughing of the ill and the weeping of the desolate.

"Boat has to go; boat has to come back. It takes time and there's an order to this, you know? Want to take that old wretch with you, got to wait longer."

"I understand, it's just...I fear we're running out of time. The orc army is going to attack and I don't want to be trapped here when it does!"

"Then leave the old woman."

"You know very well I can't do that."

Gerald looks at me now, unconvinced, skeptical, a slight curl to his lip. "I don't see why not. You think she wants to hold you back? The woman's a bitch if she does. Look at it like this: you're young, still got life to live. If this lady wants you to throw away your chance—"

"It's not like that. Of course she doesn't want to hold anyone back, but I refuse to leave her. Be reasonable. It would be like someone asking you to leave your own mother behind."

He snickers and his eyes leave me again. I suppose he might not have qualms about leaving his mother behind, but to each his own. I've no room to judge, seeing as how I got here. All I care about is getting out of Pontheugh, with the people I love in tow. This place won't be safe for much longer. The King here has not spoken—not a word of strategy or reassurance—and the castle guard struggles to maintain order among the citizens as resources continue to thin.

"There must be something you can do?"

Gerald purses his lips in a way that reminds me of Luther. A chill runs up my arms and I take a small, nearly imperceptible step back. Luther would have noticed. I think this man does too. He softens, taking me in from head to toe.

"Maybe there is something."

"What?" I ask, mistrustful but desperate.

"I know of another smuggler. Good friend of mine. Maybe we could all meet on the other side of the bridge in, say...two days? Does that sound better?"

"Two days? Really?" I chew my lip, thinking. Two days is a Hell of a lot better than two weeks.

"It isn't a sure thing, of course. He'll have to meet you first—see if you're a good fit."

"A good fit?"

Gerald grins. I feel like he's making some kind of joke at my expense.

"Look, darling, this isn't charity. It's a dangerous business and my friend isn't the type to let just anyone on his ship. Long voyage like this, he needs to know if you can handle it."

"Of course we can. All three of us are used to a hard day's work. Anything a man could do on that ship we could do too. We might not be as strong as men, but we are determined and that can get a person pretty far."

"I won't argue that point. So you'll be paying for three then? That's certain?"

"It is," I say firmly. "Me, Wendy, and Beatrice."

"Beatrice is the old one?"

I frown. "The matronly one, yes."

"And Wendy is the stick?"

I frown harder, but it only makes Gerald laugh.

"Just meet with me in two days. On the other side of the bridge. Then we'll talk."

"And your friend will take us out of here? Before the invasion?"

"You can *talk* to him and he'll decide. I can't promise more than that."

"Fine. We'll be there."

"No. Just you."

"Why just me?"

"I wouldn't expect you to know it, but that's how these things work."

I'm skeptical and Gerald can sense it.

"Listen," he explains, "if you want a shot at getting out of here before all Hell breaks loose then he's got to meet you first. A man has got to trust who's coming aboard his boat."

"As if three women would mutiny."

Gerald cocks his head, smirking. "Wouldn't be the first time."

"For goodness' sake—"

"Those are the terms. Wait it out if you want. Or take a chance in two days. But I've got business until then. You'll have to excuse me."

My heart seizes and I grab Gerald by the arm before he can depart. It's desperation that drives me, images of the destruction I've seen, the threat of death so dangerously near. I've to get the Hell out of Pontheugh, my friends too. "Two days," I agree. "I'll be there."

He leans in, that smile all too familiar, all too unsettling. "It's a date."

I wrench my hand back. "It's *business*. In two days."

He fixes his worn hat atop his head and pushes past me without any sort of farewell. I frown after him, shaking off the unsettling feeling men like Gerald always seem to leave in their wake. That feeling certainly isn't what I want to focus on. I want to think about the good news, the prospect, the hope. I've got to tell Beatrice and Wendy.

Snaking my way through the crowded tavern, I all but burst into the Matilde's kitchen. She and her daughters are there. Merry and Agnes—their hair pinned up, sleeves rolled high, everyone sweating even though it's the dead of night.

Beatrice stands before the big stoves. Sweet, elderly Beatrice. Old enough to remind me of my own grandmother. Her hair is a shock of white, clean and fresh, rolled into a bun, and tucked beneath a scarf. Her arms are bare and, despite the heat, I know they are somehow always cool to the touch. She's splitting her attention between two massive, steaming pots while Agnes and Merry peel vegetables for the endless amount of stew it takes to feed all the refugees from the orc raids. Not a full second after I fling one door open, Wendy comes surging in through the other—an enormous basket in her arms. My friend looks as if she might fall over. I rush to her aid, lessening her burden by half.

"Woof! What are you carrying, rocks?" Wispy as the girl is, she is strong as Hell. "I don't know how you managed this basket on your own!"

"Potatoes," she grunts, hefting it onto the table.

Matilde and Beatrice hurry over to peer into the basket. "Where in the world did you get all those?" Beatrice exclaims.

Wendy winks at Matilde. "Our secret benefactor comes to the rescue once more."

Beatrice huffs and wags a finger at Wendy. "Secret benefactor my ass. You better not be giving anything away for these potatoes—no amount of food is worth sacrificing yourself."

Wendy begins a protest, but it's Matilde who reassures, patting Beatrice on the arm. "You needn't worry about that sort of thing. Not here. Not in the best days and not even in a time of war."

Hand over her heart, Beatrice hobbles back to the bubbling pots set over hot stoves. "War! Has it truly come to that? In all my life..." She laments to herself while the rest of us remain huddled around the basket as if peering into a pot of gold.

"I don't even know who he is," Wendy admits to me and the girls. "Matilde gives a time and a place and the basket is always there, waiting. Must be rich..." she adds.

"Rich, yes. But an absolutely horrible man," Matilde declares with a flourish of a wooden spoon. "Consider yourself lucky you don't have to deal with him."

"How horrible can he be?"

"Plenty!"

"We wouldn't eat without his aid. There'd be no soup for us, nor all the sad souls out there, if it weren't for Mr. Horrible's vegetable endowments."

"Trust me on this," Matilde insists. "There isn't a *sourer* soul in all of Pontheugh. I tell you, I'd like to spurn these damned potatoes, but I don't have the luxury at the moment."

Wendy ties an apron around her waist and joins Merry and Agnes at the table, playfully bumping them each on the hip to wiggle her way in between. The sisters must be close to womanhood now and Wendy is only a year or so younger than me. And yet somehow, I feel so very old around them.

Unlike many young women, Wendy wasn't widowed in the raid on her village. She remains unmarried—and by all accounts happily so. Beatrice on the other hand, had lost her husband. Only, it was many years ago that it happened. Long before the orc attacks. Both women were living independent and free lives —happy, with good, safe homes, and friends to rely upon. All that was lost when the orcs came. I met the pair in Willowbend and we have been together ever since.

Reluctantly, I pull my own apron off a hook. I'm dying to speak of the good news. Just...not here. Not in front of Matilde and the girls. They've been so very kind and if it weren't for the impending attack of the Orc King's army, I could see myself staying in Pontheugh forever. I've certainly felt more at home in this place than I ever did in Aberdeen. But, alas. The Orc King advances. The sky is already black from his fires.

To Matilde and her daughters, this tavern is more than a simple building. It is life, livelihood, their world. War or no, Matilde won't leave it and her daughters won't leave her. It's honorable, but foolish. They haven't seen what the Orc King can do. Wendy, Beatrice, and I have and we won't be staying. I emphatically couldn't, for it would be like giving up a second chance at life.

A miracle was bestowed upon me. I *survived* the raid on Aberdeen because, and only because, I murdered Luther. And if it weren't for the raid, surely my crime would have been discovered. I'd have been stoned to death or hanged. But instead, I lived and my crime was all but erased. Doubtless, there is a miracle in that.

I release a breath and fasten my apron around my waist.

"You look troubled, dear." Beatrice has her discerning eyes on me, searching for clues to my trouble. "Tell me, what's wrong?"

With a gentle smile, I offer a quiet, "It can wait."

"It will have to," Matilde chimes, tipping the basket onto its side. Potatoes pour out across the table. *Thunk, thunk, thunk.* "We've got about hundred pounds of potatoes to peel."

It isn't until daybreak that we finally have a chance to rest. A solemn line, we trudge up the stairs to our makeshift beds spread out across the floor of Agnes and Merry's room—where the four of us young women sleep. Beatrice has one of the real beds and Matilde gets the other, as she's given up her room to keep a doctor here at the tavern. It's hard to tell now, but this would be very fine living quarters if so many of us weren't crammed in. Even still, it isn't all bad. Sometimes I catch myself smiling up at the ceiling, just glad to be a part of something, to feel *welcome.*

I'm staring up at the ceiling now with a busy mind, when Wendy toes me from her nearby bedroll. "Hey," she whispers.

"How are you still awake?"

"I've got an inquisitive mind."

"So? Inquire."

"Are you going to tell me what has been occupying your thoughts all night or am I going to have to drag it out of you?"

I sigh, wondering if I should say anything. The thrill I felt earlier is gone, now that I've had the chance to reflect. Gerald's offer is far from a sure thing. Do I bother getting everyone's hopes up before I know? "I think…I think I might be able to get us out of here sooner than we thought."

"No kidding?"

"I'm not sure. I talked to Gerald and he might have another boat for us. We could be out in two short days."

Wendy gives a low whistle.

"If not, it'll be another week at least. Maybe even two, before the ship comes back."

"And there's no telling if we can get on that one." All the time more people want to leave Pontheugh. Not just the refugees who have seen what the orcs can do, but everyone. And it's the families and the young ones who get spots on the ships. Not... I cast my eyes to the bed Beatrice rests in.

"The smoke has been getting closer," Wendy whispers. With the curtains drawn I can't see her face, but I can hear her concern.

"I know. That's why I have to do something."

"I don't trust that man. There's something about his eyes, Alba—"

"He could be cross-eyed, but that wouldn't lessen our need for escape."

Wendy snorts in the dark. "No, I suppose not."

"Don't worry. I don't trust him either, but I can handle myself. I can do this for us."

"What will Beatrice say?"

"I don't think I'll tell her. Not just yet, not until it's a sure thing."

"That's probably smart. She'll worry."

"She'll think I'm selling my body, you mean."

We bite back snickers. Beatrice seems to think that's how anything happens in the world. Got a basket of potatoes? You must have let a man have his way with you. Makes me wonder about her younger days more than anything else.

Quiet stretches between us, but there is no rest in it. Not with such a threat looming on the horizon.

"I'm going to get us out of here," I say finally. "I promise."

Wendy toes me one last time before rolling over to search for sleep. I smile at her back, feeling as if I have a sister. Anything it takes, I make this promise to myself, I'm going to get Beatrice and Wendy out of here.

CHAPTER 17

Thorn

𝒯he foliage is thick, the ground untrodden. An obtuse and dimwitted orc trudges alongside me, loudly crunching leaves and branches beneath his booted feet. If he cares an ounce about stealth or silence, he hides it well

"What you say is out here, my lord?" he asks in a slack-jawed sort of way, his heavy brow furrowed—signaling the slow turning of cogs in his mind.

We leave behind the ash-white trunks of the trees that speck themselves across the land of man and cross a line, known well to me. A line of blackened trunks, marking the start to the Perished Woods.

The air is different here. I feel it on my face. Cooler. Scent memory makes my nose twitch. Wretched as it is, there is something so comforting about this wood, something that feels like home. The realization makes me chuckle quietly to myself. What irony. That this place I've tried so hard to escape can bring me peace.

The medallion's coiling tendrils worm their way into my

mind, strengthening their hold with each passing minute. But I have yet to lose my grip on my plan. The coolness here helps. A shiver rolls over me as the sweat clinging to my back chills beneath the canopy's shade. The call for the castle is still there, but it ebbs a bit as I breathe in damp forest air.

The orc soldier has his attention on the terrain as he barrels over and through it—vision tunneled at his feet. He never looks up, never searches for signs of danger. It's a shock to me that he has survived as long as he has—both in my army and in the Perished Woods before that.

I grimace at the creature, at his long face and sunken cheeks. He's got a piece missing from his nose and he's adorned it heavily with silver rings—highlighting the scar. He trips over a fallen log and curses it, his maneuvers so painfully clumsily.

"How have you fared?" I ask, mildly curious. "In this war?"

"I do pretty good, I'd say. Lots of pussy to be had. Didn't know there was so much pussy to war. Thought it was all about the fighting and the death."

I grunt.

"There's lots of death too, of course." He smiles—a tight-mouthed, round, little puckering showcasing needle-like teeth in the shade of mustard, and as he does, he gives his necklace a shake. Small bones and rotting ears. Makes me feel better about my plan.

"What we doing out here?" he asks again, looking up for the first time, squinting his eyes in perplexity.

"It is the Queen of Envercress who has decided we come." My new voice is jarring, even to my own ears. Somehow it makes me feel changed.

"Ah, she's a powerful one. Can't blame you for following her."

I tighten at this fool's suggestion. I don't *follow* anyone. I *lead*. And I go about leading this one deeper into the cursed woods.

"Little trek around the perimeter? Preparing for the attack

on the castle?" Impertinence from a simple fool. Very simple, as a matter of fact. Hopefully not too simple that her Highness will be able to discern a difference...

"There's a cave up ahead," I tell him, my temples pounding. A cloud of fear hangs over me, fear like I haven't felt before—except maybe, when Petra forced this medallion on me for a second time. What if she can sense what I'm planning? What if she stops me? My heart starts a rapid beating. I need to be rid of this curse...and *soon*. If I wait much longer I might lose myself altogether.

"A cave, huh? Got something good in it?"

"A solution, as a matter of fact."

He nods knowingly. "Something to help us against the castle, I bet?"

"Something to help me anyway."

"That's good, that's good. Need all the help we can get with what we're up against."

"And what are we up against...I'm sorry, what did you say your name was?"

"Spiteleech, sir." I frown. And I thought *my* mother was cruel in the name she bestowed upon me. Thorn, as in the thorn in her side. But Spiteleech? Someone must have really loathed the young Spiteleech.

"There it is." I raise my hand to indicate a dark shadow in the rock ahead.

"I see it! Clear as day, Sir!" Spiteleech goes running on ahead, like an overeager dog as he shouts over his shoulder. "Gonna need whatever that witch left us. The way I see it, we're up against a whole castle. Pretty soon the King—the *real* King, that is—he's going to send his army for us and they're going to be a Hell of a lot better trained than the villagers we've met so far. Won't be so easy then. But I always say, nothing wrong with a little something extra up your sleeve."

Spiteleech halts at the mouth of the cave, eyeing it, for the first time showing some form of thought, some level of self-preservation.

"Dark in there," he says.

"Indeed. Caves usually are." I arrive at his side and cast one last wary glance behind us to ensure we haven't been followed.

Spiteleech sniffs the air, but he won't smell anything out of the ordinary. I'm the only one who's been here.

"Go on in, Spiteleech."

His dented and scarred face contorted in thought, Spiteleech ducks inside. "What we looking for? A trunk, or a chest, or something?"

"You'll see it, just ahead."

"*See it?* It's pitch in here, Sir." I can hear his feet shuffling deeper, toward the back wall of the cave.

"Perhaps this will help." I strike my flint near a torch left at the entrance. Warm light casts itself across wet, stone walls. Spiteleech jolts at the sudden illumination. His eyes blink as he takes in his surroundings, until they land finally on shackles... drilled into that far wall.

"Look at this—" he starts. "Someone's been using this cave to hold people." He inspects the chains with excitement. "These don't look like they've been here long."

"No. Just since last night."

"Well, how do you know—" His question is cut short when I bring the hilt of my sword down onto the back of his head. Spiteleech falls to the ground, unconscious.

I take a deep breath, peace already seeping into me. Won't be long now and I'll be rid of this damned medallion. I'll be able to think clearly. I'll be free.

Quickly, I shackle dear Spiteleech, arms and legs both. Then, I gag him. I can't kill him of course. I certainly can't. It wouldn't serve my purpose. Petra would know instantly. She was able to sense death coming for me when I was wearing her cursed chain. What I need is a live steward. I chose Spiteleech. Stupid, weak Spiteleech. He won't be missed.

The moment I'm done preparing him, I draw near as I can. I slip my hands around the scalding and heavy chain weighing me down... Then, I am quick to pull it off—dropping it seamlessly around Spiteleech's neck. He jolts in his sleep. He doesn't wake, but a fine sheen of sweat forms on his skin.

Suddenly, I can breathe—a full, deep breath. The cave feels lovely now. A breeze from outside shifts the air. There is a crispness surrounding me. And silence! Blessed, blessed silence. Finally, I am free to *think*. Free to craft a *real* plan. For this is only a temporary solution to a much larger problem. But I do think I'll take a moment to luxuriate in the peace.

I work the torch between two rocks, then drop down onto the cool, moist soil, leaning my head back against stone. A smile spreads across my lips and laughter escapes me. Slowly, it builds. Relief is the start of it, then rage, and skating at the edges: fear.

Petra's power is greater than I could have ever comprehended. I was a fool to align myself with her. If she senses my deceit now, it will easily be the end of me.

Spiteleech is roused suddenly, perhaps by my merriment. He lifts his head, uncomprehending. The simple creature doesn't even fight his binds, nor does he evaluate his situation in the slightest. He simply arches his back, as if in immense pain. And he is in pain, for I know it well. I felt it for...hmm, I can't say. Only the Gods know how long I was enthralled by Petra's curse. It felt like years. Felt longer than my journey into Black Mountain and I'm not free yet. Not really. This is a break in the storm, nothing more.

With that knowledge looming over me, it is in horror that I watch Spiteleech. I watch his face contort and his milky eyes go bloodshot as the medallion poisons his thoughts. I think perhaps it might be harder on him, on a less complex mind. He doesn't scream against his gag, but he spasms. His limbs convulse. Piss trickles down one scarred leg.

I take it all in, peace washing over me. With a deep and relaxed breath I lean back once more, resting my head on cold stone, and I close my eyes.

CHAPTER 18

Alba

The time has come. Two days have elapsed. My hands serve stew and pass out clean blankets, but mentally, I ready myself to meet with Gerald on the other side of the bridge. With a racing heart it dawns on me that I'm giddy. Nervous, of course, but altogether giddy. There is danger in the air, and I like it! It's a startling revelation. In the depths of my despair, in the throes of Luther's violence and abuse, I never imagined my life could become so absolutely different from what it was.

In a few short weeks I've become a changed woman. For the first time in my life, I've got friends. And I've traveled! All the way to the castle, I've traveled! It's amazing really. Suddenly, I feel as if anything is possible. The world is nothing more than a series of open doors to be walked through. There are so many people here. Hundreds. Thousands even. Back in Aberdeen I knew every household. But here, that can't be done!

For the first time in my life, I am limitless. The future holds joy. All I must do is get Beatrice, Wendy, and myself out of

Pontheugh. Matilde and her daughters, they will stay. This is their home. Perhaps they would choose otherwise if they had seen the absolute destruction of the orc army. Perhaps not. But it is enough to sway us three. We do not wish to be here when the orcs attack. We've seen enough death. Life awaits in a different direction.

Wendy bursts out of the kitchen and her eyes scan the crowded tavern in search of me. I raise my hand and wave her down. With a furtive expression on her lean face, she hurries across the room to meet me.

Her hands clasp my wrists when we nearly collide in our excitement. "You have the coin?" she whispers, her eyes darting about, trying to ensure no prying eyes are on us. Most here are refugees, like us. Victims of war raged by the Orc King. But sometimes dire need can make a criminal out of even the purest soul.

"Yes. I have it. Tucked away." I pat the belt at my waist. "A thief would have to strip me nude to find it."

Wendy's eyes widen in horror. "Oy, by the Gods, never say such a thing," she breathes out.

"I'll be fine," I assure.

Her expression is cautious. "I hope that you are."

"I will return and I will return with good news."

Wendy's face is tight and her brows are drown down. "I won't know peace until then."

"Come now, my friend. Of course I will be fine."

"Who's to say? Who's to say in times like these?" Tears well in her eyes.

"Wendy, I won't be gone long." I grasp her shoulders, giving a light shake to bring her back to her senses. "This is our opportunity. We mustn't miss it."

Both of us turn, inclining our gazes to the door. It's shut now, but beyond it is the Great Lake, and beyond that—the ruins of Willowbend, and even further still—but not far enough, is a field taken over by the orcs. It's as if we both can see it. As if we can hear the war drums beating over the coughs and moans of the refugees packed tightly within the Copper Coin. The smoke from the orc fires blackens the sky more each day. Soon they will come and with the state of the castle, the silence from the King, I cannot imagine Pontheugh will fare any better than Aberdeen or the rest of them. Already there are less soldiers here. Word is they're deserting. I can hardly blame them.

"No, I suppose we can't afford to miss it." Wendy sighs, dropping her head, but still, we cling to each other.

"Hey, have some faith."

"And why should I?" She clasps her hand over her mouth. "I'm sorry, Alba! I shouldn't have said that. I'm sure you're worried enough as it is, meeting these men out in the dark of night."

"As a matter of fact, I'm not worried at all," I tell her proudly, a smile on my face.

"I don't see how that could be."

"It's simple really, I've got the best of luck."

"Well, now you're just cursing yourself. You realize that, don't you?"

I laugh with my friend. "Impossible. I used to be cursed, I'm sure of that. But I overcame it. And you know how? Bravery. I know, without a shadow of a doubt, that if I keep following the path of bravery it will lead me to the place I am meant to be. Aberdeen wasn't it."

"No, I should say not." I confessed myself to Wendy and Beatrice both, very early on. Neither woman blamed or judged me for Luther's death. I remember wiping away my tears, feeling validated for the first time in my life.

"But this place isn't it either. Danger is coming. We've got to get out of here before it is too late. There is a happy life waiting for us across the sea."

"Gods." Wendy shakes her head in disbelief. "Never would I have thought *I'd* be crossing the sea."

"It's exciting, isn't it?"

A smile breaks across her face. "Absolutely thrilling!"

"Exactly!"

"An adventure!"

I let the word dance in my heart. "An adventure. And one can't possibly have an adventure without first mustering a little bravery."

"No. I suppose not." She sighs one last time, resigning herself to this fact.

"I promise you: I will be as safe as can be."

"Fine. But take this…" Her eyes dart around once more, in that way that is far more conspicuous than she thinks. Leaning closer to me, she pulls a small kitchen knife from her apron pocket and passes it to me.

I lean in as well, completely shocked. "Wendy!"

"Just take it, what other weapon do you have? Can't defend yourself with optimism, can you?"

"No." I frown. "I don't suppose I can."

"But we both know you can defend yourself with that."

I blush. "It was mostly luck that stuck Luther. I had my eyes closed and just sort of flailing."

"It was bravery that finished him."

"Well, self-preservation."

"If push comes to shove, you've a knife to aid in your self-preservation. Just take it, Alba, take it and give me a little peace of mind."

I nod. "No, you're right. That's very clever of you."

"Well, I'm a very clever girl." Wendy smiles, but it falls away quickly. "I've got to get back to the kitchen. Beatrice is out, helping the doctor with an amputation."

"Mr. Ackermane?"

"That leg wound of his got rot."

"With any luck he'll live."

"He's in good hands."

"Indeed, he is."

Both of us hesitate. I purse my lips and pull Wendy into a tight hug and without another word, we part. She heads back to the kitchen and I tuck away the knife close to my waterskin, where it will be well hidden. Then, I make for the door.

I don't look back. I simply charge ahead, as I've done ever since abandoning my old life in Aberdeen. It's worked thus far, and so I haven't changed course and I won't until the day it stops working.

Out on the cobbled street there are few people about. During the day it is crowded of course, but now, long after the sun has gone down, people have retreated to their homes to cluster around their hearths and pretend that this silence will stretch on forever. They pretend the orcs will never come.

I stay along the well-lit path to the gate, where two guards stand, shoulders bent. They're tired. We all are.

One of them sees me as I approach and calls me to the attention of his partner. "Ayo. What are you doing out and about so late?"

I wait until I am upon them to speak and draw two coins from my pocket. Two coins I intentionally kept separate from my pouch. These coins are for bribing. The others are for paying passage. I thrust the coins into the hand of one of the young men. He is wary as he looks down at them in his palm.

"I just want out of here before they come. I'm trying to find a way for myself and my friends."

"It's dangerous out there," the guard warns. "We can't escort you."

"No. I wouldn't expect you to. You're needed here at your post."

"Isn't there a man to go in your stead?"

"We had a fellow, but he was old and wounded in the raid on his village."

"Dead?"

"Thankfully no, but he isn't well. Not well enough to travel. As we speak he's with the doctor. An amputation is expected."

"That's a shame."

"Too common a shame in these times. Still, better than death." I mutter. "Anyway, my friends are working and that leaves only me. I shouldn't be long."

"You got a weapon on ya?" the other guard asks. His face hasn't been shaved in a day or more. Makes me wonder if there is anyone to relieve them from their post. Makes me wonder when they were last able to rest.

"I've got a small knife," I whisper. "And my coin is hidden."

"Don't go about telling just anyone that."

"Not even guards," the first man warns solemnly.

I nod. "Yes, of course. Thank you."

They exchange looks and move to a door in the gate, pulling back a heavy latch for me. "In a different time, we would never allow this."

"Yes, these are strange times."

They look me in my eyes, the both of them. Good men, I can see it. They aren't like my Luther. It isn't lightly that they allow me to go on in solitude. But truly, they cannot abandon their post. Not at a time like this.

"We will watch for your return."

The guard tries to shove the coin back into my hand, but I pull away too quickly and offer him a wry smile. "Take it. You never know if you'll need it…"

"No. I suppose not."

With that, I slip through the heavy wooden door and out onto the bridge.

CHAPTER 19

Alba

*E*ven with the torches lit along the bridge, it is dark out. Dreadfully so. The moon and the stars have been blotted out by the orcs' fires. Ash flits down from the sky like snow, dusting my face and clothes.

The Great Lake stretches out on either side of the bridge. It is black and still. Silent too. No lapping of the water meets my ears. And all of it, the silence, the darkness, the complete solitude…it's a little frightening. Or a *lot* frightening. I wrap my arms around myself, fighting off a chill.

I cast my eyes back a few times to the wall and for a time I can see a light. The guards watching me. But the air is thick and soon, no light can be seen. After that, I'm forced to look ahead, to the other side of the lake.

It's impossible to even make out the tree line. But I keep moving forward with resolve. This will pass, I tell myself. Soon I will find Gerald, he will be waiting for me just as he promised. We will make our deal and then I can return to Beatrice and

TRACY LAUREN

Matilde and the temporary safety of the Copper Coin. After that? Freedom. True and ultimate freedom. I will leave Luther and this sad era behind and open myself to the infinite possibilities that the Gods have laid out before me.

It brings a smile to my face to think of it, to think of this little bit of discomfort passing, and wonder lying on the other side. It makes my steps a little lighter, a little faster, and then I see it. A golden dot of light shining just up ahead. *A lantern.*

I step faster and smile wider. Then, he comes into view. Gerald. I withhold the urge to call out to him until I am near.

"I made it!"

"Good. And it's just you?"

"For now, of course. But as far as passage—"

He holds up a hand. "I meant, there's no one with you. You weren't followed?"

"No. I'm alone."

"Perfect. Follow me."

My smile falters as something about this fellow brings Luther to the forefront of my mind. Still, I follow him, bravery and hope pressing me onward.

With no more words spoken between us, we fall into step beside one another. I, of course, creating a bit of a safe distance. We follow the path along the Great Lake, which lies to our left. And to our right is a line of trees, not so menacing in and of themselves. But we all harbor the knowledge that if one were to venture a bit farther beyond those first cool grey trunks, the bark would blacken, mist would cling to the roots, and before you could even think to run—the Perished Woods would have you.

For some reason, the haunting image of Adelaide comes to me. As a matter of fact, I dream of it often. When I watched her throw herself beyond the border, my first inclination was to believe she was mad—absolutely mad. I thought it was suicide.

But the farther I've traveled from Aberdeen, the more her actions resonate with me. I can picture her still, so perfectly, throwing herself into those woods. It wasn't hopelessness she cast herself into, it was the very opposite. When she ran beyond that wretched border, she did it with *bravery*. And she was far braver than I. As the days continue to pass, I think of it...with fondness. I hope that I might be that brave one day. And these steps I take here, on this path away from the castle, these are all steps toward bravery...and...*adventure*.

I bite back discomfort; the feeling of being cornered crawls up my spine. But of course I'm not cornered. This man is here to help me, or at the very least to profit financially off of me— which is fine, no judgment there. As long as my friends and I can get to where we are going. This isn't fear, I tell myself. It is adventure.

My smile returns, coming from a place of excitement. I'm fairly lost in the romanticism of it all, running away to a new land, when I notice two lanterns shinning just ahead. My steps stall out and Gerald speaks.

"There they are now." I cast my eyes to his face, searching— not for signs of deception, but for signs that I can be at ease, signs that I can trust. Because I want this so very badly. So badly, that my intuition is cast to the wayside.

Gerald mustn't be very old, perhaps in his mid-thirties. But his face is weathered and worn. His clothes are not the best kempt and he seems to take no notice of the last time he's shaved. But he offers a smile and I take that as a sign all is well.

The other two men come into view. There's an older one, short, with hair yellowing from too much pipe. And the third man is about the same age as my escort, but he keeps his brown locks long and pulled back into a ponytail. I think the older one must be the captain of the boat. There's something about his look, his wide gait, and the rolling way that he walks. I think very likely, he is the type of man to live his life on the sea. The other two are so very alike, I think they must be brothers. Cut from the same cloth, they are—in height, appearance, and the low level of care they tend to themselves with.

I shift uncomfortably as we slow to a halt, the four of us standing in a sort of circle. Consciously, I keep space between myself and each of them. The feeling of discomfort rises in me as no one ventures to speak.

I clear my throat. "I'm here to seek passage on a ship for myself and two friends. I am told one of you has a boat available?"

"You've got coin?" the old one asks, taking me in from head to toe. His eyes squint hard and I can all but imagine a pipe in his mouth, yet there isn't one there now. Perhaps I can smell the tobacco. Perhaps it's the way his face seems to be so accustomed to clamping something between his teeth. They're yellow teeth, like his yellow hair.

"Yes, sir, I've got coin. I'd like to confirm as expedient a travel date as possible, and seeing as my friends and I have never left this land, any information you could provide about where you will be taking us would be appreciated."

"Most are grateful just to go," the other says.

My body unconsciously tightens and I draw in on myself. "Of course we would be grateful to go—"

"Then *where* you go shouldn't really matter, should it?"

"And I suppose it doesn't."

"Then why ask?"

"Perhaps just to make conversation. Perhaps wanting to know what lies ahead is human nature. But when it comes down to it, if you have a boat that is safe and you are willing to provide passage, then there isn't much more to say."

Gerald tips his hat back further on his head and his smile widens. "The lady likes to be cordial," he says. "Seems no harm to be cordial to her."

I glance between the two younger men, trying to figure out if this is some sort of reprimand. Because I have the distinct feeling in my gut, that something is being left unsaid...in a very loud sort of way.

I take a small step back, suddenly wanting very much to be away from these men and back on the quiet isolation of the bridge to Pontheugh. But as I take my step back, Gerald does the same and I realize that somehow, the circle we all started in is still a circle, yet now I am the center of it. Surrounded.

My attention is cast to the old man. "Sir, do you have a boat or not? That is what I came here to discuss."

"There's a boat that leaves, yeah."

"Is it your boat?" He says nothing so I turn my attention to the other. He, in turn, is silent. But his smile, his terrible smile, stretches from ear to ear.

"How much coin does she got?" Without looking at me, the old man addresses Gerald.

My hand inches toward the waterskin at my waist, knowing the knife is there, tucked away. My thoughts go blank otherwise. There is no desperate desire to be back at the Copper Coin, back immersed in the safety Beatrice and Wendy offer. My heart pounds in my chest, beating at my ribcage. All else washes away. The only thing occupying my mind is survival, for I find myself surrounded by wolves.

"Get on with it, will you? I haven't the taste for this part."

Gerald has got this mirthful look about him, as if he does have a taste for this part. He stares at the ground as if thinking, trying to decide his next step. Or perhaps, he is savoring my fear. The thought of which makes me very mad.

"Be nice now, Rogers. Alba went to a lot of trouble to come out here. Didn't you, dear?" Gerald fixes that predatory gaze at me and the men position themselves to block the path in both directions.

"I take it there is no boat for me."

"Clever girl."

"Not clever enough though, is she? Coming out here in the dead of night, all by herself. Deserves what she gets if she's that stupid." The old man, Rogers, says this. As if trying to justify some evil deed that has yet to be done.

"Come now," Gerald urges us all. "This doesn't have to be all bad. Matter of fact, this could be quite nice if you're an amenable young lady."

With the path blocked, I search for an escape route. My body wants me to run. *Run first. Fight if you have to,* it tells me. There's the still, black water in one direction. And...and the obvious path ahead.

That image comes to mind again, of Adelaide thrusting herself into the cursed wood and this time, it brings a smile to my face. Yes, it is obvious, I think to myself. Blessed Adelaide. This is why she has stuck so firmly in my mind, isn't it?

"There she is," Gerald says, misreading my smile.

"What's the plan then? Rape me? Steal my coin? Leave me for dead? Don't you think my friends will wonder where I am? They'll set the guards on you."

Gerald edges forward, his boots crunching over the packed earth as he does. The sound rings so clear in the silence of the night. "Well, I'll explain that you left them of course. There was a boat and only enough space for you. They won't miss you because they'll think you abandoned them. In my experience, people can be quite self-centered. If they think you did them wrong, they'll never think of you again. Unless, of course, it is to curse your name."

"By the Gods. I think you must be worse than Luther."

"Don't know who Luther is, love, but he isn't here to protect you."

"Indeed, he isn't." I laugh at the notion.

"What's so funny?" the long-haired one says, almost complaining.

"She's losing it," Rogers suggests. "Just make this fast already, will you?" He shifts on his feet, casting his eyes all around.

My eyes are locked with Gerald's. Both of us are smiling. And then, like a sudden explosion, I cut for the woods.

"Fucking Hell," Rogers mutters, and they all hesitate just a tick before tearing after me.

CHAPTER 20

Thorn

*P*art of me wishes to run—to leave this place and never look back. But that is the way of the coward, is it not? Besides, I have unfinished business here. That much, I know for certain.

I check Spiteleech once more, ensuring his gag has not loosened, and then I trek out of the cave and into the night. I need to feel cool air on my skin. I need to be away from that suffocating camp. I need to listen to all this glorious silence.

I'm hardly stepping from the mouth of the cave, the promise of silence so dear to my heart, when a scream rips through the moonless night. I jolt. Chaotic memories of the medallion make my muscles tense and I question reality. Have I truly freed myself? Or does that cursed charm still have a hold? The scream issues again, answering my question. It originates not from within my mind, but from somewhere among these trees.

Instinct drives me toward the cry of distress. I sprint— hearing the need, *the desperation*, in that cry. I have been desperate too, have I not? *Kindred* is all I can think. That call is so familiar. I rush toward it.

The woods are dark and the undergrowth thick, but my orc blood is strong. I am silent as I move, and my eyes take in everything with inhuman keenness. It doesn't take long for me to come upon the scene. A round, old man has his hold on a woman. Her back is to me as she struggles against him, frantically trying to loosen her wrists from his stronger hands.

"Hey!" he calls. "I've got her!" I can hear two others on their way, loudly crashing through the foliage. She fights harder. One of his hands releases her wrist to wrap around the woman's waist. A mistake, I think...on his part at least. Her blonde hair whips as she wrenches to one side. It reminds me of Ellyn in a confused sort of way.

With suddenness, the shine of a blade catches my eye and the woman takes her chance—driving it into the man's neck. I can hear the spray of blood hitting leaves. He releases her, only to stumble back.

The others draw nearer. With a whimper, she retrieves her blade and turns on her heel, headed straight for me. My orc eyes are strong in the night; I see her face and am struck with recognition like a physical blow. *This* is my dear friend from the sad little village of Aberdeen. This is the girl from the grave. My heart swells. She survived. I nearly laugh aloud, but manage to keep my wits about me, for she is running headlong in my direction, oblivious to my presence.

My excitement is cut short. Cursing and thundering through the forest, the pair pursuing her come into view. These aren't old, fat men. They are young and strong. Two big men pitted against a small thing like my fair-haired friend. Though her instinct for survival is mighty, the odds are certainly against her. Or they would be, if she were alone.

But she isn't alone, is she? As luck would have it, she runs right into my waiting arms. Crashes into them, really. A look of complete shock washes over her as her eyes strain to take me in. As if in slow motion, her gaze travels up my chest, her lips begin to part—the beginnings of a scream.

She must sense however, that I am not one of them—for the others have been steadily behind her and we can both hear them approaching now. I clap one hand over her mouth, cutting off a startled yelp. My other hand, I bring to my own lips, gesturing that she must be silent. Her eyes are wild, but there is an accord made between us. One that must exist on a deeper plane of knowing. With only the slightest hesitation—a mere second, if that, she nods. I release her, my woman who smells of roses, and she doesn't run. It is as if there is only trust between us.

"Look at this," one of them mutters to the other. They make their way to the body of their friend, inspecting it. He's already dead. My girl must have got him just right. He bled out quick.

"How in Hells?"

"Bitch had a weapon."

"You should have searched her, you dumb fuck."

He cuts his hand at the other man, silencing him. "Quiet. She can't be far."

"I'm going to teach that bitch a lesson when I find her—"

And with that threat, I rise from my hiding place and stalk toward them, drawing my sword as I do.

There's an unintelligible utterance of surprise. One of the pair is quick to charge. My blade sinks into his gut. I draw it upward and slice as I pull it free. The other stands there—dumbstruck. With his mouth gaping, my sword drives him back into a tree. I force him back so hard that my blade delves deep into the bark and he's pinned there as he dies. There's something very satisfying about it all. As a matter of fact, I find myself excited—thrilled, even, to protect this girl.

I'm almost nervous as I turn to face her.

CHAPTER 21

Alba

This hero, this forest-dwelling champion I was so amazingly lucky to cross paths with, he turns toward me—having killed the last of my pursuers, having rescued me from rape, from certain death. He turns and I'm feeling quite the damsel in distress, embarrassingly flustered, and flattered, and to be honest, a little attracted to such a lionheart of a man.

A bubble of laughter escapes me and I take a step toward him. Before I throw my arms around his neck, however, I manage to stop myself.

Even in the darkness, I can feel his eyes fix upon me. Unable to make out his features, I still know by instinct how handsome he is, and I'm taken by his height. He must be at least a head taller than my pursuers. Yes, he's a giant of a man.

My lips part to offer feeble words of gratitude, when suddenly, the clouds are moved by the wind. It rustles the leaves in the trees above—a beautiful sound. Beams of moonlight permeate the forest and one lucky beam shines a spotlight on my hero just as he approaches.

"You—" saved me, is what I was about to say. But the words die on my lips as I take him in. He's handsome, yes. In the most monstrous and terrible of ways. Impossibly muscled, his skin is tinted grey—and not just by the coolness of the moon. He's got jet-black hair adorned with beads. I venture they are carved from bone. His eyes are pools of ink, so maddeningly deep. And his teeth are fangs. This isn't a hero at all. It's a monster. I snap my eyes all around, noticing now the mist clinging to the trunks of the trees. Yes…of course this is a monster. I'm in the Perished Woods and I've found myself face to face with an orc.

I'm near to fainting, I swear to the Gods I think I might faint. Instead, I raise my small kitchen blade to keep him at bay.

He smiles warmly at me. "What is it with women and knives?" he asks, his voice so rough and gravelly it makes a chill run from my toes all the way up to my shoulders.

I find my voice. "Thank you for your aid, sir, but I must ask you to keep your distance."

He holds his hands up, swearing acquiescence. His smile is wide now. And even though he is showcasing the sharpness of those fangs, there is something far less menacing about his grin compared to the men who were just chasing me. "Of course, my friend. You have my word there will be distance between us. I've no death wish and I've seen how good you are with a blade."

"You don't know the half of it," I warn.

He raises his brows in humored surprise. "Is your death tally greater than the two I am already aware of? My goodness, you are quite the unassuming assassin."

My stomach sinks. *Two?* How is the world could he possibly know about Luther? No, it's a bluff or some sort of confusion.

"I see a question in your eyes. I have an answer if you wish to ask it."

I shake my head, my arm and the blade still raised between us. "You don't know anything about me."

"Well, not near enough. I can agree to that. But I do know you are from the sad, little village of Aberdeen and that you killed your drunkard of a husband not so very long ago." He seems to be searching his thoughts. "You must forgive me; I've lost track of the time. How long ago was it? Two weeks now? Three?"

My hand is trembling. "How do you know that? How could you possibly know that?"

His dark eyes move to my waist. "That's my waterskin you have there and I venture to guess you have my coin purse hidden on your person somewhere."

My hand holding the blade grows lax. My memory takes me back to that moment I crawled from Luther's grave. I remember seeing the waterskin—what a precious gift. If it weren't for the water and the coin, I don't know that I'd have made it to Pontheugh. It meant the difference between life and death for me. And who could have left it there? I had no idea. But it could have been an orc, couldn't it have? Not one of the evil ones, part of the Orc King's army. But a good one. An orc with a heart. "These belong to you?"

He nods assuredly.

"That means you saw me...in the grave?" My words come out a hoarse whisper and I can feel my face growing hot. No one should have seen me like that.

"I did," he answers. "And the day before as well. You were in quite a state. Upset, crying..."

My eyes nearly pop out of my head as recognition hits. "You were watching me!" I cry in astonishment. "I heard you. I *knew* someone was there!"

The orc crosses his arms over his chest, laughing. But I'm taking the matter more seriously, doing the math in my head. "You've been watching me... You've saved my life twice now." The astonishment still rings in my voice.

"Well, I wouldn't necessarily say I've been watching you. Not on purpose anyway. It was all very serendipitous. But our paths do seem to keep crossing."

"What wonderful luck," I breathe out, mind reeling. I begin to pace, or something much like it, but my legs wobble beneath me.

"Whoa, careful now—" His face changes, the humor leaving. He's suddenly awash with concern. And I laugh—like a woman gone mad. With no sense of direction, or conscious thought for that matter, I begin to move—clinging to trees as I do. Mist surrounds me. I can feel it entering my lungs. I'm in the cursed woods, talking to a monster. *A monster. A monster.* This monster who has befriended me? Who has been helping me? Who was there in my village the day before the raid that killed everyone but me.

My legs give out and I tumble helplessly into the arms of the orc. Captured entirely—at his mercy. With vision tunneling, I catch sight of his face. Oh, what a monstrous face and a devilish voice to go with it. And yet, as consciousness slips away, I feel oddly safe in his arms.

CHAPTER 22

Thorn

I'm dumbstruck. She's taken the King right out of me. Right now, I'm a fool, gaping at this woman in my arms, searching our surroundings for someone who might come to my aid. I simply don't know what to do.

"Careful now," I say, for no one's benefit but my own as I lower the girl onto a mossy patch of earth. I stand erect, energy coiled inside my muscles. I should go. She's safe now. I've got far graver matters to attend to. Surely, if I'm gone from my camp for too long someone will notice. Arron might come looking. I can't afford to be seen without the medallion around my neck. Petra could have confederates among my troops.

Still…I gaze down at the girl. *My friend.* Well, I always imagined her as such. Somehow I feel as if there isn't another person in all the wideness of this world who knows me as well as this little scrap of a woman. A soft smile comes to my lips. I'm *very fond* of her—vicious thing that she is. Murdered the Hell out of her bastard of a husband and that lecherous old man back there.

Nervously, I cast my eyes toward camp, but the distance is

great and the trees are thick. I push away the anxious drive to get back and instead drop down beside the girl. "I'm a busy fellow, but a gentleman at heart. I will remain by your side until you wake." I hesitate on those words, feeling the need to make an amendment. "At least, I'd like you to think of me as a gentleman—regardless of what other people might tell you."

I focus my attention to the forest around us, searching for any signs of danger. But we are not so deep into the Perished Woods. If danger is to befall us here it will be by the hands of man, not monsters. My eyes invariably fall back to the young woman and I smirk, despite myself. Seems Ash and I both favor blondes.

My girl doesn't really look like Ellyn, I think, considering her more closely. Similar hair color of course, but the shape of the face is different. This woman has sweeping cheekbones, a full bottom lip, and a delicate nose. Her eyes, I noticed, were the palest blue and her brows laid bare her every emotion. She had this windswept look about her, not just now, from running. But she's had that same look on every occasion I've seen her. As if the most important of business is to be had somewhere and I'd loathe to stand in her way.

"Tell me, friend, while I've got a moment of your time, what is your name?" I wonder aloud.

"Alba," she groans and I startle.

"Oh, you're up then? I thought you were still fainted."

Alba tries to push herself up, but fails and contents herself with rolling onto one side to face me. "Of course I didn't faint."

I'm forced to laugh. "Well, then you took a very sudden and short nap."

She frowns, her distress evident as she presses fingers to her temples.

"I don't mean to tease."

She waves away the concern, her attention on a headache perhaps? Suddenly, her eyes snap to me. "You're an orc."

I hold my hands out to show her that yes, indeed I am.

"And you were with the army that raided my village."

The smile falls from my face. Did I kill someone she loved? Destroy a future she had planned for herself? "I was, yes," I admit it. If she is to hate me, so be it. But I will not lie.

"You saw me in the grave?"

"I did."

"And you know what I was doing, I take it?"

"Trying to hide the body, I assumed. But then the raid surprised you and a grave proved to be a perfect hiding spot."

"Yes. It did." She succeeds in pushing herself up to a seated position.

"You saw me there and you...took pity on me. You left water and coin. You knew the village would be decimated and you left me the supplies necessary to survive."

My mouth opens and suddenly I'm quite self-conscious of my new voice—the roughness of it, when I wish to be gentle. So, I say nothing.

"You saved me that day," she presses.

"It was the least I could do."

"And what are you doing out here now?" she demands, her eyes narrowed in scrutiny.

I don't hesitate. "Same thing I was doing the first time I laid eyes on you. Reconnaissance."

"You *are* in league with the Orc King then?" She sinks as she says it, as if wounded.

I open my mouth, but close it again, not knowing what to say. But I know I can't stand the thought of this conversation coming to an end. I don't want Alba to hate me.

"But you're a good man—*orc-man*," she corrects, an embarrassed look on her face as she coins the term. "You're good. What has this King done to ensnare you? Why must you travel with him?"

"Well..." I hold my hands out, searching for a lie. But why

lie? I *am* the Orc King. I am the soon-to-be King of Pontheugh. What need do I have for lies? Alba pushes hair back from her face to study me. "How do you know I'm good?" I ask instead, truly wishing to know.

She shrugs in a whole-body kind of way. "Evidence, of course. You've saved me twice. Even now as I...*slept*, you stood guard over me."

"Sticking to the point that you did not faint then?"

"I have never fainted before in my life, sir, and it would be poor timing to start now." She holds her chin high and her voice is serious... I am utterly charmed by it. "Anyway, I know evil when I see it. At this point in my life I can be sure."

"Only at this point?"

"I've mounted enough experience. First through Luther—my husband."

"The drunkard in the grave?"

"How did you know he was a drunk?"

I tap my nose. "Heightened senses."

She nods in understanding and goes on. "And I saw it in these men. In my gut, I knew. I should have listened to my instinct, but I came out here on hope, you see?"

"What does your instinct tell you about me?" I ask, curious and embarrassingly hopeful.

She speaks as if the truth of the matter were plain as the nose on her face. "You're good. Obviously. Even if you hadn't proved it by now, which you have many times over, I see it in you. In your eyes..." She trails off, her gaze connecting deeply with mine. I swallow heavily, feeling the catch of the scar across my throat.

"Most humans fear eyes like mine," I point out.

"You would think I'd be afraid too," she says, half amazed and nearly breathless. "But I'm not."

I chuckle. "And yet you fainted at the sight of me."

She gasps, but I hear the gentle humor in it. "I stick to my assertation that I did not faint. And anyway, even if I had fainted, it was from exertion—not fear."

"You did just kill a man."

She grimaces. "Don't remind me." Her eyes go wide. "Oh, you must think I'm evil! A cold-hearted murderess."

Now that makes me laugh, truly it does. "Not in the slightest, my—" I nearly call her something familiar. *My dear. My love.* But that would be inappropriate, I'm sure. I smile instead. "Not in the slightest. What were you supposed to do? Let your husband kill you out of politeness? Or these men here? For the sake of what? Not coming across as offensive? No, I think you did right by yourself and the rest of the world too, for that matter."

"Good riddance to bad rubbish?"

I dip my head in affirmation and silence falls between us. It makes me inexplicably nervous. "I should go," I announce, springing to my feet. Alba's eyes widen.

"What? Now?"

"It's late—" I start.

"And we are in the Perished Woods, are we not?"

"We are."

"And you would abandon me here? Alone?" There is worry in her eyes.

"Well no, of course not." Cautiously, I drop back to my seat. Alba follows suit. But that initial ease between us falters and our eyes no longer meet. *What am doing here*, I wonder?

"You haven't told me your name," she whispers.

My heart seizes. Has she heard of me? The villain riding on Pontheugh. The leader of the orc army. If I tell her my death tally, will she be so forgiving of my deeds? "I am called Thorn," I say. If she wishes to hate me I cannot stop it. I learned that well enough with Ash.

"Thorn," she muses, her smile widening. I swear I see a blush rising on her cheeks.

"What is it?"

"It's just...my name...Alba."

Realization washes over me. "A type of rose, is it not?"

She nods. Yes, that is a blush I see making her pale cheeks turn pink.

"A matched pair then."

"Indeed, we must be."

"Then it's settled. We'll have to run away together," I tease.

She grins in amusement and leans closer. "Sounds like an adventure."

"It most definitely would be. I'm an adventurous sort and you are a cutthroat marauder yourself. The trouble we could get into together would be spectacular."

She throws her head back, laughing with such relaxed ease. It is as if we know each other so well. And for a friendless soul like me, well...I drink it in happily.

"Do you truly have no fear, sitting here beside me?" I question, a brow raised in her direction.

She considers the question. "Fear? No. I harbor a cautious curiosity."

"Allow me to satisfy it then." Silently, I pray she doesn't ask about the blood on my hands or the number of villages I've burned.

"You were there the day my village was attacked. Scouting?"

I nod.

"It is no far leap to assume you are in league with the Orc King, following him and his army to attack Pontheugh?" She looks to me for confirmation, but goes on before I can speak. "I suppose I'm just wondering why a good person would follow a beast like that? Doesn't he...well, doesn't he frighten you? Doesn't this war feel like madness? All this death and destruction, I simply can't wrap my head around it."

I open my mouth to speak, but words fail me. She doesn't know I am the beast responsible for all this death and destruction. "It's...a complicated matter. And yes, there is some madness involved."

"Help me understand," she pleads in earnest.

I look back into my mind for an answer to give. An honest answer is what she deserves. "Look at this place—the Perished Woods. It's not all bad, you know? But where it is bad, it is terrible. And then, there is the land of man—vast, fertile, safe. But it is a land my people have been banished from.

"I'm not all orc. I am half human and yet I am not welcome in your land and I've found no home in my own. I suppose I'm searching for my place. It doesn't sound like much of an explanation when I say it out loud. It doesn't lend virtue to the crimes committed, but it is the best I can offer. Perhaps that makes a selfish beast of me, to want more from life." I stare down at my hands, feeling quite lost and no closer to what I set out for, years ago, when my journey began.

Alba's soft voice breaks the silence. "I understand. It's crazy making, isn't it? To want more, but to feel such guilt for wanting."

"Do you hate me?"

She shakes her head. "How could I? Look at the lengths I've gone to in search of my own happiness. It's the same thing that drives us. How could I blame you for that, when I've got blood on my hands too?"

I look into her eyes and feel this intense sense of comfort, comfort like I've never felt in all my life. It's a vulnerable feeling and if it weren't for her small, steadying hand finding my shoulder, I might have crawled right out of my own skin. "Perhaps we should run away together?" I joke, or half-joke. Maybe I'm entirely serious.

"I might take you up on that if it weren't for my friends."

My heart sinks a little.

"Wendy and Beatrice. Wendy is young, like me. Only younger in a way. She's never been married and I don't think she's ever killed a man," Alba sends a teasing smile in my direction. "So there's this youthfulness about her, that I lost somewhere along the way. Then there's Beatrice. She's a widow, a grandmotherly type. A very good cook and she gives very good hugs."

"Survivors from your village?"

"No." Alba shakes her head. "I was the only survivor."

Her eyes seem distant and I know I've dredged up memories of Aberdeen after its fall. It must have been horrible for her, realizing she was all that was left. I drop my gaze to the forest floor. "I should have taken you from there."

There's a lightness in Alba's air. "And had me join the army?"

We both chuckle. "No, I suppose not. Anyway, you wouldn't have liked me much then. It was better to meet this way."

"I think so."

"But I take no pleasure in thinking of what it must have been for you, sorting through the remains of your village all alone."

She breathes in deeply. "It was a dark day. But it shaped me for the better and it brought me to Beatrice and Wendy. You know, they are my only friends in this whole wide world? Before that I had no one. I was alone. But now I have them."

I can't help the ache in my heart, wishing I was a part of her circle. But I force a smile to my face, for Alba's sake.

She looks at me, considering. "I wish I could ask you to come with us."

"Back to Pontheugh?"

She shakes her head. "No. We are getting out of Pontheugh, before the King and his army arrive. Please don't say anything, but the castle doesn't stand a chance. There's been no word from the King or the Chancellor. Complete silence. The guard has lost faith, half of it has already deserted and the other half—"

I hold up my hand to stop her, feeling as if this is information I should not have. She certainly wouldn't be offering it to the Orc King. "Stay in Pontheugh. You and your friends. I can protect you when the army comes."

Alba frowns. "I don't think I can do that, Thorn. I've seen so much death. Too much. You might be able to protect us, but I can't stand the thought of the streets painted red with blood and all the homes and buildings being burnt down to their bones." She shakes away some image plaguing her mind. "No. We've got to sail away from this land."

"When do you leave? Perhaps I can make sure there is no attack until you and your friends have gotten to safety?" I can make certain of it, as a matter of fact.

"Well..." She motions toward the bodies. "These men were supposed to tell me of a boat."

I grunt. "So there is no boat coming?"

Alba turns, her body desperate to convince me that there *will* be a boat. "Oh no, that's not the case. There will be another. But it is hard to get on, so many are fighting for space. They have been sending families first."

"Two young women shouldn't have a problem."

She drops her gaze. "Yes, but we have Beatrice."

"Ah, and she's elderly."

"We won't leave her," she asserts bravely.

I nod in understanding. After all, it's a family I want most in this world and if I had someone, I wouldn't leave them behind. "I think I might be able to help you." A plan forms in my mind, but it isn't the plan I should be thinking of. I should be plotting against Petra. I should be focused on how I can protect myself from her power. How to escape, once and for all, from the succubus-like hold of that wretched medallion. Instead, I plot to see Alba again.

"Really?"

I study her face with great solemnness. She is like water to a man dying of thirst and I am desperate for any drop I can get. "I can warn you, before the attack comes. Perhaps…perhaps I can even buy you time."

Her eyes well with tears. "You can do that?"

I nod and Alba does the most amazing thing. She squeals and throws her arms around my neck, *hugging me*. She smells fresh and cool, like flowers, and I am scared to touch her, so worried that I might elicit fear. Very carefully, I place one hand on her back and I close my eyes, enjoying the sensation.

"You are sent by the Gods themselves, Thorn." She pulls away, leaving me cold. "How will we do this?"

"Are you able to meet me here again?"

"When?"

Soon. I want to see her soon. "Tomorrow?"

She considers. "Yes, it…it just takes coin, to give to the guards and I only have what you gave me." She digs for the pouch as if to show me what she has left, but I stop her hand.

"You need the coin for passage on the boat?"

She nods.

"Coin isn't an issue."

"Oh, but Thorn, it is—"

"I have coin for you."

Her mouth snaps shut and her precious brows draw down.

"I don't want to upset you."

"No, of course you haven't. I just feel…embarrassed."

"Embarrassed?"

"To take your coin."

I grin. "Coin means very little to me, but it can mean something important for you and your friends."

"Well, I am not a beggar—usually."

"But these are dangerous times."

"They are," she agrees, still looking troubled.

"Then allow me to help where I can, Alba, please?"

"But how can I repay you?"

"Just meet me here tomorrow, that is enough. And please, you mustn't tell the guards."

Her eyes widen. "No! Of course not! They'd—" Her words fall away.

"They'd kill me?" I'm amused by the notion.

"They would."

"They would try to anyway."

She shakes her head vehemently. "I'd never do that to you, Thorn. You must believe me. I mean it, I mean it truly, when I say you were sent by the Gods."

My eyes go wide.

"How else can this be explained?" Alba persists. "Our paths crossing time and again, so that you might protect me time and again. You must trust me when I say I'd never do anything to hurt you."

Her words are spoken with such conviction, it softens me to my core. I reach over to brush a strand of hair away from Alba's face so I can admire the sincerity there. She leans in to the touch, ever so slightly, then that blush rushes to her cheeks again and she pulls away.

"Well, what now?"

I look up at the mostly clouded over sky. "I judge there are still a few hours until daylight."

"And you are my protector until then?"

"I'll protect you for as long as you have need of me." I want to promise forever. Instead I clear my throat. "Rest, Alba, I'll wake you with the sun and escort you to the border."

"I'd rather sit up and talk with you, if that's alright?"

My own cheeks feel hot and I look at the ground. "I wouldn't mind that at all."

CHAPTER 23

Alba

*I*t is at daybreak that Thorn and I part ways, just along the tree line, beside the path that I fled only last night. It feels as if it's been days, my perspective has shifted so drastically.

On the path once more, I pause before leaving him and find that I am unable to suppress a smile. "This has been—" I pause, searching for the right word and I find myself searching the wide span of his chest, his deep grey flesh, old scars, new ones, the long black hair that falls around his shoulders.

"Terrifying?" he offers, slightly amused.

I look back to the path, to the place I imagine I stood with Gerald, where his friends waited to rob and rape me. "Oh, well I suppose some of it was. But that isn't what I was going to say."

He leans against the trunk of a tree, offering me time to find the word that fits this feeling. "It's been magical, Thorn. Truly, something magical."

His brows rise, one of them has a slice in it. This is one of the old scars. It's hard to contemplate the stories behind all these wounds. Perhaps they should be off-putting, but they aren't. I find each of them filled with intrigue. If only I could stay here another night with my beast and press for stories of this wild and enchanted forest, tracing those beautiful scars with my fingertips. He straightens, his expression serious. "I wasn't expecting you to say that."

I bounce my shoulders lightly. "I've never met a monster before." But "monster" isn't the word I want to use. It doesn't fit. "Monster" is for Luther. Thorn...Thorn's a hero. I've never met a hero before this and the experience has shaken me to my root.

"Wasn't it what you imagined?"

I shake my head. "No. It was better." Something in him seems to tense and I regret my openness. I must seem like a foolish girl to him—naïve to be so easily enchanted by the mystical.

"Tomorrow night," he says with that deep and raspy voice. Yes. Business. The massively important business of not getting stuck in the orc raid on the castle.

"I'll be here." I smile. "It would take an army to stop me."

"You won't have to worry about one tomorrow. And you won't ever have to worry about coin again," he reassures. "I will provide for you and the others."

"Won't you get in trouble?"

Oh, and his smile is wide at that. "Who must I answer to?"

I inch a little closer, lingering pitifully long. Yes, I must be so utterly transparent in my enchantment. "The Orc King, of course," I whisper, a chill running down my spine at the thought of a good man like Thorn having to face a real monster. I don't care if my hero is half-orc. Thorn is good, right down to his core. He shouldn't have to be confined to a cursed forest, or forced to follow an evil master in the hope that it might one day lead to his freedom.

"Trust in me," he says simply, but with such conviction that it makes me swallow hard.

"Tomorrow night." I take a step back and another. He watches me go, still leaning against the smooth blue-grey bark of the tree and I hurry along the packed dirt path, every step crunching.

The clouds don't seem so merciless today, beams of welcomed sunlight pour through. I see the bridge and the castle walls not so terribly far away. And the water dances this morning, lapping musically at the rocky bank. The hope that I've been nurturing inside me feels different. Today it feels as if the small seed that it was has blossomed—resulting not in just one solitary flower, but an entire garden—lush and vibrant.

I turn back to steal one last glimpse of Thorn, but the tree stands alone—no magical orc-man, sent to me by the Gods to help steer my path. I squeeze my eyes shut and bite my bottom lip, everything inside me thrilling. He is absolute magic. My heart races. I can still smell him on my hands, on my dress...

Making haste back to the castle, I finally allow my mind find its way to Beatrice and Wendy. They must be worried sick, me gone all night like this. I'm sure they believe the worst.

My assumptions are proved correct when I enter the Copper Coin from the kitchen door. Wendy is sitting at the table, spine curled in sullenly, and Beatrice is standing over a pot at the stove—only she's got a faraway look about her, as if deep in thought. Their eyes shoot to the door and when they see me it is a mad rush.

"Alba! Sweet Alba!" Beatrice's voice cracks as she wails. She embraces me and Wendy's got a hold of my arm, shaking me with near violence.

"Where have you been?" she exclaims, her own eyes red and wet. "Gods! Gods, I thought you were dead!"

"I'm fine," I assure. "Completely fine."

"What happened, dear?" Bea is gripping me by the cheeks now, scrutinizing my face. Probably looking for injuries or some other sign of mistreatment.

"Hells," Wendy breathes out. "You've got blood on you."

I look down at myself. Indeed. Quite a bit of blood. I did happen to stab a man in the throat last night. I flush, feeling ashamed at …well…not feeling ashamed. "Everything is alright. I'm fine now."

Beatrice's eyes implore me. "Did he hurt you, love? I'll kill him if he hurt you."

A laugh bubbles up and tears spring to my eyes. I wrap my arms around Beatrice, believing her entirely. She would protect me with a mother's love. "I know you would, you sweet, vicious woman. But I assure you, I am fine."

"What happened?" Wendy demands, still clinging to my sleeve, holding on in any way she can—as if in being tethered no harm can come to me.

"Well, we were right to be wary of Gerald. That is as clear as day now."

"Tell me what he did," Beatrice says. "We'll go to the guard and if the guard doesn't do something, I will. I may not be as strong as I used to be, but I make the food around here and I've no aversion to poisoning a man."

"How delightfully macabre, Beatrice, but not necessary in the least. Gerald is dead, thanks to the kitchen knife Wendy forced me to bring." My smile is suddenly tight as I lie to my friends. I don't like twisting the truth, but I can't speak of Thorn. They wouldn't understand. He's an orc. He represents all the danger we are trying so desperately to escape. They don't know this feeling in my heart. I wouldn't be able to explain it. If they were there, if they would have met him, they'd have trusted him implicitly, just as I do. Of course they would. Thorn radiates *trustworthiness*. He's a hero, damn it. He's saved my life and he's going to help save all three of us.

It's settled. I make my smile authentic. Thorn will be my secret.

* * *

THAT NIGHT, with the constant din of the tavern downstairs, I move to the window of my shared bedroom to stare out at the sliver of Great Lake I can see beyond the wall. The forest is to the left. A black silhouette on an already dark night. And to the right is the orc camp. Fires burn and smoke billows. It used to spark such terror in me, such dread. My fingers find the icy glass and I stare past my own reflection—my thoughts on one orc in particular.

Thorn.

It's madness, isn't it? Allowing my mind to be fixated so on a…a…*beast.* Still, I hope he's alright and his absence from camp wasn't noticed. It will be hours before I know for certain, before our rendezvous on the edge of the wood—a dangerous endeavor on his part and mine. Full of risk. And yet, despite all logic, my heart thrums in excitement and I *will* for time to pass.

CHAPTER 24

Thorn

whip my cloak free from its hook, securing it around my shoulders—concealing my bare neck. The warm light of sunset illuminates my tent and all I can think of is the girl. If ever I was mad, the time is now.

All my efforts should be concentrated on the problem at hand: that damned Eternal Princess and the cursed medallion. She seeks to control me, to have power over my mind. I cannot allow that to come to pass again. I'd rather die than be a slave. What I need is a plan and I need it quick. I do not know how long this ruse will fool her or how severe her wrath will be once she finds out I've been free from her curse. As it stands, I cannot overpower the witch. I haven't the skill with magic nor do I think I could get close enough to her to utilize my strength.

How does one defeat an adversary who has been at this game for so many decades? I wouldn't know. For my mind has had an uncanny and ill-timed focus on a certain blonde-haired beauty with a penchant for murder.

Even in my tense state, the thought of Alba brings a smile to my lips. *Alba*. As precious and as delicate as the flower she's named for. But that's not all there is to her. She's got an instinct for survival and a spirit of conviction. Amazing really, when one thinks of it—of how lovely she is. And she's mine. Perfect and mine, if only for a short while. And though I should be focusing on the more dire problem at hand, I've simply got to see her. I pause before a trunk, one of the few things I did not destroy in my rage, and pull a hefty coin purse from it, weighing it in my hand.

Alba... Why have our paths continued to cross? What lesson lies hidden there? What fate draws us together?

Tying the purse to my belt, I toy with the idea that perhaps there is some greater purpose—a message from the Gods, just as my darling asserted. But what God would wish to speak with a degenerate like me? No, meeting Alba has been nothing more than cruel luck. Everything I have ever wished for...at the worst time imaginable.

I close my eyes, and the woman I adore, I see the way she looks at me. There is no fear reflected in her gaze, nothing fake, nor conjured. Alba looks at me and she *sees* me. Not the Orc King, but *me*. *Thorn*. And she doesn't turn away. No, when Alba looks at me there are stars in her eyes...and why? I don't know. She has every right to be disgusted, but she isn't. I think she feels what I feel and I can't let that go so easily. I scrub a hand down my face and laugh. Look at me, a slave all over again. But gladly this time.

I've got to drink Alba in as much as time will allow before fate calls on me to finish what has been started with the witch from Envercress. One night, I tell myself. Tomorrow I will focus on solving the problem of Petra Gunnora. And with that, I depart from my tent—heading with purpose straight for the Perished Woods. Yet, to my tremendous dismay, I am stopped before I can take two full steps.

"Your Highness is looking fine today," a woman's voice coos.

I sigh heavily as Honora blocks my path. The witch's tone is thick and seductive and her eyes are filled with degenerate promises. I grimace. If ever there were a confederate among my ranks, it would be this woman. She reeks of coercion and duplicity. I've no wish to deal with her now nor do I want her to see where I'm going.

Drawing to a halt, I consider the woman before me and the level of danger she might present. She is scheming, that much is certain. But is it Petra she serves or her own circumstances? "What do you want, woman?"

Her features tighten at the harshness of my tone, but she recovers quickly. "You are busy, my lord. I had no intention to obstruct. Perhaps when you are free, I can join you in your tent?"

"For what? Speak your mind now for I am busy *always*."

She dips her head in a modest bow. "I thought I might check your wounds." Her chin lifts and she gazes up at me with heavily coaled eyes. "And any other needs that might require my attention."

"I have no need for you."

"Perhaps I have need of you?" she offers, her hands suggestively trailing down her body.

I bare my teeth and snarl at her. "I did not realize it was my job to attend to your needs."

She flushes and is quick to rephrase. "No, of course not." Honora saunters closer with feigned meekness. "It is desire that brings me to you, Thorn. I've missed your body terribly. I came only to offer myself, but seeing that you've no need of me I will lower myself to begging. *Please*," she whispers. "There is no other who can satisfy me as you do."

With that, she raises her hands to my chest, but I snatch up her wrists before she can touch me and the empty space where the cursed medallion should lie. "What is this insolence? Who do you think you are to touch me unbidden?" I growl.

Her mouth forms an O of surprise and her eyes bounce between mine. *She knows,* I think to myself. She can sense a change. I push Honora away. "Go! Take yourself from my presence. I've no wish to see you."

She doesn't move. Her mouth works, searching for words—but I don't want her treacherous eyes studying me.

"I said, be gone! Obey my order or I will expel you from this camp!"

Honora takes a staggering step back and before another word is spoken, Arron is at her side—his grip on her elbow as he leads her away. I stare after them, wondering at her goal. Is she in league with Petra or is Honora simply conniving? A wretched woman seeking a higher station through sex and lies?

Paranoia seeks to gain hold of me but I push it away through clenched teeth. I have neither the time nor desire to place energy into worrying about that woman. I've larger problems on my plate and other things I wish to give my attention to.

Arron still pulling her, I hear Honora's outraged voice exclaim: *"He can't mean that!"*

"His highness has his moods," my general soothes in a way that is quite exceptional for an orc.

"Yes..." she replies, seemingly appeased. "Of course. He just needs time. I'll try again once he forgets."

"He will send for you if he has the desire—"

She protests, but her words are lost on the wind. Scowling, I stare after that miserable woman. *Once he forgets.* How long has she been seeking to manipulate me? And in what ways has she succeeded? I search my mind, but the past months are clouded. There are only two instances in which I have maintained any sort of clarity—in my memories of Ash and Ellyn (which I wish I didn't recall so clearly). And...in every lovely second that my eyes have set themselves upon sweet Alba.

I set myself back to the task at hand. Casting my attention about, I search for anyone who might have me under their watchful gaze. But my army seems well occupied—drinking, dining, fucking, and fighting. Orcs. There are so few of us whose minds crave more than the primitive pleasures.

I long to escape—to go to a place where I am understood. That pleasure lies with Alba alone. She is out there somewhere now. Conscious of the time perhaps, watching daylight steadily slip away. Is she as anxious as I am, yearning to reunite? Though I wear a scowl on my face, my heart is aloft. I feel as if I am on the precipice of flight. On some level I sense: this woman is meant for me.

Pulling my hood down low, I depart from camp just as the sun dips below the horizon—casting all into darkness. My lofty heart leads the way, searching for that twin light it so desperately wishes to connect with. Alba...all these years, it is love that has been calling me.

CHAPTER 25

Alba

"You again?" the guard asks.

I wince, wishing someone else had been on duty. But there are so few of them left. "Me again."

"No luck yet? As far as passage?"

"I'm working on it," I offer.

The other guard is leaning against the wall, his brows pulled down in pity. "Haven't gotten yourself into trouble have you?"

I flush. Yes, I must indeed be in trouble if I am sneaking out to meet an orc in the cursed forest. "No, no trouble. The opposite of trouble, I hope."

He pushes off the wall to look earnestly upon me. "If you're meeting someone out there who is coercing you—"

"No, no! It's nothing like that, I promise."

"Well, if it were," he presses. "Even if it were a man promising love or marriage…if someone is saying those things to get you to *do* other things—"

"Oh no! It certainly isn't that!" A shy laugh bubbles up as I imagine Thorn whispering sweet nothings in my ear and I put my hand over my heart to bring calm it to all the fluttering going on there. "Nothing like that at all." I give the guards truth —or as much of it as I can. "I am meeting an old friend who's promised to let me know if a boat is coming soon. Just information. Nothing more."

"This is a man you're meeting?"

"It is."

"And you trust this man?"

I stand taller. "With my life, sir."

They look at one another reluctantly and nod. "We can't stop you—and I wouldn't want to if this leads to your getting out of here. But a word of advice? Be careful. These are strange times —even the people we think we know best can show us a different side."

A different side? A powerful and sexy side perhaps? My blush deepens, for I am thinking of the striking orc with long, jet-black hair, and wild scars that make the most thrilling chill run over my own flesh. A good woman shouldn't be excited by such things. And yet …

I clear my throat. "I understand your meaning perfectly, but I like to think I'm a very good judge of character—"

The guard holds up his hand, stopping me. "No need to explain, love. Just take care of yourself."

Nodding, I dig for my purse—Thorn's purse—and shove two glittering coins at the guards. They pause, but I thrust out my hand. "Take them, please. Strange times and all." Hesitantly, they do.

"This is a lot of coin you've passed to us at this point. Perhaps too much if you're seeking voyage for yourself—"

"Myself and my friends."

"Oy, we can't take this—" They try to hand it back, but I draw away.

"No, it's fine. I promise. The man I'm meeting has promised to give me more."

It's meant as an assurance, but one of the guards rubs at his forehead and the look of pity deepens on the other. "Love, you sure you aren't in trouble?"

My mouth gapes. "Oh, the coin! Oh my. No, I didn't mean... he isn't giving me the coin in *exchange* for anything. Truly, there's nothing lewd—" I break off, not knowing what to say to make them believe me. "I look like a common prostitute, don't I?"

"Just *please*, for the love of the Gods and for the sake of your reputation—be careful who you tell about these meetings."

"Yessir." I nod, eyes on the ground, face crimson with embarrassment. They allow me to pass through the heavy wooden door and, silently, I curse myself all along the bridge. I've no head for subterfuge. Why was I so honest? I chide. I should have lied. Now they think I'm out here meeting a lover. Or worse...*a client*. And why, oh why, did I say he was giving me information? What if they start talking about that? What if they have questions? What if they want me to pass along the intelligence I gain from Thorn about the orc army? What then? That puts Thorn in danger. He intended only to help me, Wendy, and Beatrice. Never once did he say he wished to put all of his people at risk for my sake. And why should he? It's a whole race that's been banished to a treacherous land. I'm no traitor to my own people —but I don't expect Thorn to be a traitor to his.

The orcs wish to be free of the Perished Woods and I can't blame them. After all, I wanted to be free of Luther and just look at the lengths I traversed to do so. Murder. Outright murder. Sure, Thorn and my friends understand my course of action. But would a court? Not in a hundred years. If anyone in Aberdeen had found out what I did, I'd have been stoned or hanged on the spot.

Suddenly, I ponder what would be done to me if it were

discovered I was associating with an orc. I wring my hands, considering my predicament, hardly aware of any danger that might be lurking in the shadows. My mind is reeling far too quickly. I increase my pace. I simply must speak with Thorn and get his advice. If I'm to meet him out here again, I need a stronger story. And...and I *do* want to meet him out here again.

CHAPTER 26

Thorn

 *T*here's still time before Alba's arrival. Time that I planned for. Though the woman occupies my mind, I have that miserable Spiteleech to consider. The crux of my plan falls heavily on his existence. If the vile creature were to die or be discovered, Petra would invariably come to discover my deception. Then I'd be fucked. Completely fucked.

So, I've got check up on his state. Ensure a bear hasn't made supper of him. And I'd very much like to do that *before* Alba's arrival. I don't know how I'd explain to her fair self that I've got an orc held captive and I'm essentially torturing the bastard. No, that's another fun little fact that I'd like to leave out of our conversation. That and my true identity. She need not know me as the Orc King. I'd much rather be Thorn when it comes to that little rose.

Dipping into the cave where I left Spiteleech, I can sense his presence immediately. Silent as he is, there is an unmistakable aura about. I think it must be the medallion. It is like a pulse; I can *feel* it. Drawing nearer to the back of the cave, I lift my torch

—illuminating a contorted face. I'm hit with the putrid scent of piss and defecation. I shield my nostrils against the assault.

"I take no pleasure in your pain, Spiteleech. I want you to know that." I wonder vaguely about Petra. Did it really have to be this way? I could have been her ally. I was willing. Hells, I still am. But this torture, this puppeteering? I can't abide by it. I'm not a beast to be chained.

So, why does she play it in this way? Is the Queen evil? Or is she simply that controlling? Possessing not an ounce of trust in another soul. She's got to do it all. I suppose her reasons matter not, for she's proven herself to be my enemy.

"And what do we do to our enemies, Spiteleech? We defeat them."

I tear open one of the waterskins I packed and carefully attempt to pour the contents between Spiteleech's clenched teeth. Most of it spills down his front, but I am content that he will not die of thirst today. With nothing else to be done, I leave him alone once more, putting out my torch just before the mouth of the cave.

I'm ready to leave this behind me and find a breath of fresh air in Alba. My eyes are quick to adjust to the darkness and I start for the place where the human trail butts up to the forest. Not three steps do I take before I hear the snapping of a branch. I halt abruptly, training my ears.

Silence. All around me silence. I don't like it. My hand goes to the hilt of my sword and then—*SNAP!*

A smile spreads wide across my lips and my shoulders relax. Out amongst the trees, Alba releases a build-up of laughter.

"Come out, you beast," I call to her.

She appears from behind a tree, buckling with laughter. "Did I get you?" she asks hopefully.

"Indeed, you did."

"Turn about," she says.

"It is fair play." We walk to meet each other and I want

nothing more than to draw Alba to my chest and hold her. But we don't know each other so well, do we? "You got the drop on me," I say. "That doesn't happen often."

"I came early," she confesses. "I saw you come this way."

"And naturally, you decided to follow me?"

"Naturally," she says, eyes twinkling.

"And after that, your only logical course of action was to...?"

"Play Thorn. It's a game where one spies on another while snapping twigs. I'd never heard of it until recently, but it seems to be all the rage among orcs."

"This orc anyway. Fine. You got me at my own game, woman. Very admirable."

Alba gives a short bow at my approval.

"What are you doing out here so early anyway? Trouble in the city?"

"Oh no," Alba says, seeming shy. I don't want her near the cave, so close to my secrets, so I lead her away at a causal amble. "It's just..." she sighs, still not looking at me.

"What is it?"

"I was eager, I suppose."

I swallow and the ugly scar sprawled cross my throat bobs as I do. Rubbing at it, I say, "I'm sure you and your friends are ready to leave this land."

"Hmm? Oh, well yes. That too."

"But that wasn't your meaning?"

Our steps stall out. "No. It wasn't," she says in breathless sort of way.

"Can I take it to mean you were eager to fraternize with the enemy?"

Pulled from our reverie, Alba gasps and grips at my arm. "That's *exactly* what I wished to talk to you about."

I raise my brows, encouraging her to go on.

"I simply don't know what I'm doing—"

"Fraternizing with the enemy."

"No, no. I mean with the guards at the gate. I started talking and words began pouring out, I don't think any of it was particularly incriminating, but if they get to thinking about it, if they decide to ask any questions—"

"What have you told them thus far?"

"That I was meeting with an old friend and there was a bit of discussion about coin and I left with the sense that they assumed I was behaving in an *immoral* way."

"What are you saying?"

"Well, I take it they thought I was a prostitute. A new and inexperienced prostitute maybe, but a prostitute nonetheless."

I'm taken aback and I feel a bit of heat rising up inside me. "They didn't proposition you, did they?"

Alba's eyes shoot wide. "Oh no! Nothing like that. On the contrary, they were quite worried about me. Wanted to make sure I knew what I was doing, that I was safe, that no one was coercing me—that kind of thing."

"Oh. Well, good." But I find this information makes me just as angry. I should be watching out for Alba's wellbeing, not these other men.

I take her in, scrutinizing my woman and her beauty—that lovely, windswept look she's got. The steady flush to her cheekbones. She glows, really, she *glows*. Could it be the moonlight she catches so perfectly? Then there are her lips. Like petals on a flower heavy in bloom—full and yet fascinatingly delicate. Human men must adore her and she lives among an entire hive of them. Possessiveness threatens to overwhelm me.

"I told them that my friend, *you*, were giving me information on possible opportunities to leave Pontheugh and then after I left I thought to myself, well that was quite foolish. What if they start asking questions, looking for details. I think I put my foot in my mouth on that one, but I thought an honest lie would be the very best kind, considering..."

"Considering?"

"Considering I can't exactly tell the honest truth."

I cock my head, enjoying her distinction between the two. It sort of covers my ass, now doesn't it. For it isn't as if I can give her the honest truth about myself. Instead, I can offer an honest lie. The part about me leading the orc army will have to be left out. The rest though, the other parts I share...those are the absolute truth.

"Well?"

"Well, what?"

"What should I tell them if they start asking questions?"

"Tell them you have a lover."

She swats at me in consternation. "Thorn! They'll definitely think I'm a prostitute if I say that."

"Why? Tell them you're in love with a dashing young man and that you'll just die if you don't get to see him."

She purses her lips and takes me in from head to toe. "Dashing yes. But *young?*"

I clap my hand over my heart, laughing. "You wound me! I'm young!"

"Well, I wouldn't call you old."

"I'm only 103 in orc years."

Alba gasps. *"A hundred and three?"*

I can only keep a straight face for a moment before my grin takes over. "No. There is no difference between orc years and human years. I am thirty-three, to be honest. *Completely honest,* not the half-honest type of honesty you seem to favor."

She swats me again, this time her hand lingering on my forearm. "You cad. You had me for a moment."

"Only a moment?"

She blushes.

"Orc years?" I tease. "What in the world is an orc year?"

"How would I know? You're the orc. I have to trust your word on all things magical. I haven't the slightest familiarity with it."

My hand covers hers. She is so damned soft, where I am calloused and as coarse as sand. "I am half-human..." I murmur the words, not quite knowing where they came from. The human half isn't a side I ever resonated with and yet here I am using it to appeal to a woman. Not just any woman. My woman. The woman I want. The woman my soul has been chasing.

"You think that's why we get along so well? Because you're half-human?"

"What do you think?" I ask, reeling over the fact that she too thinks we get along well.

Alba winks. "I think it's my bestial nature that connects with you so readily."

I feel my heart lift with joy. Something about the way Alba talks, it makes me feel...*accepted as I am*. I don't think I realized how badly I desired acceptance and here is a woman who gives it freely, despite my appearance...which I know has gotten quite harsh over the years. "I think that works quite nicely. There's a little beast in the both of us and a little human nature too."

Her fingers slip between mine, fitting perfectly. "Fast friends. Or, partners in crime," she amends.

CHAPTER 27

Alba

"There were so many things I meant to talk about."

"We talked all night."

"But our time is up and I can't tell you a single thing we spoke about that was of consequence."

Our fingers are still conspicuously intertwined. It's silly, isn't it? Like young lovers, only Thorn hasn't made a move. We simply walked, talked, and held hands all the night long. It almost seemed we feared the idea of letting go as much as we feared the idea of moving forward.

"It was all of consequence," he tells me. "I know you are allergic to milkweed, that you're inexplicably fond of liverwurst, you've reccurring nightmares of the world freezing over, and that you've never had a pet that your father didn't butcher at some point."

"But that wasn't what we were *supposed* to be talking about."

"I liked hearing about you. Anyway, what were we supposed to be talking about?"

I mean to say that we were supposed to be talking about my

escape from this land and the nearest available boat. But instead, the words come out: "But I don't know a single thing about you."

Thorn takes my hands in his. "Meet me here again tonight and I'll tell you all my darkest secrets."

"All of them?" I inquire.

"Well, all the ones that make me sound favorable anyway. That I can promise you."

I laugh and lean in, foolishly close, wishing he would take the lead and embrace me. But Thorn is the picture of a gentleman. All except his appearance, of course. But in manner, the man nears sainthood. If all his kind are like this, I don't know why they were ever banished from the land of man.

A little voice somewhere inside me screams: *but they can't all be like this, can they?* Otherwise there wouldn't be so many villages burned to the ground. I bite my lip, worrying over the seriousness of all this.

"What's wrong, Alba?"

"This is all well and good, Thorn, it is. It *really* is. It's better than well and good as a matter of fact. It's absolutely lovely and I want more of it—"

"So, you will meet me again tonight?"

"Well, of course I will," I say impatiently.

"Then what's the problem?"

"I suppose I just don't understand. You are in league with the Orc King. He's evil, by all accounts."

Thorn opens his mouth as if to protest, but shuts it again promptly.

"What in the world are we doing out here? Meeting like this? Is it a true help to Wendy and Beatrice? Or am I wasting time?"

"Do you feel like this has been a waste of time?"

"No, of course not. I had a splendid time. I want to do this all day and all night."

"So, we are back at running away together again. I knew it

would circle round eventually and I agree entirely. Seems to be the only logical course of action."

"Oh, it certainly does not."

"Then where have we landed?" he asks.

I cast my eyes about. "Quite literally, we are on the edge of the Perished Woods, on the edge of a war, both of us pretending there isn't a problem in the world."

"Let's pretend for one more night," he urges, his beastly eyes so impossibly earnest.

I nod, in full agreement. "Yes. Let's." My hands remain in his and I stare longingly at them, feeling half-mad with admiration. "I think we might as well say it."

"Say what?"

"The obvious. A year or two ago I was a different girl."

"I very much doubt that."

"Well you haven't known me long."

"Still, I think I know you quite well. Better than most, even."

"There's truth in that. You certainly know all my secrets. But I was different before all this."

He shakes his head. "Younger, but not so different. I am of the firm belief that our compasses know from the start what direction we wish to be set in."

"Then how did I end up so astray?"

"I could ask myself the same thing and you know what my answer would be?"

"Please tell me."

"Foolishness. Utter foolishness. And stubbornness to boot. If I'd have only been more honest with myself...perhaps allowed myself to be more vulnerable..."

That settles it. "Well, here's the truth of it then—for the sake of my compass and in the face of my foolishness. I'm absolutely insane about you. Crazy. Like a schoolgirl, I've got a crush so big I don't know what to do with it. And I happen to think it's a very inopportune time to feel such a way. Not to mention with such an inopportune individual as yourself—well, what are you going to do about that?" I demand, feeling foolish despite myself. And perhaps a little vulnerable and defensive too.

Every second of silence is complete agony, though there may have been only two or three. Thorn—in all his wild and intense masculinity—cups my face in his hands and draws me to his lips. *Oh sweet agony.*

CHAPTER 28

Alba

"*W*hat in the name of the Gods has gotten into you?" Wendy demands.

I'm practically sleepwalking and yet elated at the same time. My brows fly up in what I hope is convincing surprise. "I don't know what you mean."

Matilde's daughter Agnes snorts and shoots her sister Merry an amused glance. Wendy looks at them accusingly, her hands fixed at her hips in anger. "Do they know something?" she presses. "How could you, Alba? Tell them before me? I thought you and I were like sisters."

My look of surprise has grown authentic and I gape at Merry and Agnes.

"She hasn't told us a thing," Agnes assures.

"Anyway, we can see for ourselves."

Wendy's eyes narrow at the pair. "Well? Who's going to tell me?"

"I'm absolutely sure I have no idea what any of you are

talking about." I rise from the table, bringing potato peels with me to dump into the compost pile.

"Come on! It's obvious!" Agnes sidles up to Wendy and grips her by the chin, adjusting her gaze squarely onto me. I try to make myself busy with the chopping of vegetables.

"Do we have any more carrots from that anonymous donor? Now *that's* a topic of interest. Who do you suppose it is?" Not a one of them takes my bait.

"Make that face again for us, Alba," Agnes requests.

"What face?"

"The dreamy one, like your mind is a hundred miles away, recollecting something utterly enjoyable."

I force out a laugh and focus as deeply as humanly possible on chopping potatoes. Assessing eyes will see nothing other than the intensity with which I cut potatoes for stew.

"Now pair that look our friend is trying so hard to disguise with her absence at night."

"Two absences, if my memory serves me," Merry puts in pleasantly.

But Wendy's brow is still furrowed in confusion and her lips are puckered by Agnes's hold. "I don't understand," she says through pinched cheeks.

"She's met a man!" Merry exclaims, unable to hold back.

Wendy shakes free. "Impossible!" I know my friend well and the way her mind works. She's tallying my absences and one of the two is accounted for. "Where? How?"

"They're insane. Don't listen to them," I tell Wendy, scooping my diligently cut potatoes into a bowl and sweeping across the room to deposit them into the stew pot.

At my words, Wendy draws in a gasp of shock. "You liar!"

My mouth hangs open. I don't know what to say.

"I can hear it in your voice!"

I snap my mouth shut and slap a hand over it for good measure.

"Who is he? Why do they know before me? Best friends in the world, you and I are supposed to be—"

Agnes and Merry are looking on, amused. But they can't know! I can't tell them I've been meeting with an orc! It will be the end of Thorn and me, and I'm simply not ready for the end. I grab Wendy by the shoulders and drag her out into the alley, Agnes and Merry laughing innocently as we go.

The fires from the orc camp haven't been so active lately. It seems more daylight has been sneaking past the smoky clouds and the whole alley is cast in a warm, sunny glow. "A man? Who is it? One of the guards at the gate? A patron of the Copper Coin? Who? Why haven't you said anything?"

"Hush!" I insist, pressing my friend's back against the wall as I search the alley for anyone who might overhear what I'm about to tell her. And what in the world am I about to tell her?

Pleadingly, I fix Wendy with my gaze.

"You've got to promise to be very open-minded."

"Name one time I haven't been!"

I cover her mouth, quieting my friend. "I know, I know. I've been a cad."

"How long has this been going on?" she demands, wriggling free of my hold. I let her go, feeling highly self-conscious of her eyes on me.

"I mean, I've only just realized myself."

On my heels, she presses, "Well? Spit it out. Tell me everything."

I'm fidgeting with my nails. How much do I confess? "I met him the night I was attacked."

"Three days! And you call yourself my best friend!"

"You *are* my best friend! My very first friend in the whole wide world and I love you like crazy."

"Then tell me all your gossip, damn it. That is the primary unspoken agreement between all best friends of the world—

unconditional access to gossip. And you've held out on me for three whole days!"

"I tell you, I only realized my feelings last night."

"Still, far too long."

"You'd have to live in my head to know any sooner!"

Wendy crosses her arms over her chest and I'm beat.

"Fine. You're right. I was keeping secrets." I hang my head in defeat. I'm absolutely rotten at lying.

Wendy pulls up a rickety old crate and takes a seat, recrossing her arms in anger. "I appreciate your admission of guilt. Now, I demand details. The juiciest details. Spare me nothing!"

I groan. "Oh Wendy. You're going to hate me."

"Hate you?" The anger slips away and is replaced with immediate concern. "You can't be serious. There's no action, nor magic, nor force of the Gods that could make me hate you, love. You're family to me."

Mustering bravery, I face her. "I'll tell you everything, okay? Just promise not to tell Beatrice. *Yet* at least."

"On my honor."

"I was being chased that night."

"By Gerald?"

"Yes, and his two friends. They'd split up and the older one came upon me first."

"You made fast work of him." Wendy gives a curt nod of approval.

"I did. But the others, they were younger men. Faster, stronger. If they'd have caught me...I might not have made it out."

"But you did make it out..."

"With the help of a friend."

"A friend? *Who?*"

"Well, to be fair—when I ran into him I thought he was a stranger."

"Where did you run into him?"

"On the border…of the Perished Woods."

"The Perished Woods!" Wendy nearly shouts the words.

I wave calming hands at her, urging discretion.

"It was the only place I had to run. Any other direction and I'd have been caught straight away."

"Still, that must have been absolutely terrifying."

"It was," I agree, suddenly quite conscious of a nagging little feeling. It was terrifying. But there was something else there too. Something I almost enjoyed. Exhilaration perhaps? The thrill of adventure?

"And you ran into this strange friend? How?"

"I didn't say he was a *strange* friend. I said I thought he was a stranger, but it turned out he was a friend."

"I'm suspicious of him already," she declares.

"Fair enough…anyway, I ran headlong into him and without a word—I don't think he even recognized me at that point—he stepped in and rescued me from the other two. Killed them both."

Wendy's expression is intense. "What happened then?"

"Well…I certainly didn't faint. After that, we got to talking and he remembered me."

"From where?"

I press my fingers to Thorn's water pouch at my hip. "This is his. The coin purse too. He gave them to me."

"You said someone left those for you beside Luther's grave."

I nod meaningfully.

Wendy's eyes shoot wide. "He saw you there, hiding…"

"With Luther's corpse. And he deduced everything. Said he could still smell the liquor on him. I suppose Thorn took pity on me and left those things."

"Thorn? What kind of name is Thorn?"

I grimace and give Wendy my back. But she doesn't seem to notice, the wheels in her mind are turning. "One second. The waterskin, the purse…those were left *during* the raid on Aberdeen."

"Yes…"

"How did he sneak past the army? Is he some kind of rogue knight?"

"I mean…one *might* say that…"

I can feel my friend's eyes boring into me. I press on.

"After he saved me from those men—saved me now for a second time—he sat with me until the sun rose. He wanted to be sure I could make it back to Pontheugh safely."

"Quite the gentleman," Wendy says, her tone laced with suspicion.

"But before we parted, Thorn offered to help me further—or *us* rather."

"How?"

"Information and more coin, to get us out of here once and for all."

"He promised you coin?" Her brow lifts as she throws me a sideways glance. "In exchange for what?"

I huff at her. "Not in exchange for anything. He *did* ask me not to tell anyone about him."

"So he could abduct and murder you without leaving a trail?"

"No, of course not. If he were going to harm me he could have done so a dozen times over by now. But he hasn't. He's been an absolute gentleman."

"So last night, you went out to get information or to go on a date?"

I hesitate. "I don't know."

"What do you mean, you don't know?"

"He and I had agreed to meet on the basis of information."

"And?"

"He asked me about myself. Pretty soon he knew all my favorite foods, and colors, my allergies, and dreams…time flew and we didn't speak at all about the war or anything pressing."

"So, he's a liar?"

"No! We simply got sidetracked. When I meet him tonight we'll try again."

"Tonight?"

"Yes tonight. I mean, the whole point is to get us out of here and Thorn has information."

"Is that the whole point?"

"Of course it is."

"What kind of information does he claim to have?"

"You know…about danger…on the horizon…"

"How?"

"How what?" I'm wringing my hands, trying to buy time, trying to think of how I can say this without upsetting Wendy.

"How does he know about danger on the horizon? How would he know more than, say…one of the guardsmen, for example?"

"Thorn is in a unique position."

Wendy waits patiently for me to go on.

"He's got access to the movement of the army. He'll be able to warn us before anything happens."

Wendy rises up off the old crate and strides to me with purpose. Gripping my arms, she pins me with a look of intensity. *"How?"* she demands, but I think she already knows. Who could have left me gifts during an orc raid on my village? Who could know the inner workings of the orc army?

"I trust him, Wendy. He's saved my life twice now. *Twice.*"

She releases me and starts pacing up and down the small alleyway, her palms pressed firmly against her temples. *"Shit, shit, shit.* Alba, this is bad."

"No…not really…"

Incredulous is the look she sends me.

"Hear me out. Look, orcs are rotten, yes?"

"Emphatically, yes!"

"But to be fair, they don't want to live exiled in the cursed forest. Who would?"

"They were exiled for a reason, Alba. They're rotten, like you said. They kill everything they touch."

"Not Thorn! Thorn has saved me. Look, I'm just saying I personally understand wanting to escape from a bad situation. *And* I understand bad method. Should I have killed Luther? Maybe not. Maybe I could have left a long time ago, snuck away when he was drunk at the tavern. I could have left him to his own devices and gotten on with my own life."

"It happened the way it happened—"

"I know, and I'm not particularly sorry for it. But it has imparted on me the perspective of understanding. And that is the lens I view Thorn through."

"How benevolent of you—"

"I'm not trying to be benevolent."

"Good, because it will get you killed and viciously so, by a rotten pack of murdering orcs."

"Wendy!"

"What do you want from me, Alba? What you're doing is dangerous. Foolishly dangerous. Even if this Thorn fellow is good, you're playing with fire."

"He is *good*, Wendy."

She sighs. "I trust you. I trust your stupid benevolent lens. It's the other cogs in this machine that I worry about." Wendy lowers her voice to a whisper, suddenly fearful someone might be listening in. "If anyone else knew you were meeting with an orc, if the guards knew... You see? It isn't just orcs you need to worry about. Align yourself with one of them and suddenly humans are your enemies too."

We stand there in the alley, our eyes locked on one another's, clutching hands in white-knuckled grips. "He kissed me," I blurt out.

All severity slips from my friend's demeanor and with twinkling and mischievous eyes, she begs, "Tell me everything!"

CHAPTER 29

Honora

$\mathcal{E}$arly morning in an orc camp is really just a synonym for a very late night and the only time to get anything of worth done. Very few soldiers straggle about in the grey light of dawn. It is a simple task to slink over to Thorn's tent unnoticed. I pause, clinging to one of the weapons caches as a guard passes. Then, I dart out—sprightly on my feet. One last glance is thrown over my shoulder. Seeing no one, I slip into the addled King's tent.

My demeanor changes immediately, from stealth to seduction. I strike a pose, waiting for Thorn to notice me. But...the tent is completely silent. Silent in that way where one knows very quickly that it is unoccupied.

I relax my body. "Well, shit. Where is he?"

Walking without pretense now, I inspect my surroundings. Things have changed since I was last here. His hoard, the towers of furniture and pillaged goods, have dismantled. It appears as if a storm hit just inside this tent alone. The rubbish of what once was still stands however. Broken bureaus and dressers, wardrobes and desks, cast dark shadows in all directions. I take up a candlestick and illuminate the uninhabited tent.

All this *stuff*...why he collected it is beyond me. Gold, I understand. But this? It's finely crafted, that's for certain. Thorn only took the best of the best. But what's the point once we occupy the castle? It will be trash in comparison to what awaits there. I sigh over the matter. Such a waste. Thorn really is quite mad, isn't he?

I peruse a row of broken vanities, mirrors shattered. Still, I check all the drawers. One never knows what some high-bred woman might have left behind. Very quickly that takes my thoughts to the Eternal Princess. So young. So rich. So much ungodly power. I could swoon.

I wonder what sort of curse it is that she's put on the medallion. I know it's her magic that makes Thorn the way he is. Gods...what I wouldn't give to have power like that. Perhaps one day—I smile. Being Queen of Pontheugh will certainly give me a leg up on the matter.

I find a stray lipstick in one of the drawers and smear it across puckered lips before tucking it away in my pocket. Stepping back, I admire my reflection. I've certainly got it, don't I? The body and face of a Queen. I let my fingertips glide over sultry curves. If I could stop the ticking of time and remain exactly like this...*forever*, just like that Eternal Princess. Well, more womanly, of course. No one wants a stick. Men desire curves and Thorn, he'll want *my* curves. If I can just get him to sit still for long enough to get his dick hard. He's so damned distracted lately.

I click my tongue, wondering about my course of action. Could logic appeal to the feeble-minded orc? If I could get him to hold the idea in his head long enough, I could sell myself as an ally—an aide—which is what he's clearly in need of. I wouldn't ask him to be faithful of course. *I* certainly won't bother with such a formality myself. But maybe I could talk him into the idea that all Kings are married, it's just something one does when becoming royalty. Besides, it's best to show up with a woman of the wood and put these man's land folks in their place. Yes, there is logic there. Thorn should be able to understand that.

Mulling the idea over, I make my way to the bed. Last time I was here, that disgusting pig Ellyn looked on. Her nose all screwed up in disgust. Jealousy is what it was. Must be absolutely awful being a stuck-up prude like that. I don't know why Thorn became so fixated on her. Must have been the stupid brother's doing.

I slip down onto the fluffy, feather-stuffed quilt, luxuriating in the feel of it. I should be in this bed every night. Instead I'm sharing a tent with the common whores Thorn keeps for his army. I'm not one of them. That much should be obvious. *I deserve more.*

From my waist pouch, I draw out my little bottle of perfume and give it a sniff before promptly dousing Thorn's pillows with it. The fool will be dreaming of me tonight, I laugh. The charm I conjured will see to that.

It will take all my tricks to pull Thorn's attention from the castle for long enough to trap him. Which is no fault of mine. It's the Envercress witch. Her curse is strong, all-encompassing. But I'm strong too—in my own way. A little bit of coercion and a lot of wet and ready pussy. I've just got to keep up the doe eyes and get him at the right time.

I should have done this weeks ago, when his mind was clearer. But that damned brother. "Fucking Ash," I curse. Ever since he showed up, Thorn has been an absolute mess. It makes it harder for me. Thorn needs...drawing out.

I run my hand over the pillows, spreading my scent and the magic mingled within. It's potent, even to me, and I spread my legs, dipping my fingers between them—seeking out the wetness of my folds. So wet.

Squeezing a nipple with one hand and fingering my cunt with the other, I envision myself being filled by a long line of orcs with fat cocks, studded and pierced. They jam their dicks into me roughly and I imagine the coarse feel of their weathered hands running up and down my body as they use me in the most delicious ways.

I'm moaning, writhing on Thorn's bed, letting my cream seep out onto the blankets...when I'm interrupted by a harsh and guttural voice. Not the one I was hoping for, but any dick will do at the present.

"Arran," I coo.

"You aren't allowed here, Honora."

Shhh. I press my finger to my lips and incline my body so he's got a view. "It can be our secret," I offer, still fingering my cunt. It's wetter now that I have an audience and it makes obscene noises as I plunge in and out. Biting my lip, I study Arran's face, enjoying the coldness I see in his eyes. That's the kind of beast I like to fuck—a little bit of anger just beneath the surface, anger that he can take out on my body.

I spread my legs wider, inviting him to feast upon the sight of me pleasuring myself in our King's bed.

"You need to leave."

"You need to cum," I suggest, with a throaty laugh. "Let me help his majesty's general. Unless you think it would make our King angry?"

"Finding you here will anger his Highness."

I smear my juice across the bed and rise to my feet, hands still touching myself and my gaze fixed on Arran's eyes.

"Arran," I purr. "It's been so long since I've been fucked properly. Perhaps you could do me the honor—" I reach for his loincloth, but his hands are fast, grabbing my wrists to halt them. A wide grin spreads across my face. "There could be only one reason why you wouldn't fuck me."

He awaits my answer.

"It would upset Thorn. Say it, it is the truth."

"Nothing could be further from it."

"Then why won't you put that big dick in me?" I pout.

"Probably for the same reason he won't."

I rip my hands away from his touch. "Get off, you disgusting beast. A woman tries to do you a favor and this is how you repay her? I didn't want you anyway. Probably have too small a cock to do any real damage." I huff and head for the tent flap, but Arron pauses me with a slight motion of his hand.

"You were told once already, do not come here unless you are called upon."

"As if *he* could keep a thought in that wormy brain of his for longer than a minute. If I want Thorn I have to come to him."

"What you want is of no consequence to the rest of us."

"You ass," I hiss. "Don't think you're better than me. We're both here for the same reason. Can't you see that?"

Arron stares at me with stoicism.

"*We* follow Thorn not because he is some great leader. This is about *power*. We want power and Petra Gunnora is oozing it." I hold out my hands as if warming them over a fire. "She's *chosen* him and no one would follow that dimwit half-blood otherwise."

Arran's stony jaw seems to grow harder still. "I followed Thorn before the Envercress witch discovered him. I followed him through the belly of Black Mountain and *that* is why I follow him still. He is the greatest leader I've ever seen and he possesses a brilliant mind. *You* are the dim and vacuous whore who can't see greatness when it stands before you."

I curl my lip in disgust and jerk my skirt aside to show Arron what he's missing out on. "Your precious King will bow to this pussy before we reach the gates of Pontheugh. You've got my word on that, and I think my first order of business as Queen will be to cut out your insubordinate tongue."

"You don't know this about him, because you don't pay attention, but Thorn is forgiving. More forgiving than I could ever claim to be."

"Is that supposed to be some kind of veiled threat?"

"I've vowed to uphold what I know he would want. And he would never want you. But he also wouldn't want harm to befall you—that is the kind of person he is. So, I offer you this one last line of forgiveness, in his name. But if I find you here again, disobeying our King's orders, I will have a band take you back to the heart of the wood, tie you to a tree, and leave you there."

I bite back a scream of hatred. "You're a fool. We could have been allies, Arran. Thorn is a sinking ship and you will drown right along with him. But that will happen *after* he makes me his Queen." I scoff. "A brilliant mind? He's a puppet and his brain lousy with holes. It could be worse though. He could be you and have shit for brains." I look down my nose at the burly orc, hating him to his core. I realize I hate Thorn too. I think I might just poison him after our marriage is official. "This is going to be easy," I say, tossing the words over my shoulder and exiting the tent.

I step out into the hazy morning, literally shaking with rage. "Who does he think he is?" I mutter. Garbage, all of them. Orcs are utter garbage. I'm going to have fun with this, indulgent fun —ruining Arron and murdering Thorn. I think it will be more delicious to let Arron live, knowing he failed his precious master.

Stalking through the mud, not wishing to go back to the tent I share with the others, I make for the edge of camp—needing time to breathe, to find a steely calm I can use to serve my purpose.

Brilliant mind...the suggestion makes me laugh aloud. They really aren't much more than animals. Arron wouldn't know a brilliant mind from a stone. I reach the pikes on the outskirts and grip them, wishing I possessed the physical strength to run an orc or two through with the sharpened ends.

Arran. The ass. He was suggesting I *couldn't* win Thorn's affection. Of course I could. I could do so at any time. It's only been difficult because of the hold Petra has. Because of Ash and Ellyn distracting him. That's why his eyes are increasingly vacant, why his memory struggles so. And that damned medallion gets louder all the time. Practically hums...

Yes, I tell myself, if he weren't so addled he'd be mine already. He can't remember all the good times we've had. It's the other girls who are right—regardless of his failing memory, it is *me* who Thorn comes to when he craves the touch of a woman. *I* am the one he wants, whether Arron will admit to it or not.

I jerk one of the pikes, still mentally cursing Arran. Probably inclined toward the male anatomy, I reason. He's jealous that Thorn wants me and not him. It's the only explanation. I nod, feeling the tension ease from my body. I'm just about to really focus in on an articulated plan to wrap Thorn around my little finger when movement near the forest catches my eye.

I fall back, finding a tent to crouch beside. Someone is coming out of the trees. Someone who doesn't wish to be seen.

I watch the figure pause, searching our camp. The wheels in my mind turn. How can I use this to my advantage? If I catch an interloper, I might be able to gain favor with Thorn, accolades or some such thing...

But the bastard pulls his hood back, exposing his face and I see it is none other than the King himself. Disappointment washes over me for one slim second, before my heart stops cold. Thorn scans suspiciously all along the perimeter of our territory, but that wretched gaze of his isn't the vacant one I've grown accustomed to. No. His eyes are clear, radiating focus and intent.

Seeing no one, he makes his move, crossing the field

between camp and the tree line, and I drop down lower so as to not be noticed by the sneaking Orc King.

My brows furrow. Now, this is interesting. Where was Thorn last night? And how is it, after months of mindlessness, does our King finally seem to have awoken? I bite my nail and fixate on the problem, for I feel the key to my future is hidden somewhere within.

CHAPTER 30

Thorn

$\mathcal{B}$ ack at camp, I set out promptly to find Arron and I find him giving orders to a group tending to the horses. He approaches, anticipating my orders perhaps, and I pause, checking myself. What would I say if I were still under the influence of the medallion?

"They are anxious for blood," he tells me.

I grunt, knowing it to be true.

"It's been too many days of waiting, Thorn."

"Our fight is not something to be rushed."

"We aren't rushing. We're stalling."

He isn't wrong, but what else is there to do? I've no intention of bearing down the weight of my army onto a castle when my precious Alba is inside. "I've thinking to do, Arran—before I make any moves."

He doesn't look at me—pointedly so—as he picks up a brush and begins scrubbing it down the side of a sturdy, brown horse. "I might be able to distract them in their restlessness." He makes a subtle nod to the orcs shoveling horse shit. "But what about the Envercress witch? How long is she going to wait, Thorn?"

I study Arran's back as he works, wondering about him, about how much he sees and knows. "What do you propose?"

"An attack on the castle."

I shake my head. "Impossible."

"Impossible?" His tone is calm. Curious.

"Now isn't the time."

My general sets aside the brush and rises to his full height to look at me. "And if she were here to ask why, what reason would you give?"

I haven't an answer. "I am at a loss, Arran." My words are a confession—honest vulnerability that I hope he mistakes for madness. Only, I think Arron sees more than I've realized.

"You are the only one who can decide."

I frown, staring out at the orcs trudging through ankle-deep muck, backed by a grey skyline. "It isn't much different, is it?"

He shares my gaze. "Black Mountain all over again."

"We seem to bring it with us wherever we go. Perhaps that is why we were cast out of this land?"

"Are you having second thoughts?"

For the first time in a long while I am free to actually explore my own thoughts. But I don't tell Arron that. There are limits to my openness. "I just need more time."

"I trust you," he says simply and our eyes meet. There are so few things I recall clearly. But I seem to remember a long famil-iarity with Arran. There is a younger version of him in my mind, visions of him fighting by my side as we forced our way deeper into the belly of the mountain.

"But if you were to make a suggestion?"

"A small attack. Something superficial to distract them and the Queen."

I nod. "Give me one more day, Arran. One more day and I'll be able to think clearly." Only, it's really one more day with Alba that I'm after. Arron gives a dutiful nod and I head for my tent, my mind hungrily replaying my last moments with Alba again and again.

She feels it too. This uncanny drive, this undeniable emotion. I search my mind for a way that I might keep her, but my temples throb with fatigue.

Sleep is what I need. A slim bit of rest. Then I will be able to think, to put all of this in order. Petra, and the war, the throne, that cursed medallion, darling Alba, and her friends whom she loves so much. There's got to be a way to put all of this in order.

I dip into the darkness of my tent and very quickly stop in my tracks. *What is that putrid odor?* Like smoke and weeds—a woman's cheap perfume. I wave my hand before my face, trying to air out whatever is offending my senses. But the motion feels catching, as if my hand is sticking to air. My spine prickles with a different kind of awareness.

Petra.

Before I can make a move there's an ugly snap. Tension builds and then bursts, a nearby shard of mirror cracks like static and ice. A wave of energy passes through the room, through my very being, and the reflection in the mirror begins to cloud.

There is no hiding. So, I make my way toward the shattered glass, just as Petra's face forms in the clouds therein. Fractured.

The Queen's jaw is set and her eyes are like weapons, aimed at me. All she need do is wish it and she has the power to bring me to my knees. My heart races and I pray to any Gods that might still have me: *don't let her see the medallion is gone.*

"Petra. I wasn't expecting you."

"That much is clear."

"To what can I owe the pleasure of this visit? Or half-visit, as the case may be." I tap the mirror, a light expression on my face.

Resolute cruelty is what she sends back in my direction. "I see nothing on the horizon, Thorn."

"Bit cloudy in our neck of the woods—" I start. She cuts me off.

"The sky should be black with smoke. But that's not what I was referring to."

"Spell it out for me, if you would."

"Do you not already possess your orders?"

I tap my temple. "Hard to keep things straight in here. I'm sure you understand."

"Days now and I've heard no progress. You sit outside the castle and you give them time to plot and plan against you. Inaction could lose this war." Her voice is strained.

"Is that what the stone says? Is that the future it has presented you with?"

Petra thrusts her hand out and I hear a succession of vials and trinkets spill across the floor, some of them shattering. "It presents me with nothing!"

I stagger over that bit of information. "What do you mean, nothing?"

She points a finger in my direction, curling her body over it, looking tense and haggard. "It's your inaction. You're distracted again, aren't you?"

I shake my head, not wanting her to come here. "There are no distractions."

"Then explain to me why you have not yet mounted your attack?"

I rub at my throat. "I'm still recovering—"

"LIES!" she bellows, rising from her seat to glower at me through the broken mirror.

I'm taken aback. I've never seen Petra so unhinged. She's usually such a calculating fiend, everything under her control, deep in a game of chess she's plotted to perfection.

"I don't know what you're doing," she hisses, "but it isn't what I want. I *want* you to take that castle for me. I *need* the King and his daughter."

TRACY LAUREN

"What do you need them for?"

She practically growls and her eyes flash red—red like the stone around her neck. *Magic of some kind?*

"My seeing stone tells me *nothing*. Nearly a hundred years I have worn this stone and *never* has it been so silent. Then, I look to the horizon—and where I wish to see towers of black smoke billowing into the sky? There is more of the same. *Nothing!*" She spits the words. "If you dare scheme to betray me you have got another think coming, indeed."

"I would never betray you, Petra. We have an alliance, you and I."

She scowls, narrowing her eyes at me. "Tell me, Thorn, do you remember what I do to people who betray me? Search that clever brain of yours."

I do remember, but I stand silent, taking in this cruel and ageless witch. Images of her garden flash to mind. Statues, empty cages, haunting reflections in the pond. I've allowed this problem to go unattended—terribly unwise on my part.

"I'll do everything in my power," I tell her. "I'll bring them to you."

Her shoulders sink, as if finally allowing her body a breath of air. Still, no mercy comes to her eyes. "I *need* them, Thorn."

"The King and his Princess," I echo.

"No more distractions."

CHAPTER 31

Honora

$\mathcal{I}$ remain there, in my hiding place. Squatting in the mud, absorbed by my meditations on Thorn sneaking from the woods. With a furrowed brow I realize...*this isn't the first time.* He's done this before, hasn't he? Been gone all night. Alone. What curious behavior... What was he doing out there? What business is this?

I search our most recent interactions for clues. Could it be Ash? Is he out there? Or Ellyn perhaps? Of course it could always be something to do with this war...but I'm not inclined to believe that.

I simply don't know what Thorn has been doing. But there is one thing I can be certain of: the anger rising in me. White-hot, anger. I put my hand over my belly and feel it growing in heat. *May the Gods damn Thorn.*

Instinct nags. There is something foul here. Whatever he's doing, I don't like it one bit. Not one bit at all! It's keeping him from me and me from his bed.

With clenched fists I damn him and his distractions! That

feeble-minded fool! I don't know why he was ever chosen for the task of taking this castle. The man is weak. I want to scream it at the top of my lungs. I want to scream the words into his hideous, scarred face. If only Thorn were *normal*. A regular orc, with a regular mind. I'd have him in the palm of my hand. But he goes off on these tangents. First his brother and Ellyn and now…whatever *this* is.

"What are you doing down there?" a voice calls. I look up to see Marie coming past with a basket of wash under her arm. Annoyed by her sudden appearance, I bring myself to my feet, still deep in thought and completely uninterested in company.

"Things used to be different," I tell her. The words come out like a challenge. And I dare her to deny it. "Tell me they weren't."

"What's that?" She squints, the hot and terrible sun breaking through the clouds.

"Thorn," I growl. "Things used to be different between him and me."

She makes a face and shifts her weight from one leg to the other. "Isn't it a little early in the day to be thinking of men?"

I wave my hand at her impatiently. "He used to have me nearly every night."

"There was a time, yes," she agrees. I pin Marie with my eyes and study her expression.

"Seems something is lingering on your tongue. Spit it out."

The look about her is placating and it does nothing to quell my growing rage. "There was a time when Thorn took you into his bed often. But consider, perhaps, that time has passed—"

"He ebbs like the tides. You know that as well as I do. Thorn will come back to me."

"Yes, he still might."

"*Might?*" I spit at Marie's feet and watch her struggle for patience. But it is not patience I seek. "I am not a woman to linger on hope. *I* make things happen."

"That's fine and all, but we're talking about the Orc King."

"You think I cannot make him mine?"

"I didn't say that, love. I'm simply pointing out his unique...*mental capacity*," she says the words gingerly, lowering her voice so as not to be overheard. "We all know he's half-mad."

"Magic," I say.

"Obviously, it's magic. That beast in Envercress has him under her thumb, but there's nothing any of us can do about it."

I cross my arms over my chest and turn toward the forest, staring at the spot Thorn emerged from. "There is something else going on. Something keeping him from me."

"Honora...you act as if you're already married to the man. But tell me, how long has it been since you shared a bed?"

I shoot a hateful glance at Marie before turning back to the woods.

"It was Ash and Ellyn who got between us," I mutter.

"They're gone now."

"Are they?"

"What do you mean? Of course they are."

Marie sighs at my silence and places a hand on my shoulder.

"Consider a possibility for me. I'd never say this in front of the others, of course, but consider...we might never be anything more than entertainment to them."

I round on Marie, roughly knocking the basket of wash from her hold—sending clothes across the mud and filth. "*Entertainment?*"

Her jaw tightens, but she maintains composure. "I'm *trying* to help you."

"By spitting curses? I don't need your help, you awful wench."

"Curses? I'm merely suggesting a possibility, one you should prepare yourself for. And it's not a bad possibility at that: consorts to a King? That's what we've been from the start and it's been fun! He'll take care of us, Honora, I'm sure of it. And we'll be far better off than when we started."

"I don't want a simple step up in life. I *want* to be on top. I *want* to be Queen."

"Well face the facts: Thorn might not want you!" She's raised her voice now, effortfully trying to force this curse upon me, to deny me of my destiny. What a friend Marie has proven to be, lingering close, hoping only to watch me fall.

"I will be Queen, I tell you. If I have to lie, cheat, steal. If I have to *kill*—I will be Queen."

"Who do you think you're going to kill? The Queen of Envercress? Good luck. You don't have half of the power she has."

"I didn't say the Queen of Envercress."

Marie scoffs and turns her back on me, picking up mud-soaked clothes one by one and depositing them into her basket. "Yeah? Who are you going to kill then?"

"Wouldn't you like to know?"

"You're all talk, Honora," she says plainly. "If you aren't careful it's going to bite you in the ass one day."

With a clamped jaw, I grip one of the long, sharp pikes.

"Listen to reason, will you? Being consort to a King is more than any of us ever counted on in life. Be happy with your blessings and let go of that damned fantasy, before you get hurt."

If Marie had planned to say more, I'll never know. Her thoughts were cut short by a sudden force jarring her forward. Slowly turning to look over her shoulder, her eyes connect with mine. Then, they travel down to her gut...where I've run her through. "You think I won't go to whatever lengths necessary?" My voice is quiet, grave.

Marie wraps her hands weakly around the bloody piece of wood protruding from her abdomen. I give it a final shove and send her face first into the mud. She's garbage. I curl my lip at her in disgust.

"Bitch."

The urge to scream nearly overwhelms me.

Just beyond this camp is the great *stinking* lake that separates us from the castle. Thorn will take that castle; he'll take it because the Witch Queen herself wants it and she will make it so. Time is short, but before we get there, I *will* make him mine. I will tie that half-blood bastard to me so there's no getting away. "I've got power of my own, damn it. Power, beauty, cunning. That's all I need to get what I want."

I cast one last disdain-filled look at Marie. Then, I make for the woods.

CHAPTER 32

Petra Gunnora, the Eternal Princess, the Witch Queen
Meanwhile in Envercress...

Cold seeps from stone walls. The room is windowless, lit by candles. Black ones. I wasn't always a witch. I hardly even think of myself as one now. These are simply the things I do...to help save the world.

It's not a task many people understand. As a matter of fact, I don't think anyone could comprehend the lengths I go to—the sacrifices I've made. I've never met a soul who did. My stepfather, the King of Envercress...he was a good man. But he couldn't do what I do. Too trusting, too simple. He loved my mother dearly, from the moment he set eyes upon her—a poor, widowed, peasant dressmaker. They were quite precious together, really they were. Their story had all the makings of a fairytale. With the exception of a "happily ever after" of course.

The King was...*removed* and the crown fell to his son, the Prince. Oh, but the things I saw the Prince capable of. My stone shows all. All possible outcomes. My stepbrother could not be allowed to lead. I had to put an end to that. The stone told me what to do, it showed me how to stop his reign before it even began. That's when I first started using magic. But it wasn't really me, was it? It's hardly me now. Yes, it's just the tasks that require doing to stop bad from happening.

My stepbrother would have brought ruin upon the land. He had a disgusting and wretched heart in him. There was no choice. I put an end to all the evil things he hadn't even conceived of yet. I couldn't kill him, of course. I was still just a girl. So I cast his soul into the pond. And he exists there, even now. Though he can't hear me. So, I can't explain how necessary it all was. Years pass...his anger never seems to dwindle, but gazing upon his reflection doesn't bother me like it used to. I just feel sort of...empty inside. It was so very, very long ago. And the potential threats to this land...they have never ceased to unfold. Even if I could talk to him, he wouldn't care.

The stone cares. The stone cares as I do. That's why it shows me, I think. The stone was meant for me and I was meant for the stone. It came in the form of a gift, long, long ago. When my mother married the King. He wanted to give me something that belonged to the royal line, to show me I was as much his child as Belric and Meredith were.

He chose the piece haphazardly, in the same way he led the kingdom—with his heart. No thought, just a simple man's emotions.

Little did he know, it was more than a pretty bauble. It was a window. A massively powerful window into every possible future. A terrible curse to hang round the neck of a child. Particularly considering the type of child I was: concerned, watchful, calculating. Before the King married my mother, it was only the two of us—she and I. I was used to responsibility and I took that stone as my own personal obligation, as well as the terror it laid out.

Over eighty years, I've worn this necklace, carried this burden. I've done everything in my power to avert danger, to exist long enough to keep averting danger, to keep this kingdom alive and prosperous. And we have prospered. It's been an age of peace. Totalitarian, yes. But peaceful nonetheless. All my people are fed, clothed, they have clean homes, and roofs over their heads. They want for nothing. Still, they look at me with *fear*.

It doesn't matter. I didn't take any of this on to be liked. I did it for them. Because I care that much. And there is no one else in all the world who could care for them as I have. I know. I've searched for someone to pass the burden to and come up empty. So I remain accountable to my obligation and the stone rewards me by showing the way.

Only, about a year ago...some of the visions...they became *clouded*. I looked to Pontheugh and I...I couldn't see their future.

I think it is their King. Disgusting thing. Absolutely wretched. But I left his Kingdom to him and focused on my own. I can only do so much. I am but one woman, stretched thin. Pontheugh is on the border of my land. They have the power to impact us. So I check on them, of course. Through the stone, as often as possible. One must be vigilant when ruling a kingdom.

I looked at my stone and I saw Pontheugh shrouded in fog. Their castle dark. Upheaval. Death. I could smell the blood. But I couldn't *see* what was happening there. The darkness could spread. It could touch my land. I won't allow that.

That's when I began to search for a course of action that could shed light on the land. That's what led me to Thorn. I saw Black Mountain in my stone. I saw the orc warriors being birthed deep in its belly. I set a door for one. A special one. Whoever made it through, I would know, *he* would be the one.

Thorn came to me. It felt right. I could see our path. I could see war. There would be death, much death, much destruction.

But it would be for the greater good. And haven't I already sacrificed so much for the greater good?

"I know what you were telling me," I whisper to the stone round my neck. "You wanted me to take this path. I know that you did. So why...why do you fall silent now?"

I whisper the words, terrified. So many years the stone has shown me the way. What would I do if the magic ran out and I had no window? I wouldn't know how to protect my land and the people here—the families. They count on me to protect them, to make all the right decisions. I can't let them down.

I squeeze my eyes shut, feeling hot tears build at the prospect of failing my people. In my mind I can see all those awful visions—visions of how this land would have looked if Meredith or Belric wore the crown.

Pestilence, famine. Grey days with no sun. Generations of darkness. My garden...my garden withering and my statues crumbling. I press my hands to my face, shaken by regret. I didn't know what I was doing in those early days, it was all just a scramble. I had to stop them, I had to stop them as quick as I could. I didn't think things through, I didn't know the magic well enough.

Meredith, shallow, unassuming Meredith. She had no evil in her. But no depth either. She was fond of pretty things. So very fond of the pretty. It was a transformation spell I used on her. I was trying to be kind...I really was. I couldn't put her in the pond with Belric. No, he was an evil sort. He might have hurt her to get back at me. So, I settled on a transformation spell. I thought I could make her something truly stunning. It worked of course; I had the help of the stone. But poor Meredith aged inside that magical bird. Stunning bird. Unnatural. Not something you could find anywhere in the wide world...not without magic. I fancied that I would put her on display and the villagers would come to see her. I fancied she would like that. But they wouldn't come. The rumors had already begun about me.

Tragedy in the castle, mysterious circumstances. I never thought that putting her soul in a living creature would be different from putting a soul in a pond. I didn't know she would age.

Meredith died a bird. A *fucking* bird. I knock over a tray of instruments and they clatter, sprawling themselves across the stone floor. The noise threatens to make me snap and I bury my face in my hands to force back the sob desperate to escape. I'm about to break when the girl on the table moans. It pulls me from my dark memories and anxious thoughts. She lifts a hand toward me. Her mouth works, but she is pale as chalk. She can't speak.

"You are supposed to be restrained," I say icily as I draw the straps tighter.

Sniffling away my tears, I bring a smile to my face and take her fingers in mine. With limited strength she tries to turn away. But she can't. Her eyes roll back in her head. "Hush," I tell her—stroking her cheek. "You do a great service to the land."

Blood fills the gutters round the edge of the table and I tilt the axis slightly. It goes rushing toward the drain, toward my precious stone.

I don't really consider myself a witch. I simply do what the stone requests of me. I do whatever necessary to protect this land and my people. When Pontheugh began to cloud over, I knew. It was time I took care of Pontheugh as well. And wouldn't that be easier? Take this whole world under my wing — I grimace…picturing Meredith in her final, repulsive state… That's what set me onto the statues. Quite easy to preserve a soul in a statue. At least Meredith taught me that. Her death wasn't in vain. And she was so melancholy as a bird. No flight, no song. And then, one day, she was dead.

"You'll be dead soon too," I explain to the virgin peasant girl. "And just like Meredith, your sacrifice won't be in vain. Your blood will breathe new life into my stone. It will lift the veil and show me everything I need to do to protect both kingdoms. Isn't that wonderful? You should be very proud of yourself." I would have been proud I think, if I had found myself in her shoes as a girl.

Her head lolls to the side. Her pretty, pale cheek is already cold. But it's cold here in the dungeon. I could light a thousand candles in this room, but the walls are stone and the ceiling is high. There is simply no way to warm it.

Carefully, I undo the bindings and drape her slender hands across her stomach. But I am anxious to follow the blood to the top of the table, to watch the last of it drain through the spout and pour itself into the bowl beneath. Crystals, ash, potions. All the knowledge I've accumulated over the years, and then some, I put everything I could think of into this spell—to renew my stone.

It's got to work.

I shift on my feet, wringing my hands, feeling nervous in a way I haven't felt since childhood, since those first glimpses into a horrid future. What if I lose those visions? I picture the darkness again—it's too much to endure and I hastily delve my hands into the blood and ash, pulling up the stone. My hands stain red. I wipe away the excess blood and search desperately for a vision.

My breath shakes when the stone begins to form a picture, I can see light within, the swirls of electric indigo taking form. "Show me Pontheugh. Show me the future of Pontheugh!" I want to see Thorn taking the throne for me. I want to see him taking the King and his daughter captive. I want them brought here. I know what to do with them. I will keep them from harming this land. I will fortify the stone with their blood and it will serve me for another 80 years. Their deaths are a small price for another 80 years of peace and prosperity.

No one cares for this land as I do. No one cares for the people. This is for the better, I know it.

The image in the stone takes shape. I wipe blood away once more, trying to get a clearer image. I see the castle. Cold, silent. I don't see Thorn. I don't see his army. I see grey. I see a haze. I see...*NOTHING*.

"Nothing!" I scream the words and kick over the bucket of blood and ash. It spills across the floor. And I scream again, my cry echoing throughout the big, round, stone room, with the lengthy, spiraling staircase circling up, up, up.

And I do the most foolish thing since that mistake I made with Meredith. Stone in hand, fear and anger overtaking me, I pull back and throw with all my might. My precious stone hits the ground with a clink and slides.

Instantly, I am filled with regret. I dive after it, muttering apologies. "No, no, no...I didn't mean to do that."

On hands and knees I clasp the stone tightly, drawing it to my chest. When I have courage, I polish it with the velvet of my skirt. But right down the center, where the lines are usually indigo...there is a vein of amber...A crack.

Sobs shake my being. "No, no, no, no—"

I clutch it to my heart, furious at myself.

"So stupid. I'm so stupid!" I wail.

There's only one thing that can help. I need Thorn to finish his task. The stone though, it didn't show Thorn taking the castle! It didn't show his army. I push to my feet, securing the precious chain round my neck, then I take to the stairs, one hand protectively over the stone the entire time.

I can't believe I did such a wretched, wretched thing. What was I thinking, I lament. Bounding up the stairs two at a time I make it to the door, winded, and push it open. Stepping into my private room. I race across to the balconies, tearing back curtains, flinging open the doors. I rush to my spy glass and point it at Pontheugh.

"Come now, orc. Don't fail me. Please, don't fail me." I search the horizon. No smoke. Throwing my head back, I scream again.

"FUCK!" What is he doing? I told him to attack and he whines about healing. Healing? Healing! The castle needs to be in my control and he bullshits me about healing! He'd be dead if it weren't for me and now he wastes my time, he draws this out. The job needs finishing. He must not think I am serious.

I will have to show him then. I think it is time for a face-to-face conversation. With a whisper and a breath, the candles across my vanity flicker to life.

"No more distractions for the orc. Thorn needs to be taught how to focus...once and for all."

CHAPTER 33

Honora

Charging through the woods with determination and a sure foot, it's rough land like this that I am accustomed to. My mother before me was a witch. She lived in man's land. That was her first mistake. Villagers are never to be trusted with what their small minds can't comprehend. Add religious zealots to the mix and you've got a dead witch on your hands. That was my mother's fate. I was but a small girl at the time. Still, I was used to going into the wood with her, collecting ingredients, chanting incantations, living freely. But one day they came. They condemned her. She, the woman who supplied them with their tonics and salves to secure good health and long life. She, the woman who brewed the occasional love potion for a desperate villager. Yes, there may have been a curse here or there, a death brew that was the collapse of everything. But my mother had done plenty of good. A bit of bad—but they had asked for it, hadn't they? They came to her, they begged for those potions. And how did they repay her in the end? By a burning at the stake.

I watched. Old man Broin at my side. Fool. Damned fool. How holy he thought he was, rescuing me from a wicked woman. I hated that man from the start. But my mother didn't raise an idiot. I pretended. Of course I did. Who wouldn't after that fire? After hearing my mother's screams. I pretended for a long while. But I couldn't be changed. I was born to be what I am. A witch. But I am not like my mother. I never had any desire to be the *village witch* as it were. An old hag with a cat and a garden, tossed a couple of coins to cast a spell when the Robinsons' farm wasn't doing well, given a cake or a meat pie when a child was ill and needed healing. That's small and I am meant for greater things. Far greater.

I was bolder with my potions than my mother ever was. Always more willing to reach for the next limit. I had to be a bold little thing with Broin watching me. I think he might have guessed at the darkness inside me. I could see it in his eyes. He watched a little too closely when I played with the other children. It was as if he could see I was different. I think sometimes he was afraid that I might hurt them. But he couldn't prove that, could he? No. No one could ever prove a thing.

As I grew older I began to sneak back into the woods, to the places my mother had taken me. She taught me well and the Perished Woods is a ready teacher for those willing to learn. That was a long time ago now. Broin has been dead for years and all his incessant praying is nothing more than a comical memory. Just the start of a much greater path.

I trudge back into the Perished Woods, wondering. Did I think I would never come back here after I took up with Thorn's army? I don't know. I hadn't thought about it when I decided to come with them. I knew it would take me away, that it would lead me to greater things and better opportunities. I suppose...I *had* thought I wouldn't come back. I packed my trunk and little else. I didn't look back on the hut I called home. I just left. It was like leaving old Broin. Old, dying Broin. Froth and spittle dribbling down his chin, a choked prayer, his eyes wide, locked on that dead rabbit.

The memory drives me forward with force. I was strong as a girl. I'm stronger still as a woman. No one, and I mean no one, will get in my way. It's the only reason to come back to this place I have outgrown. There is something out here. Something standing in my way. I'm going to find out what it is and bring it to its end. Thorn will be mine. I will be Queen. I will reign over Pontheugh and use my crown to accrue more power. More and more until I am as powerful as that beast from Envercress. Stupid rich thing, with her fine dresses. But she's never had to fight for her power. It was handed to her. Everything has been handed to her.

The thought makes me scowl. I imagine sticking a knife into one of her pretty dresses and twisting it, just to see her perfect face screwed up in knots of pain. One day, I'll kill her and take everything she has. It's so real to me, so palpable. It isn't a dream or a foolhardy desire. It's the future. *My* future. Mine for the taking. Already in my grip. All I need is Thorn's attention, just for a moment, I need to grasp hold of his attention so he can't see anything else. Not his brother, not that feeble woman he kept with him, not the castle, nor the army, *just me*. If I could get him to see *just me* for the slimmest moment, I could claim him, lock him into my grip and secure my future—the one I was destined for.

I drive onward, traversing this forest like I never left it. Ellyn couldn't do this. And what would Thorn want with a woman who didn't know the woods the way he does? There's something pathetic about it. I clench my teeth, I ruminate, murderous rage simmers just beneath the surface. My destiny is so close, I can feel it.

CHAPTER 34

Honora

y dreams threaten to slip through my fingers. I can't stand the not knowing. Not when my fate is so close at hand. I should be Queen. I will be Queen—the moment I find out what Thorn is up to, the tables are going to turn.

It takes tracking skills to find where he has gone. A broken branch here, a boot print in the mud there. Then, a clearing. I search it. I scan every square inch for a clue. Something to indicate what has been going on out here.

He's been distant. Not in the typical way. Not the insanity that worms its way through his mind. No. He's been more...*alive* as of late. I can picture his eyes now. Clear. Focused. I snarl in anger. After much searching, I am satisfied there is nothing to find and I turn to waiting.

Crouching among the trees, I sit and wait. I turn every interaction over in my mind, inspecting it. I lose myself in thought. An hour passes. Maybe more. My eyes focus on stones in the distance. I train my ears for the sound of approaching footsteps. There's only silence.

Those stones stare back at me. I ignore them and focus on my plot against Thorn. Disgusting beast. I'll remember all he put me through once I have more power. I'll have power like the Envercress witch one day soon and then he'll be sorry.

A squirrel comes slowly up one of those stones, pausing to greedily shove a seed into its mouth. Absently I am watching, not truly paying attention. Then that little squirrel continues on his way, turning round a curve in the rock that I can't quite make out from my angle. He disappears—never reappearing on the other side.

The cogs in my mind turn slowly. I am so very absorbed in rage...but eventually, my curiosity is sparked. *Where* in the world did that little squirrel go?

I rise from my place at the base of the tree and slowly head toward the pile of grey rock. Making a wide berth around to one side, I see an opening. *A cave.*

I curse myself under my breath for missing such a thing. "Doesn't matter," I whisper. "I'm clever and I found it."

Striding onward, I'm not worried about my steps being overheard. Thorn is back at camp. There's been no movement from this cave in all the time I've been here waiting. What's inside must be some kind of secret then. And I mean to find out exactly what this secret is.

Tucked close to the opening is a torch. I take it up and, rubbing my fingers together, it's lit. A simple bit of magic, but I'm feeling proud of myself. I'm feeling clever. I'm feeling like a real witch. The kind of witch that wields power as if it takes nothing from her.

Blazing stick before me, I venture inside. The little squirrel darts past my feet. "What secrets are you hiding, you wretched creature?" Slowly, I delve deeper into the cold hollow of the mountainside. Water drips and echoes around me and the hint of another sound nags at my consciousness. *What is it?* I search my mind.

Breath. It sounds like ragged breath. And just as it comes to me…I see it. I see his majesty's dark secret.

Chained to the wall is the contorted body of an orc. Tall, lean, lanky. Do I know this fellow? I narrow my eyes, wondering if I've fucked him. But it is so hard to tell. He's skin and bones, rib cage protruding, encased only by the thinnest layer of skin. He's got dark bags under his eyes. His cheeks are hollow. His mouth is gaping but his jaw is so tight it is pulled to one side. He looks dead, but I can hear low, craggy breaths escaping him.

I hold my torch closer. His eyes are unseeing. There's a glint in the darkness, in the long shadows of the cave. The golden shine of a medallion. *Thorn's medallion.*

Inching closer. "What's wrong with you?" I demand.

The orc is silent. I reach my foot out and kick him. He makes a sort of death moan but otherwise is immobile. My confidence is high and I get close enough to reach for the medallion— thinking it might behoove me to just take it. But when my fingers graze the metal, they are singed. My breath hisses and I hug my fingers to my chest. Angry and accusing eyes shoot to the orc.

"Wake up!" I demand. "Who put you here? Was it Thorn?"

Silence.

"Was it the Orc King?"

Still, no response.

I press my lips together, enraged. Then, I thrust the torch out, grinding it into the orc's shoulder. He moans and his jaw swings to the other side. Smells like burnt flesh. I watch his skin blister, break, and peel back. But he still seems to be stuck in some sort of twilight.

"Thorn wanted you here?" I demand. The orc says nothing. "Well, to Hell with what Thorn wants."

I thrust the torch out again and hold it to the beast. I hold it for a long time. His moaning builds into a howl—wretched dog. With skin like gauze, he burns with surprising ease. Screams echo off stone walls. Black smoke billows overhead and my heart races. With wild eyes, I watch the orc die. I watch his pain. I watch bits of his body melt away. It thrills me. I'm shaking with delight. My breast rising and falling with gleeful and rapid breaths. Thorn is all that is on my mind. Thorn is next.

The orc fights feebly against the chains until life fails him. I watch for a while longer. I watch the moment the chain around his neck becomes too heavy for a burnt corpse to hold. There's a snap. His head rolls. The chain and the medallion hanging from it falls to the floor. It's too hot to be touched so I hook it onto the torch and head for the light of day, laughing to myself.

A breeze hits my face. I feel charged, every vessel in my body is tingling with delight. What a prize I have found! My fingers twitch. So much power, so close at hand. How can I use it? Blackmail Thorn? Hold this cursed thing over him—if the Envercress witch finds out, there will be hell to pay. Or...do I go to the Eternal Princess herself?

I bite my lip, grinning as I traipse back to the clearing. Maybe I earn the witch's favor. Maybe she makes me Queen of Pontheugh?

Drunk on delight, I drop down onto a mossy patch of earth to think over my options. It's only the castle I can think of. The riches. The power. The clothes I will wear. The jewels. I stare at the medallion. Pure gold, I bet...

The breeze slips around me again. A bit stronger this time. Like the stone and the squirrel, I pay no attention. The leaves overhead tremble, but I am faraway in my mind, wearing a blood-red gown, my throat dripping in rubies, music playing, men lining up to dance with me—to fuck me, to make my toes curl all night long while I drink only the best wine. The wine Kings and Queens drink.

It isn't until the earth starts shaking that I rip myself from my fantasy.

CHAPTER 35

Thorn

*I*t's far too early, the sun has not yet touched the horizon and still I make my way to our spot. I feel young again. Thrilled in a way I've never before felt. It is like I am touching life. And it is easy to leave behind the camp—the ugliness of it, the stench, the endless mud… It burns away with every step I take in Alba's direction.

I don't let myself think about the future, or her leaving for a new land. Now is all I can consider. I'll kiss her. I'll hold her against my chest and she'll hold me back. How can a girl like her, a precious thing like Alba, love me back? I squeeze my eyes shut, the unfamiliar sensation of joy washing over me. She is a killer, yes. But she is all virtue. An angel with a streak of strength. A flower…with a thorn…

One more night, then I will face reality. I will focus on Pontheugh and Petra. I will solve that problem once and for all. But for now…Alba. Alba. Alba. My Alba.

The wind picks up pace and I grin. A storm is coming. My

woman will be cold and I will have to hold her to keep her
warm.

CHAPTER 36

Alba

*I*t's too early. I know it is. But I can't wait. I want to be with Thorn. I need to be by his side, I need to breathe him in and marvel at my beast from the Perished Woods. I laugh to myself, nearly skipping down the path to our spot.

I think of the future. I try to bend my obligations to fit with my desires. Maybe Thorn can come with us? Maybe we can secure our own boat. He is strong, a fighter. He can protect me, and Wendy, and Beatrice. We can be a family and go to a new land together. Maybe in a faraway place Thorn will be accepted? We can have a little farm and take care of ourselves. Take care of each other...

I squeeze myself, remembering my man's touch. He's magical. Completely magical. And I can't believe someone so lovely would love me the way that I love them. I'm nearly laughing thinking of the contrast between Luther and my orc. Luther was the beast and everyone loved him. Thorn is...an orc and *I* love him.

I see the familiar trees ahead and fight to hold my hair in place as a harsh wind whips against my face. I look up and the clouds overhead churn and swirl in an unsettling way. The hair on my arms stand on end and the first sense of trouble begins a nagging at my mind.

Concerned thoughts go out to Thorn. I don't know where he is, but I hope he'll be here soon. I wish there was a way to go straight to him, to communicate. But there isn't. I hover on the edge of the wood, remembering there is danger in the world. There are other orcs, violent ones. The Orc King even. I tremble at the thought. If I came across a beast like that they would cut me down just as they cut down my village.

But the woods seem to hold a measure of safety, don't they? The same woods I was taught to fear my entire life. Only, Thorn is of these woods. So they can't be all bad, can they? And as I stand between two worlds the ground beneath my feet begins to shake.

Gasping, I cling to a tree, trying to keep myself upright. "By the Gods—" It feels as if the earth might just open up and suck me inside. There's a rumble, like thunder, it's loud enough to make me loosen my grip on the tree and slap my hands over my ears. I scream. Maybe it's Thorn's name that I scream in my confusion and terror. But one can't tell—the rumbling is so loud.

I see nothing from where I stand, but hear snapping, crashing, and chaos. The horror of it is followed by deafening silence. Something has happened and the man I love is out there. That thought brings me more terror than I've ever known.

"Thorn—" With trembling hands, I think only of my love as I thrust myself past the border of the Perished Woods.

CHAPTER 37

Honora

A beast. A flying devil. A red dragon. It circles in the sky, screeching. Everything around me shakes. I snatch up the medallion, ignoring its magical heat. My flesh burns but there's no time to hesitate and I'm not leaving my prize behind.

I bolt towards camp.

But the dragon descends, ripping up trees with its talons. Massive trunks snap and wood splinters. I scramble over rocks and lose my footing more than once. All the while the dragon draws nearer.

Rational thought escapes me. All I can do is flee.

The trees thin. It isn't much farther. If I can make it to camp the army will have to fight the beast and I will be able to hide.

My hopes are dashed when the dragon claws its way across the tree tops to maneuver itself in front of me. I grind to a halt, falling in my efforts. The dragon screams again and I see its fire-red eyes shoot to the medallion sticking to my burned palm. I draw it quickly behind my back. No beast is going to keep me from becoming Queen—not an orc and not a dragon either.

Massive clawed feet begin striding toward me but with each step there's a shift, there's a flurry of smoke, there's a change in perception. The dragon shrinks. It becomes more human. I notice one heavy scale at the throat turn to stone. And by the time this beast stops before me, it is a woman. The Queen of Envercress. Her hair is wild, her eyes even wilder.

I drop to my knees and bow deep—forehead to the ground.

"Your Highness—" I start, speaking in my most God-fearing tone.

She grips me by my arm, twisting it around in an impossibly strong hold. I think she still must have talons, because I can feel my skin being punctured.

"I brought it for you—" I start, but she silences me with her eyes.

"Did you kill him?" she asks.

I shake my head, thinking she must mean the orc I burned alive. "No! No, I would never offend you. I killed no one. I would not kill unless you requested me to—"

"If you did not kill Thorn, how did you get this?"

"Thorn? Thorn wasn't wearing it."

Her brows raise high and I try to draw back, but it only makes her hold grow tighter. She leans close and smells me. When she draws away I can see disgust on her face. "I have smelled you in his tent."

I feign a blush. "Yes, ma'am. Thorn and I...we love each other."

If I thought this might appeal to her compassion, I was wrong. She clenches her teeth, glaring at me with menace and a swirl of black smoke envelops us both. All the air is sucked from my lungs and I feel as if I am being turned inside out.

CHAPTER 38

Thorn

*W*hen the ground begins to shake, my thoughts shoot to the cave. To my prisoner there and the burden around his neck. I know in my gut: something has gone wrong. Regret washes over me. I waited too long. I've no plan. And Alba...she is at the castle now, in danger.

"Fuck!" I curse myself. I should have gotten her out of here. I've been so selfish, clinging to each moment with her. The second I started to feel for the girl I should have sent her and her loved ones away. I should have protected her.

There's the cry of a beast. Trees snap, I see them fly up into the sky—discarded by something monstrous. "By the Gods," I utter, then I turn back to camp. There's only one person who can help me.

Sprinting at full speed, my thoughts and reality align. Ahead I see Arron running, right for me.

"A dragon," he shouts once close enough.

"*A dragon?* There are no dragons."

"There is a dragon now."

I grip my friend by the shoulders. "Petra?"

He nods. "It must be magic and she is the only one strong enough. I saw it, heading for camp."

"Arron, I must confess—" I search his face, desperate to know I can trust him. He's the only person I can trust, isn't he? "There's a girl. I've fallen in love with her."

He shakes his head, trying to figure out who.

"She's from the castle. She's soft, Arron, delicate. She needs protecting."

He nods with decision. "I'll take care of Petra. You take care of the girl."

I shake my head. "No. Petra is my problem. But I beg you, Arron, you must find my girl. Find Alba."

"How? Where?"

"I meet her in the clearing..." I point back the way I was headed when the world came crumbling down. "If I know her well...she will come searching for me."

"Is she mad?"

"She says she loves me. So yes."

Arron nods. "I will protect her with my life."

And with that, we part ways. Arron heading for Alba and me racing toward camp.

CHAPTER 39

Thorn

I expect pandemonium—bodies, fighting, gore. Instead there is a crowd gathered round the dais and the silence is disarming. I free my sword from its scabbard and the crowd parts. Their milky eyes on me, faces blank.

That's when I see Petra...Petra as I have never seen her before. Her face is haggard, her hair wild, and her eyes... It's so startling that I lower my weapon.

"*You,*" she says, her voice shaking with accusation. Reaching behind her skirts, she drags the struggling body of a woman. Honora. She's got her by the hair—the long black locks hang over her face like a curtain. The camp whore fights to free herself but there's nothing she can do.

"Let her go," I say, feeling more myself than perhaps I ever have. "There's no need to harm that woman."

She laughs, an icy laugh. Shivers run over my skin. "How valiant!" A sudden and rough shake parts Honora's hair and a glint of gold catches my attention. She's got the medallion around her neck.

Petra must see recognition in my eyes and she points a clawed hand at me. "Missing something? I think you must be."

"It's cruel, Petra, to put a thing like that on her."

"Cruel? *Cruel?* You must not be paying attention. It isn't cruelty that I deal in." She squeezes her eyes shut and the madness of the Eternal Princess dawns on me. "I cannot afford to lose. Do you understand that? Do you understand the sacrifices I have made to protect this land? I'm not cruel, Thorn. I'm selfless. More selfless than you could ever comprehend. The fate of this world rests in Pontheugh and you threaten to ruin everything for this?" She shakes Honora.

Poor, pathetic Honora. Her face is contorted in fear, but she still has the capacity to struggle—she is stronger than the orc I left in the cave. She must have found him, I reason. Honora went out there, found the orc, disturbed the medallion...and now Petra is here. I feel pity for the camp whore, but it is my concern over Alba that shakes me to my core. How easily could she be the one in Honora's place?

"We need to find a way out," I say, hoping against hope that reason will get through to Petra... If it comes to a fight I don't know that I stand a chance against her magic.

A hollow laugh escapes her. "There's no way out. The stone shows me every angle and there is only one way: forward." She looks to the castle on the grey horizon.

"I'll get you the castle, Petra. But we have to stop all this bloodshed." I'm thinking of Alba and her people behind the walls.

Petra sneers at me. "When did you become the hero, Thorn?"

My stomach tightens as the magnitude of my crimes dawns on me. If Alba knew what I really was... "I'm no hero. But let me at least do this. Please, Petra, I can get behind those walls, I can get into that castle, I can take it in your name without more needless death. Isn't that what you want? Don't you want to protect the people?"

"I do *everything* for the people."

Slowly, I lower my sword. "Then there's no reason for us to be at odds. You have my allegiance, as you always have."

"I have your allegiance?" She curls a finger under Honora's chin, showcasing my discarded medallion. "Then explain this."

"That medallion is poison and you know it!" I snarl.

"It is a promise. It keeps you from being distracted!" She shakes Honora again, with violent strength that doesn't seem to match Petra's small frame.

"You have no idea what you're talking about."

"You will wear the medallion—"

"I WILL NOT! That thing is a poison on my mind, woman. If you want the castle, I go in with clarity!"

"You do as I say."

"You cannot control everything."

"You don't know how far I'm willing to go."

"Send me in there with a cloud hanging over my head and Pontheugh will never be yours."

She hesitates. I can see it for just a moment in her tight features and hysterical eyes. I pounce.

"Does your stone tell you this is the right path?"

"I have conversed with the stone."

"That is not an answer."

"I am not required to answer to you."

"But you *are* answering, aren't you? The stone hasn't told you this is the way."

"You. It's your fault. The closer you get, the more silent it becomes."

"Perhaps it is time you listen to an actual ally and not a rock around your neck!"

She laughs. "You? An ally? You're a monster, Thorn, and you're only good for one thing: killing."

Her insult hits harder than it should. I wish this wasn't what I was good at. I wish I were a simple man, good at farming, good at loving, good at being a part of a family without driving everyone away. "Please, Petra. Let me do the thing that I'm good at." I sheath my sword.

"There are consequences to your disloyalty."

"There are consequences to everything, Princess."

"You have one day. I'll let you go in with your clear mind—"

"Thank you—"

"No medallion and no camp whore to distract you." With a swift jerk of her arm she snaps Honora's head down so hard it breaks her neck. She falls lifeless and limp.

I gape, thinking more of Alba than the sad woman on the dais. "Why...you didn't have to do that."

"I could smell her in your tent. The place reeked of her. I need you focused, Thorn. You can't allow something so small as a woman to distract you from what's truly important."

Petra pulls the medallion to her with nothing more than a wave of her fingers. It disappears somewhere among her skirts. Walking to the dais, I scoop Honora's body into my arms. I didn't love her. I didn't particularly like her, but damn, how I pity her.

"Don't be angry with me, Thorn," Petra says in a softer tone. "It's for the best. The less you engage with them, the less it hurts."

"Them?"

"The people."

"And these are the people you are trying to protect."

She shakes her head in a sad sort of way. "It's best not to engage. If you love something, love it from afar."

I want to tell Petra she's mad, but I say nothing as I stare up at her ageless face.

"One day. If you don't bring me the King and his daughter..." She scans the army gathered around to watch. "I'll start killing *all* of them. From here to Black Mountain. Do you hear me?"

I think of Ash out there somewhere with Ellyn, perhaps a child with orc blood growing in her belly and I nod gravely.

Petra takes a step back, then another, and another. She tumbles into my throne, her face buried in her hands. She looks exhausted. Black smoke curls and she's gone.

The world is silent and when I turn to face the orcs, they are silent too.

CHAPTER 40

Alba

I know the way of course, to our spot in the clearing. To that spot where Thorn saved my life. But when I get there, I can hardly recognize it. There are gouges scraped up out of the earth, trees torn from the ground and tossed aside. I stumble to a halt, shocked to my core. What could have done this? I search my memories for some story of the Perished Woods I might have heard of as a child. Trolls, orcs, will o' wisps, spiders...nothing that could have done damage like this.

I am surrounded in silence. I bring my arms around me and hug myself tight. I don't know what to do now or where to go. Twilight is falling over the land. *Where is Thorn?* Is he safe? It isn't as if I can go to the orc camp and search for him. No. I had better stay here and wait. He'll come for me. I know he will.

I sneak close to a tree and huddle against it, half from fear and half for support.

Thorn is nothing like Luther. This thing between us...I can *feel* how different it is. This is love. This is the kind of love you hear about in stories. I haven't known him long. But with love like this…it doesn't take long. Wherever he is now, whatever he is doing—he is thinking of me as I am thinking of him. He will come. He will find me. And then…and then we'll run away together. That's what we'll have to do. I can get my coin to Beatrice and Wendy, and Thorn and I will run off. If I have to live in the Perished Woods, I'll do it. Wherever we can go to be safe and be together. We'll run away from this war and live happily ever after—together.

"Thorn…" I whisper. "Please hurry. I need you." I need him by my side. I need to tell him what I've resolved to do—to be with him always.

There's the sound of boots running fast in my direction. Pounding against the ground. *Thorn!* I spin round the tree, showing myself, ready to crash into my love's arms. But it isn't Thorn I run into. It's a monster. A giant. An honest to goodness orc.

I crash into his rock-hard chest. His strong arms grip my shoulders, I crane my neck up and scream. I scream as loud as I can. I try to wrench myself free, but it is as if I am wrestling against solid stone.

"Alba?" He growls my name.

I freeze, wide-eyed. Fear for my own well-being escapes me. I think only of Thorn. This must be the monster who tore up the clearing. This vicious beast must have hurt my Thorn. "I know who you are," I gasp.

He raises a scarred brow.

"You're…*the Orc King.*"

His face hardens. "Are you Alba?"

I hold my chin high. "What have you done to Thorn?" I demand.

He shakes his head at me—underestimating. But I've faced monsters before. I rip one of the battered axes from the beast's leather straps and plunge it in his direction.

"Where is he?" I scream as the beast lurches back, losing his

balance with a look of utter astonishment. He tumbles, clumsily at first and then with practiced athleticism. He bounds back to his feet, keeping a safe distance between us.

"Delicate my ass," he grits out before diving at me. I swing the heavy axe and it collides with something—what, I don't know. I had closed my eyes.

Arms like tree trunks wrap around me, my hand is twisted and the axe falls. I cry out, more from distress than pain. Then I demand once more, "What did you do to him?"

"Thorn sent me here to protect you, you banshee."

I open my eyes, bewildered. "He did what now?"

"Thorn sent me here to watch over you," he growls. "Until he could come."

I relax and the beast lets me go. "You're lying?" I ask carefully.

"No," he hisses. "I'm not lying." He's checking is side. I see there's blood dripping down. Plenty of it.

I suck in a breath. "I've hurt you! Oh no, no, no! I'm so sorry!"

He waves my concern away, but I can see him grimacing.

"No, please. I'm so sorry. I had no idea. I would have never—I just, I had thought you..." I wave my hand at the forest and it's state of disarray.

The orc laughs, shaking his head. "You thought this was my doing?"

I roll a shoulder. "You're the Orc King, aren't you?"

He stops laughing. "No. I am not."

"Well, you're big. Biggest monster...*man* I've ever seen."

"I am a monster," he corrects.

"If you're Thorn's friend then I don't mind what kind of monster you are. Please, can you tell me if he's alright?"

"Last I saw him he was fine."

I peek at the orc's wound. It looks bad. "Where is he?"

"He went after the thing that did this."

TRACY LAUREN

"Why?"

With a troubled gaze, the orc stares at me long and hard. "I don't know."

"But he'll be back?"

"If he survives."

"*If?*"

He waves a hand and drops down onto a freshly unearthed tree. I kneel, to tear away a bit of my underskirts. "What are you doing?"

"That needs bandaging."

"I'm fine."

I shake my head. "It's a lot of blood."

"I've seen more."

"I won't ask about that," I whisper, approaching him with hesitating movements. He doesn't try to stop me, so I wipe away as much of the blood as I can, find the slice, and press the material down over it. "I think it needs pressure. To stop the bleeding. If you let me..."

The orc takes his twin axes, and with suspicious eyes, sets them out of my reach. Then, he holds his arms up, giving me access to properly wrap the wound.

"I wasn't planning on cutting you again."

"I should hope not. You're far too good at it for comfort."

"I've had a bit of practice."

He grunts and I finish tying off the makeshift bandage.

"What's your name?"

"I am Arron. General to the King."

"Oh...and friend to Thorn?"

"His oldest friend."

I try to picture a younger version on the man I love and smile at the thought.

"He's the best warrior in the world," Arron says suddenly. "If anyone can find a way to win this, it will be him."

I kneel beside the giant of a beast. "I don't know what danger Thorn is facing, but we should help."

Arron shakes his head. "We wait. I promised Thorn I would protect you."

"But who will protect him?"

Arron laughs. "Didn't you hear me, girl? He's the best warrior in the world and now that is mind is clear…" He sighs. "He'll be fine. I'm sure of it."

I shift to lean against the tree Arron is using as a bench. "I'm still worried."

"Good. It would be foolish if you weren't."

We sit in silence for a moment, but I can't keep quiet. "I'm going to run away with him."

Arron says nothing, so I look over my shoulder and see him appraising me.

"I decided."

"Did he ask?"

"No. But I don't care. I'll ask."

He chuckles, wiping at his brow. "What did he do to you?"

"He saved me. More than once."

"Ah. Then we have something in common."

I consider Arron. "We can all escape together," I tell him. "I've got friends back at the castle. I need to help them—give them some coin so they can survive. But then we can run away from here."

"From where?"

"From the Orc King and his army."

Arron stares.

"Look, Thorn is a good man. In his heart, he is good. And if you are his friend, then I know you are good too. But this army —this war." I shake my head.

"What of it?"

"It's evil. All this death? We don't need to be a part of it. We don't need to lose our lives over some mad King."

Long and hard, he stares. "Where do you propose we go?"

Sighing, I confess. "I don't know. Anywhere but here."

"There aren't many places for orcs."

"Then we live in the Perished Woods."

"The Perished Woods are cursed."

I sit a little taller. "I've been told my whole life that the Perished Woods are cursed. But I've seen evil out there, in the *land of man*. And I've seen *good* here."

He snorts. "An idealist."

"Don't be mean," I scold. "What's idealistic about wanting to survive? Wanting to find some peace and happiness?"

"It's harder to find than you think."

"Thorn keeps on finding me."

As if I spoke prophecy, there comes a sound. Arron and I are on our feet. He thrusts an axe back into my grip and stands ready to defend me. I hold my borrowed weapon and pretend I'm confident.

The shadows of the impending night are long now. And though I can hear footfalls, I can't make out who they might belong to.

Finally, a figure comes into view. Wide. Unwieldy. Not Thorn?

He steps close enough to see. It *is* my love and he carries a dead woman in his arms. I stifle something between a scream and whimper and rush to his side.

"Thorn!"

With gentleness he hushes me.

Arron takes Thorn's burden and lays the dark-haired woman on a clear patch of earth.

Thorn and I throw our arms around each other, and despite myself, I begin to sob. He clutches me against him, as if he wasn't sure he'd ever see me again. I can feel it in the way he holds me. He wasn't sure he'd make it back. I weep harder.

"I'm here now. I'm here."

"Never leave me again, please?" I beg. He strokes the hair back from my face and looks down at me with troubled eyes. He doesn't answer. "We've got to run away," I insist. "We have to get out of here."

Thorn links his fingers with mine and we all look to the poor dead woman. My throat tightens when I see the loose way her head hangs to one side.

"Who is she?"

"A witch. One of the camp whores," Arron supplies.

"A wretched thing. But she didn't deserve to die."

"Who does?" Arron asks. "But we all die, don't we?"

"Not tonight," I say, tugging on Thorn. "We've got to get out of here," I plead again.

"She wants to run away," Arron explains. "With us."

Thorn looks at Arron. I see the troubled expressions they share.

"Hear me out," I protest.

But Arron speaks for me. "She wants us all to run away from this war and the Orc King. She wants to live in the Perished Woods...with *you*."

Thorn hangs his head. My hands don't leave him. I hold him up as if he might fall. "Alba, no. I'm not what you think I am."

"I know who you are!" I cry. "You're my soulmate. I belong to you—"

"Darling—" He tries to get me to sit, but I won't.

"It's fate that's brought us together. Twice you saved my life. Listen to me, Thorn. I feel it in my bones, we need to get out of here. Please, let me save you."

"You need to get back to Beatrice and Wendy."

"I can give them my coin and then we can be together. We don't need anything grand out here. We can hunt and plant a garden—"

He gives a choked little laugh that holds no humor. In that

rough voice of his he tells me, "You have no idea how much I want that—"

"Then let's go!" I try to drag him by the hand, but he refuses to follow.

"Alba, listen to me."

"No!" I don't want to hear what he has to say. "I'm not going to lose you," I insist. I'm crying again. "I've been so alone. My entire life, I've been alone." I bang my fist against my chest. "It was like I was hollow, Thorn. There was no one in the world for me and I felt it, here. But you changed that. I don't know how to explain what I feel, but there's no denying it. I love you! I've never loved anything like I love you! And I *refuse* to lose this."

He pulls me into his arms and his lips collide with mine. The kiss is hard and passionate—it is all the emotion I was trying to describe packed into one physical action. Any other words are useless.

"I love you," he growls. "You are my soul, Alba; you are my heart. You are every dream I've ever had, every hope. But there are bigger things going on."

"I don't care about anything but you."

"That isn't true. You care about Beatrice and Wendy. They are behind those castle walls and if I don't do something, they'll die tomorrow."

"Why does it have to be you?"

"Who else will save them?"

I stammer, but come up with nothing.

"This is my fault, all of it."

"No! Of course it isn't. You just wanted out of the cursed wood. No one could blame you for that. All this terrible war, it's the King's doing."

Thorn takes up both my hands and presses them to his chest, right over his heart. I can feel it pounding like a drum. Like the orc's war drums tearing through the silence of the night. "Alba...*I* am the Orc King."

CHAPTER 41

Thorn

She blinks at me. "I...I don't understand what you're saying."

"It was me, Alba. I did all of this. I led the army here and wiped out your village. I wiped out all the villages."

"No," she says plainly, as if it simply can't be true.

I cast my eyes to Arron and he gives a nod of confirmation.

Alba starts, "No. That's absurd—"

"I'm a monster, Alba. That's all there is to it. Now I need to get you out of here. You and your people."

"I'm not going anywhere," she contends.

"You are, damn it. There are forces at play here, dangerous forces—"

"I don't care what kind of forces. I'm not going anywhere without you."

"Aren't you listening?" I demand, grabbing hold of her. "I'm evil. I've lied to you!"

"Lied? About what? About being the Orc King? What do I

care if you're a soldier or the commander himself? I knew there was death involved, Thorn, I'm not an idiot."

"You don't belong in a world like this."

"Well, I'm here and I've been here." Her eyes search wildly across my face, looking for insincerity perhaps? But she won't find it in me. "I've had a husband who *really* lied to me. Who used me, beat me, and made me feel like my *soul* was dying. He was a monster, Thorn. Not you."

"If you knew the things I've done—"

"And if you knew all *my* secrets? If you saw me at my lowest moments, would you not love me anymore? Would you think less of me?"

"That's absurd!"

"It's not, I tell you! It's the same thing!"

"You've killed two men, I've killed hundreds."

"I'm not just talking about murder. I'm talking about the weakest versions of myself, when I was alone and frightened, when I compromised my values for others. That's the conversation, Thorn. That's the heart of it. Can you love all of me? Can you forgive me where I've failed? Because I can forgive you. I look in my heart and it's easy. It isn't even a question."

I push away from Alba and cut my hands in a frustrated motion before turning to Arron. "Talk sense into her!"

Instead, he moves closer to Honora's limp body. "What would you have me say?"

"She cannot remain here, with me!"

"Why?" Alba protests.

"Because it is dangerous!"

"It's dangerous everywhere, isn't it?" Arron mutters.

Alba jumps on the comment. "The second time you came to my rescue was in this very spot, from men trying to rape and rob me. *Human* men. Tell me, Thorn, where do you propose I go to be safe?"

"Away from me, that's all that matters."

"You don't care where I go? All you're saying is that I don't belong with you?"

"Yes," I grit out.

"Well, I disagree and I'm not leaving."

"If I have to carry you back to the castle and throw you over the wall myself, you're going!"

"Carry me then! But even if you do, I won't stay."

"Fine! Go somewhere else! Go anywhere else! I don't care as long as it is far away from me. There's a witch coming, Alba, she's the most powerful thing I've ever seen. Powerful and unhinged."

She ignores my words. "I'll kill myself."

My eyes go wide, but I quickly shake off the surprise. "You will do nothing of the sort—"

She hauls up one of Arron's great axes, clumsily aiming it at her neck.

"Stop that, right now!" I shout. "You might hurt yourself!"

"I'll *kill* myself!"

Arron looks on with interest, but he is no help whatsoever.

"You can't kill yourself," I insist.

"I'll do it. If you leave me behind, so help me, I'll kill myself." She lines the blade up with the main artery on her neck and my insides recoil. I dive forward and pull the blade away, angrily tossing it back to Arron.

"Damn it, Alba, you're acting like a...like a *woman!*"

She laughs defiantly. "I'm *your* woman, Thorn! Yours! Do you hear me?"

I want to pull out my hair. "If I'd have known you were crazy—"

"I'm not crazy in the slightest. What I am is *serious.*"

"Have you thought for one second that I was playing?"

"You must have thought I was."

"You can't love an orc, Alba."

"I'm done letting people tell me what to do. I was done with that the night I killed Luther. The fact of the matter is that I love you."

"And yet you threaten to kill yourself? You hang that over my head?"

She rushes forward, crashing into me with desperate eyes. They're filled with tears. "You think I'm stupid," she declares.

"I do not!"

"You do! You think I don't know what it is you're saying? You're making me leave because you believe you're going to die. You're planning on it, as a matter of fact."

"Maybe that's what ought to happen—"

"No!" she cries.

"Is it not what I deserve? After all this death? Don't I deserve to answer for it?"

"To Hell with what you deserve! What do I deserve? Have I not murdered?"

"It isn't the same."

"Let the Gods judge me!"

"You're good, Alba, damn it, don't you see that you're good? You don't know half of the ugly things I've done and you certainly don't belong here—to pay my crimes."

"I'll stay where I want to stay. I'll pay for what I wish to pay for. And I tell you right now, you will *not* go off to your death. Try to and I'll kill myself."

"You've all but captured me and now you're holding me hostage. No. I won't allow this. You have no concept of what you're getting into."

Her hands go to my face and she holds me in place. Alba. A fucking angel...I don't know what she sees in me. "You feel it, don't you?" she asks. "This thing between us?"

"If I said I didn't, would you leave?"

She shakes her head.

I sigh. "Alba, this witch—the Queen of Envercress—she'll kill you with a wave of her hand. She killed Honora because she thought I was distracted by her. What do you think she would do to the woman who..."

"Who what?"

"Who I love, damn it." I pull her hard against my chest, not wanting to let go.

"You feel it," she says, her voice muffled by my embrace.

"Of course I feel it. I don't think I ever felt anything before you and now I can't control myself. This feeling—it consumes me. It's more consuming than...than that damned cursed medallion!"

"That medallion changed you, Thorn," Arron says suddenly.

My eyes snap to him, but my throat is too tight to speak.

"You mustn't blame all this on yourself. The witch, she had you under her control."

"I don't know that for certain. There's so little I can remember...Ash, flashes of you, and Black Mountain, and Alba."

Arron looks down at Honora. "Why did you bring her?"

I shake my head. Staring down at the lifeless body while clinging to my woman. "I couldn't leave her with the others. What would they do? Throw her on the fire? Leave her to rot in the mud?"

"And what will we do?"

"Bury her," I say.

Arron nods. "That is the Thorn I know."

"It's the least—"

"It is more than what most would do."

"And what do *you* propose we should do now?"

He rolls a massive shoulder. "What happened with the Queen?"

"I asked for one more day. I told her there needn't be more bloodshed. I'll go to the castle and get what she asked for. The King and his daughter."

"If you don't deliver?"

TRACY LAUREN

"She starts killing and she starts with the army. She said she'd murder every orc from here to Black Mountain."

Alba gasps.

"Is that so bad?" Arron questions.

"Yes!" Alba cries, snapping her gaze between Arron and me.

"Do you not care for your own life, old friend?"

Arron laughs. "She would have to find me to kill me."

"Fair enough, but my brother is out there somewhere, Ellyn too, and suppose she is with child?"

"There's got to be other orcs, like you. Orcs who don't deserve to die," Alba reasons. I don't tell her what a violent race we are. Resolutely, she adds: "So, all we have to do is give her the King and his daughter."

"No qualms about that?"

"Consider me a desperate woman."

"Yes. If *I* want to appease Petra Gunnora, *I* have to deliver the King of Pontheugh and his only heir—the Princess."

"We are in this together."

"I haven't agreed to that."

"You don't need to," she says with narrowed eyes.

"How did a woman like you become so fierce?"

"A woman like me?"

"Your nature is a delicate one..."

She shakes her head at me. "All women are fierce, Thorn, when pushed."

I press a kiss to the top of her head. Maybe she is a little murderess, but she is still the most precious and gentle thing I have ever touched.

"It's going to be problematic," she says with a sigh.

"What is?"

"Getting to the King."

"I can infiltrate the castle."

"That's fine, but I've been in Pontheugh for weeks now and I haven't seen the King once. Nor his daughter. I was beginning to wonder if they even existed."

"Of course they exist." But the mere statement makes me question myself.

Alba says nothing. I look to Arron and he is silent as well.

"Petra would know if they didn't exist. Of course they exist! Who would rule if they didn't exist?"

"Well, it's the chancellor and the mage—" Alba starts. My mind is reeling.

"What if that's why her stone doesn't speak?"

Alba stares in confusion.

"Some sort of counter magic—from this mage perhaps?" Arron offers.

"I don't know…"

"There's something strange there. I'd bet on it. It's odd that a King, with his kingdom in lockdown, would not speak to the people or even show himself to his guardsmen."

"Hasn't shown himself even to the guardsmen?" I question.

Alba shakes her head.

"That is odd."

"But we have a plan," she says.

"I don't know that we have a plan—"

"You said we will break into the castle, find the King and his daughter and—if possible—deliver them to this Witch Queen of Envercress."

"That is a plan for me. A plan perhaps for me and Arron. But not a plan for the three of us."

"I think you'll have to reconsider."

"If I have to I'll leave Arron to guard over you and I'll go alone."

"I'll kill Arron."

I scoff. "You will not."

Arron lifts his arm to show me the bandaged wound on his ribs. "Came damn near already."

"You lie. Alba did not—"

"She did. She thought I'd done something to you." Arron's tone is as dry as ever and yet I feel somehow that he is teasing me. A ghost of a memory flits through my mind. Perhaps there was a time when we laughed more.

"Well in any case, now you know to watch out for her."

"And if she tries to kill herself?"

"I will," Alba insists.

"Arron, you will stop her."

He gazes at Alba, considering. "I might be able to. I might not."

I throw my head back and sigh. "Was I not King only a short while ago? Aren't the orders of a King meant to be honored?"

"You've been overthrown," Alba tells me. But her words aren't the joke she means them to be. Her tone is far too sad and her eyes, far too wet. "Please, Thorn...I've been so lost. And I've only just found where I'm meant to be. I can't go back to the way things were before. I mean what I say. I'll die without you."

"I can't let that happen."

"And so there is only one path forward," Arron says, deciding for us. "We leave for the castle before dawn. In the meantime, we bury Honora, and we plan."

"I can tell you about the castle. I don't know much but I can give you a general idea of where things are. Possible ways in."

I press another kiss to Alba's head and she leans heavily into it. Truly, I don't know what a precious thing like Alba is doing here with a wretch like me.

CHAPTER 42

Thorn

*A*rron does most the work of burying. I try to say a few words about the woman, but I find it difficult. All I can think of is how easily it could have been Alba up there, in Petra's grasp. My woman must sense my struggle and speaks for me, offering kind words to a terrible witch that she herself never met.

We make a small fire and have a meal of rabbit while Alba draws a figure of the castle in the dirt. "There's a door here, down this alley. It's small, unobtrusive. Matilde would send us to pick up baskets of vegetables. I don't know who put them out. A cook maybe? But it isn't a main exit or entrance for anyone and there was never a guard. I think that's why the baskets were left there. It was a secret or something, that someone in the castle was giving food out. I think that's the best way in. I can't imagine anyone would notice us—not in the dark anyway."

"That's good," Arron tells Alba with an approving nod. She

blushes and her eyes dart to me, twinkling with pride. I keep my arm wrapped around her. *Mine*, is all I can think. Mine, mine, mine. She's a good woman and she's mine. She's a good woman and by some miracle she wants me. I'm probably the worst bastard in the world for wanting to keep her, for ruining such perfection. But I can't help being selfish when it comes to my Alba. I never want to let her go. Fuck castles, and power, and kingdoms. All I want is her.

I press a kiss to her head, terrified of how precious she is. "You should sleep," I tell her.

Her eyes are pleading when they look into mine. "I want to stay up with you."

"Afraid I'll abandon you?"

She shakes her head. "I wouldn't let you." But I know, she is afraid. Hell, I'm afraid. So I pull her onto my lap.

"Sleep, love, and if I move you'll know I'm trying to escape."

She beams a smile at me and wraps arms around my neck before tucking her head against my chest. I caress her back and after a while her breathing becomes slow and even.

Arron stares at the fire and the silence between us feels weighted.

"Maybe you run things for Petra? Once we secure the castle."

He snorts, a wry look in his eyes.

"No desire to be King?"

"I've as much desire to be King as I've desire to die."

I grunt in reply. "Does seem rather empty, doesn't it?"

"Seems like torture. Who would want to sit on a damn throne, everyone looking at you..." He shakes his head in dismay. "Always having to make decisions."

"I suppose I wanted that."

"Well, you always did want something grand."

I raise a brow and Arron shrugs.

"It was the *wrong* grand thing you were after. A distraction I think." His eyes go to the sweet Alba.

"Ash reminded me what was really important."

"He reminded you of what you were looking for from the start. Of course that's only my opinion of it. You were lost for a long time, Thorn; I couldn't get through to you. But when Ash came, there were sparks. I could see it. Sparks that were fighting with that witches curse."

"Why did you follow me out of the Perished Woods?" I ask.

Arron pokes at the fire. "Saved my life more than once in Black Mountain. Ain't got family. You were always closest thing to it." Arron speaks as if it's the most unimportant thing in the world. I get the sense that he *feels* differently however. "Besides, always wanted out of the Perished Woods. Didn't sound so bad at first. Reclaiming man's land, orcs running one of their kingdoms."

"But you changed your mind?"

He curls his lip. "Just feels like we brought Black Mountain with us. I wanted something different and it was more of the same. Tried though. I'll always be glad we tried."

"What comes after?"

Arron snorts again. "Let's just get through tomorrow."

"Do you think we will?"

His milky eyes go to Alba again. "Easy to get through something when you have a reason to."

"Let's give us all a reason. After this, we are farmers, Arron. Together. We find a nice, safe plot of land, and we make our own kingdom. Won't be as adventurous as Black Mountain or going to war with man."

He tosses his stick in the fire. "Like I said, I just want something different. At a certain point, settling down and farming sounds more like an adventure than..."

"All this death and destruction?"

Arron nods. "How about we get through tomorrow with as little death and destruction as possible, just for a change? See what it's like."

"Agreed," I tell him and I bury my nose in Alba's hair, just to breathe her in.

CHAPTER 43

Alba

Thorn's touch wakes me. Gentle fingers pulling my hair back from my face.

"It's time, love."

I blink. It's still dark out and the fire isn't more than embers. I glance around. "Where's Arron?"

"Went back to camp to grab a few weapons and some horses."

"We're alone?" I breathe out.

Thorn nods, but before he can speak I pull his lips to mine. There's a moment of surprise before he takes charge of the kiss. Kissing him is like nothing I have ever experienced.

Luther's kisses, when he bothered, were harsh. His stubble cut at my face. And they never felt like affection. They felt more like a cruel taunt.

There were a few other boys I kissed when I was young. Just little things—a peck that gave a foolish girl a thrill. But when Thorn kisses me, it is entirely different.

Thorn's kisses make me feel like a woman. I feel desired. I

feel soft and feminine. I feel owned in the way I *want* to feel owned—as if he has taken full possession of me. I trust him with my body. I feel safe enough to let go, knowing I'm in the hands of a real man, knowing that he loves me.

Fear dictated most things with Luther. But I feel no fear with Thorn. I feel completely and utterly safe...right down to my soul. His hands grip me like I'm precious.

"You'll never forget to love me?" I ask, my lips still pressed against his.

He squeezes me tighter. "I've been searching for you, Alba. All my life I've been searching for you."

"It took so long," I say, nearly weeping.

"Gods, it took too long. I needed you; do you know that?"

"I do. I know." I know because I needed him too. Desperately.

He pulls away just enough to gaze into my eyes with unfiltered emotion. "How could I ever forget to love you? You are everything to me. The only thing that matters."

"And you won't leave me?"

He shakes his head solemnly.

"I swear, I will kill myself if you do."

"I know you would."

"How?"

"Because I'd do the same."

"Are we crazy?"

He grins in a sad sort of way, a way that highlights all the beautiful scars across his face. "I might very well be."

I run the pad of my thumb down the scar that runs from his brow to his jaw. "I don't mind."

He swallows hard and as vicious and battle worn as my orc looks, I know there is more. I know he has a tender heart and that he is as desperate for love as I have been.

"Let me love you," I plead.

He laughs. "You have my permission."

I pull him down toward the mossy earth. "Like this."

He looks out into the night. "Arron…"

"Do we have time?"

Thorn looks at me and a low growl rises in his throat. "Yes."

Then, he is more animal than man. He is like a wolf devouring me. His hands push up my skirt and slide over my thighs. He touches me as if my hips alone are the most erotic thing in the world. As if the mere sensation of my skin against his sustains him, body and spirit. We nourish each other. I throw my head back and he attacks my throat. His breath is hot and it makes my skin tingle in excitement. I wrap my legs around his waist and he fights to tear the front of his pants open.

"I need you," he tells me. "This time is about need. Next time, I will explore every inch of you."

I nod, feeling every bit as needy. I think we might very well die today. And if we do, I need this. I need it very much.

Thorn slows and unlaces the front of my dress. My breasts fall free. Pink nipples pebble in the chill of the night. I arch my back and he kisses me there. He runs teeth and tongue over me. He does it with passion and hunger. I moan and cling to him. Nothing could feel so good as being desired in the same deep way that I desire.

He fits his cock against my pussy. I'm wet and I wiggle, sliding his hot manhood over my soft lips. He groans and it makes me melt into him. His cock sinks deeper and deeper. I whimper at the girth. The delicious girth of him…

"You feel so good," he tells me. "You must be made for me."

I nod. "I am."

I wrap my arms around him and he thrusts into me, his cock sending thrilling shivers up my back and down my arms and legs. My heart swells. Thorn's hands search me. They hug and hold me. I notice him inhaling deeply of my scent. In every motion, there is a wave of passionate love. And even though the threat of death lingers in the back of my mind, I don't think I have ever been so happy in my life. If this is all the happiness I get before I go to my grave, it is enough.

His mouth is teasing one of my tits when I cum, his hands gripping my ass. I cry out.

"I can feel you," he growls, pumping harder. "I can feel my woman's pussy squeezing. Did I make you cum, Alba? Did you cum for me?"

I half scream his name and he lets his own pleasure come to a climax. Thorn cums so hard I can feel it too. A wave of wet heat. The pulsing of his cock. Pleasure washes over me.

Slowly our bodies grow still. Thorn hugs me against him and I think I'd be happy to stay like this forever. Let the forest grow around us. Thorn and I could lie here for eternity, just holding on.

"I filled you with my seed," he says.

I wiggle. "I can tell."

"You know what that means, don't you?"

I raise my head to give him a droll look.

"I just don't want you to be surprised if..." His words trail away.

"If I become pregnant? I know how conception works, Thorn. I'm not an imbecile."

"No, I didn't mean...I just want you to be sure."

I smile at him and he nods.

"We are sure."

There's the sound of someone approaching followed by a whistle. Thorn returns the call then shouts, "Just a moment!"

He helps me right my skirts and retie my bodice then produces a scrap of cloth.

"To clean with," he says, offering it to me.

But I don't want to clean his seed away. I want to feel the memory of him, and maybe it's primitive of me, but I want to know who I belong to. Thorn left his mark and I want it to stay.

I squeeze his hand, but don't accept the cloth. Thorn calls for Arron and he appears from out of the darkness laden with weapons, including a belt for me that has six blades fitted into it —five knives and one short sword.

"That's a lot of knives," I note, wide-eyed.

"They're easy to lose," Arron says. "If you have to leave one in a body, you know you have another to fall back on."

I nod with severity. I will kill for Thorn.

"Hopefully, it doesn't come to that. I want to avoid needless death at all cost," Thorn says.

"With the exception of the King and his daughter," I point out.

"Their fate might be something else."

He answers the question in my eyes.

"The Queen has a garden where she keeps her victims."

"Oh, well that doesn't sound so bad."

"She turns them to statues or traps them in ponds. Things like that."

"Oh, my…" That is bad.

"Not us though. It won't happen to us."

I nod, agreeing with him. Thorn puts out the last of the dying embers from our fire and Arron leads us to the horses. Dawn draws ever nearer and we ride toward Pontheugh.

CHAPTER 44

Thorn

*W*e help Alba mount the wall and leave our horses tied off where they can't be seen by the guards. Arron brought with him two heavy cloaks, which we hide our appearances with. But it seems hardly necessary. Behind Pontheugh's walls the city is sleeping.

A few beggars make their beds in the alleyways and we see only two guards in the distance, posted by the main gate.

"Many have deserted," Alba whispers. "With the King silent…there isn't much faith."

Lights in taverns are lit, warmth exudes.

"Why don't they all leave?" Arron asks.

"People have been leaving. In droves. The ships are overwhelmed. My friends and I haven't been able to secure passage. And with the farms not sending any food—"

"There are no farms left," I point out. My army saw to that.

Alba gives me a soft smile and places a comforting hand on my arm. So easily does she chip away at all my hardness.

CAPTURED BY THE ORC KING

"That's the Copper Coin," she whispers, a bright grin lighting up her face. "It's where I've been staying with my friends." The smile falls a bit. "If we can...I have the coin I want to get to Beatrice and Wendy. It's hard for women on their own to get a start."

"We won't forget," I assure. Arron makes note of the building and we proceed silently down the alleyways, Alba leading us.

Eventually we near the castle itself. I gaze up at it, searching for some ghost of my past obsession. Some internal desire to dominate this place. But there is none. I want only to be done with it, to escape with my woman and start life anew.

"There," Alba whispers, pointing to a wooden door, nearly obscured by shadow.

"Are you sure?" I ask.

She nods vigorously.

Indeed, there are no guards to be seen. Arron tries the door, but it is bolted on the inside. He motions for Alba to give a knock and she does. Only silence follows. Arron puts his finger to his lips and then uses his shoulder to bust the door in. It is a loud endeavor.

I expect a guard to call out. I expect hurried footsteps on stone. An alarm being sounded. But there is nothing. We step into a dark and silent room that smells of mildew. Alba strains her eyes to see.

"Everything look normal?" I ask.

She shrugs. "I've never seen inside. The baskets are always just waiting just in front of the door."

"Where are the guards?" Arron wonders.

"The men at the gate have been there for weeks. I've seen them sleep in shifts."

Alba finds a torch and we light it, holding it out to show us a long, stone stairway. There's a stillness here that I don't like.

Up the stairs we go. I expect at any moment to be discovered, or at the very least to cross paths with a guard. But we get to the top of the stairs and to a service door without encountering so much as a sound.

I take care with the next door, but we find this one unlocked. It leads into a massive kitchen that is just as cold and silent as the corridor was. There aren't even lingering odors from last night's dinner.

"What is this?" Alba asks. But neither Arron nor I know.

We find our way out of the kitchen and into a massive dining hall. Our footsteps echo and Alba treads ahead to wipe her finger over the long table. With a frown, she holds it up to show us. In the light of the torch we see...*dust*.

"Maybe I was misinformed, but I always thought castles were well-kept. They have enough maids, don't they?" she queries.

"It seems as if no one has been here in a while. A long while."

Double doors lead us out of the dining room and onto the main floor. There isn't a single candle or torch lit. Nor is there the whisper of a guard or nobleman.

"It's deserted," Alba says, her face horrorstricken.

Arron and I hardly believe it, and my general lets out a wild call. It echoes off tall ceilings. All three of us brace ourselves, weapons drawn. But no one comes.

Alba takes the torch and sets to work lighting candles until the hall is bright.

"What now?" she asks, trouble in her eyes.

"We search," Arron says.

"That's all there is to do."

We make our way up an elaborate staircase. The walls are marble and gold, with statues carved into them. Paintings hang in alcoves. The floor is carpeted in red. Crystal chandeliers hang in abundance. And all of this opulence is like a nightmare, without a soul here living among it.

Door after door, we come up empty. Arron takes one hallway and Alba and I take another.

"Look!" she cries after sometime. My eyes are brought to a set of double doors, more ostentatious than anything else we've seen. "Do you think that might be the King's rooms?"

"Only one way to know." I push the doors open. They creak heavily and dust swirls in the light of our fire.

Alba walks in and begins drawing back curtains. Outside, the sun has broken over the horizon. My love pauses her work to grimace at the bed with me. It is empty, but the covers are all torn back as if someone left in a hurry.

"I always make my bed," Alba says. "I do think Kings have people to set things nice on a daily basis. Seems odd to be left like this."

"I agree."

"Did everyone just...*leave?*" she asks. "Did they flee? Abandon the peasants to be taken by the orc army?" She's tearing curtains open as she asks, clearly perturbed. "It's low. There are women and children out there, the elderly. How could a King just leave people to die?"

She yanks a curtain back, but instead of a window, on the other side there is a door. She gasps in surprise when she sees it. I rush to her side and fling the door open. The corridor is tight and dark. Cobwebs hang and the dust here is even thicker than it is everywhere else in the castle.

"Careful," I say, as Alba follows me in. She hitches up her skirts so they don't catch the old spiderwebs.

The corridor is long and winding. Eventually we get to a small door that even Alba has to duck through.

There's a bed—a made up one. That's the first thing we see upon entering. But the air in this room is stagnant. Terribly so. It has been some time since anyone occupied the rest of the castle, but even longer since anyone has been in here.

TRACY LAUREN

Alba gets to tearing open curtains again. I scan the room as she does and quickly come to a halt.

There's a large glass case.

"Alba," I call to her. She hears my tone and turns. A gasp escapes her when she sees what I do.

"Is that what I think it is?" she rushes to my side, linking her fingers with mine. Together we approach the casket.

Alba utters a little gasp, covering her lips.

"It's the Princess, isn't it?"

Inside the case is a young woman. Perhaps near in age to my own beautiful Alba. She has been dead for a while, though preserved decently. You can see it though, in the flat tone of her hair, in the hollows of her cheeks, the long nails gripping a crown against her breast.

Alba utters a curse and my eyes snap to her.

"The Envercress witch. This is what she wanted, isn't it? I mean, this is *who* she wanted."

"Yes. But I don't think she wanted her dead. Not to start with anyway."

Alba frowns. "What does she want with them? The King and the Princess, I mean?"

"I don't know for certain, but blood magic is powerful. Even more powerful if the blood belongs to royalty. I think she needs them for her spells."

"Will a dead Princess work?"

"I'm not sure."

"But the missing King is another problem."

"It is."

Alba sighs heavily. "We find Arron, tell him what we found and then we search the rest of the castle for clues as to where the King might have gone."

"I only have until nightfall."

"Then we better get to work. Unless you have a better plan?"

I consider. "We make a run for it."

Alba turns the idea over. "We search first, if it gets dire, then we run. " She draws up short. "What about the witch's threats? Will she begin killing people if you don't deliver?"

"She will."

"But we won't fight. We'll run?"

"I haven't decided yet," I confess.

She nods. "That's fair. Come on. Let's go find Arron."

CHAPTER 45

Alba

The next hours pass quickly and uneventfully. We find nothing but empty rooms. There seems to be evidence that treasure was packed and a group fled toward a private access to the great lake.

"How long ago did they desert us?" I demand, furious at this point. The position of the sun in the sky is inescapably pressing. We'll have to leave soon. The thought is on all of our minds, I'm sure of it.

"Perhaps she will be happy with the Kingdom alone," Arron suggests, but he doesn't sound convinced by his own words.

I pace, thinking of the dead Princess in her casket. "We should leave the body out, so she can find it and hopefully realize for herself what's gone on here."

Arron rises and strides from the room. I stare after him.

"Does he need help?"

"It will come down to a fight," Thorn says, his rough voice sounding far away.

"She's stupid," I say.

His eyes smile when he looks at me.

"This is the fault of Pontheugh's King. If she wants to kill you over it then she's foolish and vindictive. Like a spoiled child insisting on having what she wants. It isn't as if you can materialize this King, or bring the Princess back to life."

"She's losing her mind. I could see it. She was consumed, like I had been when I wore her medallion. I think that might be the cost of magic like this."

"I've heard magic always has a cost."

Thorn nods, still staring out the window, across the great lake, to the dark blight on the countryside. His army and their path of destruction. I join him.

"It might have been your sword, Thorn, but she was the one spurring you."

"I don't mind taking the blame, love. There's a thousand things I could have done differently. I let her drive me to my madness."

I run my hand over the back of his neck, trying to soothe him. He smiles and I melt my body against his.

Arron returns a short while later. "It's done."

"What now?"

The sun is dropping so quickly. This is nearly the time I went looking for Thorn yesterday. I was out on the other side of the bridge when the whole world started to shake. It was Petra Gunnora, I know that now. The witch Queen of Envercress.

"I've got to get my coin to Beatrice." I pull the pouch free from its hiding place along my belt.

"Let's do it and go," Arron says.

"Go where?"

Thorn answers. "Deep into the Perished Woods. It's our only chance."

I nod, and just as we turn to start for the door, there's a great quaking in the distance. The three of us look out the window. I draw in a sharp gasp. Something, out in the muddy field, is growing at an inhuman rate.

"She's turning back into a dragon!"

My brows rise high. *"A dragon?"*

Thorn has my hand in his and before I have time to process a single thought, we are racing through the castle.

"We should have left earlier," Thorn laments. But I don't agree. We tried our best here. We searched for answers. We did as right as we could by the cruel Queen Petra.

Running through the castle is like a nightmare. Every room, every hall, from top to bottom, is vacant. Only the candles I lit make this place seem half alive. But it is more dead than anything else. The castle echoes memories of death. They are practically coded into the very walls. I long to be free of this place, but we can't seem to run fast enough.

Finally, we make it to the main doors. Still clad in his cloak, strong Arron uses his massive shoulder to push them open. Out in the courtyard, I see the place he moved the glass casket to. In the shade of a flowering tree, yet still visible for anyone who might come looking. A feeling of affection for the beast fills me.

Just as suddenly, however, my coin purse is ripped from my grasp.

"Arron!" I cry.

He doesn't look back. I nearly stumble to a halt, but Thorn pulls me onward. Veering me in a different direction from Arron.

"The Copper Coin," is all Thorn says.

I shake my head. "He can't go there alone. They'll…"

"He will meet us at the horses. If we make it to the horses…"

Suddenly, the last of the sun is blocked out as the shadow of a dragon falls over us.

CHAPTER 46

Thorn

I throw Alba behind me and shout, "Get back to the castle!"

Precious woman. She ignores my demand and pulls the short sword from her belt, holding it in front of her as she trembles like a leaf—her eyes on Petra's dragon form the entire time.

"Get out of here," I insist again—necessity requiring me to keep my focus on Petra.

"I'm with you," is all Alba says. She's too brave for her own good. Or perhaps too scrappy. She was born a soft woman and this world has forced her to fight. I've seen the ways she's fought for herself and now she wants to fight by my side. I'm humbled. I don't deserve her in the least.

I scan the courtyard, searching for a place to hide her. I've got to hide her away before Petra—

The dragon lands on a stone archway—blocking our path down to freedom. She lets out a vicious cry. In the distance the screams of villagers can be heard. I think that soon the last of the guardsmen will come. What will Petra do then?

She fumbles on the arch and stones come hurtling down. Massive stones. They crash into the ground; Alba and I are sprayed with debris. I push my woman back just as the top half of a stone figure comes careening toward us. Petra is unhinged. Her wings stretch to their full expanse as she tries to keep her balance and she snaps wildly in all directions. Finally, she catches sight of me.

Black smoke curls. I see through the magical guise, as if peering through a veil. I can see Petra and I can see the dragon. Moreover, I can see the stone.

"The Princess is dead!" I bellow, my sword still out in front of me. I incline the dragon's attention toward the casket.

What have you done? It's a screech that I hear only in my mind. But I think Alba must hear it too, because she drops to the ground and covers her ears.

"I didn't kill her. I searched the castle. It's empty save for the corpse. The King is gone. He's fled. Abandoned his people."

The dragon screams a terrible scream into the sky. The grey clouds overhead churn and swirl. A wind stirs up and everything seems to be spinning.

Lies.

"No," I tell her. "It's the truth. It shouldn't matter though. The castle has no monarch. It's yours for the taking."

I needed the King! I needed his heir, his blood, and now I have nothing! You did this to me. You plotted against me, you tried to foil my plans, from the start you were against me, working against me, I'll kill you, I'll kill everything you love, I'll kill every orc on this planet, I'll burn this kingdom to the ground and start it fresh, the King, I needed the King, I needed the Princess...

Her thoughts bombard me. Alba screams, clutching at her temples and writhing as if in terrible pain. Far away, I hear more screams.

"Stop this!" I cry, and I jump onto the base of the stone arch, running up it like a stair. I search the clouds of my memories for reference. I've fought awful things before, haven't I? Surely I've fought something like this in the belly of Black Mountain. That place is the gateway to Hell. The birthplace of all full-blooded orcs. I survived there for how long? Yes, surely I've fought a demon or something like this and survived. Surely...

I throw myself through the air, my sword overhead, I bring it crashing down onto Petra's shoulder. I may as well have hit stone. Pain shoots through my arms and my sword flies back. I fall. The tiled courtyard is unforgiving.

Petra shifts, nearly falling from her perch. Her long neck bends down in my direction and her great jaws snap at me. I roll back and out of the way, but my sword is left behind. My eyes go from the shining bit of metal to the dragon. Wind whips my hair. Leaves and branches swirl round the courtyard. Petra prowls closer, descending from the arch. She paws her way right on top of my blade and I'm reminded of a cat, readying itself for the pounce.

And just when I think it might happen, a rock hits Petra right in the snout. She flinches, swatting helplessly at her own face. Another rock hits, and another. With surprise, I see Alba is on her feet issuing this assault on the dragon. It buys me the distraction I need.

Not wasting the opportunity, I roll forward, grabbing up my sword as I do. In one fluid motion, I come up and bring my blade crashing into the big rounded scale on Petra's chest, the one concealing the stone. It's a glamor, nothing more. I know what lies inside.

There's a crack, like thunder. The sky seems to open up and all the wind is sucked straight up into it. Alba screams, but the sound is carried away. All that can be heard is the rushing. Black smoke issues all around the dragon, the veil lifts and returns. Her face is shock, horror. She clutches at her chest. And just when I think she will fall back into the form of a woman— everything grows still. The wind stops and the dragon remains.

The promise of death is in her eyes, but her gaze is shifted away from me and onto my dear Alba.

"No!" I scream and I attack. This time, her scales are no stronger than a basilisk's and my blade plunges into them. Still, she is a massive and mighty thing. She twitches, and with her great tail, she swings me away. I'm thrown into a defunct fountain. Alba screams, not the scream of a cowering woman, but a fierce battle cry, and I scramble to get to her. Sweet girl, after all she's been through, she doesn't know how soft she still is.

And just as I've recovered myself, just as I'm ready to attack once more, just as Alba dives for the dragon, her tiny blade in hand—arrows come flying into the courtyard.

The guard, what's left of them, they've arrived. Hope swells in my chest and with every bit of energy and strength in my being, I make my way between Alba and the dragon.

Petra rears up on hind legs. Arrows tear through her thin and leathery wings.

You don't understand, you fools, you don't understand, who will save you? Who will protect you? No one loves you as I do...

I crash my sword into the stony scale one last time. In this instance, when it cracks, I can see slivers of light trying to burst through. The cry that escapes Petra is a death wail, a cry of pure sorrow. The black smoke rushes around her. She falls to the ground, shifting like the reflective surface of water, from woman to dragon, dragon to woman.

Her crazed eyes finally seem to take in the casket and she half slithers to it in desperation. Wrapping an arm around it, smoke envelops them both. They vanish.

Alba and I stand there, breathless, staring at the spot where the dragon once was. But not for long. For we can feel the heavy weight of eyes on our backs.

I turn to face two dozen castle guards.

Alba takes up my cloak from the ground, desperately trying to wrap it around my shoulders, but it is too late.

"An orc," someone says, anger in their tone.

Alba jumps in front of me before another word can be spoken, her arms held up in a halting motion. "This orc just helped save Pontheugh!" she cries, her voice trembling. "It isn't the orc army we need to worry about. It was the witch at Envercress! She possessed the orcs and drove them here to kill and to take the castle. She wanted the blood of the King and Princess."

"Where is the King?"

"Gone," Alba answers. "The castle has been abandoned for weeks." She doesn't mention the dead Princess.

"Abandoned his people?"

"Yes," Alba says gravely. "And if it weren't for this orc, the whole kingdom would have been lost."

"An orc killed my brother," one man shouts. He's got a white-knuckled grip on his sword.

"Burned the village I came from," another says.

"Alba," I try to caution her, but she does not heed me.

"Not this orc! Today, this orc saved all of us."

One of them steps forward, just a faceless human to me, with a ragged and tired look about him. I sense recognition between Alba and this man. He nods to her.

"We all saw what we saw. There's no denying that. That dragon turned into a woman. Now, I don't know if we could have stopped her on our own. But I can bet not all of us would have made it home if it would have been human against beast. And I *did* see this orc finish her off."

"Orcs can rot in—"

"Now," the guard goes on. "I'm going to look out this way toward the village, I'm going to do that for about a minute. And when I turn around I'm going to search that damn castle to see who's in charge around here. If some of the people who helped defeat the dragon happen to be gone, well, that's no concern of mine. I'm concerned with Pontheugh and the carrying on of its

King and citizens. And anyone who don't belong here might as well be getting on their way."

With finality, he shoves his sword into its scabbard and crosses his arms over his chest as he stares out toward the great lake. One by one, the other men begrudgingly turn. Alba grips me by the arm and together we run back toward the side entrance to the castle that we came in through.

"I could have bested them," I tell her.

"I know that just as well as they did. Why do you think they're all staring at that stupid lake?"

CHAPTER 47

Alba

We make our way to the spot where we left our horses. Arron isn't there, but his stallion still is. The minutes pass agonizingly slowly. Inside the walls of the castle, there is mayhem—screaming and people running about. The bridge across the great lake is flooded with people trying to escape—they think the war has come, or perhaps they saw the dragon and don't know that particular threat has passed.

"We can't stay here much longer," Thorn says, his features tight.

"Arron—"

He readies my horse for me. "We go back to the clearing, last night's camp. When he's able to, he will meet us there."

I don't want to go, but I fear for my love's safety as well. Orcs aren't welcome in Pontheugh. I'm sure he could best a dozen tired guardsmen, but if he were swarmed by an angry mob? Reluctantly, I accept aid up onto my horse and Thorn mounts his own.

"Arron will meet us there," he promises and I nod in agreement. Arron is big and strong. He will escape. We will all escape together.

Thorn in his cloak, we make our way to the bridge, taking special care riding alongside the masses trying to escape. There are so many who are dirty and injured. Thin refugees from the orc raids scramble away from Pontheugh.

"Where are they going?" I wonder.

"The docks up the lake?"

"There aren't enough ships, if there's anything at all."

"The panic will settle," Thorn assures. "When they see they have nowhere to go they will return to their homes."

Finally, we make it to the end of the ever-so-long bridge. Those escaping Pontheugh go left up the path that leads to the ocean's shipping docks. Thorn and I go straight, continuing onward toward the trees.

I cast eyes over my shoulder, searching for another cloaked rider, but there are only people. Hordes and hordes of people. And no Beatrice, no Wendy, no Matilde, no Merry, no Agnes. No familiar faces at all.

We reach the tree line and cross through it, finding our spot quickly on horseback. Neither of us dismount however. We sit atop our horses, waiting, anxiety making our bodies tense.

"You're sure he will know to come there?"

"I'm sure," Thorn promises.

But time passes and night falls. Eventually, Thorn jumps down and reaches a hand up to help me.

"I should build a fire," he says, pressing his waterskin into my hands. I take a sip and pass it back to him. We do three rounds of this, staring into each other's eyes, both of us unable to speak our fear aloud.

"A fire would be nice," I agree, scanning our surroundings. Though they are far away, I can still hear the citizens of Pontheugh, a cry here and there, the gentle hum of conversation, feet stumbling down the packed earth path.

Thorn gets to work rebuilding last night's fire.

Before it's lit, I sniff the air. "Smells like smoke."

He grunts. "It's coming from camp."

My brows lift. "Oh? The orc camp?"

He nods, is expression grim.

"Will…will you go back there?"

"No. There is nothing for me back there."

"No friends?"

"I had only Arron."

"No…lovers?"

He freezes, his eyes locked onto my face. "Only you, Alba. All my life, there has only been you."

"Surely you've had other lovers."

"You redefine the role, my dear."

My heart stirs and I go to him, slipping my arms round his waist. Thorn holds me tenderly.

"You're precious," he whispers, over and over again, his hands running over my hair.

"Were you scared?"

I can feel him nod. "Yes. Very. Were you?"

I laugh. "Intensely."

"I couldn't tell."

Grinning, I look up at Thorn, the Orc King, the warrior who defeated a dragon before my eyes. "You lie."

He beams a wicked smile back at me. "Never. Your bravery moved me, Alba. Your willingness to stand by my side."

"It's all I've ever wanted in life, to stand by someone. To be welcomed to do so."

His hands cup my face and I feel as precious as he declares me to be. "I've longed for the same. You have no idea how I've longed for the same."

"Will you kiss me, Thorn?"

"Promise to marry me first."

I nod vigorously. "I promise, with all my heart, I promise."

"Promise to be with me always."

"Yes, I'd like that very much. Please."

"Be my family, Alba, and I'll be yours. Every day, from this moment on, it is me and you."

Tears well up in my eyes. My heart aches with joy…and with grief. It is like a very old wound is just starting to heal. I surrender to it. I lean into the joy.

"You've captured my heart, Thorn."

"And you have captured mine."

Finally, he kisses me—long and passionate. And I know, this is where my story begins—with happily ever after.

CHAPTER 48

Thorn

The night passes without silence. There are screams, angry and arguing voices, rustling in the trees not far away. Alba dozes, but wakes with a start every few minutes asking for Arron. He doesn't come.

When dawn arrives, she asks. "What will we do?"

I don't know. But I say, "We'll have to check the camp."

"And check to see if his horse is gone?"

I agree, but through the long night anyone might have taken it to make their own escape.

"The problem is, I don't want you near camp."

"Yes. That is a problem, because you've promised to always be by my side."

"Well, I suppose I've got to show myself to be an honest man for my wife."

Alba rewards me with a smile so bright I think I can see stars in her eyes.

I put her on my horse with me and make sure she has her knives, then we ebb slowly toward my old camp.

I don't plan to draw too near; I'm looking only for some kind of sign or indication that Arron has been through—however slim the chance. But I find something quite unexpected.

Alba strains her eyes, shielding them from a dim sun struggling to break through a haze that's been present for...as long as I can remember. "That doesn't look right," she says, and she isn't wrong.

To her, the camp appears vacant. But to my half-orc eyes, I can see grey bodies littering the mud. With a heavy sigh I tell her, "We have to go to the camp."

"Won't it be dangerous?"

"I doubt there will be much, if any."

"Do you think Arron is there?"

"I hope not."

When we get close she sees the devastation. Though I don't know if devastation is the right word—for there were no good men among them. Regardless of their morals, they are all dead now. My army was slaughtered by Petra Gunnora—before or after our fight, I do not know.

"We should check them," she whispers, staring at bodies face down in the mud. "See if there are any survivors."

"Noble of you," I whisper back. "But I can't allow it."

We comb the camp and find no one alive. More importantly, we find no sign that Arron has been through.

"Back to the castle then, to see about his horse."

"And then?" I ask.

"And then back to the clearing."

I sigh.

"Don't give up on him, Thorn."

I nuzzle my woman. "I won't." Even if we don't find him, I won't give up.

And we don't find him. Arron's horse is gone, but that could mean anything. He isn't back at the clearing either. We wait through another night, but can wait no longer. The castle guards ventured out into the decimated orc camp to start burning all the bodies. Alba and I are forced to leave, lest we be discovered.

"Is there somewhere we can go that Arron might think to check?"

"There might be. But my memories..." I shake my head, angry with myself. "If only I could remember a place that he and I visited together or at least spoke about."

"Think with this," she tells me, her small, pale hand over my heart.

I close my eyes and think, think, think. I search my heart for the right place to start the rest of our lives—someplace we could make beautiful...*together.*

"There's one place. I don't know if I told Arron about it, but it's all I can think of."

"Where?"

I wince. "It's not beautiful. *Yet.*"

"I don't care where we go, as long as it's together."

"It's the place where I grew up...with my brother."

"You have a brother?"

"It's a long story and not a very good one, I'm afraid."

"Will I meet him?"

"I don't think I will ever see him again."

Alba shakes her head, not comprehending.

"When I was in my madness, cursed by a medallion Petra forced me to wear, I hurt my brother. I was cruel to him and the woman he loved—"

"That's not your fault—"

"I think it is," I tell her. And I do. I think I could have done better for Ash. I think I should have.

"Growing up, Ash was all I had."

"What about your mother? Your father?"

I shake my head. "My mother was a witch and my father an

orc. He came only a few times and then…he never came again. But my mother…"

Alba squeezes my hand. "My father hated me," she explains in a knowing kind of way and I see that she understands. "You had Ash."

"I had Ash. But we grew apart. We went our separate ways. And when I found him again…" I shake my head. "That's all done now. There's no changing it. But I think I would like to go back to the place I came from."

"Yes," Alba says. "We can do that."

"I want you to know though, it was never a place of happy memories for me. It was dark, and sad, and lonely—"

"We can change that."

"It's already changing, Alba. When I look back at it now, I don't see the things I was lacking—the mother who hated her sons and cared more about magic. I look back and I see me and my brother—playing together, I see myself teaching him to throw knives, and to use a bow. I see the times we were sick or injured and cared for each other. I remember fishing with him in streams and scavenging for mushrooms. There was good there, Alba, lots of good that I was too blind to see. But it's all different now. I'm different. I think if we go back there, we can bring light to it. I think we can make it a home. We can clear the trees and start our own little farm, raise our children where my brother and I raised each other."

"We can teach them to throw knives and use a bow?" Alba gives me wry grin.

"We can teach them to farm and to fish, we can teach them how to be happy—a skill I am only just learning."

Alba throws her arms around me, nothing but excitement in her voice. "It's perfect, it's everything I ever wanted!"

"You wanted to live in the Perished Woods?" I tease.

"I wanted to live happily ever after."

I hug my woman back. "Me too."

EPILOGUE

Thorn
Many months later...

The house was grey when we came upon it. Aged and falling apart. Alba looked at it like a diamond in the rough. I can remember that day so well. The valley my mother's shack stood in was dark even in my memory—overgrown with trees, a hundred-year-old blanket of leaves carpeting the land. It was even worse after years of abandonment. But Alba saw a blank canvas. Alba saw a future.

Her excitement drove me. We started on the shack. Swept out the leaves and cobwebs, disposed of all the magics my mother had left behind. I built new furniture from fallen trees, Alba painted windowsills and planted flowers. Then, we turned to the land.

Clearing the trees brought light in. Sunshine—a commodity I once thought rare for orcs. Then, we began to plant. I had no idea what I was doing. Alba declared she was known for being quite poor at gardening. And together we managed to kill our first crop of beanstalks. But to our surprise, the potatoes took hold. Carrots and onions too.

We crossed paths with an orc family one day, orcs who hadn't ventured out of the Perished Woods when I called for an army. They remained behind...to farm. We talked at length about the soil, I learned much, and then the beanstalks began to grow. After that it was cabbage, and radishes, cucumber, and squash.

Alba and I had our first good harvest—enough for a vegetable feast. That's another night I remember well. Staying up so late that the candles died on us—talking, laughing, eating our fill and then eating some more. It's the night we conceived.

Time went on. Her belly grew. The garden turned into something resembling a true farm. And those orc neighbors, we discovered there were more of them, and not so far away. Families, like ours. With young children. Strange to see the neighbors' boys playing together by the stream. Three of them. I think of Ash and Arron often when I watch those boys play. They're happy. And I pretend that Ash, Arron and I all grew up happy together. Or at least, I wonder what it would have been like. I wonder what it will be like for our children. Will their memories be bright and joyful? Certainly not dark and clouded like my own. No, not with a mother and father and a household full of love.

Shovel in hand, I smile down at my work. It's back-breaking and I couldn't be happier. I certainly beats fighting all the time. The sun beats down on me all day long. I come into the house with filthy boots and filthier hands. And Alba loves on me, pulling off my dirty shoes and heating water for me to wash. Still, she looks at me with stars in her eyes, as if she can hardly believe how lucky we have been. And I marvel at it all as well.

"Daydreaming?" Alba calls, baby Bea on her hip.

"You caught me," I say with a grin.

"What are you thinking about, handsome?"

My smile grows wide. She's mad. No one else in all the world would call me handsome, not with a scarred face like the one I've got. But Alba says it and she believes it. Bless her, she actually thinks I'm handsome. "Children."

"This one?" She pats Bea on the head. "Or this one?" she asks, patting her still flat belly.

"A little of these two wonders and a little of the past," I tell her.

Her smile softens. "Ah. Ash?"

"Ash and Arron both." But it was Ash who I wronged so intensely. Ash who will never forgave me. We may never know what became of Arron, but certainly Ash is out there somewhere hating me right now. I wish it wasn't so.

Alba reaches out to squeeze my arm. Her touch grounds me, brings me back to the joy of this moment. The awe of it. Baby Bea coos in delight. She has our attention when a call comes from up the path.

Errol, one of the young orc boys, comes hauling up as fast as his little legs can carry him. "Mister Thorn, Mister Thorn!"

"Haven't I told you to call me Your Highness?"

The boy laughs between heavy inhalations of breath. "You got a visitor coming!"

"A visitor? Is it your father?"

The boy shakes his head vigorously. "No, it's a stranger!"

I consider who it might be. "Isn't a dragon, is it?"

Errol laughs. "There's no such thing as a dragon."

"Oh yes there is, haven't I ever told you the story of how I defeated a dragon?"

Errol brushes my words away as jest.

"Fine, but it better not have been a woman. A human-looking one with a crown and impossibly perfect curls."

Errol's face grows serious and he blushes, cutting eyes to Alba. "Well—I...I'm sure I didn't see no woman coming to visit you." We have neither heard from nor seen Petra since that last day at the castle. Though she certainly frequents my night-mares. I think that witch must have a grudge against me. If she is still out there in the land of man, I wouldn't know, so deep are we into the wood. "Anyway it was a man."

"A man you say? What did he look like?"

"Short or tall?" Alba shouts, getting into the game.

"Just regular looking, I guess. Only...kinda looks like you now that you mention it."

Beside me Alba tenses. "What is it, my love?"

She turns to Errol. "Anything else about him? Any weapons perhaps?"

Errol nods vigorously once more. "You bet he has weapons! Whole coat full of knives. He gave me one if I promised to use it only for good and not evil.

With fear, my eyes cut to Alba. "It couldn't be." I'm searching my brain, wondering how Ash might have found me and what type of revenge he is looking for. "Get back to the house and lock the door," I tell Alba. "You too, Errol, get out of here and get out of here quick!" But Errol takes his lead from Alba, and she doesn't move an inch. I do happen to notice that she wears no look of surprise.

"What's going on here?" I demand.

"Maybe it's nothing."

"Errol, did he say his name?"

Errol casts his eyes down. "I was so excited I forgot to ask. But he was like you, you know?"

"Like me?"

"Half—" He doesn't finish the word, worried it might offend.

"You can say it, little man, I am only half-blood."

"Nothing wrong with that," he mutters.

"Now, Thorn, don't get mad. But I have a little confession to make..." Alba says cautiously.

"You mean this fella *is* coming to see the missus?" Errol cries in shock.

"No, no." Alba brushes away the concern with a laugh. "I suspect he's here to talk to Thorn. Our guest is his brother after all."

"Alba, what do you know about this?"

"I wrote a few letters and sent them out. It was months ago. I hadn't heard back, so I assumed it didn't work..."

"What didn't work?"

"Letters for Ash and Arron, I hoped it might eventually help them make their way here." She doesn't have much more time to explain, because a figure appears on the rise. An all too familiar figure. I could live a thousand years and know my brother from a mile away. He pauses, taking in the scene, seeing our valley, our mother's wretched little valley, transformed into something beautiful.

I drop my shovel.

I'm frozen in place as he comes down the hill and joins us. Errol breaks the silence with more ease than I might be able to muster. "I told 'em you was coming!"

"Thank you, young man," Ash says with a jovial smile. His eyes are on Alba. "I take it you are Alba? Alba of Aberdeen?"

She nods. "Yes. And I see you got my letter."

Ash takes a folded and yellow piece of tattered paper from of his coat's inner pocket. "I did. Wasn't sure what to do about it at first, but my wife sent me."

"I understand if you don't wish to be here," I say.

Ash winces. "Your voice! You have a cold, brother? There are teas for that."

I swallow hard when I hear Ash call me his brother. I don't know what in the world to say.

"I came to see my niece *and* to make sure you didn't cast a spell on this poor woman." He indicates Alba with a nod.

I'm about to defend myself when Alba laughs. She plops Bea into Ash's arms and says something about brewing up some tea. She drags Errol along behind her, leaving Ash and me alone.

There is silence between us, but he coos and plays with Bea
—fitting his finger in her small hand.

"I want to say I'm sorry. Terribly sorry for all I put you and
Ellyn through."

"I had a hard time coming, if I'm to be honest with you."

"What happened?"

"My wife encouraged me."

"That's generous of her." I toe the ground. "So, you married
Ellyn?"

"I did. And I wanted to see what kind of batty thing would
marry you."

"Alba is not—"

Ash waves the comment away. "I know she isn't. I only tease.
Judging by her letter, she is lovely and that too made me want to
come and see for myself..."

"I've changed," I tell him.

"I can see that. Looks like a lot has changed."

I nod, and together we stare back at the house.

"It's so different. Did you do all this?"

"Yes. Alba helped. She inspired all of it really."

"I like it. It's different and different looks good on you,
brother. Or should I call you Your Highness?"

"I feel pretty good about you calling me brother."

Ash smiles, first at Bea and then at me. And after a moment,
he reaches an arm around my shoulder and hugs me against
him. Bea coos in delight. "You'll have to show me around. I have
a feeling there are a lot of changes around here."

"Only changes for the better, I can promise you that."

He smiles gently. "I believe it. But Thorn...you know we
have a long way to go before we get back to where we belong."

"If it takes a hundred years, I'll keep trying to make things
right between us."

Ash slaps me hard on the back and lets out a heavy sigh. "I
missed you, Thorn, for a long time, I've missed you."

"I'm here now."

"Good." One last family hug and we head for the house. Inside I can hear Alba taking the kettle off the fire and I'm thrilled. I cannot wait to sit down and introduce my little family to Ash—my brother. And I catch myself marveling once more on the way life keeps on getting better here in the Perished Woods.

AUTHOR'S NOTE

*T*hank you for reading Captured by the Orc King. If you follow me on Facebook you know the tragic background of this book. I was finished writing and working on edits way back in June 2022, when my computer completely obliterated the entire manuscript. It was a 100k word document that took me four months to write. The loss was *devastating. Sickening. Heartbreaking.*

ALREADY THIS BOOK was hard for me to tackle. I get so many lovely emails from fans asking about the next installation of The Perished Woods series and, to be honest, it made me nervous. I wanted my story to be amazing. I wanted to make readers proud and happy with what I created. But nope! The technology Gods had other plans.

WITHIN A DAY or two of the loss I started rewriting Captured by the Orc King (version 2.0). Only, I decided to make it completely different. The idea of trying to recreate what I had lost was grating, so I made it brand new. Fun fact, Alba murders her husband in both versions. With 2.0 my hope is the same: that you found this story exciting and engaging, that you could relate both with aspects of Thorn and Alba, and that you might be looking forward to knowing what has become of Arron (his story is set to release in May 2023).

I HAVE a lot of big feelings on this book. So many that it's hard to know exactly what to say here, how to articulate the journey I went on with this baby. But I learned a lot. It encouraged me to try new things. And...TO MAKE PLENTY OF BACK UP SAVES!!!!

THIS IS THE YEAR, my friends. A year of abundant creativity. I can't wait to share all my stories with you. Special thanks to Aquila Editing, cover artist Madelene Martin, and to all of you who sent emails and messages encouraging me to return to the Perished Woods. Happy reading.

THE BEST WAY TO keep in touch is on my website: https://www. tracylaurenromance.com where you can join my newsletter for FREE Tracy Lauren swag items and up to date release information! You can also follow me on Facebook for promos and events: https://www.facebook.com/tracy.lauren.148 or join my group, Lauren's Lair: https://www.facebook.com/groups/ 280490619460186

ALSO BY TRACY LAUREN

The Perished Woods

Tamed by the Troll

Enthralling the Orc

Captured by the Orc King

The Alien Series

Alien Instinct

Alien Bride

Alien Ascension

Alien Gift: A Christmas Novella

Alien Bond

Alien Surrender

Alien Attraction

Alien Holiday: A Christmas Novella

Alien Prison

Brides: Tales from the Alien Universe

A Bride Worth Fighting For

The Sovolians' Bride

Rescuing his Bride

The Hunting Series

Hunting Faith

Hunting Purity

Stand Alone (for now...)

In the Arms of an Android

Android Blue Christmas

The Frog Prince: Cosmic Fairy Tales

My Alien Roommate

Demon Realm

Enchanting the Mage

Allied to the Archer

Sexy Stuff by my Alter Ego Lana Taylor

Filled by the Troll

Seduced by the Satyr

Ganged by Goblins

Printed in Great Britain
by Amazon

20818455R00192